THAT ENCHANTRESS

by

DORIS LESLIE

THE BOOK CLUB
121 CHARING CROSS ROAD, LONDON, W.C.2

This Edition 1951

PRINTED IN GREAT BRITAIN BY
EBENEZER BAYLIS AND SON, LTD., THE
TRINITY PRESS, WORCESTER, AND LONDON

FOR
MY HUSBAND

CONTENTS

BOOK ONE
(1698–1701)

'Oh, I could tell you ten thousand things of
our mad politicks, upon what small circumstances great affairs have turned. . . .'

Jonathan Swift: *Journal to Stella*

CHAPTER ONE

"Two o' the clock and a fine clear night . . ."

She was startled from her first uneasy sleep by the voice of the watch beneath the window.

The wandering light of the watchman's lanthorn revealed in brief but fervent interlude the dingy room and its familiar objects; the gaunt age-blackened chest that once had stored her father's wealth, empty now of everything but dust; a high-backed chair covered with worn tapestry, a film of tarnish on the gilt-framed mirror. These, and a portrait of her mother above the mantel-shelf, were more graciously presented as the light in that second lingered; the eyes in the picture, to her fancy, seemed to glow and the lips to move before the light passed on and the room sank to darkness.

Beside her in the great canopied four-post bed on which their mother had borne them and on which both their parents had died, her sister Alice Mary slept but she could not. All sleep for her had fled. She must wait now for dawn, and the day when she would set out upon her journey—into what? A new, an unknown world.

The prospect was both dismal and exciting. Who could have foreseen that within the space of one short week her future would be so decisively resolved! And to think that had she waited three days more she might have been spared this last extreme to which desperation had driven her. Yet while she would have sooner starved than have done what she did—for the sake of Jack and Alice, she could not let them suffer want of food. So she had cut off her hair and sold it for a guinea to a dealer of periwigs in Drury Lane. A poor enough exchange, but it had sufficed to fill their empty bellies for a week. And now she must enter her ladyship's service shorn: a rare figure of fun!

9

1*

A sob tore at her throat and was buried in the pillow. Let that be the least of her troubles. The past year had brought her enough.

Although the joint ages of herself and Jack and Alice amounted to little more than forty years between them, the two younger children had turned instinctively to Abigail when their mother's death left them penniless and orphaned.

Francis Hill, their father, had amassed a vast fortune in Levant merchandise and lost it in rash speculation. He died soon after, of the smallpox, more happily for him than for Mary, his widow, to whom he bequeathed a family of four and very little else beyond his debts.

She had battled bravely with disaster. Her Hampshire house and almost all its contents together with her jewels, her horses and her coach, went to pay the creditors. The surplus she retained for the upkeep of her children. Through the influence of Lord Godolphin, who had been acquainted with her husband, she had managed to secure for her eldest son, Richard, a post in the Customs Office at Southampton. But he, although now self-supporting, could not, on his lean earnings, support her. Mary Hill was unused to economy. Notwithstanding her removal to London and a modest habitation near Ludgate, she found her limited means insufficient to meet her expenses. Nor was financial embarrassment the poor lady's only anxiety. She had contracted a consumption following a fever, and feared she would die before she could make adequate provision for the future of her family. The governess whom she had engaged to teach her daughters the usual smattering of French, High Dutch, a little music on the harpsichord, and those certain household duties encumbent on a gentlewoman's education, was, she decided, a luxury with which she could dispense. The governess must go. She went; but Jack's tutor remained.

If this estimable gentleman, one Mr. Richard Johnson, evinced less taste for academics than for taverns, Jack had no cause to quarrel with his tutor's predilections. And it may be that in after years Brigadier John Hill, known among his men as 'Fighting Jack', felt himself indebted to his kind Mr. Johnson, from whom he learned a great deal more than geometry and classics. He learned, besides good sword-play, and, most shockingly, to swear, that a gentleman might use his fists to some advantage. Sparring contests in the attic between the master and his pupil were conducted as part of Jack's curriculum.

If Mary disapproved these methods of tuition she had deemed it wiser to refrain from interference, until it seems that Mr. Johnson, to pursue his methods further, took Jack to see the prize-fighting at Hockley-in-the-Hole. They finished off with dinner at the sign of Shakespeare's Head in Covent Garden.

And Mr. Johnson, to Jack's sorrow, was dismissed.

But despite that Mrs. Hill was now saved a tutor's salary, since Jack was left to educate himself, her children must be clothed and fed, her rent was in arrears, and she knew she had not long to live.

It was then she had appealed to her niece Sarah.

To swallow her pride and go guardedly begging of one who so near was yet so far above her, must have cost the timid Mary no small effort of courage. Sarah, renowned throughout the land for her fame and name and beauty, had, till then, ignored her aunt's existence. Mary could not, however, complain of her welcome nor of Sarah's concern for her misfortunes; nor of the repeated assurance that while Sarah lived she would care for, guard, and cherish her aunt and her aunt's children. She would be their comfort and salvation.

Mary, in her mourning black, sipping bohea in the beams of magnanimity, sat overwhelmed with gratitude and wonder. Sarah, at that time, had been allotted a suite of rooms in St. James's Palace. The magnificence of this establishment, the gilded pillars, moulded ceilings, mural paintings, lackeys, Sarah's jewels, no less than her benign commiseration, bereft Mary not only of speech but of sense. To her it was incredible that she, so insignificant and plain, could be blood-tied to such an exquisite, incomparable being.

And as if she had taken that thought from her, the Lady said: "How strange that you and I are aunt and niece."

Mary wet her lips and answered nothing.

"Strange," Sarah had, with winning grace, conceded, "because I think you must be younger than myself."

"By six months," ventured Mary.

"Ah, yes! My grandfather—*your* father—Sir John Jennings—let me offer you a ratifee cake. Princess Anne's French chef, Centlivre, makes them to perfection. My grandfather," Sarah told her, when the cake had been accepted and Mary's cup refilled, "must have been prodigious prolific. My father—rest his soul!—was one of twenty-two. He came at the top and you were at the tail."

Her laughter was infectious. Mary tremulously smiled.

"Dear sweet aunt—no! I cannot call you 'Aunt'. We are of one age. Your name is——?"

"Mary."

"Mary. To be sure! But tell me, Mary, when you married, were you not well endowed? I understand my grandfather was wealthy. Did you," persisted Sarah while Mary still sat mute, "receive no marriage portion?"

"I had five hundred pounds, but"—Mary managed to articulate —"it was lost with—when—my——"

Her voice halted and was stuck upon a crumb. She spluttered, choked, induced a fit of coughing.

"Hold your breath. Look up," commanded Sarah, "and count twenty."

Her attempt to do as she was bidden lamentably failed. Sarah frowned and tapped a toe, while Mary, stammering apologies, fought for breath and wiped her mouth and folded, hastily, her handkerchief to hide its crimson stain.

"Bohea is an acquired taste," commented Sarah kindly. "And an expensive one, believe me. I bought this infusion of Gary, the druggist, at the Bell in Gracechurch Street. It cost sixteen shillings the pound. I call it outrageous."

Mary too, silently, called it outrageous. The price of a pound of Mr. Gary's bohea would have supplied her three children with food for a week. At which reflection Mary, for the life of her, could not restrain her tears. Sarah held her patience till the sobing had subsided.

"Come, come!" she urged, "don't fret yourself. 'Tis barbarous that your husband's creditors should have turned you out of doors and seized your patrimony, but I'll see you righted. We will make amends."

Amends were made; embraces passed. Mary left the richer by ten pounds.

She died before the last of them was spent.

But that interview, faithfully recorded, had left a deep impression on Abigail's mind. With her last breath her mother spoke of Sarah.

"I leave you three to God," she said, "and her."

For weeks thereafter Abigail waited for a summons from the Lady or an answer to her prayers, while she sought to provide sustenance for her dependants. She sold, with pangs, her mother's clothes to an 'Old Taffety' who gave her seven shillings for the lot. She knew she had been cheated, but Jack and Alice must be fed. She sold the household silver; she sold a china teapot. She sold her father's snuff-boxes; and then she sold her hair.

If only she had waited three days longer. . . .

Lying in the darkness watching for the dawn, she recalled that afternoon a week ago. She was mending Jack's torn breeches while Alice pressed his shirts, when they were disturbed by a commotion in the street.

Alice went to the window and peered out to report: "A coach. Postilions. Footmen in scarlet liveries. Abbie, come and see."

Abbie came and saw: a splendid equipage drawn by six Flemish horses whose prancing hooves scraped the cobbles to raise sparks. From every window in the houses opposite heads peeped; and in the road had gathered a small crowd composed of beggars, dogs, and butchers' boys, an orange girl: and Jack.

He was in tatters and bare-headed, his hair tousled, his nose bloody and spreading half across his face. One eye was plum-coloured, and the other fixed with admiration on the coach and its fair occupant.

"He looks as he's been fighting," observed Alice.

Abigail hurriedly withdrew. She had glimpsed and recognized, from her mamma's description, the face of the Lady who, as the footman had prepared to hand her out, appeared to hesitate when confronted by a heap of muck and refuse in the gutter. Lifting daintily her quilted petticoat to display her slender ankles encased in green silk stockings and embroidered satin shoes with high red heels, she had gazed up at the unprepossessing façade of the house.

"I think," Alice said laconically, "that she is coming here."

Not for the first time, and more than ever at that moment, did Abigail envy her sister's pachydermatous approach to life's surprises. While Abigail wore her stoicism as an armour of defence against the pitiless adversities of fate, Alice was by nature philosophic. Nothing short of hunger could disturb her equanimity. So then, when their whole future had swung upon the whim of a great lady while she debated whether she would or would not soil her shoes to act the good Samaratan, Alice had stolidly maintained her position at the window. It may have crossed her mind that the advent of the Lady heralded a change in her condition, or at least a good round meal of mutton collops, syllabub, a pie. Circumstances had reduced her weight but not her optimism.

So while Alice watched, hoped, wondered, saw visions of a pie, Abigail, in the flutters, had set the room to rights. She hid Jack's breeches in the clothes-basket; shoved that beneath the table, bade her sister: "Stir yourself for pity's sake—and fetch a duster."

"I've dusted round already once to-day," objected Alice. "Your hair looks frightful."

Her hair!

Abigail had forgotten her cropped hair.

Dragging forth and placing a stool beneath the wall-mirror, she had climbed on to it and stood tiptoe to survey this new horrid sight of herself. Her reflection had not been reassuring. A pair of white-lidded gooseberry eyes stared reproachfully back at her out of a pinched, freckled face, too small for its high-bridged intelligent nose. Her slab of a forehead, pale as dough, was surmounted by sand-coloured elf-locks that, although silken soft, were too short to lie flat. Yet before it had been cut her hair was so long she could sit on it.

"I'm a monster," she said to the face in the glass, and to Alice: "Don't stand gaping there! Give me a clean cap from that drawer."

Alice gave her a clean cap from that drawer, and as Abigail hastily covered her head a thunderous knock had echoed through the house to shake the walls. She scuttled to the landing, leaned over the balusters, and returned with palpitations to say:

"She's coming up!"

"I told you so," said Alice.

There was the sound of a light footfall on the staircase, the rustle of a petticoat, a smell of musk and amber . . . The Lady had entered the room.

"My footman," she announced with smiles, "found the front door open. I walked in."

She had seemed to glitter, not so much from the sparkle of her jewels, the sheen of broidered raiment, as from some inner, indefinable illumination. She was flame-like. Her hair, to Abigail's dazzled fancy, had appeared as the halo of gold crowning the heads of pictured saints. Her eyes, blue as bluest water, were shadowed by stupendous long dark lashes; her voice, vibrant with compassion, caressed the air in a mellifluous contralto.

"Poor motherless, lost, lonely little lambs!"

Behind Abigail's speechless awe arose the involuntary comment: Four L's. Alliteration.

She had often remarked and deplored in herself this same disconcerting inconsequence. It was as if she were not one but two persons, each propelled by the same moving spirit and in essence co-related, yet each functioning in opposite directions, unidentified with and, seemingly, quite independent of the other: a case of the Right and Left Hand. Only at moments of crises did this phenomenon occur: as when at her mother's deathbed one half of her had performed dispassionately, coldly, the last rites, while her stricken double writhed in anguished sorrow. And Alice, who for once had shown emotion, broken-heartedly declared her hard and callous; for even at the funeral she had not shed a tear.

So when the Lady, exuding sweetness, spoke, one of these two Abigails, inly and schoolgirlishly had been compelled to giggle, while her twin, with eyelids lowered, curtsied to the visitor in worshipful respect.

"I have but just heard of your most sad bereavement." The Lady's sympathetic, comprehensive glance had embraced the impoverished parlour, its comfortless furnishings, rickety chairs; a broken pane in the window patched with rags; the clothes-basket under the table, the flat-iron upon it, the pewter plates on the dresser alongside a loaf of bread and the remains of a herring: Jack's dinner. From this noisome skeleton, and with a faint shudder, the Lady averted her eyes.

"I am come," she said deeply, "to help you. I promised my aunt, your dear mother, that you should never want. You never shall."

If she had found the fixed regard of her silent audience discouraging, she persevered. Her teeth were like white seeds in ripe red fruit.

"You"—she addressed herself to Alice who was open-mouthed, agog—"you are the elder, I presume?"

"No, madam."

"No?" Her smile rested brightly upon Abigail. "You then must be the elder. You are so small. I—h'm——"

She had paused to scrutinize this inappreciable midget; its austere white cap, its wan, obsequious, submissive personality that Abigail hazarded the Lady thought to be no more nor less alluring than a turnip.

"How old—or how young are you, my dear?"

"Fifteen years and six months, madam."

"An awkward age. Now tell me, can you read aloud, write letters? Can you sew?"

Abigail raised her eyes.

"I have been educated, madam."

"Which," returned the Lady graciously, "is certain by your bearing."

Abigail offered her a chair.

"Thank you, child. I abhor to stand."

She sat, produced a fan, and waved it to and fro before her face as if to dispel the odour of the herring. Admittedly it stank.

The Lady, fanning vigorously, had then proceeded to expound her plans for the removal of the sisters from 'this garret'. Her friend, Lady Rivers, who suffered from the gout, was seeking as companion a young gentlewoman of good family who would attend her, read aloud, and make herself in every way agreeable. She would write to her ladyship at once to let her know that she had found the very person for the post. The house was at Penshurst in Kent. Abigail's coach fare would be paid. "You will need"—her keen blue gaze skimmed Abigail's childish body as if to strip it naked—"you will need," she had pronounced briskly, "some new clothes. I will see what I can do for you. My younger girl, Elizabeth, is just about your size. Your sister——"

She stayed her fan and tapped a nail to a tooth while she considered.

Abigail had covertly appraised her. Her gown of rose satin was looped above a petticoat of silvery brocade. She had pearls at her neck and rings on her fingers; and on her head a 'fontange' —the latest thing in caps—made of lace and stiffened muslin spreading in a circle from above her creaseless forehead to display her glinting honey-coloured curls. She might have been a play-actress; she might have been a queen. She was beautiful beyond imagination. Her eyes pensively regarded the clothes-basket, and as if from that humble source she had derived her inspiration, she exclaimed with buoyancy, "I have it!" and then she turned to Alice. "You can goffer, wash linen? You know how to starch, I am sure."

Alice blinked. "Yes, madam, I do."

"You see how I recognize your qualities?" the Lady had insinuated sweetly. "Not from second-sight, but from observation. I'll warrant you've been busy with a flat-iron this morning."

Following the direction of the Lady's smiling look, Abigail saw the pile of freshly laundered linen exposed where Alice had left it, forgotten, on a chair. Jack's shirts; Alice's night-shift, and other and more intimate apparel. To the tip of her nose Abigail pinkened; even Alice was constrained to blush.

The Lady rippled into laughter.

"Thus the smallest trifles resolve the greatest destinies. I have been exercised how to play you to advantage. Now I know. I will find you a situation as a laundry-maid."

If this concession did not meet with the gratitude that it deserved, the Lady remained gracious and still smiling.

"Well, and what have you to say?"

Alice had nothing to say.

The Lady shrugged a shoulder, and spoke to Abigail with a sharpness in her voice.

"I take it your rent has been paid?"

Yes, the rent for the December quarter had been paid in advance by her mother . . . Yes, notice had been given to the landlord that there would be no renewal of the lease. All then that now remained to be disposed of were their personal effects. The sale of these, the Lady did not need to emphasize, would barely provide them with sufficient for immediate necessities. She would gladly contribute a loan or a small gift of money for their current expenses, if desired. As to their salaries, she had assured them she would see that they were granted at least the minimum of weekly wages for their service.

Then she had got upon her feet, and taking Abigail's small mouse-hands in hers, had declared her to be honest, brave— "You'll be rewarded. Henceforth the pair of you are *my* responsibility. I must give you a jar of my special orange-water cream to rid you of those unbecoming freckles . . . But wait a moment." She spun round. All her movements were mercurial, decisive. "I understood there were three of you here. Is there not another girl?"

"No, madam," it was Alice who answered, "a boy."

He had come tiptoe up the stairway in the hope of sneaking past the parlour door to clean himself before he should be seen. The Lady was too quick. She hailed him delightedly.

"A boy? A giant! Two yards high if he's an inch. Come in, sirrah, and show yourself."

Unembarrassed by the parlour spectacle that he presented, Jack advanced. Abigail, wishing she might sink through the floor, cast a glance of agonized apology at the Lady, who had no eyes for her.

"Faith! 'Tis as pretty a fellow as ever I saw." As pretty, her tone had unconsciously implied, as his two sisters were plain; and this despite his purple eye, his swollen nose, his filthy shirt, and the grime of sweat and battle on his face.

The Lady twinkled.

"How come you, sirrah, to be so scarred and battered?"

"I have given," Jack replied, and his mouth was one wide grin, "a great hulking brute his fair due, madam."

"Fair due? For what foul purpose?" she, amused, inquired.

"For rough treatment of a bitch, madam."

"Fie!" The Lady flicked his cheek with her fan. "There's many a bitch I could name might deserve what you give to your bitch's chastiser."

"Madam," Jack parried, "this bitch was in whelp. Would you have had her tormented?"

At which the Lady had laughed loudly.

"A bold lad, forsooth! A knight errant, a defender of bitches. Go to, you young rascal! How old are you, sirrah? . . . Twelve years? You might be twenty. Ecod, I'm of a mind to wish you were."

And Abigail's heart had swelled with love of him; pride of him.

For all his black eye and the blood on his nose, he was handsome. His hair, tawny-gilded, was bleached pale at the temples with exposure to the sun. In his gipsy-brown face his teeth were white as almonds—or the Lady's.

"You're a slubberdegullion," she had told him, "a vagabond out at your elbows—not to say out of your breeks. For the Lord's sake don't grow any higher!" Jack had reddened at her mocking look that raked him up and down. "I'll have you clothed and put to school. Can you read? Can you write? What do you know?"

He had surprised her.

"Madam, nihil scire est vita jucundissima."

"Lud, the boy speaks Latin! Now, sirrah, construe."

"I said, madam, that the happiest life is to know nothing."

She was enchanted.

"Why, sir, if you know nothing, then you don't know who I am."

"Yes, madam, I do." He had swept her a bow; he had charm to melt stones. "You're my cousin . . . The Countess of Marlborough."

And now the day that Abigail sleeplessly awaited had arrived. So soon as light came stealing through a moth-hole in the curtain she was up and dressed. She wore a gown of green cloth over a holland petticoat that true to her promise the Lady had sent; and a pair of shoes, almost new, and thread stockings. The Lady had given her, besides, a snuff-coloured camlet cloak and hood. She need not now go shabby. Of her shoes she was particularly proud; fashioned of moroccan leather, with modish red heels and steel buckles, they added a good two inches to her height. Excitement had lent a flush to her cheeks and a sparkle to her eyes, and but for her cropped hair which entirely spoiled the effect of her new clothes, she could almost have believed—unless her mirror lied to her—that she was not uncomely.

Since the descent of Cousin Sarah in their midst, as of a benignant Aphrodite come to scatter largesse from Olympus, the Lady's efforts on behalf of 'my three waifs'—so she had described them to her dear friend 'Mrs. Morley'—were unflagging. Within an hour of her first appearance at their door, a special messenger from Sarah was on his way to Kent and she upon her way to Camden House.

There she interviewed one Mr. Jenkin Lewis, attendant on Prince William, Duke of Gloucester. As a result of these activities her ladyship had managed to secure for Alice a situation in the Royal Laundry at a salary of two hundred pounds a year.

So far, so good, but Jack fared even better. Her ladyship had borne him off with her that very day of her arrival, all in rags and tatters as he was, to St. James's Palace. There she had him scrubbed, groomed, tailored, fitted for a suit, breeches, shirts, and the Lord alone knew what of elegant apparel.

Abigail had not seen him since, but she was told that the Lady intended putting him to school at St. Albans, near to Holywell, her country residence.

As for Abigail, it appeared that Lady Rivers had expressed herself delighted to secure her services as 'femme de chambre'. True, the wage was negligible when compared to that of Alice, whose appointment, Lady Marlborough had declared, would not necessarily enforce domestic duties other than the starching of the Prince's bands and cuffs. Moreover she would occupy at least two private rooms at Camden House and be waited on by servants.

It was obvious to Abigail that her sister's prospects offered more advantage than her own. She did not greatly relish the post of 'femme de chambre' to a lady addicted to the gout; and Alice, who received her elevation with habitual placidity, was more than ever platitudinous and vexing. Almost daily she reminded Abigail that 'Life has its Ups and Downs', that 'Beggars can't be Choosers' and that 'Abbie should be Thankful for Small Mercies'.

Abbie was, upon her knees on this last morning, thankful for small mercies; thankful that no longer would she have to scrape and screw to make ends meet, and satisfy the lusty appetites of Jack and Alice.

And to her sister, who was grunting in her sleep, she said: "Wake up! It's six o' the clock and we'll have to leave here before eight."

Alice, yawning widely, woke, rubbed her knuckles in her eyes and turning over on her back, asked: "What's to eat?"

"Pigs' trotters," Abigail answered briefly.

"Hot?"

"Cold. I'm not cooking breakfast to-day."

Raising herself on her elbow, Alice stared and remarked: "You look so fine in that new gown, Lady Rivers'll think you're a duchess."

"Get up," urged Abigail. "There's a mort to do. You haven't near finished your packing."

"Yes, I have. I've packed everything except my sewing-bag, and I've nothing to do but fetch in the cat. I'm not leaving her here. She's going to have kittens."

"They may object at Camden House, to your bringing a cat and her kittens."

"If they do object, they do," was the irrefutable reply. "And she hasn't had her kittens yet. I'm not leaving that cat here to starve."

As this appeared to be conclusive, Abigail had no more to say than to bid Alice: "Make haste."

While Alice, who never made haste, lethargically bestirred herself, Abigail mounted with the aid of a chair to the top of the tallboy and thence to the mantelshelf, in attempt to detach their mother's portrait from the wall. These singular manœuvres prompted Alice, half in and half out of her shift, to inquire: "What in the deuce are you at?"

The question, although reasonably pertinent, served to distract Abigail's attention sufficiently to cause one foot to slip from its perch and send her crashing, with the picture, to the floor.

"You might have known that would happen," said Alice. "Are your hurt?"

Abigail picked herself up. She *was* hurt. Her elbows and knees were scraped raw. She had a cut on her chin, a bruise on her forehead, and had torn a great hole in her stocking, but: "At any rate," she said, "I've saved the picture."

"What do you mean," asked Alice, "by 'saved'?"

"Don't you remember she told us she would sell our furniture and personal effects and give us what was left when she had paid our expenses? I'm not going to let her sell this."

"Then what'll you do with it?"

"I am giving it," said Abigail solemnly, "to you."

"Me? Why?"

"Because I can't take it where I'm going, and you can. She said you were to have your own apartments. You must hang it on the wall. 'Tis a lovely likeness. I wouldn't lose it for the world. Mamma used to say it was by Sir Peter Lely, but 'tisn't signed, so we shall never know." Abigail stifled a sigh. "Now do," she added brusquely, "get dressed. You'll never be ready in time . . . I shall have to mend this stocking. Where's your sewing-bag?"

As she threaded a needle she heard a soft unmistakable sound. Glancing up she saw her sister, shaken from her customary phlegm, standing in her stays and very little else, while two fat tears rolled slowly down her cheeks.

"I doh—don't want," she sobbed, surprisingly, "to—to leave you. I doh—don't want to live with strangers, even though they may be roy—royal. I doh—don't, truly. I'd sell winkles on a bah—barrow suh—sooner than leave you!"

This outburst from her wontedly impassive sister aroused in Abigail a remorseful twinge. Alice, then, was not so lacking in the tenderer susceptibilities as she had always supposed. Relinquishing her stocking, Abigail slid an arm round Alice's plump shoulders. "Don't," she whispered. "Dear. Don't cry. We won't live apart for ever. And listen. If you save your wages for a year you'll have two hundred pounds. That's a deal of money. I'll save my wages too, and with what is left us from the sale of our things——" she faltered, swallowed a rock in her throat and proceeded resolutely, "we'll have enough to set up house again together. You and Jack and I."

"And maybe Dick," said Alice, snuffling, "will help us find a lodging near—or with him—at Southampton."

"Yes, maybe."

On some such slender hope the sisters, more devoted than demonstrative, faced the wrench of separation. Alice dried her tears and ate a hearty breakfast of pigs' trotters, cold, and apple-pie washed down by a tankard of small ale. Abigail darned her stocking and ate nothing.

Lady Marlborough had arranged to send a post-chaise to fetch Alice and take her to Camden House,* near the village of Kensington. Abigail was to accompany her part of the way, as far as the Cross Keys Inn in Wood Street. There she was instructed to await the coach for Kent.

Soon after eight o'clock Lady Marlborough's chaise arrived, and with it a tall footman in powder and plush to carry down their inconsiderable baggage.

"Is this h'all?" asked the footman disdainfully.

"All," Abigail answered, "except that." She pointed to the portrait of her mother, around which she had draped a strip of sacking. "Have the goodness to see that this is hung upon the wall in the bedroom of my sister, Mistress Hill, at Camden House."

"Ho!" quoth the footman, "hindeed. And 'oo, may I harsk, is givin' horders?"

Abigail looked at him.

"I am."

*   *   *

When the chaise set her down at the Cross Keys Inn an hour before the arrival of the coach, she found the inn yard abuzz with activity, and herself very much in the way. The ostlers at their grooming, stable-boys filling and emptying buckets, maids darting in at one door and out at another, carrying trays with cups of chocolate, mugs of ale, steaming dishes, had no word nor time for the small pale girl in a snuff-coloured cloak who stood in a corner clutching her bundle.

* Originally the seat of Lord Camden, situated on Campden Hill.

The sight of the trays, however, reminded her that she had eaten no breakfast. She was about to approach one of the tripping damsels with the request that she might be allowed to buy a cup of chocolate and a rusk, when she encountered a formidable horse. To be sure he was led at the end of a rein, but his prancing and snorting, the roll of his eye, the red flare of his nostril, and his attendant's terse warning to: 'Stand on one side, 'e be vicious', sent her flying into safety.

Flattened against a doorpost, removed from immediate hurry and scurry, Abigail watched the comings and goings of postboys, waggoners, baggage-men, and a miscellany of street vendors who, clustered beneath the windows of the guest-rooms, outcried one another with offers of their wares to lie-abed visitors above. At length when the cantata had reached its most discordant height, a window was flung open and a pallid, heavy-eyed gentleman in a night-cap stuck out his head, piteously to entreat the choristers: "For the mercy of God, cease your din and let me sleep!"

Untouched by this appeal, the itinerant purveyors of 'Hot Pies', 'New Shoes', 'Old Boots', 'Cocked Hats', 'Pickled Oysters', 'Dutch Biscuits', and 'Green Cowcumbers', renewed their clamour, while a ragged ballad-monger, stinking to high heaven joined the raucous throng with serenade. At which the pallid gentleman, slapping hands to ears, withdrew his head, slammed the casement on confusion and retired.

With the arrival of more passengers awaiting the coach, none of whom was unattended, Abigail, more than ever hungry and disconsolate, wandered out into the street in search of food. She bought a mutton pasty from a pieman, and spreading her handkerchief upon the cobbles to save her gown, she sat, and ate . . . And wished that she had never sold her hair.

Her hunger satisfied, she hugged her knees and unobtrusively crushed against the wall, watched the early traffic of the city, to which she, country-bred and born, was still a stranger. Purposeful gentlemen, dodging each other for right of way, hurried from their homes to their houses of business. The more prosperous drove in a coach and four, some in a hackney carriage; some walked, but all appeared bent on their lawful occasions. The corruption of the night and its vicissitudes had vanished with the day. The women of the town were gone to their lairs, the footpads and thieves to their holes. Only an occasional chair with a periwigged fop boxed inside it, and sniffing daintily at his lace-trimmed handkerchief to keep away the stench of the common folk, was borne homeward from some late adventure; or a hackney, loaded with drunks, comatose, sullen, boisterous, or bilious, according to the quantity of wine they had consumed or the luck of their night's gaming, would rattle by from more fashionable quarters.

The October day was fair and sunny. A breeze, like a mischievous urchin, whisked at the rags and tags of straw, scraps of paper, vegetable refuse and other matters rotting in the gutter, to raise a grit that prickled the throat and spiked the eyes and set up a squeaking and a groaning as of protest from the gaily painted signs above the shops.

On the threshold of a doorway a slipshod apprentice was sprinkling sand, while a rosy-cheeked maid mopped the step. A hawker, hung around with the corpses of rabbits, bartered 'Coney skins for ladies' hats, bobbins or shoe buckles'. A noseless man with a hump on his back and a tray of little toys announced himself to Abigail as : 'Ha, Ha, Ha! Poor Jack!', and begged her to buy a pair of his 'Fine Singing Glasses for two pence.' A Billingsgate drab offered 'Flounders, fresh flounders!' But their smell, and the request that the young lady should keep an eye on her barrow while she went to fetch another load of fish from the market, gave Abigail to think that the flounders were nothing so fresh as she cried.

There were orange girls and milkmaids and stout farmers' wives from nearby villages with their baskets of butter, eggs, and poultry, quick and dead: a cowherd, driving his slow unwilling cattle. Here and there an out of work and out of pocket soldier; and a water-carrier, a garbage-cart, a coal-heaver, a sweep. To him Abigail bowed and said: "Good morning Master Sweep"— and crossed her thumbs; for, as everybody knew, a chimney-sweep to whom you bowed and said 'Good morning', brought you luck. Then, of a sudden, in the midst of these diversions, doubling to avoid the overhanging pent-houses, darting under horses' heads and in between the barrows, Abigail sighted a tall lad in a fine suit of mulberry cloth, white breeches, lace wristlets, silk stockings—a beau: and none else but her own brother Jack!

She sprang to her feet. He dashed up to her, breathless. "Thanks be I've come here in time! I heard her tell the footman that the coach would start from the Cross Keys Inn. I sneaked out before the household was awake and I've run every step of the way. Gemini! I'm hot."

He took off his elegant three-cornered hat to fan himself. His bright hair, brushed and shining, hung in curls to his shoulders; his face was rosy and beaded with sweat.

Her heart twisted. She loved him to distraction that to part from him was torture. To hide her pain she told him, sharp:

"It was very bold of you to come."

"I wanted to come." He beamed down at her, wiping the wet from his forehead. His steinkerk had slipped under one ear, his shoes were white with dust, his hands so dirty that where he rubbed his face he left a smudge.

"Jack! You haven't washed this morning."

He grinned widely.

"No, I couldn't wait for that."

"Oh, dear!" She gazed at him helplessly, half-laughing, half-crying. "What if they miss you?"

"Whisk! Let them. See this!"

He dived a hand in his pocket and pulled out a pink ribbon. "I bought it for you to tie in your hair when it grows again. Although," he hastened to add as he saw her face crumple, "you're better with short hair than long. 'Tis more uncommon and makes you less of a girl than a boy." And because he saw she could not, just then, speak, he went on speaking for her. "You know I'm going to school at St. Albans?"

Controlling the shake in her voice that she couldn't keep out of her chin: "Is she," asked Abigail, "kind to you?"

He nodded dubiously. " 'M. She's kind when she wants to be, but when she don't—God help us! You should hear her screeching to his lordship and the servants."

"So you know his lordship too!"

"Well, in course," Jack began very slightly to swagger. "He lives with her at St. James's when they're not at Holywell. The Princess Anne often comes to their apartments." He winked an eye. "We're very royal. Very high and mighty now. They let me sit at table. I listen to their talk. She says she'll make me page to the Duke of Gloucester when I've been at school a year."

"Jack!" Abigail sparkled. "What an honour! You never hoped to aim so high."

"Honour? Boo. My aim is higher than to dance attendance on a codlin—Prince, Duke, or whatever, with a head over big for his body. I've seen him."

"You've *seen* him!" echoed Abigail, marvelling. "Gracious me! You've not already been presented?"

"Not to say presented." Jack confessed. "I peeked through a window when he came to call with Prince George and the Princess. They say he plays at soldiers and leads his own regiment of boys. He drills them. But I don't want to be his page and fight mock battles. I hope we'll have another war, then I'll enlist myself and go to't. I swear I will."

"I swear you won't. You go learn your lessons, that's what you've to do. And there isn't going to be another war."

"Is there not?" Jack nodded sagely. "That's as may be. I keep my ears wide open, and I know——"

"You know too much, my lad, and not enough." Abigail screwed her eyes against the sun, and gazing at him through her lashes, said: "Remember this. When you keep your ears wide open, shut your mouth . . . I don't believe my lord and lady talk in front of you."

"They do." Jack raised himself on his toes and then sank down again. "They talk all manner of stuff."

"What manner of stuff?"

"Well . . . *He* talks mostly about the cost of food and living. He's Comptroller of the Duke of Gloucester's household, but 'tis she who hands out the appointments. That's how Alice comes to be placed in the laundry. She should have put you there and sent Alice to this Lady Rivers. I wish she wasn't sending you so far away."

Abigail wished so too.

"What do you think of my new suit?" Jack turned himself about to show it off. "It belongs—or did until she gave it me—to her son, Lord Churchill."

"It fits you like a skin. Take care not to muss it. We can never be grateful enough for"—Abigail looked down at her shoes—"for her goodness."

But Jack's attention had now strayed and was focused on a difference of opinion between a water-carrier and a coal-man. The latter had shoved his barrow against the water-carrier's knees, thereby spilling the contents of the buckets slung from a pole across his shoulders. This mishap resulted in a volley of abuse from the injured party to the effect that the coal-man was a lousy, misbegotten son of a Bridewell bawd, and why in the devil's name could he not watch his way? "You will pay me," the water-carrier demanded, "the price of those two full buckets, or I'll take their worth in coal."

With which he made as if to seize a sack.

"So will you! May your guts rot on the gallows!" was the coal-heaver's prompt retaliation as he reclaimed with force his property. Go sing your stinking water—you'll not sell it. 'Tis a-crawl with slime to turn the stomach of a sow. I had the right o' way."

"Why, yer mangy gobbet o' dung!" roared the water-carrier, "Did you or did you not ram me with your barrow?"

"I did *not*, seller of pig's sop. And if there's any talk o' ramming, then I'll ram your teeth into your poxy snout!"

At this gentle threat the waterman detached himself from the encumbrance of his buckets and fetched the coal-heaver a blow beneath his jaw to lay him flat; but only for a second. The next minute he was up, and seething, hurled himself at his opponent to the immense delight of the onlookers and Jack.

While Abigail shrank, with covered ears, from the interchange of pleasantries between the combatants, Jack, fairly dancing with excitement, urged the waterman: "Go to't, sirrah! Have at him. He bumped you first—go *on*!" until Abigail clapped her hand over his mouth.

"Quiet! Come away. They'll start you fighting next." Which might well have been, since Jack was in a fret to join the scrimmage, but for the belated arrival of the coach.

"Come," repeated Abigail firmly, "I must go." And tucking her hand under his arm, she dragged him from the scene of the disturbance.

The coach was in the yard, the coachman on the box, her fellow-passengers already in their seats, when the guard approached her with the query, "Name of Ill?"

"Yes, if you please."

Producing a grimy paper, the guard looked it over, to tell her: "Back seat. Name of Ill. Booked for Penshurst."

She turned to Jack who was holding her bundle, threw her arms round his neck and whispered, "Thank you for my ribbon. Be good. God bless you. And . . . don't *fight*!"

He hugged her heartily.

"I won't promise not to fight, but I'll be good."

Gulping back her tears, she took her bundle from him and was hoisted by the guard into her seat. The coachman cracked his whip across the flanks of the right leader, and with a clattering and rattling, a jingling of steel, and a roaring cheer from the spectators, the coach and its four sturdy horses went rollicking out of the yard.

Abigail leaned from the window to obtain a last glimpse of Jack running in the wake of the wheels, till a cloud of kicked dust and the mist in her eyes obscured him from her sight.

CHAPTER TWO

AT the same time that Abigail in the coach was carried off to Kent, a small boy with a large head reviewed his troops in a Kensington garden. Thirty stalwart grenadiers in paper caps and scarlet coats, with wooden swords at their sides and muskets on their shoulders, presented arms to their Commander-in-Chief, Prince William, Duke of Gloucester.

Slowly, with careful step, he passed along the line. He walked slowly and was careful because his ankles might at any moment let him down, and that would be unseemly in a General about to lead his forces into action. His left eye, too, was troublesome and watering again; and although his three veteran officers, Captains Churchill, Boscawen, and Bathurst, knew well that he had a weak eye, his recent recruits might almost believe he was crying.

In order to disabuse their minds of any such fallacy he halted, and straddling his legs to secure a firmer stance, addressed his men at the top of his lungs, in the way they had in the Army.

"Stand—at—*ease*! Now, gentlemen, we all know the issues at stake. Yesterday we fought and won the second and glorious battle of Campden Hill, but our losses have been—— Hey! You at the end of the line there—don't pick your nose on parade!"

The subject of this address, a raw recruit, who had not yet been equipped with uniform, since none could be found small enough to fit him, continued, blissfully, his occupation.

"Damme, sir!" roared the righteously outraged Commander-in-Chief. "Are you deaf? . . . Captain Churchill, who is this insum-borndinate fellow?"

Captain Churchill, three years older and a head taller than his General, stepped forward to salute.

"His name, Sir, is William Gardiner. I recruited him because he beats the drum."

"Where is his drum?" demanded the Duke.

"You, Gardiner—Hi!" bawled Captain Churchill, "Where's your drum?"

The grenadier, aware for the first time that he was called upon to answer, and whose clarity of diction was somewhat impeded by the loss of his milk teeth, replied that he had left it at home.

"Then go fetch it," shouted his Commander, "and return here within five minutes."

Nothing daunted at the attention he had drawn upon himself, the recently appointed grenadier displayed his depleted gums in the happiest of smiles, and scampered away as fast as his short legs could take him.

The Duke staunched the flow from his watering eye and turned it coldly upon his Captain who was grinning.

"What's his age?" he rapped out with a frown for this levity.

Captain Churchill composed his face.

"Six years—and a half, Your Highness."

"Six! What the pox," exploded the general, "do you mean by recruiting a child?"

"Why, Sir," Captain Churchill reminded him, "you remember we've been searching for a drummer."

"Yes, but not below the reg'lation age." Which the Duke had raised to the minimum of nine, since he himself had now attained that level of maturity.

"I understand, Sir," was Captain Churchill's defence, "that Mr. Lewis is acquainted with his father, who reports him to be equal to the ablest drummer in——"

"This"—the Duke thumped the butt end of his musket on the lawn—"is most irreg'lar. Lord Churchill, go back to your place. Gentlemen, I was about to say when I was int'rupted, that yesterday, despite our victorious beginnings, for which I heartily commend you, the enemy has not yet been routed and is making ready for reper-prisals. But we are sadly lacking in arms. Since the first battle of Campden, when we took two guns from the enemy, we have managed to muster between us"—drawing a paper from his pouch, he announced the list, "twenty pikes, seventeen muskets, a dozen swords and six cannon—two small and four large. Of those six cannon, gentlemen, the enemy has two, one of which, besides our own—that somebody broke—is jammed in the breech-bolt and will need to be mended before we can fire it again. It is imper-impereritive that we capture those two cannon to-day, otherwise we shall have to use squibs. We must *not*, on our lives, use squibs. We will now proceed into battle formation of four platoons. I'll lead the first, Churchill the second, Boscawen the third, Bathurst the fourth——"

"Your Highness," Captain Bathurst came out of line to pluck at his General's sleeve. "Look." And jerking his head in the direction of the house he produced a hideous, if significant, contortion of his features.

At this audacious interruption the Duke stood for a second in amaze, then: "S'death and deuce!" he expostulated loudly, "Why do you make me these grimaces? . . . Eh? . . . What?" His voice faltered on a distinctly subdued note. "Where?"

"There." With another backward jerk to rick his neck, Captain Bathurst added, sotto voce: "At the window."

A sidelong glance confirmed his officer's report, and identified the black-clad emaciated figure in a monstrous periwig, standing at the casement that overlooked the terrace.

"Yes. Um . . . Well," muttered the much deflated General, whose ears were now as scarlet as his coat, "d'you think he heard me?"

"The window is wide open, Sir," was Captain Bathurst's comfortless reply, "and Your Highness's voice carries."

The Duke turned to his battalion.

"Gentlemen, His Majesty the King is here, and I will have to go. Company dis*miss*! . . . I'll expect you on parade at this same time to-morrow morning."

Chapfallen, and with no attempt now to conceal his lagging step, the Duke walked up the avenue of elms towards the house. These visits from his uncle and godfather, King William, were always unexpected and never very welcome.

As he drew nearer to the window whence His Majesty watched his approach, William perceived the rotund countenance of his tutor, Dr. Burnet, Bishop of Salisbury, peering like a rosy moon above the narrow shoulders of the King.

William's face lengthened. He knew what this visit purported. His Majesty had come to question him upon the progress of his schooling under his learned instructor. He would be cross-examined, made to repeat in Greek a chapter of the Gospels, or discuss his views on the present international crisis, or the cause of the past Revolution.

On this subject William hoped he would not be too closely pressed. It was a sore one and excessively awkward to answer, inasmuch as it involved the abdication and flight of his grandfather, King James II, and had placed on the throne this Dutch uncle, who—in his heart William dared confess it—had no right at all to be there. True, Mr. Jenkin Lewis, William's equerry, had never ceased to remind him that he, William of Gloucester, was the future Prince of Wales and would one day be King. But despite the envisioned splendours unfolded by his gentleman, William persisted in his choice of a military career in preference to that of a monarch. While Mr. Lewis was at pains to restrain these war-like sentiments, his mother, Princess Anne, who believed that every thought, word, deed of her beloved one surviving son denoted an intelligence and perspicacity akin to genius, encouraged not his martial pursuits only, but his every whim.

Having arrived beneath the window, William shouldered his musket and stood at the salute.

The King curtly beckoned him closer.

"Villiam, did I hear you svear?"

As the Duke tilted his chin prepared to reply, his paper cap fell off. The sun, shining full on his face, made his eye water again, but he answered unflinchingly: "Yes, Sire."

"And vy, Villiam," the King asked with ice, "do you use this shameful langvidge?"

William shuffled his feet, looked all ways at once, then back at his inquisitor.

"For no reason, Your Majesty, other than that swearing is a trooper's priv'lege."

A shocked 'hem' escaped the Bishop, a sound betwixt a chuckle and a cough issued from behind the hastily raised hand of the King's gentleman, the Earl of Albemarle; but the face of the King was an expressionless mask, dry and withered as a medlar.

"You are not a trooper, Villiam. Yours is a line regiment."

"Yes, Sire, because I have no live horses for my men—only dead ones."

The King's beetling brows twitched above his nose in humourless interrogation.

"Dead?"

"Wooden horses, Sire."

"So! No horses save wooden horses for your men. That is a sad deficiency."

The King's low-lidded glance explored the small stunted figure from its head of flaxen hair, fine as spun glass, to the spindle-weak legs bravely straddling the turf; and the granite eyes softened.

"You vill have your horses on von condition, Villiam—that you do not use again bad langvidge. Ven you play vith your friends you may forget you are a Prince, but you never must forget you are a gentleman. Now come in. I vish to speak vith you."

In the Great Parlour he stood for an hour while the King fired his salvo of questions. There were some who suggested that the abnormal growth of the Duke's head was the result of the combined efforts of the King and his tutors who had stuffed it so full of scholarship that it had swelled; but the doctors called it 'water on the brain'.

Having dealt with a résumé of Plutarch's Lives, made him repeat a few verses of St. John in Greek, and give an account of the beneficiary and Feudal Laws appertaining to the Gothic Constitution, the King turned to current politics.

"Vat are the suggested terms of the Partition Treaty, and vy are these considered necessary to the maintenance of European peace?"

William, who had by this time had enough of it, whose ankles were aching, whose eye was bloodshot with persistent moisture, wanted mightily to sit and rest his legs. His head ached too, and felt uncommonly like an over-ripe boil ready to burst, but since he was asked he must answer.

"By Your Majesty's leave, I understand that King Carlos II

of Spain has willed his Empire to Prince Joseph Ferdinand of Bavaria."

"And how," asked the King as he paused, "does this affect the balance of power in Europe?"

Send me patience, prayed William. Who cares? But he said:

"Because, Sire, Spain would then remain independent of France and Austria, and they—France and Austria—would be more content, being both afraid and jealous of each other's power as fighting cats."

At last the immobile face of the King relaxed its tension.

"Fighting cats." He slid a look at his gentleman and added, wry-mouthed; "How charmed vould be the Sun King to hear himself so lucidly described. Go on, child. Vat next?"

"Well, Sire, has it not been decided to award consolation prizes to the two unsuccessful candy—candind-dates for the throne of Spain?"

"Can*did*ates. Do not use vords you cannot pronounce. Vat prizes?"

"Naples and Sicily for France, Sire, and——" the wall of the room dipped and curtsied; William's forehead was suddenly damp. He wanted to say—and thought he had said—that Milan would be offered to Austria; but his tongue played him false and:

"Please, Sire," he stammered, "I think I will have to . . . sit down."

And down he sat, on the floor, in a faint.

The Bishop hurried forward; Lord Albemarle knelt and raised that large, lolling head on his knee. The Bishop, bending fussily over the little limp body and making clucking noises in his throat, was peremptorily bidden by the King to: "Give him air and send for Mr. Lewis."

As the Bishop, hastening to obey his Sovereign's command flung wide the door, Mr. Lewis appeared so promptly that one might have believed him posted on the mat.

Sparse and swarthy, misanthropic, with a mane of black hair that he chose to wear unwigged, Mr. Lewis had but two loves in his life: the one his native Wales, the other the child Prince, whose every trivial activity he faithfully recorded in his Journal.

Without a word or look at the King, Mr. Lewis, strode into the room, lifted the sagging William in his arms and, followed by Lord Albemarle, carried him out.

"O, dear! Dear me!" fussed the Bishop, in two minds whether to go or to stay. "I have never before seen His Highness affected by the heat."

"Heat? In October? How can it be the heat?" the King

crushingly retorted. "No. I am to blame. I qvestioned him too long. Von forgets, in the pleasure of examining this so receptive virgin mind, how that he is not——"

He turned abruptly to the window. Drumming his sensitive long fingers on the sill, he gazed upon the avenue of elms, thinned with faint autumn gold. Presently, and without moving his head, the King spoke.

"My Lord Bishop, ve desire that His Highness rests from his studies for this veek."

Folding his hands over his paunch, the Bishop bowed.

"His Highness is indeed so exemplary and so industrious a scholar, so far advanced in learning that it is a God-given joy to be thus privileged to——"

The King wheeled round.

"Qvite so. I vill send Doctor Radcliffe to examine His Highness . . . Vell, Keppel?"

"Your Machesty," Lord Albemarle, who at that moment had re-entered, reported in his execrable English, "His Highness is recoverdt andt sendts his apolochies thadt he cannot return to pay his respects to Your Machesty. His Highness's nurse puts him in his bedt."

"Tell Mr. Lewis to come back."

Widowed, childless, this alien King, who conscientiously performed the thankless task of sovereignty in the land of his adoption, had, even as his subject Jenkin Lewis, but two primary loves in his life: the one his native Holland, the other the boy who was his dead wife's nephew. This child, whose soldier's play he deliberately encouraged, symbolized for him a golden age for England's future. A warrior King, allied to a supernormal intelligence, might yet prove to be another Rupert, crowned.

While fully aware of and indifferent to the unveiled abhorrence in which he was regarded by the vast majority of his people, William III, Prince of Orange, had endeavoured to maintain an impartial attitude to the domestic feuds of Whig and Tory. A temporary cessation of hostilities abroad had brought about a renewal of hostilities at home. Nor was the proposed reduction of his standing army to a paltry seven thousand the least contentious factor in the transitional crisis that had followed the Peace of Ryswick. Faced with the problems of post-war adjustment, the King found little support from a Cabinet predominantly Whig in a Parliament predominantly Tory.

This singular state of affairs had been largely induced by William's misinterpretation of the democratic principles he doubtfully professed and zealously attempted to uphold. That he failed in his purpose was due less to misplaced judgment than to the distorted shadow of frustration that dogged the life from birth to death of this sagacious and extraordinary being.

On his erased palimpsest no hosanna is inscribed. While the reign of his successor resounds with the glories of Blenheim, Ramillies, Oudenarde, and their forceful moving spirit, the great Marlborough, his song remains unsung. Yet those immortal victories he did not live to see, he may not only have envisaged but promoted. That chill taciturn exterior he presented to the world masked one burning and indomitable passion—to curb, quench, and ultimately to destroy the power of the French Apollo, Louis XIV of France.

As a posthumous son of his father, the unhappy youth of William, Prince of Orange, had been warped by the dominance of a termagant grandmother, Amalia of Solms. A loveless marriage of convenience to the English wife whose throne he had shared, nothing lessened his inherent aversion to women. That he lavished much wealth and little attention on his mistress, Lady Orkney, served as the flimsiest disguise for the more subtle affection he bestowed upon his gentlemen. The disgruntled, disregarded ladies of his Court nicknamed him 'The Monster'; while she who of them all could claim the right of precedence, was systematically slighted by her brother-in-law, the King.

Anne Stuart, his heiress apparent, was the chief obstacle to William's secret scheming for the future of her son, unless, as her father before her, she too could be excluded from her place in the succession. That, ruthlessly he reasoned, might yet be brought about, despite the staunch support and loyalty of the English people for their native-born Princess. To the Calvinistic and sub-atheistic William, Anne's High Church and High Tory principles were not only anathema but worse; the portent of another dynastic upheaval in the shape of her half-brother, the present, unacknowledged and exiled Prince of Wales. With the ashes of a Revolution still smoking on its pyre, it needed but the merest spark to light a blaze.

He stood now at the window of Camden House on that fair October morning, and gazed upon the misted spaces of the garden, the sunlit bronze and gold of leaves about to fall; he saw the faded lavender of autumn daisies, the blue above, the green below, the crimson splendour of a dying rose. He saw, unseeing, with a detached observance that registered externals while he coldly savoured the sweetness of the day. So later, towards evening, he would savour the Schnapps he had introduced to a beer-drinking England. And standing there in that lingering stillness, broken only by the clamour of birdsong and the lowing of distant cattle, his thoughts, like furtive wasps sneaking around a beehive, hovered to probe the problem of the Hanoverian succession which in the event, God forbid, of Gloucester's death without issue would bring to the English throne a German King. Well, they already had a Dutchman.

The King snickered, breathing down his nose. Yes, and how they loathed him! But no more than he loathed them for their conceit, their bawdy jests, their asinine false chivalry to women, their drunkenness on Gallic wine and ale. He could have forgiven them a taste for Hollands gin. A race of uncultured, unimaginative clods, who passed for gallants with their furbelows and rouge-pots. Pah! There again the influence of France. They copied Paris fashions. Yet they had a noble tradition to maintain which must not, if he could help it, be dissipated by the antics of two amorous she-asses, and one, forsooth, the heiress to Great Britain . . . 'Mrs. Morley' Queen of England. Excellent! Superb! A fitting foil for the might and arrogance of Louis, Roi Soleil. With such grace, such dignity and with so diplomatic and so charming an ambassadress as Mrs. Sarah 'Freeman', one could prophesy the absolute collapse, not of France, not of Spain and all her Popish satellites, but of this miserable fog-bound island its beer-sodden, bull-baiting inhabitants—these boors who called him so reluctantly their King.

The snicker in his nose broke in a laugh, to rap his throat and halt his breath and bring on an attack of his asthma. His narrow body shook as if with ague; his face became encrimsoned in the fight against the overwhelming sense of suffocation. With one hand he clutched the window-sill, while with the other he dug in his pocket for his snuff-box.

The Bishop, in a further fuss at His Majesty's abstracted inattention to himself, took this opportunity to sidle up. "Sire! I trust Your Majesty is not unwell?"

"Unvell," gasped the King, "because I—laugh? Is humour so rare—in me, Bishop?"

"No, no, indeed, Your Majesty." The Bishop glanced uncomfortably away from that cadaverous fixed smile which bore so startling a resemblance to the grin on the face of a skull.

"I vill have tulips planted in these beds," announced the King, inhaling a pinch of the Spanish 'Sabilla,' a brick-red concoction specially blent for asthmatics. "This garden is an eyesore. You have no idea in England of horticultural design. The art of making gardens beautiful vent out with Elizabeth."

"That is so, Sire, alas!" The Bishop sighed extensively, then bethought himself in haste to add: "But Your Majesty's expert knowledge of flowers has brought a welcome revival of——"

"You admire then my garden at Kensington?" Gazing, not at the Bishop but out of the window, the King took another sniff of Spanish snuff.

"Admire!" The Bishop waxed ecstatic. "Your Majesty has performed wonders in what was little better than a wilderness."

"A vilderness." The King passed his tongue over his dry lips with a faint grimace as if the taste were bitter. "So vas this whole land a vilderness ven I came into it. A maze of conflict, with as many tortuous paths as in the Maze at my Hampton Court Palace. You prefer—in this country—to cultivate ridiculous kinder-gartens composed of blind alleys that carry you nowhere, rather than lay straightforvard simple paving-stones of solid vorth be-tween vich bright flowers—such as my tulips I bring you from Holland—may blow and bloom. My garden is not yet in the good order I vould have it, though the plants that I have sown vill live long after I am dead."

"Yes, yes—no, no," agreed and contradicted Bishop Burnet in a hurry. "'Tis an admirable garden, but"—he wagged a coy finger—"Your Majesty must not speak in terms of death."

"Vy?" The King turned his head and stared at the Bishop with that in his eyes to chill him into silence. "Vy should ve not speak of death, vich is the tvin sister of life? I have to die—you have to die—but for myself I do not care if I am dead to-morrow."

"Sire!" The Bishop expressed profoundest shock. "Let us not anticipate so dreadful a calamity."

"Ach, pish!" The King hunched his bony shoulders. "Vy make such a Thing of death? I cannot understand this negative approach to vat is after all as natural as birth. You know, as I know and as my doctors know, that this house of flesh vich I am privileged to occupy for an indefinite period, is in deplorable condition. True, my roof"—he touched the grotesque periwig that adorned his head—"does not leak, but its foundations are tottering. Here," the King laid his hand upon his chest, "these vindows, my two lungs that breathe God's precious air into my body, are being slowly destroyed by an horrible disease that my good doctor calls 'phthisical fever'. I am also asthmatic, mal-formed, and I am dropsical. It is difficult to know vere this dropsy can find the room to svell in the meagre limits of my body, vich, unlike my dear sister Anne's, gives not much space for expansion. She too suffers from this hideous ailment. Hers is due to brandy and mine is due to gin. So"—the King treated the greatly per-turbed Bishop to an exhibition of his yellow teeth—"you, my

Right Reverend Father in God, vill understand vy I wish to think sometimes of my escape from this house of bondage that I, on a short term of lease, inhabit, and dvell upon the possibilities of my continuance on some happier plane."

At this appeal the Bishop, now on surer ground, placed his finger-tips together, lowered his chin, lifted his eyes, and prepared to offer ghostly counsel.

"If Your Majesty has the least possible doubt that you, God's Anointed, will not ascend to the highest——"

"Come, come!" the King with suave impatience interrupted, "the mere fact that oil vas poured on my head and equally on that of my late—lamented—vife at our Coronation, is no guarantee of my admittance into Paradise. That exalted state of being is, ve know, *your* ultimate revard for the purgatory of existence here on earth. But is it mine?"

"Your Majesty, I . . ." the Bishop attempted feebly.

"It is," the King's perpetual smile flickering about his pale sardonic lips, echanced rather than detracted from his grimness, "a difficult qvestion to answer, even for you, my good Bishop. Ve vill therefore leave it in abeyance, and I vill ask you this. Do you believe that love is akin to hate?"

"Sire!" A gentle dew appeared upon the Bishop's forehead. "At the risk of Your Majesty's displeasure I am bound to dispel these—hem—this iconoclastic suggestion. I can admit no comparison between love and hate. The one is good, the other evil. Is not love the fundamental law of life? Did not our Blessed Saviour die for love, the love of humanity? Did He not adjure us 'Love our neighbour' as ourselves?"

"Exactly. But I do not love my neighbour. I detest him."

The worthy prelate found himself in greatest trouble now. As a pillar of the Whig Party he was torn between the dictates of his conscience and ambition. He owed his Diocese of Salisbury to the favour of the King, but he had set his heart on Winchester as a stepping stone to York. He must tread warily along the line of least resistance. . . . May God give me strength, the Bishop prayed, to guide His Majesty in the paths of righteous thought. And why, for pity's sake, did not Lord Albemarle return to save him from this most awkward situation?

"Love and hate," the King was saying. "You believe them to be *opp*osite, and I believe them to be *app*osite. There is but a hair's breadth of difference between these two, how you say?—conceptions? Emotions? Passions? Yes, passions." The King's eyes rested meditatively on the Bishop's distended paunch. "For there can be no milk-varm half measures between liking and disliking. If I do not love, then"—his voice rose to a metallic emphasis—"I must, must *hate* my enemy."

"No, Sire, no," soothed the now profusely perspiring Bishop. "Your Majesty has no enemy."

"No?"

The King smiled.

"No." Shuffling his feet, the Bishop glanced in the direction of the door.

"Only von," the King said, with that smile. "Only von in a vorld composed of incalculable millions. Am I not to be permitted then this small luxury—" the sombre eyes dilated—"of hating my life-long and most powerful antagonist, this painted popinjay whom I have sworn to overthrow and beat to his knees ven ve shall meet again?" He crushed his palms together as if between them he enclosed a noxious insect. "Though I admire him more than any man alive, though he has proved himself to be a gallant loser and a great gentleman, I must hate Louis, and must hate him —till I die!" As he spoke a shudder contorted that ravaged frame and swept the mocking smile from his face; then in a second it re-appeared as his eyes swerved from the staring Bishop to the door.

"Here I think," the King said gently, "is Lord Albemarle." The Bishop breathed deep thankfulness . . . "Yes, Keppel, come in."

Arnold Joost van Keppel, Lord Albemarle, a graceful youth with incredible eyelashes fringing his empty blue eyes, came in.

Since he had supplanted Bentinck, Earl of Portland, as King's favourite, honour after honour had been heaped upon this former page. Although he had never drawn a sword in battle, he was Colonel of the Dutch Carabineers, Governor of Bois le Duc, Baron Ashford of Ashford in Kent, Viscount Bury in the County Palatine of Lancaster; Earl of Albemarle in the British Peerage; Knight of the Garter and Master of the Robes.

"Vere have you been all this vile?" the King inquired petulantly. "I have to amuse myself *en épatant* the Bishop. My good Burnet, you must forgive my little, *litt*le joke. Do you not know that I am far too serious to be taken seriously? Arnold, vat have you done with Lewis? I asked for him."

"He is here, your Machesty." Keppel beckoned the Duke's gentleman into the room.

"How is His Highness now?" asked the King.

Lewis answered glumly that His Highness was asleep.

"Lewis," the King paused to take snuff. "I understand that a new appointment has been made in the Household of His Highness."

"Yes, Sire. In the Laundry."

"Vy vas I not consulted in this matter?"

Lewis stood in silence.

"*Vy?*" the King repeated.

"I do not know, Sire."

"Who introduced this person to the Household?"

"My Lady of Marlborough, Sire."

The King stretched his lips.

"Qvite so. The name is——?"

"Hill."

"Ven did she arrive?"

"To-day."

"Vat are her duties?"

"None, Sire, whatever."

And Lewis buttoned his tight mouth as if he never meant to open it again.

The King waved the hand that held his golden snuff-box. "You may go."

Lewis went.

Turning to Keppel, who was razing his dimpled chin between a finger and a thumb, the King spoke low-voiced to him in Dutch, while the Bishop, straining his ears, greatly deplored that he had neglected to teach himself more than a few words of the language. Though the King, he reflected, was a considerable diplomat, his manners were appalling . . . *Épatant*! The Bishop spoke French, but *épatant*? Surely the verb '*épater*' meant in English to break a glass? Or, more correctly, the base of a glass? He failed to see the connexion.

"My Lord Bishop," the King extended him two fingers, "I compliment you on His Highness's progress. Ven he resumes his studies, I vish him to be carefully instructed in the political history of France since the beginning of the reign of Louis Quatorze."

The Bishop bowed above the fleshless hand. Keppel opened the door and stood back. The King linked his arm in that of his young gentleman, and the two went out together.

*   *   *

On her arrival at the posting-inn at Penshurst, Abigail found that no conveyance had been sent to meet her, and that if she wished to reach her destination before nightfall she must walk.

She walked: a good three miles.

The sense of depression that had accompanied her throughout

her journey was nothing lessened by her first glimpse of Chafford House. This, the seat of Sir George Rivers, Baronet, was an early Elizabethan manor set amid wooded grounds and surrounded by a high bricked wall. A pair of wrought-iron gates supported by stone pillars, each topped by a bull at gaze, guarded the entrance to a gloomy drive bordered with thickets of laurel.

The many mullioned windows offered no light save the last fading glow from the sky; the oaken door no answer to her knock, until, when her arm was stiff and aching from repeated effort, a shuffling step was heard within.

Stealthily, and creaking as if encased in rust, the bolts were drawn. The door opened a few inches. In the aperture a face appeared, old, crinkled, yellow, inconceivably malign.

"Her ladyship," faltered Abigail. "Lady Rivers, if you please."

Her ladyship, the face informed her in a voice as rusty as the door-bolts, was from home.

"From——?" A host of misgivings besieged her. "Is her ladyship not—then—is she not expecting me?"

"I've told you," the face, with every indication of dismissing her, insisted, "that Er ladyship's from Ome." Then in after-thought it acrimoniously supplemented, "at the Bath."

"The——?"

"Bath," the face mumbled, "for the waters."

"Oh . . . The Bath."

She had forgotten that ladies of fashion who suffered from the gout were wont to take the waters at 'The Bath'.

"Did her ladyship not leave me any message?"

"I couldn't say," replied the face with shocking nonchalance, "I'm sure."

Abigail gathered her courage to force her way in if needs must. "Is there no one in this house who has been told of my arrival here to-day?"

As if obscurely touched by this appeal, the face blinked its bleared eyes and volunteered resentfully that 'Mrs. South' might know.

"Mrs. . . . Who?"

"South. 'Ousekeeper. No one tells me nothing, so you had best ask 'Er."

With which the door, groaning on its hinges, swung open.

She stood in semi-darkness in a lofty hall, panelled and raftered with oak. She had a swift impression of lavishly carven screens, a refectory table, several high-backed chairs, dim portraits inter-spersed with heads of stags upon the walls, and heraldic signs upon the windows that reflected dull gleams from the dying light on coats of armour. The owner of the face, seen now in his entirety, was presented as an ancient man-servant of dwarfish stature, his back bowed with the weight of its years.

Across the deeply shadowed hall, along a corridor covered with rush matting, she followed her hobbling guide to the door of a room at the far end. Here he halted, rapped on the oak, and, without waiting for an answer, opened it and ushered her in.

"A young person to see you, marm," he croaked; and went.

The sudden illumination of fire and candle-light, the unpretentious aspect of a small and cosy parlour, drawn curtains, a polished table on which were placed a tea-urn and various dishes of cakes, invited a reassuring contrast to the gloom of the hall and her churlish reception.

In a chair by the hearth sat a large-bosomed lady in a dark cloth gown and flowered petticoat drawn up to her knees to expose her stout but shapely legs, which she appeared to be toasting at the fire. Her black hair, arranged in a redundancy of curls, showed undisguised silver at the temples; but her fresh-complexioned face showed no expression whatsoever save that of the liveliest astonishment.

"Are you—but never, surely!" was this gentlewoman's greeting, uttered in full penetrating tones.

Abigail's dejection, which at sight of the room and its occupant had vanished, returned fourfold to sink her.

"Yes, madam. The new maid."

"Would ye believe it!" And rising from her chair the lady smilingly advanced to lay hands upon her shoulders.

"Goodness gracious, child! What's amiss? You tremble. Come to the fire and warm yourself. Sure, you must be perished after your long journey—all the way from Newcastle."

"New—castle!" panted Abigail. "No, madam, London."

"Yes, yes," the lady humoured her, "where no doubt you lay the night. You look incredibly young, my dear. How old are you?"

"Fifteen, ma'am."

"Fifteen! For the Lord's sake! And you a widow with a child!"

"A widow? . . ." Abigail paled and silently entreated: Heaven help me! "No, madam, I am not a——"

"Not? Oho! I see." These meaningful ejaculations were accompanied by a look both intimate and wise, that held in it, however, more of sympathy than censure. "So! The same old story—but all's one to me. I'm no saint to set myself above a sinner."

While she was speaking, Mrs. South's hands urged Abigail to a chair. Her gestures, her rich voice that betrayed an accent easily identified as Irish, her greeting which, if incomprehensible, was hearty, persuaded Abigail to decide that if she had inadvertently entered a madhouse, she had come and was here; and would stay.

"The truth is"—bustling to and fro behind the urn Mrs. South poured tea, plied Abigail with delicious almond cake, and told her—"the truth is, my dear, her ladyship cannot be relied upon for accuracy. Lady Rivers you will find to be eccentric. In fact this whole household is, to say the least, eccentric."

Abigail could well believe it.

"I'd not be staying here another minute," continued Mrs. South, "if I could afford to take myself off—but I can't."

Abigail gazed at her dumbly.

"Sure to God, child, what eyes ye have! Green as a cat's. Very knowing. No," Mrs. South shook her head till every curl on it waggled, "I cannot, being as it were dependent on the bounty of Sir George, own cousin to me poor dead mother twice removed, and given a home when my husband—the saints rest his soul!— was killed in the Battle o' the Boyne, fighting for our King against the Dutchman. And," Mrs. South concluded with so deep a heart-fetched sigh that the seams of her bodice looked to burst, "so there it is. And," her tone lightened to a chuckle, "here am I."

"Madam," holding her handleless cup and sipping the scalding bohea, Abigail burnt her tongue and braced herself to ask: "Did you not know I was coming to-day?"

"Not at all," replied Mrs. South promptly. "Herself wrote me from the Bath, having seen your advertisement——"

"Ad . . . vertisement, ma'am?" faltered Abigail.

"In the *News-Letter*," said Mrs. South with some impatience. "She wrote she had engaged you on condition you put your child out to nurse."

Abigail gasped.

"Yes," continued Mrs. South, "she's been at the Bath these two months, and taken half the servants with her. I understood from her I was to expect you here within the next sennight."

Abigail set down her cup and lifted her eyes.

"Madam, I must tell you——" and telling her she rose, prepared to go. "I am *not* a widow. Nor am I a mother with a child. Nor am I the person you're expecting."

"Are ye not?" The housekeeper received this information unsurprisedly. "Then sure and all, her ladyship, as usual, is mistook. But if," said Mrs. South, "you're not the person I'm expecting, I beg to know—for mercy's sake—who in the world you are!"

CHAPTER THREE

By the time Lady Rivers returned, three weeks later, from Bath, Abigail had come to accept her new life with the same resigned adaptability as one accepts a climate. Mrs. South, having ascertained and been duly impressed by the fact that Mistress Hill could claim close kinship with the Quality, and the Lady Marlborough no less, saw to it that the newcomer should be accorded those privileges that she, as supervisor of the household, exacted. Thus Mistress Hill took her meals with Mrs. South in the housekeeper's parlour and occupied a bedroom on the third floor, which was a more salubrious if scarcely more cheerful apartment than the attic allotted to her predecessors.

Abigail's duties, so far as Mrs. South had seemed it necessary to advise her, would consist mainly of carrying her ladyship's morning chocolate to her bedside, of tending her ladyship's toilet, and combing her lapdogs. And since her ladyship would not permit any but Mrs. South or her personal maid to enter her room, Abigail was informed that she would have to clean it.

Lady Rivers, it seemed, suffered less from the gout than from periodic absence of mind. "Which is to say," Mrs. South mysteriously hinted, "she is not so much *out* of her mind as romantic, particularly when the moon is at the full. At such times she may be captious but never unconformable."

"You mean," Abigail asked with falling lip, "that her ladyship is——?"

"Not at all," Mrs. South assured her strongly. "Don't I tell you she's sensible—but she's not *common*-sensible. There's a deal o' difference, and for myself I'd as lief be whimsical as wise."

That her ladyship had omitted to inform Mrs. South of Lady Marlborough's intervention on behalf of Mrs. Hill* was, it seemed not inconsistent with her employer's whimsies. As for the widow, were she coming, Mrs. South decided, she must come, and be returned to Newcastle with a month's wage as compensation: which contingency, however, could be dealt with when, or if, it should arise. In Mrs. South's opinion it would not, for, to further Abigail's uneasiness, Mrs. South was reminded by the date of her

---

* The abbreviation 'Mrs.' for Mistress was, until the middle of the eighteenth century, the prefix generally used for single and married women alike.

ladyship's letter concerning the widow, that the moon at that time was at the full.

Since Mrs. South could talk enough for two and Mrs. Hill had the gift of silence, confidences passed, or may have been extracted in the housekeeper's snug parlour, of which the garrulous good-natured Mrs. South was scarce aware.

From her Abigail learned that Sir George Rivers, the husband of her ladyship, seldom opened his mouth in the house save to yawn. "But out of it—Lord!" Mrs. South raised her hands and let them fall in her lap, leaning forward. "If I tell you—though I shouldn't—he had a rakish reputation that couples him with never-mind-who and half-a-dozen more. I warn you that Sir George is ever on the itch for a new petticoat. Even I——"

Here she threw her head back and laughed to shake her bosoms.

"Even you, ma'am?" Abigail innocently questioned with a lift of her white eyelids. "Even you, ma'am . . . what?"

"I deserve to be hanged," declared Mrs. South, "for speaking to a child on such a questionable topic, but I am bound to put you on your guard."

"Thank you, ma'am. I'm much obleeged," Abigail murmured.

"Sure, 'tis only Christian charity to prepare ye for the worst," Mrs. South pursued in tones of sprightly relish that suggested rather preparation for the best. "Sir George is nothing near so mild as his manners, and although I'll allow ye're not after his taste, being small as ye are, and so pale——"

"And plain," Abigail prompted, meek.

"Not at all!" Mrs. South denied with disconcerting haste. "Pale if ye like, and not a beauty——" She ran a searching eye over the modest little creature who sat with feet crossed and hands folded, the very image of youthful simplicity—"But," said Mrs. South decisively, "you've something. You're secretive, you may be sly, but you've a *some*thing that'll drive a man to wring your neck or tumble you!"

Mrs. Hill fluttered her negligible lashes.

"Madam, O, indeed, I trust you are mistook in thinking any gentleman would wish to take advantage of an unprotected orphan."

Which faltering speech was accompanied by so artless an upward glance of the green eyes that Mrs. South believed her judgment for once to be wanting, and hastened to amend it.

"Och! Never heed me blarney! But, Lord above, I'll say 'tis a crime to send ye out into the world to earn your living with no more knowledge of man and his vile ways than a babe in the womb. Still, we all have to make our beginnings"—and Mrs. South proceeded to tell Abigail hers, from the time that she was born in County Mayo to her marriage with a brother of the Commissioner of Revenue in Dublin.

"My husband was a Tory, and his father was a Tory, and I'm as hot a Tory"—she dropped her voice a semitone—"as I'm a Jack!"

Abigail knit her brows in puzzlement.

"A Jack?"

"Yes," repeated Mrs. South with hearty vehemence, "a Jack —for the Church and King James!"

As she spoke she rose from her seat, went to a cupboard and took from it a flagon and two glasses.

"I never say his name," she reverentially avowed, "but I don't drink to ut."

Which demonstration of loyalty, to judge by the effluvium that Mrs. South habitually exhaled, must have occurred throughout each day at not infrequent intervals.

"Ah! I comprehend, ma'am," Abigail diffidently offered. "You're a Jacobite."

"I am an' all." Mrs. South filled the glasses to their brims. "And I'll drink to no King but to him that is over the water!" She handed Abigail's glass to her across the table, raised her own and drained it at a draught.

Abigail tentatively sipped. It was her first experience of wine. She found it strong, but pleasant tasting; sipped again.

"You're too young to remember," said Mrs. South, re-seating herself with the bottle at her elbow, "the day that Dutch William came over from Holland to sit on the throne o' King James. I saw ut," declared Mrs. South, now rendered more than usually loquacious by this latest repetition of her loyalty, "with these own eyes o' mine I saw ut, and I'll swear that scarce a voice was raised against him when he landed on the Devon coast and marched to London. Yes, he, the damned usurper, had the whole country at his heels and His Majesty, King James, deserted by his own blackguardly officers. And who may you suppose turned tail on him, too? None other than Lord Churchill, as then he was, may he burnt for't! And him in command of a Brigade."

"Dear, dear!" responded Mrs. Hill with suitable dismay.

"Yes, the treacherous dog, great soldier though he be, I'll not deny, soon proved himself no ally to his King. Then who of all besides should follow his example and go over to the enemy— pushed to't by her lady friend, Lord Churchill's wife—none other than Her Highness, Princess Anne. Ran off in the night with your fine lady cousin she did, and left the King lamenting—'God help

me, I'm forsaken by me own children.' 'Tis true, and—may God
help him—so he was. And the other daugher——" Mrs. South
refilled her glass, savoured the bouquet of the white Cahorze before her nose with the air of a connoisseur, and impressively continued—"the *other* daughter, the late Queen Mary, married to
Dutch William, was ready enough to take her father's place. That
broke his spirit, poor soul, and he fled. Can you blame um? He
was hounded to't, driven from his kingdom by traitors who spread
the wicked lie that our Prince of Wales, James Francis Edward,
was not the King's own son, but had been smuggled to the Queen's
bed in a warming-pan! A young girl of a Queen she was too—his
second wife—a Princess of Modena and a Catholic. Believe me,
this land o' yours, my dear, will never prosper until the rightful
King or his descendants are returned to ut. Ye'll rise up an' up,
maybe, but in God's own time so ye'll go down"—Mrs. South
pointed ominously to the floor—"an' down an' down to stew—in
the cauldron of Hell."

At which conclusion Mrs. South circumvented a hiccup and
lifting her glass cried, "Come, child, drink! We'll drink health
to the King and damnation to the Whigs."

"To the King!" echoed Abigail, guiding her glass to Mrs.
South's that wavered hazily before her in mid-air: but she was not
very certain to which King's health she drank. "And," she smiled
happily, "damnation to the—madam, what exactly, may I ask
you, is a Whig?"

"What's—why!" cried Mrs. South, completely scandalized
by this display of ignorance, "ye poor benighted child, don't ye
know?"

Abigail said she was not very sure, but thought it had something to do with false hair.

"False——" Mrs. South guffawed to ring the rafters. "False, it
is indeed. You're right. Out o' the mouths o' sucklings! False,
and cunning as the devil is a Whig. Every man of um is rotten as
shtink—ashstinkin' eggs. And if you don' know the devvy—deri-
devri——" Mrs. South pettishly sucked at her palate and achieved
with perseverance, "deri-vation o' the word 'Whig', let me tell you
'tis the Scots for sour milk."

"Sour milk!" Abigail expressed herself astonished. "Only
fancy!"

" 'Tis not fancy at all, child. Fact. And 'pon my life and liver
it well suits the mealy-mouthed, cantank'rous, come-to-Jazus
piety o' those maw-worm Whig Dissenters and the Low Church
Bishops who hand-in-glove it with the Dutchman to withhold our
blessed Catholic King from his throne. But," said Mrs South,

whose face to Abigail's wonder, appeared grotesquely to have swelled, and possessed not two, but four eyes and three noses, "But the Whigs return the compliment, begar, for 'tis from Ireland they have borrowed the word 'Tory'; and that"—Mrs. South adroitly turned a belch into a chuckle, "that word, in my country, signifies 'robber.' "

"Robber." Abigail, sipping, smiled happily. "Does it, ma'am, indeed?"

"It does. So now ye have ut. A house divided—thass' to say the House o' Parliament, and a pack o' scurvy hounds tearing the guts and entrails out o' the body o' the Church to feather their own foul nests with wealth and honours. Did ye ever hear the song bawled by the Whigs when they drove our King James from his throne?"

Abigail shook her head.

" 'Twent like this. 'Lero, Lero, Lilliburlero'——" and Mrs. South boisterously began to sing it, while she beat time in the air with one finger, " 'Lilliburlero bullen-a-lah!' Och, 'twas terrible to hear in their stinking mouths that song they stole from the folk-lore of Ireland. Yes, from our Irish peasants they stole ut and howled ut:

> 'O why does he sta-ay so lo-ont be*hind*,
> By-*hy* my shoul, 'tis a Protestant wind' . . . .

Ah! 'twas a Protestant wind that blew the Dutchman on to England's shores, and a Protestant hurricane that drove th' Shtuart from them. So thass' the way 'tis," Mrs. South concluded indistinctly, "and rape me if the bottle isn't dead again—bad cess to ut!"

None knows whence, why, or how Abigail Hill became imbued with the Jacobite fever which in after years, first secretly then openly, possessed her. It may well be that the tales told, the songs sung in Mrs. South's parlour, served to release a significant thread in the pattern of her earlier life and contributed their own share to the weaving of that complicated tapestry in which she figures, moth-coloured, unobtrusive, but persistent still, when the rival gold is frayed.

Mrs. South, who had finished her song and her bottle, got up to fetch more—"For luck and the King and a nightcap," she said, when she was halted in her progress to the cupboard by the sound of a commotion in the drive.

The clatter of wheels, the jingle of harness, an hallooing of men's voices, the yapping of dogs, a hammering upon the door and the shuffling step of the ancient man-servant treading the hall, brought Mrs. South in a trice to her senses and Mrs. Hill in a daze to her feet.

"Why, madam, what——" she faintly asked, clinging for support to the arm of her chair while the walls went whizzing round her—"what's to do?"

Superb in dignity, miraculously sobered, Mrs. South confronted her.

"There's everything to do. Herself is here a week before her time, and you're in no state to attend her. You're raddled. Fetch me the warming-pan. I'll prepare my lady's chamber. And you," said Mrs. South, "can go to bed."

She went to bed, and as a result of her unusual libations slept the clock round from the moment she laid her head on the pillow till she was awakened in the morning, to find Mrs. South, very stately, beside her.

"Dress yourself," was the command. "Her ladyship requires your attendance."

Abigail put her hand to her head which was aching to split. "I feel," she murmured, "greatly indisposed."

"You were," Mrs. South significantly stated, "indisposed, being taken—should her ladyship inquire—with the megrims."

And producing a phial, she poured its contents in a glass and offered it to Abigail's lips.

"O, ma'am," she shuddered, shrinking. "Don't make me drink again!"

"Make?" In tones of monumental incredulity Mrs. South repeated, "*make* you drink—*again*! What perfidy is here? Is this all the thanks I receive for supplying you last night with a restorative when you came to my room, white as a ghost, and so sickly you could scarce stand on your feet, begging and praying me send for the 'pothecary? And did I not, in the goodness of me heart, lay you in your bed while with me own hands I performed your duties? Disrobed her ladyship, warmed her pan, took up her supper—and now I am reproached for't. Ingratitude, thy name is sharper than the serpent's tooth, that I," said Mrs. South obscurely, "have nurtured in me bosom. So drink this. Yes, I insist. And come to me parlour when you're ready."

Abigail, whose memory of the previous night's entertainment was no clearer than Mrs. South's account of it, unwillingly accepted the proffered dose, that did, indisputably, revive her. Having splashed her face in cold water, combed and hid her hair —which was growing—in a mob, and with the private reservation that the housekeeper was likely as romantic as her mistress, she presented herself for Mrs. South's approval.

That lady, now elegantly apparelled in an ash-coloured silk petticoat, and a black bodice cut low to exhibit a wide expanse of bosom only partially concealed by a tucker, euphemistically known as a 'modesty piece', was gracious enough to express herself satisfied with her underling's appearance.

As she followed in the rustling wake of Mrs. South, Abigail was conscious of a sinking in the stomach that might have been due as much to dissipation as to nervousness. At the door of her ladyship's chamber Mrs. South paused, knocked, and receiving no answer, opened it and entered.

Her curtsy was a thing to wonder at.

"The young person, my lady," she regally announced, "recommended by the Lady Marlborough, is here."

Abigail, who for the last three weeks had swept and dusted Lady Rivers' apartment, leaving everything neat as a pin, was now shocked to perceive its disorder. Perfume bottles, patch-boxes, hares' feet, and every kind of toilet perquisite littered the dressing table; a bowl of rice-powder had spilled its contents on the carpet, in company with sundry soiled garments, stays, caps, pantoufles, and a chamber-pot whose contents obtrusively assailed the nose. As Abigail rose from the bob she received a push in the back from her instructress to indicate that she approach the bed. This contained, as far as could be seen in the sombre shadows of its curtains, nothing but a pile of pillows; and, reposing on the coverlid, a heap of sprawling spaniels of various ages and sizes. These, as she drew nearer, leapt to greet her in a veritable fury of yapping and snarling, while one, evidently the mother of a family, sprang from the bed to sniff at her toes with the utmost suspicion.

"Angel! Fie! Naughty-naugh'. Swee'—swee'," cooed a voice, indistinct and muffled as if it issued from beneath the counterpane; as indeed it did.

Abigail, in a fright, glanced behind for Mrs. South and found that she had vanished. The spaniel bitch, oblivious to her mistress's admonishment was now, with a wolfish exposure of fangs, examining Abigail's calves.

"Won' bi'. You sta' still," urged the same muffled voice.

Abigail stayed uncomfortably still, while the bitch, joined by her children who appeared to be alarmingly adult, shared a jealous guard between them of her ankles.

"You no' love dogs?" queried the invisible owner of the voice. " 'f so won' suit. Come 'ere. P'ecious life."

For a second Abigail was embarrassed to believe that she and not her ruffianly receptionist had been thus endearingly addressed, until the voice continued: "Ang'. Nast' pers'n don' 'ike you. So sh' not 'ike 'er." And flinging off the covers that obscured her face, the speaker rose up from the pillows and beckoned her hand-maiden closer.

Lady Rivers, at this first glimpse, appeared to be a woman in her latest fifties. Her hair, of no colour seen in nature but approximately orange, was in wildest disarray. Her complexion, vividly encarmined, bore the ravages of smallpox. Her shapeless lips were smudged with the paint that had left its scarlet stain upon the bed-linen.

"So," remarked her ladyship, myopically peering over the edge of the sheet, "you Sar'h Mor'bra's poor 'lation. Ar'fu' cat. Sudd'n int'rest *my* pligh'. No mai'. Sen's you. Help me. Pitifu' story. Moth'less orphans. Saves keep. Kinds' 'tention. She an' John coupla' misers. Com'cal, an't it? Take pot. Empt'. An' commode. Mind monkey."

The termination of this coherent speech threw Abigail in a state of terror. Monkey! Mrs. South had not advised her that her duties would include the care of a menagerie.

"On c'mode," her ladyship said fretfully, pointing.

Following the direction indicated by the lady's finger, Abigail discovered by the bedside the article in question; on its closed lid a cushion; and curled on the cushion a dark bundle of fur.

"Lift r'up," commanded Lady Rivers. "Gimme. Carefu'. Carefu'."

As Abigail gingerly attempted to lift her up and be careful—a superfluous injunction—the monkey turned upon her, venomously chattering, and fastened its teeth in her thumb, Repressing a scream she let go the creature, who crouched on its cushion with every apparent intention of springing at her throat.

"Ange'," tittered Lady Rivers. "Marv'llous 'telligence. Named 'Ginia for Q'een 'Lizbeth. Both virgins. Are you?" And at this question, which appeared to call for no reply, her ladyship prepared to leave her bed.

Some judicious inquiry later revealed that the singular impediment in Lady Rivers' speech was the result of a minor apoplexy. But despite that, and other of her ladyship's peculiarities, she was at heart the kindliest of creatures, generous to folly and lavish with her gifts, which for all her good intentions were almost always useless or unwearable. Thus Abigail, during her first few months of service, became the recipient of five odd stockings, three gloves, a gentleman's snuff-box, one shoe, and a turtle dove from Moco (stuffed), no bigger than a lark.

This early apprenticeship in her combined capacity of nurse and general attendant on a semi-invalid who, at the waxing of the moon would be more than ever incoherent, irritable, vague, called for tact and indefatigable patience, and proved indeed to be—as Mrs. Hill in later years admitted—the best possible training for one whose life was destined for a much higher service; one whose name is held in perpetuity as a synonym for lady's maid: the perfect abigail.

She had been some few weeks in this employment before she became acquainted with Sir George. The cause of his prolonged absence was ambiguously attributed by his wife to: " 'Fairs o' State. Purely Parl'ment'ry. Keeps 'm 'ployed. Out o' mischief. Can't t'ink wha' poor ange' finds do here. Bur'd alive 'ith me."

Abigail could perhaps have enlightened her in respect of Sir George's activities at home; for, if her report of his conduct in a letter to her sister is not a little boastful and exaggerated, we may take it she was 'plagued' by his attentions, and that she cannot tell which of the two she most cordially detested: Lady Rivers' husband or her ape.

Yet a more harmless, affable, gentlemanly gentleman can scarcely be conceived than Sir George Rivers, whose care of and apparent devotion to his invalid wife was excessively courteous and touching. She had a passion for cards, and he, we are told, was always prepared to take a hand in a game after dinner. He would even condescend, obligingly, to teach his wife's 'young person' the intricacies of Brag, Basset, Lanctre Loo, and Ombre.

"Such droll names," Abigail modestly remarked. "What, sir, if you please, does 'Ombre' signify?"

Sir George, whose face beneath the juvenile furbelow that he affected, greatly resembled a boat's, was at pains to instruct her.

" 'Ombre' comes from the Spanish, 'Yo soy el hombre', which in plain English means—'I am the man.' " This information was accompanied by a languishing look and a pressure of her toe with his under the table. " 'Tis a game that can be played by three or five, though to be sure"—Sir George glanced from his wife, who was dozing in her chair, to her handmaiden whose green eyes were fixed on his in rapt attention—" 'tis more happily played," he pressed her foot again, "by only two."

Abigail proved so apt a pupil that her presence at the card-table was required every evening, and provoked from Mrs. South the caustic comment that: 'She'd be shot before she'd waste her breath again in pity for the innocence of one whose subtle tricks were only to be matched by a Circus.'

"A circus, madam?" Abigail showed the whites of her eyes in some bewilderment, and Mrs. South her teeth in a near frenzy.

"Yes, the Circus who turned honest men into swine."

"Ah!" said Abigail, seeing light. "I comprehend, ma'am. Circe. A mythological enchantress."

"Mythological my——!" was Mrs. South's more vigorous than virtuous retort. "You can't gull me. *I'm* not sixteen, and nor are you save in your years, I'm thinking. You was born old. *I've* watched you play your cards and tip the toe under the table. 'So droll to be sure,' and 'O sir, No sir!' Twiddle me thumb and twiddle him, too, in exchange for——"

"Him? Twiddle? Exchange? O, ma'am——" Abigail clasped her hands as if to wring them, "I may be dense as a brick wall and blind as a bat, but I fail to follow the trend of these——"

"Och, crucify me if I ever saw the like of ut!" tempestuously interrupted Mrs. South. "I'm asking no questions to be answered with lies. But I'd be glad to know how you came by that new fontange, the latest thing in heads, which you bought of Mrs. Milligan, the milliner at Penshurst and wore to church last Sunday and which cost, or I'm a Dutchman, every penny of a pound. You didn't buy *that*," concluded Mrs. South, very red in the face, very full in the chest, "out o' your wage of two shillings a week."

"Why, ma'am," said Abigail mildly, "I'm not denying that I bought myself a fontange, for since my hair has grown again I have no cap to fit my head, and I cannot go to church uncovered. Can I?"

"Umph!" ejaculated Mrs. South, which temporarily terminated that discussion.

As Christmas approached Lady Rivers evinced unprecedented energy in her preparations for the festival of cheer. The gardeners were ordered to cut branches of holly with which to decorate the hall. Sir George, assisted by the lady's maid, himself supervised the hanging over doors of the "kissing berries", which was the local name, he said, for mistletoe.

These innocent proceedings again greatly vexed Mrs. South, who chose to regard them as gross interference in those domestic operations over which she, as housekeeper, presided. Indeed, Mrs. South's allusions—somewhat metaphorically mixed—to lambs in snakeskins nurtured in a bosom who played the part of Circuses disguised in a wolf's clothing, so much disturbed Mrs. Hill that she vowed and declared she would give a month's warning, and was found in tears by Sir George in the hall.

"What's this? What? Warning? Nonsense. Pooh!"

Sir George would have none of these fantods, he said; and

playfully pinching the young person's cheek he marched her off
to her ladyship's chamber.

"Here, my heart's soul, is your good little Hill talking of
leaving us. Hey?"

"Leavin'?" screamed his heart's soul, rising from her pillows.
"Sh'not hear of't. Why leave? Dogs love. And 'Ginia. Wass'
trouble? Not 'nough money?"

"O, my lady! No, my lady!" While hastening to disabuse her
lady's mind of any mercenary motive, Mrs. Hill tearfully submitted: " 'Twas only, madam, that the housekeeper does not
appear to be altogether satisfied with me, or"—she cast down her
eyes—"with my work."

"S'keeper be dam'!" cried her ladyship, extremely fussed.
"You're my mai'. Not 'ers. Ev'y sass'faction. Don' she, ange'?"

Sir George fervently agreed that Mrs. Hill to his certain knowledge gave every satisfaction, and indeed deserved a substantial
rise—in her wages.

Thereafter Abigail's position in the household, Mrs. South's
rancour notwithstanding, stayed secure. And since Mrs. Hill
desired nothing more than to retain the good esteem of Mrs.
South, and everybody else, she did not too much emphasize the
point of this, her latest triumph. Nor did Mrs. South, in her turn,
feel disposed to fall out with the cousin of a countess, poor relation
though she was and little better than a servant. On tacit understanding, therefore of both parties, the friendly sessions in Mrs.
South's parlour were resumed.

Among the few guests invited for Christmas was Lady Rivers'
daughter, surprisingly named Philadelphia, and who, Lady Rivers
informed her attendant, had 'marr'd a Baker.'

"A baker, my lady?"

"Not b'ead, child. Ol' fam'ly. Goo' match. F'end o' Harley.
Know Harley?"

"No, madam."

"Son o' Abigail Thingummy. Same name's yours. Cousin?"

"I think not, madam. I have few relations."

Her ladyship grinned slantwise. "Only Sar'h. One too many.
Vile tan'tums. Hol's P'incess so." She made a significant down-
ward gesture with her thumb. "Bleedin' whi'. Know 'er daught'
Hen'ietta?"

Abigail admitted she was unacquainted with the Lady Henrietta.

"Marr'd Godophin's son. Ten thous'n' wed' p'esent f'om
P'incess. Three more gir's. Anne nex'. Lov'ey c'eature."

"Lovely creature? Where?" cried Sir George starting from his
doze to fumble for his quizzing glass and gaze expectantly around.

"There!" His wife giggled and pointed a finger at Abigail, who blushed to the tip of her nose. "Goo' thing she an't, or we migh' 'ave 'nothiner case o' warmin'-pan 'ere!"

With the arrival of Mrs. Philadelphia Baker, her husband, a family of four and no nursemaid, Abigail was kept busy from morning till night waiting not only on the ladies but the children. Yet so cheerfully did she perform this extra work, carrying trays to the rooms set apart for nurseries and entertaining the young with such games as 'Rise Pig and Go', 'One Penny Follow Me', and playing tunes on the harpsichord with a very sweet touch to set them dancing jigs in the hall, that Mistress Philadelphia expressed herself enchanted and declared the girl to be a paragon.

"I shall tell Sarah Marlborough," she confided to her husband, "how really grateful we are for her kindness in sending so excellent a person as Mrs. Hill to Mamma, who has never before kept any one of her maids for more than a month at a time. This little Hill has worked wonders. The children positively dote on her and so does poor Mamma. . . ."

* * *

Sarah was delighted. The 'poor waif' whom of her charity she had 'rescued from a garret', had proved the greatest credit to her choice. Yet, she was delighted . . . until it occurred to her that charity were best begun at home.

She had three girls yet to settle. Anne, her lovely Anne, to whom Charles Spencer, son of her dear friend Lady Sunderland, was paying marked attention, must be presented with due formality at Court. The equipment necessary to a marriageable daughter, her gowns, her jewels, and a suitable attendant, would take the better part of the meagre quarterly dole her dearest John allowed her for the family's expenses. And now with their son so soon to go to Cambridge, to say nothing of the fees encumbent on the education of that other 'waif' of hers, the 'ragged boy' whom she had clothed and sent to school here in this village of St. Albans —a nice expense!—she would be hard put, even with the strictest economy, to maintain the upkeep of her establishment.

True, 'Mrs. Morley' had been generous above all expectation with her gift of ten thousand pounds to Henrietta on her marriage. One could only hope she would be equally as generous again when the time came to announce the news of Anne's betrothal. Anne, however, to her mother's chagrin, had shown herself to be exceedingly provoking in her objection to the suitor elect. There had, indeed, been some vexatious scenes which had sorely racked

Anne's mother, and had terminated in her hoity-toity daughter's imprisonment, as penance, in her room.

Then, no doubt invited by their sister, the two younger girls had mutinied on Anne's behalf, for which offence they too had received punishment, richly deserved.

These fatiguing annoyances at home, in addition to dear 'Mrs. Morley's' demands on her time at St. James's, had strained the lady's patience beyond breaking-point. For only God and 'Mrs. Freeman' could know how progidious tedious, tiresome, and dull were the hours, days, nights, spent in 'Mrs. Morley's' company—playing Loo for the lowest possible stakes, plaiting fringes for scarves, and listening to 'Mrs. Morley's' rhapsodies over Prince William's scholastic achievements or her complaints of 'Mr. Caliban', as she was pleased to call the King.

Nothing but copious draughts of 'cold tea', medicinally administered, could stay 'Mrs. Morley's' interminable talk, and surely to goodness for such exigent and manifold attention, 'Mrs. Freeman' merited and would receive a handsome recompense.

Thus, on a spring morning in 1699, while she sipped her chocolate in bed, and her husband stood shaving himself at her mirror, Sarah reviewed her immediate problems. That she, Countess of Marlborough, wife of the great Churchill, second lady (some said the first) in the land, must be tormented by these incessant, niggardly domestic importunities was an outrage: inconsistent with her calling, and insufferable.

Her beloved John, although the most devoted of all husbands, was inclined to be slightly *too* cautious in parting with his money. A fault on the right side that had, withal, its disadvantages. He wore his clothes threadbare, his uniforms shabby. There were incidents, bandied by the Tories, to shame her. As, for example, the time when his gaiters were soaked with the rain and had to be cut from his legs to remove them. He had bidden his orderly rip them up at the seams, that they might be re-sewn and re-worn. That tale went the round of the Clubs of St. James's, gaining nothing to its credit by embellishment.

His insistence on economy at home extended to the smallest matters, such as the careful use of candles to save tallow, so that one groped about the house after dusk to bark one's shins: his reduction of the domestic staff to a minimum, even to his own self-denial of a valet, and his meticulous examination each week of the household accounts; all this was very irksome to his wife.

She throughout their life together had striven to humour John's idiosyncrasies, which, confessedly, enhanced the thousand irritations that beset her. Every room in the house required new curtains; the girls' gowns were démodé—they needed new stays, and here was Anne behaving like a bedlamite and vowing she would sooner hang than marry that pug-nosed Republican Spencer and his boils . . . 'Cod! was ever woman in this world more cruelly used?

"John."

"My love?"

"I have had a letter from Lady Sunderland," said Sarah with a frown for his soap-lathered face in the glass. "She tells me she met at cards last week the daughter of Lady Rivers—that Baker woman with the ridiculous name of Philadelphia. It appears that my whey-faced little relative, whom I sent as maid to Mrs. Baker's mother—poor mumbling Dorothea Rivers—has proved herself a godsend."

"Goddess-sent," replied her husband gallantly; and cut his chin and turned upon her, bleeding.

"Yes," said Sarah, sharp as knives. "You'll cut your throat sooner than spend a shilling a week for a servant to raze you. I've no patience!"

"Give me some cotton, sweet life, that I may staunch it," urged John. "I seem to have shaved off a pimple."

"You'll find a clean kerchief here in the drawer of the table. I was saying—oh, for God's sake! In the drawer! Must I jump up and find it for you? Are you so helpless? No—the *other* drawer!"

"I have it," John answered, and dabbed: and smiled pacifically at his beautiful sulky-mouthed wife, who, with her silken gold hair childishly tousled, looked no older, he decided fatuously, than her daughters. "What is it you were saying of your cousin, my love?"

"Only that I must have been out of my mind to hand her over to Dorothea Rivers. She makes good use of her, who could be of better use to me. If I had not been so——"

"Tender-hearted, as you always are," her husband interposed.

"*Will you,*" shrilled Sarah, "let me speak?"

And she spoke: to such strong purpose that her husband more than ever marvelled at her perspicacity, her genius for seizing opportunities, and above all for her consideration of his purse.

"Why certainly, my darling, your cousin Hill, whom you so generously rescued from a——"

"Garret," Sarah prompted. "She has much to thank me for."

"She has indeed," assented John, who was case-hardened now to Sarah's frequent repetition of her favourite theme; how that she had found those pitiful poor orphans 'living in a hovel', and the most dire squalid circumstances; how that the boy was a ruffianly young urchin, 'fighting in the streets and all in rags'; how that one of the girls was 'fat as a dumpling and plain as a potato—the other a sly, green-eyed shuffling little creature who could never look you in the face and was only fit to wield a broom, but were all three none the less her kith and kin.'

"Which being so," said Sarah, "I have succoured them. And wonder 'tis indeed that you approve my charity to that good-for-nothing rascal, young Jack Hill, while you deny your wife and daughters an attendant. However, I consider it my duty to bring this Abigail here, where she will live among her relatives and not with strangers in a menial capacity. I am glad you agree."

John would have agreed to anything within economic reason, which might have proved as equally agreeable to his wife.

"I take it," reflected Sarah, "as a slur upon myself and my good name, that my cousin should be put to service to wait on all and sundry. Can you *conceive* my horror to learn that Abigail Hill was nursemaid to the Baker children when they visited at Chafford House last Christmas? To say nothing of the odious duties she performs for Dorothea, who is not at all nice in her habits. Lady Sunderland declares that poor little Hill has to go round with a mop. Too disgusting. She is besides, I am told, kennel-maid to the dogs and keeper to a monkey. Worst of all—wait. I have the letter somewhere."

Sarah rummaged on the table at her bedside and produced a closely written paper. "Listen, pray, to this. Lady Sunderland says—'Hill takes her meals with the housekeeper.' (Only think, John, not with the family!) 'who is an Irish Papist and a Jacobite.' Dreadful. Um . . . She then goes on to say how Mrs. Baker related to her as if it were something to Hill's credit, that 'the girl convulsed the Baker children with her mimicry of Mrs. South'— that's the housekeeper—'and her Irish brogue.' A fine to-do," cried Sarah, "that my cousin plays a pantomime, giving imitations of her fellow servants like a sawney at a fair! But that is not the worst of it. I understand also—and this is most important"— Sarah raised her voice to recall her husband's attention from his chin. "*Will* you stop dabbing and listen to me! I understand also that Lady Rivers intends to take Abigail Hill with her to the Bath, where it will be all over the town and run in by the bells and lapped up with every glass of water in the Pump Room, that Sarah Marlborough's cousin is Lady Rivers' maid. I won't have it!" vociferated Sarah, thumping the bed with such violence that the crockery jumped from the tray and the contents of the jug of chocolate were spilled upon the coverlid. "*Now* see what you have made me do!"

"I? My love," John protested mildly, "how could I possibly have caused——"

"If I had a maid to attend me, which you are too mean with your money to provide, *this* would not have occurred. Give me a towel. Not your towel, idiot, smothered in soap. There's a clean towel on the table. Fetch it."

He fetched it.

Snatching the damask from her gentle spouse, Sarah vigorously rubbed the rivulets of chocolate from the rose-pink satin.

"Damnation! Now I've made it worse. Ruined. D'ye see? It will have to be replaced. Lack of domestic service, my dear, has cost you, this morning, three times the yearly wages of a maid. Is that false or true economy? Take this." She flung the stained napkin into John's face. He caught it deftly, mastered a grin, and returned to his toilet pursued by his wife's entreaties to change his shirt. "Clean this morning and covered in blood. And if it were not that I study your purse and send our washing each week to Camden House to be laundered by that suet-pudding—the other Hill, whom I of my charity placed there—you would have to keep a laundry-woman on the premises, and that would cost a pretty penny, wouldn't it? But if," argued Sarah, "I bring this Abigail here, she can act as maid to all of us and cost us nothing but her food. I'll write to-day to Lady Rivers and let her know of my intention. She must release her. She will not dare to refuse my request. If she does, I'll go fetch the girl myself. So that's the end of it."

"If you say so, my heart . . ." John dropped a kiss upon her cheek and left the thought unspoken that this end might prove to be a bad beginning.

CHAPTER FOUR

IN the year 1699 occurred a disruptive event to menace once again the peace of Europe. Oft consulted astrologers clacked gloomily of armies on the march, of a great General's victories and of the death of a King. A not unlikely deduction since William of Orange, as everyone knew, had a fatal disease of the lungs.

But that indomitable spirit which had wrested England's crown from its rightful owner still clung, with febrile insistence, to the walls of its mouldering fortress, his flesh, despite the auguries of wizards, the grave prognosis of his doctors, and the hopes of his rival, the Sun King.

Those two crowned diplomats, to all purpose allies, to all intent foes, had sunk each his mistrust of the other in their joint agreement of the first Partition Treaty. By the terms therein suggested, their imbecile pawn, King Carlos II of Spain, had been moved to will his Empire to the young Bavarian Prince, Joseph Ferdinand, with a conciliatory clause in favour of two disappointed claimants, the princelings of Austria and France. Sicily and Naples was the consolation prize offered to Philip of Bourbon, grandson of Louis, and Milan to the Austrian Hapsburg, Prince Charles. The problem then that faced the Kings of France and England, on the chequer-board of Europe, seemed about to be amicably solved, when their game was halted by a stalemate unforeseen in their joint calculations; the death, not of the moribund Carlos of Spain, but of his young heir, the Bavarian.

Thus in one blow the pieces so carefully placed were scattered and the board re-set again.

The terms of the second Partition Treaty proposed and signed by William III, without advice from or consultation with his Ministers, nominated the son of the Emperor Leopold heir to King Carlos of Spain.

Shock, however, was succeded by shock when Leopold of Austria who stood to win for his son the better part of an Empire, refused it.

Crowned heads and diplomats received the news aghast. What would be the outcome of this idiocy, this short-sighted, high-handed rejection of almost the whole of Spain? Would Louis seize it? Would the Dutchman annexe it for the Netherlands and bring about a Papal war? Rumour went that William's army was disbanded and his Parliament dissolved.

Rumour, as usual, was wrong.

William, although at loggerheads with Parliament, had no immediate intention of calling a General Election. He had, it is true, reconstructed his Ministry by replacing certain of the Whig Junto with Tories. He had also, for some time past, watched, with secret approval, the methods of a rising politician: Robert Harley.

With the ever increasing alienation of the Tories from the King, here was one who, professedly opposed to the Whigs, was not to be swayed by party, personal or even Royal favour, but by national interest only. A man after William's own heart. He might go far. He might even, the King privately considered, be elevated to the place of Speaker in the House; that for the future. For the present, Harley must be watched.

And William watched him.

Affable, courteous, a suave conversationalist, this not so very young man—he was forty—delved in and had knowledge of a great variety of matters. He favoured men of wit and learning, was a collector of books, a master of language; above all was he master of his tongue. But despite his polished, glib assurance, he could be as secretive and cautious when he chose as could the King. The Whigs regarded him with marked suspicion, complained that he collected information through the secret agencies of spies, and preferred to ask than to answer a question; another point of contact, this, between the King and Robert Harley.

Yet not even to him did William impart the substance of his second and revised Partition Treaty. He might have saved the peace of Europe if he had.

A great era had passed; one, perhaps greater, was dawning. Along those foetid byways that sprawled eastward from the City of Westminster, highwaymen, harlots, pickpockets, footpads, were gathered together in vagabond fraternity to toast the New Year* in the raw gin brought by King William from the Netherlands, to the detriment of honest English ale.

The bloods of St. James's declared their exuberance, each according to his taste and means, in high play, deep drink, or whoring. The bells of St. Paul's pealed their chimes of good cheer. The young Duke of Gloucester came from Windsor with his parents to attend the New Century Ball in the Palace of St. James's.

To this function Lady Marlborough's four daughters and their brother, Lord Churchill, were invited; but the two younger girls, Elizabeth and Mary, had been left at home at Holywell House, and at their mother's command. They were too young, went the verdict—to dash them—to be presented at Court.

Her ladyship's decision was received with protest from the parties concerned, and with some supporting opposition from their sister Anne, who suggested that: "Mamma is studying the cost of your Court gowns, my dears, and not your tender years. I was not considered too young to attend a Court Ball—aged eleven. And you are now both in your teens. She's been marrying me off to every eligible rake-hell in and out of town since I was six!"

And now Anne was the wife of Lord Spencer.

She had succumbed from sheer exhaustion, to scenes unprecedented, to threats, entreaties, accusations that her stubbornness, her selfishness, her obstinate ingratitude, were shortening her mother's life. After all, Anne had reflected, Spencer might yet prove to be the lesser of two evils. He was too old for her, almost

* Old Style Calendar.

twice her age, "And uglier than Satan," so on her return from an unblissful honeymoon she had confided to her cousin Abigail Hill. "He has pimples. He is dirty. His breath is offensive. He has already buried one wife. Can you wonder she died—of shock, I should think—to wake and find *that* in her bed! Every night I suffer hell's own misery, but 'tis nothing so bad as I suffered at home with Mamma."

Thus Lady Spencer, who was staying at Holywell pending the removal to her husband's house. Seated at her dressing-glass with Abigail in attendance, she accompanied this remark with a supercilious survey of Mrs. Hill's face in the mirror. Abigail's unresponsive silence, her patient wielding of the comb as she coiffed the Lady Anne, her very modest and obsequious demeanour, served not to soothe but only to increase Lady Anne's exasperation.

"Hey now!" she cried, "Clumsy toad! Would you drag my hair out by the roots?"

And jerking her head from Abigail's gentle hands, she rounded on her in a fury.

"The Lord knows why Mamma insists you wait on *me* when you're here to attend on the children! . . . You poor little beast! What a hellish life you lead with us—almost as hellish as mine is with Spencer. But at least you can thank your stars you're so unlovely that not even a pug-nosed chimpanzee would pester you with his—— Oh, God! Why do you make me say these vile things?"

She seized her hair-brush from the table and flung it in a passion on the floor. "Fetch me my shoes, and take that look of a suffering spaniel off your face or I'll vomit." And bowing her golden head upon her hands, Anne wept.

Abigail, still in silence, picked up the brush.

"Your tantrums, Cousin Anne," she said, cool, "don't disturb me. I can fully comprehend your distaste for Lord Spencer, and I know—as your mamma is always saying—that what's on your tongue must come out on your lung. You follow her in that. Nor are you unkind. You're unhappy." She laid her hand, light as a leaf, on Anne's shoulder. "Why don't you defy your mamma?" she asked softly. "Take to your heels. Run away."

"Run?" Anne raised her head and mopped her eyes. "Where? Are you inciting me to leave my husband, whom I have promised to love and obey?" She laughed on a high cracked note. "What a noise I should raise—but I can't. I *can't*! Not for my mother's sake, not even for *dear* Mrs. Morley's sake, despite she's been tapped for ten thousand as my portion—but for my father's sake.

Could I disgrace him and his name? No. I'll have to bear it. I'll have to—have to—*have* to! Don't stare like an imbecile. Fasten my bodice. What have you done with my patch-box? The patch-box, fool. No, that's the rouge . . ."

Anne Churchill, the toast of the Town, and 'as sweet a creature as ever was seen'—so the eulogistic Mr. Lewis in his journal describes her—was her father's favourite, and the loveliest of Sarah's four beautiful daughters.

Abigail had been bidden from Holywell House to wait upon her cousins at St. James's; and despite her self-effacing, meek obedience as befitting her combined role of personal maid and dependant, Mrs. Hill was elated at this, her first introduction to Court circles. None, however, could have guessed what volcanic upheaval seethed in that flattened bosom beneath the close-fitting bodice that hugged its maidenly curves. None knew, while she took her orders, ran her errands and performed her humble duties, that her mind was in a ferment of excitement: that while she pressed her cousins' petticoats, caps, frills, and night-shifts, she was secretly transported: dreamed her dreams and sang her songs and prayed her little prayers, as if she too were the daughter of a great lady about to be presented instead of only Abigail Hill. Sometimes, however, she tasked herself severely for her secret hopes and aspirations. Fie, you! Look in the glass. Look at your freckles. No wonder they mock. No wonder they whisper and grin at your back . . . She ground her small molars in a sudden gust of rage. What future lies ahead for you—a servant who waits on her betters? You're plain. You've a face like a cheese. You've no charm. Oho! Have I not? Didn't Mrs. South say I had *some*thing? Was Cleopatra handsome? History gives it she wasn't: but she too had 'something'. God damn them! Damn then, *damn* them for their beastliness—and for their beauty. Let me die!

Some such tormenting perplexities, virginal fears and emotions, may have disturbed the nights of Abigail Hill. She was at that expectant age when life is either radiant or agonizing; when each momentary encounter or impression is extravagantly multiplied: when the spirit alternately seared, riven, sunk—at the loss of a pin, goes soaring to the clouds at a gift of green stockings. When the whisper of wind in the grasses, sunlight on a hill, a jest, a harsh word, a nonsensical fancy, a hope frustrated, or a fairy tale, brings equal laughter and tears. And this as much for Abigail, orphaned, humble, poor, as for any other and more fortunate young lady, was youth's part and fleeting share in joy and sorrow.

In a state then that rang the changes on anticipatory excitement, romantic tremors, and subdued defiance—for Cousin Sarah had been singularly trying and splenetic, and Abigail's patience sorely taxed—she travelled by stage coach to London in advance and in charge of her ladies' bandboxes.

Mrs. Danvers received her at the Palace.

She was awed. Her poor mamma's description had not at all exaggerated the magnificence, the unimaginable luxury of the apartments occupied by Lady Marlborough, adjoining the Royal suite.

Mrs. Danvers, who had been dresser to the Princess Anne and recently raised to the rank of Bedchamber-woman, was immensely aware of her office. Wry as a crab-apple, sour as curds, Abigail decided as she rose from the curtsy and stood meekly regarding her toes.

In a far-away tone that proclaimed at once her superior status in the Household as opposed to that of 'Mrs. Freeman's' poor relation, Mrs. Danvers gave Mrs. Hill to understand that since accommodation at the Palace was restricted, she had arranged for Mrs. Hill to share her sister's room as at Camden House.

"A chaise," conceded Mrs. Danvers, "will be placed at your disposal to fetch and carry you back and forth from Kensington to St. James's."

Than which nothing could have more delighted Mrs. Hill.

It was, however, not her place to express her satisfaction at any arrangement made for her disposal and at Mrs. Danvers' convenience. She was accepted, merely as part and parcel of Lady Marlborough's goods and chattels, baggage: which she must now unpack.

And when the gowns were hung up in the clothes-press, the kerchiefs, fontanges, frills and shifts laid neatly in the drawers; the perfume bottles, powder-bowls, patch-boxes set out on the tables, and everything ready to receive Cousin Sarah and her daughters, Abigail was free to leave the Palace.

A chaise, bearing the Royal coat of arms, awaited her. She stepped in, and was not ill-pleased to observe that a smiling, graceful young gentleman in a full-bottomed periwig and a salmon-coloured coat, with a little fur muff and astonishing calves, side-glassed her at the gates as she drove out.

It was more than a year since the sisters had met, and the better part of that night passed in bridging the time spent away from each other.

Alice was full of complaints. She was the youngest member of the Duke's Household by at least twenty years, except for his pages, who were all little boys of his age. The ladies of his Court

were old and musty; Mr. Jenkin Lewis was a boor—sullen, dis-
agreeable, always sneering. She was pushed on one side by the
rest of the staff. She had no laundry duties other than the weekly
wash, sent from Holywell by Cousin Sarah and returned by one
of the Royal couriers.

"You may think yourself in luck," she told her sister, "that
you are kept busy all day, even though they may treat you like
dirt."

"Less than dirt," smiled Abigail, "dust."

"Dust, dirt, or what you will, I'd lefer be in your place," retorted Alice. "I'd as soon be a galley slave aboard a pirate ship
and live on salt beef and maggoty bread, as to be stuck here on a
hill in a prison. That's all I am—a prisoner. Yes, you may laugh.
'Tis the truth. I never stir out of the grounds. I'm sick to the
stomach of life in this house, and I'm no more a laundress than the
cat."

"I see," Abigail straightened her face, "that she's expecting
again."

"Yes," said Alice gloomily. "Last time she had them in Mr.
Lewis's bed. He was mad as jumping beans with me—as if it
were *my* fault! Do you think I've grown fatter with nothing to
do but eat?"

She certainly had. "But," said Abigail tactfully, "you may
grow thin as you grow older. You're still young."

"I'm fifteen, and you—why you're almost seventeen! Quite a
hag. We'll become dry and bitter as sea-holly in service, you and
I. We're only upper servants after all. We'll never marry."

"Marry?" Abigail twitched an eyebrow and said primly,
"We shouldn't, at our ages, be thinking of marriage."

"Why not? I think of nothing else, as a release from this life.
A forlorn hope, since for my part," grumbled Alice, "I never
speak to a man other than Mr. Lewis, and he's thirty if he's a
minute, and as broody as a hen. And he looks at me, when I
meet him sometimes in the garden, as if I were a nasty smell. And
believe me or not, he's so loyally, fanatically Welsh that he goes
about with a leek in his hat on St. David's day and makes the
Duke, as future Prince of Wales, do the same. And that's the only
time I've laughed in all the twelve months I've lived here in this
mausoleum. Which reminds me—mentioning mausoleums, for if
ever there's a walking corpse—I've seen the King!"

"Oh?"

Abigail's dispassionate response to this intelligence piqued her
sister, albeit at some defiance, to enlarge.

"Yes, I have. They say he'll be dead in a year. Nobody here

has a good word to say of him. They call him the Dutch Monster and Usurper, and the Lord knows what. I'll allow he's ugly, but his gentleman, Lord Albemarle," Alice said with lush sentiment, "is the handsomest man I have ever beheld. I watch him through the window when he comes with the King to visit the Duke, though he never looks at me. Mrs. Abrahal says he's the King's Jemmy-Jessamy and daren't cast an eye on the ladies. What do you think she can mean?"

Abigail's glance slid down.

"I can't imagine. Who is Mrs. Abrahal?"

"O, she——"

Alice launched into a tale. Mrs. Abrahal was first lady in charge of the Laundry, and bosom friend of Mrs. Danvers at the Palace. "And they both abhor Cousin Sarah. They say she puts brandy in the Princess's tea to make her tipsy, so that she'll promise her everything she asks. They say she'll have the Crown jewels, if not the Crown, from the Princess when she's Queen. Did you know she calls Cousin Sarah 'Mrs. Freeman', and *she* calls the Princess 'Mrs. Morley'? And they write love letters to each other? So Mrs. Danvers told Mrs. Abrahal. Isn't it comic? She, Mrs. Danvers, has seen them—the letters, I mean. You've no idea how the Princess signs herself—'with Love and Passion.' Such stuff! They say she has had dozens of miscarriages, and that Prince George has given her the——"

"And I say," Abigail deftly interposed, "that you'd best keep a still tongue in your head, and learn better than to repeat such scandalous muck to anyone"—she dropped her eyes—"but me."

"There's no one but you to whom I would wish to repeat it. I don't talk. I listen."

Abigail smiled, and said: "You're growing up."

"And so are you," returned Alice. "You've changed."

"How? For the better or worse?"

This was a poser. "You're more . . . Well, you're . . . different."

And having come to that weighty conclusion, Alice gazed with marked approval at her sister where she sat. Abigail's sand-coloured hair was drawn back from her forehead in the fashionable roll and fell artificially curled to her shoulders. Her figure, in an old dress of young Elizabeth Churchill's, was trim; her mouth, with its secretive closed smile, as red as if it had been painted, as indeed it was—with the Lady Anne's lip salve.

"*You* haven't grown, but your hair has," said Alice. "It never used to curl. Has it grown curly since you cut it off? Was that why you did cut it off?"

Abigail blinked at her.

"Maybe. And now that we've talked enough of ourselves, let me tell you of Jack."

There was everything to tell of Jack. He had grown, if Abigail hadn't, and had the shoulders of a bear, the face of an Adonis—"and calves as good"—she was suddenly reminded of the beau who had quizzed her at the Palace gates, "as good," she declared, glowing, "as any blade in St. James's. O, and Alice, you'll be glad to hear . . ."

Alice indeed was glad to hear how Jack had made such marked progress at his school that Cousin Sarah had promised to appoint him page to the Duke of Gloucester in the new year.

"Page to the Duke!" Alice brightened. "That's capital news. I won't have to die from a surfeit of old women and my own company now. Jack'll be company for a dozen. We *are* going up in the world!"

Abigail lifted her eyelids.

"You are. And Jack is, but I stay where I'm placed—down below."

"At least," Alice said consolingly, "you have a good home and more food than you can eat, and girls of your own age around you."

"Yes, so much around me that I live in a constant ring-a-ring-o' bells—and belles—who order me, 'Fetch this. Take away that. Lace my bodice. Comb my hair. Careful, careful, clumsy toad! Would you scalp me? Stupid creature!' "

And distorting her small mouth into a kittenish snarl, she jumped from her seat to give a diabolically clever imitation of a young lady of fashion at her toilet, titivating at the glass, applying an imaginary hare's foot, smiting an invisible attendant, and all this in such droll pantomime that Alice lay back in her chair and laughed till she ached.

"O lud, Abbie! You'll kill me! There never *was* such a mimic. You haven't lost the art. D'you remember how you used to amuse poor Mamma when she lay ill . . . Now give me Cousin Sarah."

So Abigail gave her Cousin Sarah, deepening her voice, throwing out her arms, flashing her eyes, squaring her chin, and pronouncing her words with histrionic elocution.

"Buckle my shoe. Lace my corset. Clean up the cat's mess. Bow the knee and worship me, the great I AM—you poor lost, lonely little lamb whom I rescued, as I will never cease to tell you, from the gutter. From a dustbin. From a broom. Yes! 'I took you from a broom', as the old song goes, and I receive

3

your lowly service in return for my generous, most charitable bounty. Sew this hem! Turn this sheet—side to middle. It has a great hole down its centre, and his lordship keeps me so close that I cannot afford new bed-linen, so sit you down and darn away, you ugly, shuffling, sly little bitch—my kinswoman—God help me! Were ever two cousins so dissimilar? The one a goddess, the other a—whoof!"

She paused for breath and flopped down on a stool. Her cheeks were flushed, her eyes half closed and shining.

Alice wiped hers. "Lord!" she giggled, "how you hate her!"

"Hate her? No." Abigail knit her pale brows. "I know I *ought* to hate her, for 'tis one of human nature's most sinful and most common weaknesses to bite the hand that feeds it. But," she shook her head, "I can't hate her. She has a horrid ugly temper, she's a scold, a shrew, a tyrant—she runs mad when she's in her fits—yet one could no more hate her for that than one could hate an ungovernable child. One could pity it for its bad upbringing, but one couldn't hate it. You see . . . she's so dreadfully young. Yes, *young*. She has never grown up. Her husband won't let her grow up. He married a very young girl and she's stayed—just a very young girl. She's younger than her daughters. She's younger than I. No," Abigail pondered, "I don't hate her."

"In spite of all that," Alice stated calmly, "you do. You would not go to such lengths to deny it if you didn't. And you've every reason to hate her. She took you away from Lady Rivers, where you were happy and contented, without so much as 'by your leave'. She makes you work like a housemaid and she knocks you about, and she don't even pay you for your service."

"But," Abigail smiled, "I am accepted as a member of the family and permitted to sit at their table. I am fed, clothed——"

"In your cousin's cast-offs. I can't forget—if you can—how she let poor Mamma, her own aunt, die in poverty."

"She gave her ten pounds," murmured Abigail.

"Ten! What's ten pounds? I earn more than ten pounds in a month for doing nothing. She gave Mamma ten pounds to keep us in food and clothing for a year."

"Yet not so long ago ten pounds would have represented a fortune to you and me. And you wouldn't be here but for her. Don't forget *that*." Abigail rose to her feet and twisting a curl of her hair round her finger, said slowly: "It isn't everyone who would take a stranger—which is all I am, blood relation or not—into her household to live. If I were in her place——"

"Well?" Alice prompted, staring. There was a look in Abigail's eyes, a startled, listening, expectant look that puzzled her. Abbie could, Alice decided, be very odd and unaccountable at times. "If you were in her place," she asked, "what then?"

Abigail yawned: and that strange look vanished. "I do not know what then. I only know what now, which is that I'm sleepy and must rise early to-morrow." She went to the window and pulled aside the curtain. The night was waning. A rime of frost silvered the lawn, and a full grinning moon swung out of a cloud to hang like a witch's lantern high above a tree-top.

Somewhere in the distance a cock crew.

Abigail let fall the curtain.

"And to-morrow," she said softly, "is to-day. . . ."

A day of sun and birds at song amid the greening buds and golden catkins in the gardens of St. James's. Spring had come in a night. The saffron crocus spread her wings and fled before the trumpet-peal of daffodils. Through the open window of the Princess Anne's apartment drifted the scent of early gillyflowers, together with the sound of clashing arms and battle cries. A deadly feud between two cumbersome Turks and four nimble Crusaders, as manifested by the crimson crosses on their shields and their tinfoil helmets, was in active progress on the lawn.

The Turks, each identically uniformed in what appeared to be tunics of sack-cloth emblazoned with a crescent in white paint, had been beaten to their knees and bore with patient fortitude the violent attacks of the Knights Templars.

The Princess, after anxiously watching the fray for a few seconds, leaned from the casement to hail her son.

"William! My darling! I do not like the way you are flourishing that sword. You'll poke out somebody's eye with it. Pray, sweetheart, be careful. Drury! Wetherby!"

The Turks, who in private life were the Duke's chairman and coachman respectively, rose from their knees and stood at attention.

"How can you," the Princess demanded, "encourage His Highness to play such a dangerous game? William, my treasure, stop playing now. Come in at once, I insist."

Her treasure, as scarlet with mortification as the cross on his shield, handed it with his helmet, to his pages, Churchill and Bathurst. His sword he retained, and using it as a prop for his faltering step, marched sulkily into the Palace.

"I am here, at your command, Madam," he announced with marked chill.

"Dearest heart!" His mother gathered him into her arms "You must forgive me for spoiling your play, but——"

"*I* forgive *you*, Madam?" William sternly interrupted. "You do me too much honour. Your orders, Madam, your smallest wish, must be obeyed. But one favour only I beg——"

"Anything, my darling, if you will only go now to Mrs. Wanley and have your face washed and change your suit. You look so dreadfully dirty and hot."

William scowled.

"I crave your pardon, Madam, for entering your presence in battle-dress, but I was about to entreat that you will not again allude to the manœuvres"—he drew himself up to his very small height—"of the Duke of Gloucester's Cadet Corps as *play*."

The Princess gasped back a giggle, covered her mouth, and answered abjectly: "I know 'twas most irreverent in me to be so thoughtless, darling. You have every reason to be vexed. It shall not occur again. Now do go, love, to Mrs. Wanley, and then come back to breakfast. And don't be long. You know how Papa dislikes to be kept waiting."

"Your servant, Madam."

William, exceedingly haughty, bowed and turned to the door. His mother followed to relieve him of his weapon. "And give that nasty thing to me. That's my precious boy."

With long suffering William relinquished his Crusader's tin sword and left the room.

The Princess smiled on a sigh and carefully lowered herself to her day-bed. She was distressingly stout, her complexion veinous and pitted with smallpox, her mouth full and wide, her eyes large, brown, bovine. She had two chins and a clear, sweet, surprisingly young voice. Her once very beautiful hands were sadly disfigured with gout. She glanced down at them resting on her uncorseted pendulous bosom, and twisted a ring on her forefinger that dug painfully into her flesh. It would have to be cut since it could not be pulled off. The knuckle was turning blue and shockingly swollen. She sighed again and called: "George! Are you ready for your breakfast?"

From the communicating apartment came a guttural reply in a pronounced foreign accent.

"Yes, my love. Will you haf any objection"—the bulky presence of Prince George of Denmark appeared in the doorway—"if Mr. Masham will choin us?"

"By all means," assented his wife, "invite Mr. Masham to join us."

"Masham!" Over his shoulder the Prince addressed an unseen personage. "Her Highness invites you to breakfast."

A voice from within replied, in a tone that suggested its owner was bowing nose to knees, that he was honoured to accept the invitation.

Whereupon the Prince, whose face carried not two but four chins, advanced to bestow on his wife's placid forehead a kiss that lost nothing of its fervour because it was accompanied strongly by a breath of stale wine.

This great clumsy, flaxen-haired Dane, of exceptional height and breadth of shoulder, had, after many years of over-eating and drinking, run to inordinate fat. He was a martyr to asthma, the gout, and his kidneys. His mild blue eyes were embedded in the folds of his mauvish pink cheeks. His fingers were thick as sausages, and he could not see his feet for his paunch. But in his marred and bloated features there still lingered some trace of that beauty which had captured the heart of Anne Stuart. He was remarkable for nothing save a simple, dog-like devotion to his wife and a taste for carpentering. He would spend hours in his little workshop, sawing and planing wood, screwing hinges on doors, making curious toys for his son, none of which bore any semblance to the original intention of their creator. Bred of the blood of the Vikings with the salt of the sea in his veins, he was born to the life of a sailor; but while he may have dreamed of the ships he would never command, he would not have exchanged his stout, loving, greatly loved Anne for a Fleet.

More than fifteen years had passed since Prince George of Denmark had courted and married the niece of King Charles II. The two had been lovers then; they were lovers still. Their tragedy lay in the fate that destined her for a throne and him for a Queen's Consort, when both would have wished no happier existence than to share—not a palace, but a home, for his choice on the shores of a sea. The brooding tragedy of those many little bodies buried in St. George's Chapel had bound them ever closer in their mutual adoration for their one surviving child. In a world of petty intrigues and infidelities where love was a mockery, marriage a farce, this very ordinary man and his wife occasioned much derisive ridicule among the beaux and the belles of St. James's for their constancy and their devotion; and for the fact that they still shared one bed.

From that bed Prince George, who had overslept, had just risen. He wore a magnificent embroidered dressing-gown over his night-shift, and a hastily adjusted periwig over his thinning gold hair.

"Pull the bell, my dearest," said Anne, patting her husband's caressing hand. "I am ravenous for my breakfast, and so, I am sure, are you."

Prince George was not ravenous for breakfast. He had stayed up till the early hours of the morning playing hazard with his gentlemen, and had consumed the better part of six flagons of Burgundy and three of Hollands before he had tiptoed, somewhat rockily, to the nuptial couch and climbed in without waking his wife.

"William will take orange-water," said Anne, to whom affairs of food bore equal importance to affairs of State. "Dr. Radcliffe says that orange-water is particularly beneficial to the health of a growing boy. He is growing," she questioned anxiously, "isn't he, George?"

"He grows prodigious," agreed the Prince, whose habit it was to repeat everything twice and even thrice in paraphrase, and his favourite expression, 'est-il possible?' at every opportunity. "I too have noticed how he grows. He is growing to a formidable height. He will be a giant. He resembles my father, who also was a big man. Ach! Here he is. My brave! My William. My Crusader. Mon Chou-chou!" He was caught up in his father's arms and rapturously kissed. "How goes my Knightss Templarss?"

"I am very well, I thank you, Sir," William politely disengaged, and straightened his wig that his father's embrace had pushed awry. So small he looked and pale, that the Prince hastened boisterously to reiterate: "I swear you have grown bigger in the night. You grow like a mushroom while you sleep. How goes the battle? Have you beaten the Turk? Have you slaughtered the Saracen, my Knightss Templarss?"

"Knight Templar, Papa," William corrected. "I am not in the plural—and the battle was a draw."

"Est-il possible?" sympathetically exclaimed the Prince. "You have not beaten him? He is not vanquished?"

"I was to blame for that," said William's mother hastily. "I interrupted the game. I have promised never to do it again, but he must also promise me not to play with those horrid—— Yes, come."

A scratch at the door was followed by two lackeys carrying breakfast dishes, by two pages of the backstairs with cups and tankards; by Mrs. Wanley, to tie a napkin round her nursling's neck; by Mrs. Danvers to place a chair and footstool for the Princess at the table; by Jenkin Lewis to attend upon the Duke; and, last of all, by Mr. Masham, Prince George's equerry.

He, a graceful young gentleman in a full-bottomed wig, a salmon-coloured coat, with astonishing calves and a most amiable smile, advanced to fall on one knee and kiss the welcoming hand of the Princess.

"Your Royal Highness." He rose to his feet and bowed again, very low. "I trust Your Highness has slept well?"

"I always sleep well, thank God, Mr. Masham. Did you sleep well?"

Mr. Masham was happy to admit that he had slept very well indeed, he thanked Her Highness, and turning his smile and his bow to the en-napkined Duke he expressed the hope that His Highness had also passed a comfortable night.

"Very comfortable, I thank you, Mr. Masham," answered the Duke, whose tone of forced politeness did not at all disguise the fact that these preliminary inquiries were a ritual long custom had staled. "Did you?"

"Oh, indeed, indeed, Your Highness," was Mr. Masham's ecstatic response, accompanied by another bow and a smile that looked to split his face in two. "Such a wonderful day on which to wake after a peaceful night."

The countenance of Mr. Masham offered no indication that the greater part of his peaceful night had been spent at the card-table; that Prince George had won from him something over fifty guineas, and that his head ached to burst as the result of an over-spill of Burgundy, for Mr. Masham could not hold his drink.

"And what a good omen for the birth of the New Century," dutifully pursued the smiling Mr. Masham. "May Your Highness live to see the end of it."

"If so I should be," His Highness wrinkled his supernormally high brow in calculation, "almost one hundred and eleven years old. Even elephants don't live to be as old as that—or do they? I hope I may die at a reasonable age."

"My precious!" his mother shuddered. "Don't, pray, talk of dying."

"I was not, Mamma, talking of dying. I was only saying that——"

"Then don't say it, sweetheart . . . George. Mr. Masham."

The Princess graciously gestured her husband and his gentle-man to their respective seats. Mr. Masham at imminent risk of a tumble on the polished floor, darted forward to conduct Her Highness to her place at the head of the table.

Prince George said grace. Prince William said: "Amen . . . I'm confounded dry," and slewed his eyes round longingly at a carafe filled with orange-water on a sideboard.

"William!" His mother lifted a shocked hand to her face. "From whom did you learn that dreadful word?"

"From Jenkin Lewis," William promptly replied.

Anne summoned a frown.

"If so, then Mr. Lewis must be sent away."

"No, I didn't, Mamma—truly I didn't," said William in a hurry. "And Jenkin has already been sent away once for my fault. I won't have him sent away again. You mustn't send him away, Mamma."

"Est-il possible," exclaimed Prince George, "that my ears have not deceived? Have I heard correct? Do you say 'must not' to your mother, William?"

"I only said, Sir——"

"I do not wish for arguments. You shall not argue. Na, see, you have hurt your dear mother by using this so dreadful swear in her presence."

"Hurt her? Have I?" William jumped from his chair and ran to her side. "I didn't mean to hurt you, Mamma. It slipped out and it's nothing as bad as some words I . . . No. Well, I'll allow 'tis a monstrous wicked vile habit but, Madam, all soldiers swear. Don't cry, Mamma. My dearest dear. Are you crying?"

She was crying: her love for him ached in her heart; he was so small, so precious, so frail, so utterly and awfully her love, the only one of all her many babies who had survived his first year, that she feared every day, every hour, to lose him as she had lost those others.

"Return to your seat, my angel." And as she stroked back a curl of his periwig that dangled over his forehead she noticed, thankfully, that his left eye was not so inflamed and watery to-day.

William returned to his seat. The lackeys handed round dishes of porridge, beefsteak, mutton collops, a dish of carp, an eel-pie, and slices of cold boar's head.

The Princess helped herself to liberal pie, and her son to porridge. Her husband accepted a slice of boar's head; Mr. Masham, shrinkingly, a morsel of carp.

The conversation, between pauses for mastication, rang the changes on the beneficial qualities of porridge—which, Mr. Masham volunteered, was a national dish of the Scots—as opposed to curds and whey; on the weather; on the King's health which Mr. Masham declared to be rapidly failing, and was answered with an optimistic, "est-il possible?" from the Prince.

"Did you hear, my love, that the King's health is not good? He is failing."

"I hope not," said Anne unconcernedly. "William, eat out of your spoon sideways, my darling. Don't push the whole of it into your mouth."

"It is the general opinion, Sir," said Mr. Masham, picking at his carp, "that the King is undergoing some not unnatural anxiety with regard to the European problem." And having got that out he paused, patted his lips with his napkin, and looked from the Prince to the Princess, awaiting his cue.

"Anxiety?" The Prince goggled. "Est-il possible?"

"I do not understand, Mr. Masham," said the Princess, raising her gentle brown eyes to his, "why the King should be more anxious about the state of Europe now than he was last year. A crown," she added sighing, "is a fearful weight to carry."

"It is." Prince George gulped down his beer and nodded his great head. "A formidable weight. And the promise of one still more weightier."

He looked with doting affection at his wife, where she sat colossal in ruby satin, her low-cut bodice amply exposing her bosom. A probing sunbeam touched a curl of her mahogany-brown hair and burnished it richly to bronze.

"The sun shines bright to-day," remarked the Prince. "It is a sunshine day. May the sun always shine so bright for you my love, and make of your hair a crown. A lighter crown to wear than one of gold. Yes? Is not Her Highness's hair a crown of glory, Masham?"

"A heavenly crown, Sir," acquiesced the eager Mr. Masham. "I think I never saw so beautiful an effect. The light on Her Highness's hair reminds me of——"

While Mr. Masham racked his brains to decide precisely of what Her Highness's hair reminded him, other than a horse's mane, he was spared this tax on his inventive powers by the announcement of a page at the door.

"The Countess of Marlborough, Madam."

"Oh!" Anne half rose from her seat. "I did not expect her ladyship so early. Danvers, go tell her ladyship that I will be with her directly."

As Danvers curtsied herself out of the room Prince George, whose face had turned the colour of a beetroot, said with unwonted temerity, "She must wait. You must be allowed to finish your breakfast, mon ange."

"I have finished my breakfast." Anne's eyes, pointedly directed at her husband, held in their gentle depths a sudden gleam like the spark from a tinder-box. "And when you have finished yours, my love——"

Her tone suggested he should be finished now.

"Presently, presently, heart's delight." The Prince beckoned a footman. "Give me some of that excellent bifsteak. I will

3*

have that red cut, underdone. I like well the bifsteak. It is good."

Beefsteak was served. The Prince conveyed a chunk of the juicy meat to his wide cavern of a mouth. His appetite, never long absent, returned with the savoury morsel. He chewed, gobbled, bolted with the utmost relish, and insisted that Mr. Masham should also be served with beefsteak.

Renewing his smile, Mr. Masham fortified himself to follow his Prince's example. But the effort of swallowing food so substantial was too much for his stomach; his gorge rose, the meat stuck in his gullet. His attempt to dislodge it with a draught of beer was his undoing. Mr. Masham choked into his cup, gave a loud whoop, and returned the little he had eaten to his plate. Whereupon the kind Princess, forgetting her momentary displeasure, herself rose to pat the abject Mr. Masham between his heaving shoulders.

Mr. Masham's shame was worse than death.

William, taking the opportunity afforded by this unfortunate disturbance to dispose of his loathly porridge, scooped up what remained on his platter, deposited it under the table, and replacing his spoon on his empty dish said brightly:

"I am finished, Mamma."

"Then, if we have all finished"—the Princess removed her hand from the Prince's empurpled gentleman—"Poor Mr. Masham. How very distressing. If we have all finished—— Give Mr. Masham a glass of water."

"No—ouch! Ma-Ma-Madam! I assure you 'tis—'tis—noth—ouch! 'Twill—ow—ow—ow!"

But despite his paroxysms Mr. Masham succeeded, though almost bent double, in reaching the door to bow Her Highness out.

"And all this," reflectively remarked the Prince, picking steak from his teeth with a finger-nail, "all this—my breakfast spoilt, my gentleman in a fit—yes, my good Masham, you are certainly choking yourself into a fit. Come, come! Drink some water, pray, or you will bring up your guts."

"Ow—ow!" croaked the exhausted Mr. Masham.

"And all this," said the Prince with heartfelt disgust, "because *dear* Mrs. Freeman comes to call."

"My dear Mrs. Freeman!" was Mrs. Morley's greeting. "How more than kind of you to be so punctual."

"Not too punctual, Madam, I hope?" Mrs. Freeman, with slight asperity, rejoined. "I recollect that I particularly emphasized

the request, which Mrs. Morley has graciously granted, that I
wished to see you on a matter of some urgency at ten o' the clock
this morning."

In her verbal, as in all her written communications with her
mistress, Mrs. Freeman evinced a dexterous and superb disregard
for her pronouns.

"Mrs. Freeman could never be too punctual," admitted Mrs.
Morley, with, however, some misgiving for the impatient toss of
Mrs. Freeman's head. "Pray be seated, Mrs. Freeman."

Mrs. Freeman sat.

"I trust," ventured Mrs. Morley, "that Mrs. Freeman has
breakfasted. If not——"

"Breakfasted! Why, Madam, I have been up and about my
business since dawn. I break my fast every day of my life at eight
o' the clock."

"Which is the reason why you retain your beautiful figure."
Mrs. Morley glanced ruefully down at hers. "Mine——"

"Yours is your own fault, my dear Madam. Am I not at continuous pains to impress on Mrs. Morley the necessity for regular
exercise? You should ride to the hunt in Windsor Park—not
follow in your pony-chaise. *That* is no exercise. Ride here." Mrs.
Freeman waved her hand in some vague direction. "You have
hundreds of acres of greensward on which to gallop. But no! You
prefer to be driven. Mrs. Morley is certainly much too stout for
your age. Lud, Madam! You are four years younger than I, and
you look at least twenty years older."

"I am sure I do," Mrs. Morley agreed with a sigh. "I carry
far too much weight. I certainly must take more exer——"

"However," interrupted Mrs. Freeman, "I have not sought an
audience with my beloved Mrs. Morley to discuss your obesity,
but to beg a favour that is not wholly personal, although it affects
me as much as every other of her devoted subj—er—*future*
subjects."

Her penetrating fixed regard held the hapless Mrs. Morley as
some gigantic captive moth is held impaled on a pin.

"Anything within my power—my favour—none——" ineffectually murmured Mrs. Morley, "no favour is too great, as my
dear Mrs. Freeman must——"

"Yes, yes. Exactly so. But this is less a favour that I ask you,
Madam, than a duty of which I am bound to remind Mrs. Morley.
You have, most unwisely, let it be known all over the Court, and
carried, I have no doubt, by Danvers, *out* of the Court to her
gossip Abrahal at Kensington, and God alone can tell where else
—for already the news-sheets are full of it—that Your Highness

will not appear to-night at the Ball. The most important function of the year. Nay!" cried Mrs. Freeman, dramatically gesturing, "the first and the last of its kind that you, I, or any one of us is like to see. The celebration of a century's birth and death. Lord, Madam! You must, you positively *must* appear to-night."

"I would indeed," was Mrs. Morley's hesitant reply, "be most happy to appear to-night, but that Dr. Radcliffe says I am not yet fully recovered from my miscarriage. The afterbirth did not come away as it——"

"What Dr. Radcliffe says or does not say," Mrs. Freeman shatteringly intervened, "doesn't alter my opinion one tittle. Dr. Radcliffe has never borne a child and you have borne sixteen."

"Seventeen."

"Sixteen."

A slight movement of Mrs. Morley's head accompanied her repetition: "Seventeen. With William."

"Ah, yes! I was counting those you lost—not the one precious cherub who has, God be thanked, survived. Therefore as I was about to suggest if I am graciously permitted to speak, you should understand yourself and your condition better than Dr. Radcliffe or all the court physicians put together. These doctors—foh!" The medical profession in general and Dr. Radcliffe in particular were relegated to nihility by Mrs. Freeman's scorn. "Dr. Radcliffe is mollycoddling my beloved Mrs. Morley out of existence. He doses you with purges, pills, and smothers you in plasters. I never heard of plastering a woman after her confinement."

"I was not plastered," Mrs. Morley dared to object. "Dr. Radcliffe advised a binding to support me——"

"Fiddle-faddle! I believe in letting Nature have its way. Did you ever see a cow swathed in bandages and plasters after calving?"

"My dear Mrs. Freeman," Mrs. Morley raised her heavy chin, and Mrs. Freeman had the grace to lower hers. "I am bound to resent your somewhat ill-chosen——"

"I merit Your Highness's rebuke," Mrs. Freeman hurriedly allowed. "But Mrs. Morley should know me well enough to realize that Mrs. Freeman's speech outrides her choice of words. Does not my dearest Mrs. Morley understand the love, the ever anxious guardianship that prompts her Freeman to watch and cherish Mrs. Morley's every action? Do you not know that I would as soon cut myself to pieces as speak aught that savours of irreverence to Your most adored Royal Highness?"

Mrs. Morley leaned forward to take Mrs. Freeman's gesticulating hand in both of hers and tell her softly, soothingly: "I know, I know . . . You are completely guileless and utterly my friend."

"I am that indeed," was the indulgent reply, "which is the reason I advise Mrs. Morley to dispense with the services of Dr. Radcliffe and employ in his stead my good Dr. Garth, who is a man of highest qualities and parts."

"And a Whig," supplemented Mrs. Morley.

"Whig?" echoed Mrs. Freeman, glaring. "Why certainly, Madam, Dr. Garth is a Whig. And what of it? Good heavens alive! What in the world have politics to do with medicine?"

"Nothing, to be sure. But . . . What I meant to say . . ." faltered Mrs. Morley.

Mrs. Freeman said it sternly for her.

"What you meant to say, Madam, is that because this hoddy-doddy of a Radcliffe has persuaded Mrs. Morley to believe yourself an invalid, you refuse to make a brief appearance at the Ball to-night. Frankly, Mrs. Morley, you provoke me."

Mrs. Morley flushed.

"I exceedingly regret that I provoke my good Mrs. Freeman, but I am bound to follow my doctor's advice."

"And set the whole Court clacking? Lord, Madam, conceive the disappointment of your guests! Conceive the slight you put upon them by your invisibility—to say nothing of the slight to His Majesty the King. And, Madam, have you forgot"—Mrs. Freeman strategically plugged the last loophole—"have you forgot that my beloved Anne, Your Highness's god-daughter and name-sake, is to be presented to-night for the first time since her marriage?"

Mrs. Morley's face lighted. "Ah, yes! How remiss of me. I had indeed forgot. Dear Mrs. Freeman, why did you not remind me? Nothing now will keep me from the Ball. I'll wear my silver brocade and my pearls."

"If I may suggest, Madam, your rubies. You are pale. You will need colour if you insist on wearing white."

"Silver."

"Silver or white, 'tis one and the same. Why split hairs?"

"I am not splitting hairs." Mrs. Morley's underlip bulged obstinately outward. "Only I wish to wear the silver and my pearls."

"And who am I," queried Mrs. Freeman, syrup-sweet, "to circumvent Your Highness's command? Who am I to express the smallest contradictory opinion against Mrs. Morley's wish, who am but your faithful, loving and adoring servant?"

She curtsied to the ground. Mrs. Morley, at once contrite and tender, raised her up.

"Not my servant. My friend. My dearest friend." She held out her hand. Mrs. Freeman covered it with kisses.

"My sweet mistress! You will be the belle of the Ball."

"La, Mrs. Freeman! I? The belle?" Mrs. Morley smiled; a slow, pleased smile. "Come, come, dear soul, I've heard that love is blind, but I—truly, Mrs. Freeman, your eyesight needs attention. Look at me!"

Mrs. Freeman looked and blinked as if her sight were dazzled.

"Madam, you are ravishing. You have the Stuart charm, which is always irresistible. Your mouth, your eyes, your lovely hair . . ." But if her words convinced to flatter, her thoughts were far away. She was wondering if she could possibly contrive to borrow Mrs. Morley's pearls for Anne.

"*I* the belle of the Ball," Mrs. Morley's smile lingered. "There is only one who can claim that distinction. You, my sweetest. You."

"What?" Mrs. Freeman returned her errant thoughts and bobbed again. "I dare to differ, Madam. Mrs. Morley honours me above my worth. I am faded now, and old."

"No, never old," murmured Mrs. Morley, fondling Mrs. Freeman's hand. "Perennially young. *So* beautiful!"

"I will dress you," Mrs. Freeman said, "à merveille. In your silver, with your rubies——"

Mrs. Morley's smile vanished.

"Pearls."

"Rubies. Pray permit me, Madam, to know what best becomes you. The first lady in the land must outshine in jewels and splendour the ladies of her Court. 'Tis fantastical," cried Mrs. Freeman, "that Your Highness should appear in pearls that are more suited to a young girl or a—or a bride. I beg Mrs. Morley to consider your position. You must wear your rubies."

"I will look," pouted Mrs. Morley, "like the Queen of Sheba."

"You will look divine. Rubies. On that," Mrs. Freeman said decisively, "we are now both agreed. I knew, Madam, you would see it must be so."

And so it was.

Mrs. Morley wore the rubies and Mrs. Freeman's daughter, Anne, the pearls.

* * *

From the gallery that overlooked the ballroom Abigail and Alice watched the guests assemble. Nearby, but sufficiently removed from contact with the Hills and other unimportant persons to emphasize their social and functional superiority, a triad composed of Mesdames Danvers, Abrahal, and Wanley, provided a sibilant accompaniment to hidden music.

Candleshine reflected from a myriad crystal lustres poured a shower of light on rich brocaded gown and broidered coat, gold lace and dainty sword-hilt; struck diamond sparks from jewelled heads and buckles, subdued the garish overtones of paint and rouge and powder.

On the velvet-covered dais at the end of the hall stood the three Royal chairs still unoccupied; but the tiers of seats ranged along the tapestried walls were already filled with privileged spectators.

The Hills were not privileged spectators. Mrs. Danvers had clearly stressed that point, when, on request of Mrs. Abrahal, she had granted the sisters entrance to the gallery. Mrs. Danvers, who as the Princess Anne's Bedchamber-woman was accorded a seat in the ballroom, had been gracious enough to leave her place of prominence below to mingle with obscurity above.

The fine distinctions of Court etiquette were, however, wasted on the Hills. Squeezed close to Abigail's side, Alice, all eyes for the pageant, all ears for the comments of the ladies Danvers, Abrahal and Wanley, was breathing open-mouthed and heavily down Abigail's neck.

The persuasive murmur of stringed instruments, a boy's voice singing clear and sweet, the tinkle of laughter, the momentary articulation of a face, a form, emerging from that lively chimera to be at once dissolved in new enchantment, brushed Abigail's consciousness with magic. Wonder-charged, she stood surrendered, lost. The trials, tribulations, of the day were all forgotten; yet not two hours since, she had fled, crushed, from the wrath of . . .

"The Countess of Marlborough."

The voice of the Lord Chamberlain announcing arrivals, and Alice's redundant observation, "Cousin Sarah!" returned her to reality.

She shrank.

A stir below, a louder buzz of whispering above, a craning of necks, from the seated heralded the Lady's entrance on her husband's arm.

Exquisitely gowned, the fairest of any, shining, bejewelled, with gold dust on her hair, none to see her exchanging curtsies for bows and radiant smile for smiles, could have guessed her but recently rageful, so loud that her cries, lamentations and scoldings might have been heard from St. James's to Kensington Palace.

The first mutterings of thunder had resounded at noon when Anne's dress for the Ball had not been delivered, though promised. Abigail, who had volunteered to fetch it, was despatched in a chair to the Exchange. On the way along the Strand one of the chairmen, who had evidently been celebrating—in anticipation—the New Century, stumbled and let the chair fall. The door, insecurely fastened, had unlatched itself, and Abigail was flung into the gutter. Worse than that, so was Anne's gown. The mantua-maker, in her hurry, had omitted to tie a cord round the bandbox, from which the lid parted to disgorge its contents in the mud.

Amid the jeers of spectators and profanities hurled at his mate from the other and more sober chairman, Abigail had scrambled, unhurt, to her feet. Horror crept in as she surveyed the damage to Anne's gown. The quilted satin petticoat, the gold-laced bodice with its fall of Mechlin, were woefully stained and bespattered. What to do? Smuggle it up the backstairs and sponge it? That would mean another two hours at least of delay. Confess the truth and brave the storm? Or take coach for Southampton and Dick; but he had lately married and his wife might not be eager to welcome a superfluous sister-in-law. . . . Or she could drown herself: the Thames was near at hand.

In the end she was persuaded to be bold. Though life with Cousin Sarah had its disadvantages it was preferable to poverty or death. But her faithful account, and the unsightly evidence produced, of the mishap, did not assuage the spleen of Cousin Sarah. Abigail, chagrined to see such poor reward for virtue, wished she had resorted to apocrypha and come to the Lady with a tale: how she had been set upon by footpads, robbed, and gagged, the chairmen murdered—any like to save her face, and the accusation of duplicity and wickedness unparalleled heaped upon her luckless head. Despite all pleadings to the contrary, Cousin Sarah was convinced that deliberate malevolent connivance, and not accident, had wrought this shocking havoc to Anne's gown.

"May you burn for a liar!" the Lady had shrieked. "How could you fall from a chair, unless you were drunk. *Were* you drunk?"

"No, madam . . . The man," bleated Abigail, "was, I think . . ."

"Hear her!" had then cried the Countess to heaven. "Listen to this vile object, who damnifies an innocent servant, one of the Royal servants forsooth, own chairman to Her Highness—you low, sneaking, ill-bred, miserable—Hah!" With which the Lady had thrown herself upon a day-bed, laughed, wept, and tumbled her hair in a violent fit of the vapours.

His lordship, coming from his dressing-room to inquire the cause of the disturbance, was called to witness how 'this sly minx, this shuffling, sneaking little cat, who had been taken from a broom and placed above her station,' repaid her benefactress. "Anne's gown," besought the Countess, "will you look at it? Ruined! Covered in mire and filth. This wretched girl you see before you has dragged it in the dirt, from what devil-guided motive only Satan himself can tell. Look at it. Look!"

And springing from her couch, the Lady had dangled the gown in front of her lord, who vainly strove to soothe.

"My dearest, I am certain Abigail would not have deliberately contrived to——"

"Would she not? I say she would and did! Look how she stands, with no word to say in defence of herself. She *has* no defence. There's guilt in her eye. I must have been out of my mind to bring her into my house to defile me and my children. That comes of taking pity on a poor relation. She serves me with evil in return for every kindness. Why, the very clothes she wears I give her. Every morsel of food she puts in her mouth is paid for by you. Yes, by *you*! Which means so much less for our own. Go, get you gone, viper. The sight of you sickens me. Go! Go! Go!"

And with each repetition of the word the Lady had fetched a clout on Abigail's ear to turn it blue.

Whereupon Anne, who had entered the room in time to witness this assault, turned upon her mother blazing protest.

"Mamma! I will not stand by and see my cousin so abused. I heard you shouting as I came along the corridor. Every word you said will be carried by the pages of the back stairs to make us all a laughing-stock. Is it likely Abigail would have purposely spoilt my——"

But having dared thus far, Anne was allowed to dare no farther. Her ladyship, aboil, seized her by the shoulders and shook her till her teeth rattled like dice in a box. Whereupon Lord Marlborough, who had hurried to his daughter's aid, hustled her and Abigail out of the room and closed the door firmly upon them.

In the privacy of her own chamber, Anne, betwixt laughing and crying, had apologized for her mamma's behaviour.

"You must believe she does not know what she is saying. I admit it is shocking to see her so beside herself, but Mamma has always been incapable of guarding her tongue, or her temper. You must forgive her."

"It is not for me to forgive her," Abigail, with uncommon tartness, had rejoined. "I am here to take her orders."

"But not," flashed Anne, "her blows."

"Oh, that! So long as I keep my hearing, your mamma may

loose her tongue. Words don't hurt." And then she smiled. "Let's forget it. I believe I can remove these stains . . ."

Which she did to such good purpose that when Anne had at last been laced into her green and white gown not the slightest mark impaired the delicious effect.

"You look like a white tulip folded in green leaves." Stepping back to survey with pride her handiwork, Abigail had pinned up a curl of Anne's hair. "If I were one thousandth part as lovely as you, I would be so . . ." She paused and pinkened.

"Well, what?" Anne leaned forward to criticize herself in the mirror. Her skin had a delicate shell-like transparency; her crystal-blue eyes stared out from the perfect oval of her face with a blank, dazed look.

"I," Abigail had whispered, "would be . . . happy."

"Happy!" Anne uttered a short mirthless laugh. "Then let us envy each other. I vow I would sooner be you for all the wretched life you lead with us, than I, who——" She swung round on her stool. "I'll tell you this——"

But what she had to tell remained untold. The door had burst open as if by a whirlwind, and Henrietta rushed into the room.

"Abigail! Is she here?"

Lady Rialton, the Marlboroughs' eldest daughter, had inherited some of her mother's beauty, but more of her disposition. Brusque of speech, downright in manner, impulsive, self-opinionated, she was the terror of her two younger sisters and continuously quarrelling with Anne.

"Is Abigail . . . Ah, there you are! I've been hunting for you high and low. What are you doing here? Why are you not with Mamma?"

"Because," Anne had provokingly replied, "she is with me."

"You're dressed and Mamma isn't. She says she won't go to the Ball. She swears that Abigail dragged your gown in the gutter out of spite—which I don't doubt she did, and now she's thrown her hand-glass at one of the footmen and smashed it to atoms."

"That's seven years' bad luck," pronounced Abigail calmly.

"What?" Henrietta turned upon her. "Here's wickedness! Calling down curses on us like a heathen! If there's any bad luck to come to our family you'll have brought it on us, you sly snivelling little rat! Go to my mother at once. Go! Hurry!" And chasing Abigail to the door she had slammed it after her.

As she fled down the corridor Abigail had heard Anne's voice raised high and clear: "You should be ashamed, both you and Mamma, the way you torment that poor girl. You seem to forget she's our cousin—our own kin. She's every bit as well born as we are, if not better. The Hills are related to——"

Related to whom? She had missed that. Pausing in her flight, Abigail had tiptoed back to listen at the keyhole and heard Henrietta say: "Ho! So! You're mighty set above yourself, my girl, since you became a Toast of the Kit-Cat. Pooh! You a Toast. Ha-ha! 'The little Whig.' The Whigs must be in low water to drink *you* with their wine! Who gave you those pearls? Not Spencer, I'll warrant. He's more like to give you nothing but the——"

A word indistinguishable here had been interrupted by Anne's meditative and inconsequent remark:

" 'Tis a pity you should have chosen such a hideous shade of lemon yellow for your gown, though I'll allow it fadges well with your sickly complexion."

There had followed an explosive sound from Henrietta, a scream from Anne, and a crash as of a chair overturned.

"At least," said Henrietta shouting, "my jewels are my own and not borrowed—or worse!"

So those two were at it again. . . . And at that remembrance Abigail's shoulders shook in soundless laughter. But for Anne, she told herself hotly, she would leave Cousin Sarah and Holywell House and be done with the Churchills for ever. On the other hand, she reasoned, a girl without a penny could not quarrel with her bread and butter, even though her bread were a butterless dry crust. Yet the time might come when she could make return in fullest measure for every slight and blow, and every insult offered, and every stinging tear that she had shed.

And here they all were, guests of honour. Cousin Sarah strewing sweetness in her path like some bountiful Ceres with two attendant Persephones; yet to be sure Henrietta more resembled Medusa, with her hair dressed in snaky curls and that scowl upon her face. Yes, and lemon-yellow, Abigail was encouraged to agree, could *not* have been a more unhappy choice. Her husband, Rialton, son and heir of Lord Godolphin, underwent in his turn a critical survey. What a gross, mottled face was his: how pompous his bearing. How he strutted, pigeon-chested, eyes everywhere searching, but never once did he look at his wife. In the wake of her sister, came Anne with Lord Spencer.

Pasty-faced and inclined to be corpulent, no figure of romance was he. Talk gave it he had married Anne Churchill not for love of her but of ambition, and the glory to be reflected in the future from the altitude to which her mother, it was augured, would be raised in the next reign.

Anne, decided Abigail, looked as she were walking in her sleep. No trace of the recent scuffle with her sister lay in the cool transparent stare of those ice-blue eyes, or in those close-folded flower-like lips. Her bearing was erect; her gold shining hair fell caressingly upon her shoulders; her throat was no less white than the necklace of pearls that adorned it.

Murmurs of admiration greeted her; men's glances hovered, paused; women looked and turned to whisper. Unseeingly she passed to her place.

Mrs. Danvers was mindful of hers.

"Ladies, I must leave you. Her Highness will appear at any moment. My attendance is required."

The attendance of Mrs. Abrahal and Mrs. Wanley being thus, by slender implication, *not* required, Mrs. Danvers offered a gracious amendment.

"I have ordered supper to be served to you both at midnight in the ante-room yonder."

"Obleeged, ma'am, I am sure."

The ladies bobbed. Mrs. Danvers inclined her head. Resplendent in fuchsia-red fronted with purple, fringed with gold net a yard deep, and with all her petticoats hissing as if they housed beneath their folds a colony of serpents, Mrs. Danvers, ignoring the Hills, departed to take her seat among the highest.

"Do you think *we* will be served with supper?" whispered Alice. "I'm mortal hungry. I had no time to eat a proper meal before I——"

A fanfare of trumpets rang through the hall to silence her and rouse a buzz of expectation. Voices hushed; all heads turned towards the folding doors at the right of the dais, where heralds awaited the approach of the Princess.

Lady Marlborough advanced to stand immediately below the dais and above her husband. The musicians played a lively march; two silver-clad pages flung open the doors simultaneously with the Lord Chamberlain's announcement:

"Their Royal Highnesses the Princess Anne and Prince George of Denmark."

"His Royal Highness the Duke of Gloucester."

The Princess was magnificent in silver edged with ermine. Diamonds flashed in her hair; rubies, like crimson jets of blood, girdled her short neck, shone on her extravagant bosom, clasped her plump wrists. Leaning heavily on the Prince's arm, and with remarkable dignity for one so stout, she passed slowly along the ranks of courtiers to the end of the hall, and turned to walk back again to the dais followed by two pages carrying her train.

Her hand encased in a jewelled glove, waved repeated acknow-
ledgment to down-bent heads and curtsies. When she smiled she
showed dimples.

"I told you she was fat," whispered Alice.

So fat, poor soul, that despite the combined efforts of her pages,
her husband, and Lady Marlborough, who was in the fore to offer
assistance, she could scarcely mount the velvet-covered steps to
her seat, and was seen to flush as red as her rubies, then turn so
pale with a hand to her heart that she appeared for a second to
swoon. But she instantly recovered and was hoisted up and
lowered down and placed upon her chair. Prince George, monumental in velvet, his chest glittering with Orders, his smile a trifle
anxious as he watched his wife across the space reserved for the
most ornate of the three gilded seats, beckoned his son to the stool
on the dais which none but those of the nearest Blood Royal was
permitted to occupy.

The Duke, in sky blue and a white owlish wig, manfully controlled his wobbling legs and mounted gaily to his seat, attended
by four pages headed by young Lord Churchill.

"Our cousins," commented Alice, "appear to be uncommonly
well favoured. They might be royalty themselves, the way
they—— Ooh! you spiteful——"

A pinch, deftly administered to the fleshy underpart of her arm,
wrenched tears of pain from her eyes and the words from her
lips.

"Then stop gaggling like a Greek chorus," threatened Abigail,
"or you'll have worse done to you than that."

In the absence of Mrs. Danvers, and with the private circulation
of a bottle, hitherto concealed, and produced from beneath the
ample petticoats of Mrs. Wanley, she and Mrs. Abrahal did not
now appear to be entirely indifferent to the presence of the Hills.
Mrs. Abrahal, indeed, condescended to bestow on Abigail a smile
and the hope that she had a good view of the hall; which kindly
patronage embolded her to sidle nearer with the question:

"Madam, who is the gentleman bowing and smiling behind the
Duke of Gloucester's pages?"

For despite that he wore a full-dress furbelow in place of his
periwig, and had exchanged his salmon-pink suit for one of amber
satin, she had recognized him instantly. His calves were more than
ever astonishing: stupendous. Padded surely?

"That is Prince George's equerry, Mr. Masham," she was told.

Masham! Of all droll . . . Abigail had barely imbibed this
information before another, louder fanfare swept the hall. There
was a multiple stir among the spectators; heads peered and dodged

behind, above obstructive shoulders, jostling for a nearer view. With skirts swung wide and looking for all the world like a twin border of multi-coloured peonies, the double line of ladies billowed to the ground. The music twanged and throbbed; the viol and flute vied with the harpsichord in an orchestrated pæan of praise, as the doors were flung open to admit a short solitary figure in black.

"His Majesty the King!"

The bladelike silhouette of his profile was etched in bas-relief against the vivid walls, while his head in its preposterous furbelow turned this way, that way, acknowledging with curt nods the dutiful applause that greeted him. Mounting the steps of the dais he extended his hand to the curtsying Princess, raised her, pecked at her cheek, and took his seat between her and the Prince.

His Majesty's entourage followed.

Alice jogged her sister's elbow. "That marvellous handsome young gentleman who came in first after the King—that is Lord Albemarle. Isn't he handsome, Abbie. *Isn't* he?"

But Abigail's interest was not centred in the handsome Lord Albemarle, nor any more in the smiling Mr. Masham. Another had claimed her attention; one who, unobtrusively, had entered upon the heels of the King's attendants: a tall man with a long nose, a womanish mouth, and keen, heavily-hooded eyes. In that ornate assemblage he was remarkable for the simplicity of his sombre-hued dress in contrast to the gaudy sheen of satin, gold, and silver. He wore no jewels save the sparkle of a diamond half hidden in the fall of lace at his throat. But it was not his outward person that caused Abigail's heart to beat with the sense of memory revived: of a face envisioned in the veiled distance of a child's consciousness, partially defined and never quite forgotten, formless as the face of the loved dead. . . . Her flesh crept and she shivered, glanced aside at Alice. Did she see it too? Alice, however, saw only Lord Albemarle.

Reason returned with commonsense to advise her that this man was vital, living; no spirit harassed by her wrongs, risen from the grave to fright her with paternal pity and consolatory care. No ghost was this, though he resembled one, with so strange, compelling a likeness that her heart fainted to see it, and seeing, feared again to question this merest chance resemblance to . . . her father!

"You will never find him," Mrs. Wanley was saying, "very far from His Majesty. He . . ."

Abigail strained her ears.

". . . one day. If the King lives."

"Who?" asked Mrs. Abrahal.

Mrs. Wanley passed the bottle.

"I've just told you. Mr. Harley."

"Which, ma'am," Abigail asked, "is Mr. Harley?"

"Him. He's looking up."

As Abigail from her perch was looking down.

Seen from the lofty elevation of the gallery, the colourful figures far below appeared now to have dwindled to elfin proportions forming a brilliant fragmentary pattern, elusive, yet perfectly co-ordinated. In rhythmic movement to the strains of flute and harpsichord, and the aching solo of a violin, they bowed, curtsied, parted, to converge again, presenting to the spellbound Hills an empyrean vision, preternaturally endowed.

Enthroned on the dais between the decorative amplitude of the Princess and her Prince, the King in his sable trappings looked not unlike a seedy raven perched between two Titans. His face surmounted by the towering black wig, had the greenish pallor of the drowned. So motionless he sat that only his eyes seemed to live, save when he struggled to control the harsh spasmodic cough that persistently attacked him.

To another more astute observer than Abigail Hill, the King appeared to be a desperately sick man. Leaning against a pillar and taking no part in the dance, Robert Harley watched; and wondered . . . Would the King last out the year? If not, the Speakership, an office which his supporters more than once had suggested should be his, might go a-begging to be snatched by that fellow, Thomas Littleton, in fair running for the favour of the Whigs. Yes, and there he was, sidling up to homage Madam Marlborough. So *that* was how he had attained his entry here! When she should take her stance behind the throne of 'Mrs. Morley' the Government would look to sink in petticoats, hagridden. Ah! If the King could be granted a new lease of life and a twist of his perverted mind to right it, what a political giant could be raised from the cast skin of this puny yellow dwarf. . . . The long peculiarly sensitive fingers toyed with the lace of his cravat, and the womanish lips tightened till they looked to have been grafted upon steel.

"Mr. Harley!"

Albemarle, flushed with rouge, exquisite in cherry brocade, postured before him. "The King is pleasedt to sendt me to express his satisfaction at your presence here to-night and to commandt vit you an audience to-morrow at ten hours in Kensington Palace."

Harley lowered his chin and raised his eyes.

"I humbly thank His Majesty. I shall be honoured to wait upon
the King." He bowed. "Your lordship's servant."

"Mine duty, sir." With a flutter of his overwhelming eyelashes
Albemarle glided away.

Harley pursed his mouth to a silent whistle. What, he conjectured, could this approach from the King portend? It was not
unexpected, nor was it his first summons to a private audience,
although nothing to his favour, or against it, had as yet been
openly declared. He had sailed pretty near the wind when he had
steered a middle course through the storm of controversy raised
around the question of a standing army. To be or not to be—
and it had been reduced, under his leadership. A tricky business
that, to fly in the face of Parliament and hold his own against
monarchical and governmental opposition. But he had succeeded
in resolving that dangerous crisis which had looked to make or
break him. Was he made? Or were his sails to be furled and he
to be docked—in the Lords? Never that—at least not yet—
although he would have to be prepared for all contingencies, refuse
all baits, and play for time, since only time could tell.

Harley's hooded eyes betrayed a sudden gleam as they pursued
Lord Albemarle winding his graceful way among the dancers,
till he halted at the dais directly below the King. The almost imperceptible nod of His Majesty's head was not lost on Mr. Harley.
Resuming his position by the pillar, he folded his arms; but under
his elbows the hidden fingers clenched, and his lips parted to
hum beneath his breath a doggerel brought by his agents from
Scotland.

> 'Wilful Willy, Willy, will ye,
> Wilt thou be wilful still?'

The musicians played a minuet. The King left his seat to stroll
among his guests, with a word here, a gesture there, displaying his
yellow teeth in his contortion of a smile, stretching his claw-like
hand to be kissed by bashful young maidens presented by eager
mammas.

The Princess leaned her head against the gilded chair-back.
None saw, except her anxious husband and one watchful young
person above, how her face had paled.

By his pillar Harley waited.

The small watcher in the gallery poked her head over the rail
to see the King turn his in the direction of the tall gentleman who
stood remotely separate from the rest of that glittering throng.
And it seemed as if a signal as of eyebrows raised, a nod, a word-
less answer, was exchanged.

The stately dancers bowed, advanced, retreated, with measured step, turn of white shoulder, rustle of silk, whisper of slippers on the polished floor. In the dusty light of candles the scene possessed an eerie beauty. Voices were muted, the music sighed and sang; colours merged in a bewildering confusion of saffron and purple, crimson, rose, the rowdy overtone of orange, the fresh green and white of Anne's gown, and one thin narrow streak of black as the King edged his way to the dais.

The music ceased on a low lingering chord; the dancers dispersed. The King was halting, Prince George rising, the Princess swooning, her ladies hurrying, the Countess of Marlborough issuing orders: "Vinegar! Hartshorn! Open a window. Do not crowd around Her Highness! Air—give her air!"

And all this occurred in less time that it took the impassive Mr. Harley to hum an impromptu variation of:

> 'Willy, Willy, will not—will he?
> Willynilly, yes, he *will*!'

The dais was now thronged with ladies flapping handkerchiefs: with Prince George in a great fuss: with Mr. Masham murmuring instructions to the pages, offering assistance, and in everybody's way, to be swept commandingly aside by Lady Marlborough who raised the Princess, now recovered, from her chair and led her out.

The Prince whose lobster-red face had, in his agitation, faded to the colour of a shrimp, whispered something to his son, and followed his wife. The little Duke returned to bow before the King, who lowered an ear to him and nodded. Then, raising his hand for silence, he addressed the excited assembly.

"My lords, ladies, and gentlemen. Her Highness finds the room to varm for her comfort and has retired to her apartments. She bids you all to supper in the banqveting hall, vere Her Highness vill presently rejoin you."

"She will not." Mrs. Wanley wagged her head despondently. "She should never have come to the Ball. Dr. Radcliffe was against it, but Someone Else had the last word—as she always does. I could fancy a bite to eat, ma'am, couldn't you?"

Yes, Mrs. Abrahal could.

"And so could I," confessed Alice, as the ladies withdrew, "I'm sinking for want of food. They might have invited us."

But they were not forgotten.

Having sampled their repast supplied by Mrs. Danvers, the

ladies despatched a page with the remnants of it on a tray, and two glasses of wine for their underlings.

The hall had emptied. A distant clamour of voices and clatter of plates denoted that the guests were at their banquet. Yet it is likely that none who ate of golden carp, roast turkey, sucking-pig, stuffed boar's head, and every kind of sweetmeat, enjoyed one half as well his feast as did those two, unseen, unheeded, who sat together on the floor of the gallery munching lollipops and picking goose-bones in their fingers. Nor did any who at midnight raised a cup to the New Century, drink with more zest than did the sisters Hill in their concerted treble:

"To this year of grace, seventeen hundred!"

CHAPTER FIVE

WHEN at the end of that festive week Abigail returned to Holywell House, Lady Marlborough remained in attendance at St. James's. Thus, the normal course of life that involved certain menial duties besides the care and mending of her young ladies' clothes, was for Abigail rendered if no happier decidedly more peaceful by her ladyship's absence. So soon as her daily work was done, her mind, ever active, went searching and discovered fresh matter to engross it in the library at Holywell.

Browsing there among the fusty volumes, she lost herself with Rosalind in Arden's Forest, went with Juliet, frolicked with Puck, laughed as merrily as any Wife of Windsor at fat Falstaff's antics, learned history from the Henrys, and philosophy, that somewhat too severely taxed her understanding, from Sir Thomas Browne. Finding a dose of 'Urn Burial' too dry, she turned for sweeter comfort to the limpid lyrical verse of Robert Herrick, who assured her that:

> 'Never was day so over sick with showres
> But that it had some intermittent houres.
> Never was night so tedious but it knew
> The last watch out and saw the dawning too.'

But her 'intermittent houres' often suffered rude disturbance. Her young ladies were exacting, and when they missed her they would seek until they found her, to drag her forth from her concealment in a window-seat.

"Here's our little misery—in the dumps again! Why, what's this? A book of verse? O, Mary, listen what she reads!"

And snatching Master Herrick from Abigail's hand, Elizabeth with giggles would recite:

> 'Begin with a kiss,
> Go on, too, with this
> And thus, thus, thus let us smother
> Our lips for a while . . .'

"So *that's* how she passes her time, in day-dreams and slobber! She's love-sick and full o' tears. She's cried her nose red, and all for the love of a—— Who is he? Tell us, Abbie? Look, Mary, how this poem is titled. 'Uptailes.' Ohoo! For shame! Uptai—— Hah! Would you show your claws? I' faith, a wild cat!"

For Abigail, smarting, had leapt to her feet and made a grab for the book, which Elizabeth, laughing, raised high above her head out of Abigail's reach. She was tall for her age and Abigail little.

"I'll thank you," Abigail said between her teeth, "to give me my book."

" 'Tis not *your* book. 'Tis my father's book. You have no right to read his books without his permission. I've half a mind to report you to Mamma."

"I, too, can report you to your mamma. Who wore her mamma's best cap to church last Sunday dressed to kill, patched and painted like a play-actress, and the parson sermonizing on the sins of Jezebel with all the congregation staring hard at *you*! Wouldn't my lady like to know?"

Betty blenched.

"You'll not go sneaking to her, Abbie!"

"I will if Parson doesn't."

"No!"

"Yes!"

But Elizabeth knew she never would.

In June Lady Marlborough obtained leave of absence from the Court and reappeared at home in high good humour: presented each of her little daughters with a new gown, Abigail with an old one, and was full of quips and jests at the expense of certain gentlemen whose names, Abigail gathered, were not insignificant in courtly circles.

Seated at the table, speaking only when addressed, to answer a complaint or to obey an order; or, in her ladyship's withdrawing-room while Mary and Elizabeth played a subdued game of cat's cradle, Abigail's presence was as little heeded as that of a fly on the wall.

The lady talked, his lordship dozed and Abigail lowered her eyes to her tambour frame and heard:

That the Princess Anne's physician, the celebrated Dr. Radcliffe, had been struck off Her Highness's list in consequence of his refusal to prescribe a certain medicine which Cousin Sarah playfully referred to as 'Cold Tea'.

"And—ah—very right and proper too," was his lordship's yawning comment, to call forth an indignant reply from his lady.

"Right? Proper? When 'tis the only beverage that sends her to sleep and gives me some respite from attendance?"

Cold tea? Cold. Now what, Abigail wondered, was harmful in tea taken cold, unless it were better digested when hot? Or was there any truth in the tales brought by Alice, gleaned from Mrs. Abrahal, that the Princess inclined to flavour her bohea with stronger waters? Which was, however, no concern of Mrs. Hill's.

And now other names came into the discussion at which again Mrs. Hill pricked up her ears.

Lord Albemarle: he, Cousin Sarah declared, had bled the King of immense estates in Ireland to the tune of something more than a hundred thousand acres. Bentinck, too, Lord Portland, had been granted even more land. Ruvigny, Earl of Galway, had likewise consumed his share.

"Mr. Caliban," chuckled Sarah, "is, for all his Calvinism, mighty Catholic in his tastes. Two Dutchmen and a Frenchman, and Betty Villiers of Orkney have between them swallowed near upon three-quarters of a million."

Lord Marlborough rubbed his chin.

"They'll not digest it. Commissioners have been appointed to look into the case. You wait. They'll spew it up."

"But 'tis scandalous of Caliban to hand over Crown property!"

"Popish property in Ireland, my love."

"Tory, you mean. They're at the back of it—to be caught in their own trap. The Bill of Resumption will net them, we hope. And it may also net you. The King don't approve of the Bill. You'll find yourself in bad odour if you choose to support it. Mark me."

Although this, to Abigail, was about as comprehensible as Sanscrit, she concentrated her attention on her needle—to learn more.

" 'Tis a monstrous misplacement of justice that wealth and land and honours should be heaped on a parcel of foreigners, to say nothing of his doxy, the Villiers, who, God knows, serves him as good as a stuffed image for the little use he may put her to—which I'll wager is not in his bed! And all he's given you in recognition of your service other than this paltry earldom—is as much as would sit on a farthing. Where is *your* land? *Your* mansions? And where, Lord help us, is your income? Does he expect you to work unrewarded, except for a pittance?"

"I ask no reward," was the somewhat sententious reply, "but the privilege of serving my King and my country."

"Pah! Privilege! There you go, tilting—like that Spanish Don what's-his-name at windmills—seeing armies in the clouds and fighting visionary battles. You'll never be content until you're on the march again to break my heart. *You'll* never lead in politics, that's sure. All you do is to float like a straw in the wind of 'em. I've no patience!"

He gave her the smile he reserved for her alone.

"The wind may blow me higher than you think."

"Not high enough for me while there's one whose cunning seeks to bring you low. Yes, you know who I mean. Robert Harley."

"Harley, my dear, is my friend."

"Harley is nobody's friend. He walks alone, like a cat. And he works in the dark. He has spies."

"Spies?" His lordship's smile broadened. "Who has been gulling you with such immitigable stuff?"

" 'Tisn't 'stuff'; nor am I easily gulled. You're the one who is more like to be that. I know what I know, and what you, seemingly, don't. He has bad blood in him somewhere. Is he not the son of Abigail——"

As she uttered that name Sarah checked herself and turned to the silent figure in the corner, who was so diligently bent on her embroidery that she started like a frightened fawn when her ladyship addressed her.

"What? You still here? And the children not abed? Must I be for ever on the watch? Look at the time. Past ten o' the clock. Betty! Mary! Leave your game, my chucks, and kiss good-night. Sleep well."

But Mrs. Hill did not. She lay long awake in her narrow bed, with that unfinished sentence burning in her ears: 'The son of Abigail . . .'

Abigail *who*?

*   *   *

In June Cousin Sarah rejoined the Court, and with her went Jack Hill promoted now to the post of page to the Duke of

Gloucester. Abigail sped him on to Kensington with embraces, her blessing, and the hope that he would make the best of his opportunities and write to her once a week.

Most grievously she missed him. She missed the walks they took together on his holidays; the tales he told her of his fights with older boys, in which, according to Jack, he was always victorious: his mimicry—they both had a gift for that—of 'Sheepshanks', as he was pleased to dub his tutor. He told her of his future plans. He had mapped out his career. He would go for a soldier so soon as his term of office at Camden House was done. He wouldn't for ever stay attendant on a child, Prince or nothing.

"The Prince won't always be a child," Abigail had reminded him. "And one day he'll be King. You must look ahead to your advantage. There's more to be gained as King's favourite than as a common soldier."

"I may begin as a common soldier," Jack had loftily retorted, "but I'll end in command of an army. I'll win my spurs in the next war—you'll see."

"Why will you always be talking of wars?" cried Abigail. "We've done with wars in our time, please God."

"So you think. I know better. There's a mort o' trouble brewing on the Continent, and when it comes I'll go to't wherever I may be. I've no taste for the life of a lickspittle courtier, bowing and scraping at the beck and call of Princes."

She did not doubt he would succeed in any walk of life. If his good looks, his fearlessness, his charm and, yes, his impudence, had found favour in the sight of Cousin Sarah, he would win his spurs and all else that he desired. Yet, though she rejoiced in his good fortune, she could not but compare it with her own, and wish that fate—or Cousin Sarah—had dealt with her more kindly. It wasn't fair that Jack and Alice should have all the sugar plums, while she ate dust and ashes. She tried not to feel bitter, nor to grudge the two she loved most in the world their happier lots; and consoled herself with the few laconic letters she received from Jack. These gave her, besides a glimpse of the distinguished company in which he now associated, some alarms.

He saw much of Alice. She had grown fat as a tub and never stopped eating. Jack had introduced a new method of training to the recruits of the Duke's Cadet Corps by drilling them in the use of their fists before they took to the sword and pike. He was teaching the Duke the first rules of boxing, but the Princess had forbidden what she called 'horse-play'. The Duke was game for anything: a likely lad if he were not so spindle-legged. Mr. Jenkin Lewis, the Duke's equerry, had lately departed for France. There had been a rumpus between the King and Mr. Lewis, who had expressed his opinion that the Duke's tutors crammed him too full of book-lore at the expense of his health. John Churchill was now Master of the Duke's Horse, a stout fellow, the best of the bunch by far. Jack had been presented to the King—how Abigail's heart had swelled at that—who looked like a cadaver and was about as cheerful as a hearse. Yesterday, Prince George of Denmark had dined with the Duke attended by his gentleman, Mr. Masham, and Jack had served behind the Duke's chair. The Court was going to Windsor in July. Jack hoped he would go too.

But he didn't.

When the Princess, her Court, her husband, and her son went to Windsor, Jack was left behind at Camden House.

On July 24, William, Duke of Gloucester, celebrated his eleventh birthday with a review of his regiment, a Trooping of the Colours, a letting off of squibs, and a grand march past—up and down the terrace—to the glowing admiration of his parents.

This was followed by a banquet, over which the Duke presided. It is likely he ate too much of the good fare Monsieur Centlivre had been at pains to provide; or he may have too often responded, in wine, to the toasts, but whatever the cause, by nightfall he seemed greatly excited; and when Mrs. Wanley had tucked him up in his bed and was about to leave the room he called to her: "I'm thirsty. My throat's dry. I can't sleep."

Kicking off the covers he sat up. "*What* a happy birthday I have had!"

"May Your Highness have many more birthdays equally as happy. There, my precious, drink this. Let Mother Wanley hold the cup."

He frowned up at her. 'Mother Wanley'. Why would she still persist in treating him like an infant in arms? And he in his twelfth year to-day!

"How strange," he said, and drank; and asked for more.

"What is strange, Your Grace?"

"That I'll soon be in my teens. Tempus fugit. But I don't want to be a man. I would like always to be a boy and never grow old and fat. And ill. I feel ill now."

And to his hot forehead he laid his cold hands.

"Your Grace is over-wrought with your gay doings. You're tired. Will my treasure lie down and let his Wanley cover him?"

"I won't be covered."

"There, there! His precious Highness must be a good boy and

go to sleep. If he is warm he mustn't take cold. Let me wrap this round you."

He was wrapped.

"Shall Wanley read to Your Highness?"

"No. I'll read to Wanley. Sit down. And don't *fuss*! Give me that book."

There was always a book at his bedside.

He gleamed at her with eyes very bright and cheeks very flushed.

"This is the work of a great poet and satirist who lived more than sixty years before the birth of Our Lord. His name is Horace. Take note of it."

"Horace," obediently echoed Mrs. Wanley.

"Now listen." And in his clear piping voice he began to read: "Dum licet, in rebus jucundis, vive beatus; vive memor, quam sis ævi brevis.' Which is to say, 'While time permits live happy in the midst of pleasures; live mindful also that your time is short.' Yes!" He nodded with gay mystery as he closed the book and tossed it aside. "Our time is very short. We must live and enjoy while we can. That's what Horace advises, and *he* should know."

His teeth began to chatter to put Wanley in a fright.

"Come, my love," she coaxed, "lie down."

"Buzz, buzz." He wriggled away from her touch and hoisting his knees he clasped them. "I feel as if cold water is running down my back, but I'm hot—I'm hot as Hades. No! Let us not talk of Hades." He crossed his fingers with a shudder. " 'Give us a taste of your quality . . . Come, a passionate speech.' *That's* not Horace. That's Hamlet, Prince of Denmark, my ancestor, or he would have been my ancestor had he lived, which he did not save in the mind of an immortal god. I think Shakespeare must have been a god so great he is. Greater than Horace. As great as Socrates. Yet England hails him only as a strolling player. One day he'll be recognized. He'll live when all *our* bones are dust. *I'm* dry as dust. More to drink, good Wanley."

"God save Your Grace, you've had too much to drink already. It's that nasty wine that's put you in this state."

"Then give me a grape. A purply black one."

He nibbled a grape and spat it out, complaining that it hurt his throat to swallow, shivered and was hot, burned and was cold, and refused to be covered until Wanley sent a page to fetch his mother.

She came and saw, and feared to see what the nurse did not.

" 'Tis nothing but a touch of the sun, Madam, and the wine he drank. His Grace is over-tired."

"He is in a high fever."

"Yes, Madam, but children run to fever very easily when they are excited."

"Send at once for Dr. Radcliffe."

"Doctor Rad . . . Madam, has Your Highness forgotten," stammered Wanley, "that you have dismissed Dr. Radcliffe?"

"Send for him. *Send!* And tell the Prince to come."

All night the parents watched beside that bed: all night the broken voice, no longer clear but hoarse and unintelligible, babbled fragments of the Gospels, Shakespeare, Latin, Greek, spilled harvest of a mind too young to hold the sheaves of learning. And every so often he reviewed his troops and called for the absent Lewis. "Lewis . . . I want Lewis!" To soothe him they brought his friends Churchill, Boscawen, and the brothers Bathurst to the door. They were not allowed in the room. The physician in attendance, pending the arrival of Dr. Radcliffe, had declared the Prince's illness symptomatic of the smallpox and bled him of a pint.

When Dr. Radcliffe came at dawn he diagnosed the case as scarlet fever, and asked what treatment had been prescribed. His colleague admitted to bleeding.

"Which," Radcliffe said, "has destroyed him . . ."

Yet while he lived the mother hoped. None was permitted to wait upon him but herself. She would not rest nor eat. She did not see the food they offered, did not hear her husband's prayers. She saw only her child's smitten face upon the pillow and the feeble tossing arms; heard only his gasping breath that grew weaker, till he sank at last into the passive quiescence of unconsciousness. And still she sat, in her agonized composure, unheedful of the father's sobs, the wailing of her women, unmoved and hopeful still: for while he breathed he lived. His forehead was cool and damp and his sleep natural. He would waken . . . Hoping, tearless, prayerless, long after hope had fled.

And when they told her he would never wake, she rose without a word and left him where he lay.

She went to her room and, in the icy calm of her despair, wrote a letter to the exiled King, her father; a letter of penitence, a confession of guilt.

'Heaven,' she cried in her anguish, 'had punished her for her cruel treatment of him when he most needed her love and support. She had failed in her duty as a daughter. She had played the dual parts of Goneril and Regan, but never of Cordelia. Heaven had now demanded for her sin the supreme sacrifice—her son.'

She ended with the promise that she 'would use her utmost power to effect the restoration of the brother she had denied, and if ever she were forced to take the throne she would only accept that dignity to be held in trust for him. . . .'

She wrote till the night closed in with shadows. She wrote till her hand was numb; and as she read what she had written her frozen heart was splintered in a cry, distraught, unhuman, as that of some wild woodland thing trapped to its tortured end, a cry that echoed through the silent Castle and brought her stricken husband to her side.

*   *   *

William of Orange and England was at his Palace at Loo, enjoying his summer vacation, when he received the news of Gloucester's death. He received it unmoved, sent no message of condolence to his dead wife's sister, against whom he had nursed dislike till it had turned to loathing. But to Marlborough he wrote: 'It is so great a loss to me as well as to England, that it pierces my heart with affliction.'

Did it?

Pacing unattended the flagged paths of his garden where fountains played and tall hollyhocks—for it was long past tulip time—stood sentinel against the trim box-hedge, he may have indulged in the haunting evocation of a small flaxen-haired figure whose weak legs bravely straddled the lawn, whose voice piped shrill incongruous oaths . . . 'Villiam! Did I hear you svear?' Or he may not.

Sic transit! He had more to do than snivel for a child's death when his own was near at hand and he must set his house in order, or rather Britain's house of which he was the tenant, and which looked to crumble and might fall with this fall of the last male Stuart. No! *Not* the last.

His thoughts swung to another Prince, whose claim, prior to that of his own, or his wife, or his wife's sister, had been so hotly supported by the Jacobites. And in God's name, why not?

The thin cheeks flushed, the sunken eyes glittered as the astounding notion leapt, to halt his step and strike him motionless at the sheer surprise of it. Yet was it so surprising? Had not this probability lain dormant as a last resource, to be uncached in event of a crisis such as had now arisen, and which he knew with a prophetic certitude, he had always feared, foreseen? . . . His little, *lit*tle William in whom he had pinned his faith, his hopeless hope, whom he—pity of Christ!—had loved as he had loved no man nor any woman, had been foredoomed from birth. And must he now watch his own bodily corruption, his slow, yet welcome sinking to the grave, knowing there was none but that dropsical fat woman to succeed him; a weak, vacillating, brandy-sodden simpleton . . . None other? Yes, one other. If he could reclaim him from his Papistry and crush once and for ever the idiot voices that clacked of a changeling smuggled to the girl-wife of James II in a warming-pan!

A short staccato laugh escaped him, and with it his dry, rasping cough. Blood oozed from his mouth and fell in crimson petal drops upon his hand. He rubbed the stain against his velvet breeks and smiled . . . Not long now, but long enough to bring his plans and that boy to heel: another boy to watch and guard and train in his own way for kingship. James, exiled Prince of Wales, a Royal Stuart, could be brought here to Holland and reared in the Protestant Faith, to succeed him. For if not he, who else, after Anne, was left to Britain's throne, other than that ancient hag of Hanover, the Electress Sophia, granddaughter of James I?

Clasping his hands behind him, the King resumed his walk. The sun blazed down on his uncovered head, that, weighted by the smothering wig, drew beads of sweat from his brow. He turned impatiently towards the Palace, his eyes searching up at the open windows.

"Bring me my hat!"

A page came running with it.

"And send Lord Portland here."

Up and down the flagged path strolled the King and his gentle-man, Hans William Bentinck, Earl of Portland, late Ambassador in Paris; a pompous fellow he, whose rosy puffed cheeks had the gloss of a wooden soldier's; and wooden too was his bearing. His stiff immaculate dress that showed no crease, no sign of wear, might have been brought that moment from a bandbox. But behind his carven immobility the astute mind listened, alert to restrain or advise; to question, as no other dared question the King; not as King's courtier, not as King's favourite, but as King's comrade and friend.

He was blunt.

"If you think you can save Britain by promoting the son of the Papist James in Anne's place, you are asking for trouble." He spoke in Dutch, and in Dutch the King answered him.

"Pah! You're over cautious. I'd hazard a chance."

"And bring about another Revolution?"

"I may not be there to see it." The King coughed again, spat a gobbet of red slime on the paving stones: and smiled. "The enemy is already at my gates. He will force his entrance soon."

"Sire!" Bentinck laid a hand, gentle as a woman's, on the shrunken shoulder. "Since you have been here in your native air, Dr. Fagon reports a great improvement in your health. If only you could live here always."

The King dabbed his mouth with his handkerchief and shoved it in his sleeve. "If only I could die here and be buried here—but they won't even give me that. They will lay my bones in their Abbey at Westminster. I would like to lie beneath the tulips . . . over there." He pointed upward and beyond the box-hedge. "So you would say I am straining at a gnat?"

"Yes, Sire. To swallow a camel."

"A camel!" William broke into hoarse laughter. "You think the Electress Sophia of Hanover is like a camel?"

"Very like a camel," said Bentinck stolidly.

"My Hans!" William slid his narrow hand into Bentinck's and gripped it tight. "You are a never ending joy to me. You have so much sense and so little, *lit*tle sense of humour. My dream then is a nightmare?"

"It might well be, with a rude awakening. If you take my advice you will settle the succession before the Papists do more mischief at St. Germains."

William withdrew his hand.

"I might have known you would advise me play for safety."

"I advise you, Sir, to obey your conscience."

"If I had obeyed my conscience I should not be King of England."

"Obey it now, Your Majesty, and make him King of England who will preserve the soul of England—and her Church."

"Do you believe England and her Church will welcome a German princeling whose wife languishes in prison for fornication with that handsome young rascal, Königsmark, murdered by his father's whore, the Platen? A prince who comes queenless to the throne?"

"He has an heir, Sire."

"And half a dozen mistresses."

Bentinck gave a shrug.

"He can leave them behind."

"He can, but he won't. They'll attend him and be turned into English Duchesses." William snickered. "You will see. He will follow the precedent of that arch-womanizer, my merry Uncle Charles, whose bastards are strewn all over Holland, where he rested on his 'travels.' And how do we know that this son of Hanover, the German, is not the son of Königsmark, the Swede? A fine stock to hand Britain!"

"Whether he is or is not the son of Hanover, we know he is a Protestant," said Bentinck.

The King drew a deep breath, checked a cough, and turned his steps towards the Palace.

"You are extraordinarily wise, my Hans, for such a blockhead as you look. Come in with me now and write a letter, couched in terms of cousinly affection, to Sophia the Electress and George Lewis, her fat frightful son. We will invite them both to visit us. At Loo."

Thus, by the death of a child, was the Act of Settlement decided that Passed the Crown to Hanover and changed the face of history.

And as the ripples caused by a stone cast into a stagnant pond widen, lingering upon its ruffled surface, so did the issue of one swift tragic circumstance diverge to affect, not a nation only or a Cause but individuals.

Lord Marlborough, Comptroller of the Duke's Household, was deprived of his office: the Duke's servants, by the King's command, were deprived of their wages. These, however, were refunded by Anne, who in her bereavement could still remember those who had served her son.

Mrs. Abrahal, the Duke's Chief Laundress, was installed as Her Highness's Starcher. Alice Hill, to her astonishment, was granted a pension of the same yearly sum as her wages, and permission to retain her rooms at Camden House. And Jack was appointed page to Prince George.

As for Mrs. Freeman, more than ever exacting were the demands on her time and service of her 'poor unfortunate faithful Morley', so the Princess now in all her letters signed herself. Mrs. Morley had given up card-playing, seldom stirred from her apartments—"And I," Mrs. Freeman complained to her John, "must be ever at her side to hear her prayers, her bemoanings, and her ceaseless wailings of her duty to her father. She has an obsession about *him*. And I assure you if she don't lose her reason, I'll lose mine. I can't stand much more of this. . . ."

Nor perhaps could John.

He wanted his wife to himself, as much and as often as she could be spared from her attendance. He knew, if she did not, that their home life together might at any moment be disrupted. He expounded his views, for her enlightenment, on the European situation.

The continued obstinacy on the part of the Austrian Emperor Leopold in his refusal to accept the terms of the Partition Treaty, had raised once again the spectre of war. He who had rejected three-fourths of Spain for his son, had now changed his mind and was prepared to fight for the whole of it. There must be no division of territory. But the Spaniards, whose King had taken so long to die and was at last dying, had more cause than any for alarm. Only the Pyrenees protected Spain from France in event of invasion. To whom then could she look for aid? Not to Austria, whose Emperor was behaving like a madman . . . "Not to England!" Sarah's voice held fear, "for England and you, my dearest, are synonymous." This was her true self, her tenderest side, that all but unmanned him. "O, love, my love," she whispered, "I cannot let you go again. I can't."

"You will, my heart, if I am called."

"But why? Why?" she persisted. "You speak as if war were imminent. Life goes on as usual. There is no talk, except among the scaremongers, of war. The Spaniards have nothing to fear save Louis. Why don't they take him for an ally—offer Spain to the Bourbon since Leopold refuses to accept the Treaty terms?"

"They have," said John calmly, "offered Spain to the Bourbon."

"What!" she gaped at him.

He smiled. " 'Twas your own suggestion, sweet."

"Foh! Much should I know of these matters. A guess in the dark."

But within a week the news had come to light. The Church, represented by Cardinal Porto Carrero, had been called to witness the Will signed by the hand of Spain's King as he lay on his death-bed; the hand of a lunatic who willed his Empire to Philip the Bourbon, grandson of Louis of France.

The seeds of the War of the Spanish Succession were irrevocably sown, to reap a harvest of bloodshed and victories immortal that would ring the name of Marlborough through the ages for all time.

His call would come, and he awaited it. But while he waited he must have his wife beside him here, not there, in London or at Windsor, serving on bended knee the silver ewer in which Mrs. Morley washed her hands; tending her swollen feet, harking to her chat and plaiting fringes. Such trivial duties could surely be undertaken by a lesser woman of the Household.

"Is there not someone can serve her in your place, so that you serve me?"

He was like a petulant schoolboy, leaning back in his chair, glum-browed, with his hands in the pockets of his breeches; still greedy for the sweets she offered—and which for him had never staled.

Sarah leaned over him, ruffling his hair.

"I love you best without your wig. You look no more than ten. You are the youngest thing for your age I ever saw."

"Do you not see yourself?"

He snatched her hand and pulled her to his knee. She laid her lips to his cheek; her throat ached with unshed tears. "O, love, how long can I keep you here with me? How long before you take command again? How am I to face it?"

"You are a soldier's wife, my darling. You will face it."

"Yes." She kissed the tip of his blunt nose. "But I am first a woman."

A timid knock at the door sent her guiltily flying.

"Madam."

Abigail stood in the doorway, curtsying.

"What do you want?"

"The week's laundry, madam. Will you be sending it to Camden House as usual, since Mrs. Abrahal is not . . ."

"Oh ! No . . . Yes." She nibbled a nail. "Your sister is still there. You can send it." But she was evidently not concerned with the week's laundry. Her eyes were fixed on Abigail, standing deferentially downcast to take her orders.

"Come here."

And as Abigail shrinkingly advanced, Sarah's face broke into smiles. She flung back her head, laughed loud, and turned to John.

"You said . . ." between her laughter she hysterically spluttered, "you said 'someone'! A serving-woman who would hold Mrs. Morley's basin, wash her feet, listen to her dirges and plait fringes for scarves till her fingers drop off. Here she is! Will you wait upon the Princess Anne and relieve me of my duties? Will you be my deputy, Abigail Hill? Well? Have you no word to say?"

No word.

White-lipped she stood in silence, while the blood drained from her heart and surged upward in a drenching torrent to fill her ears and drown her foolish voice that struggled, bleating:

"I . . . madam, I . . . thank . . ."

"Ho! So! She thanks . . . she thanks me, John! Do you hear her?" Sarah cried, and she was laughing still. "I beg you not to thank me. You'll be doing me a service. 'Tis I, my dear, who will have to thank *you*!"

In her attic room under the eaves, Abigail knelt upon the window-seat and watched the blossoming sky where a young slip of a moon lay on her back among the stars. No sound broke the stillness; no breath of air shook the heavy-laden heat of a summer that had long outstayed its time.

Her small pointed face, uplifted in the starlight, had a strange, spriteish look. Her eyes mirrored the thin moon's ghost; her hands were clasped as if she prayed, but no prayer came from her lips.

Tranced, motionless, she knelt. The stable clock struck two, and three . . . And presently the dark matrix of the night was pierced by a shivering gleam that trembled eastward through gossamer cloud-veils. A chill swept over the sleeping earth; and in the quiet garden the pale discs of flowers, lost shapes of trees unmoving, the dream solidity of shadows, velvet-masked, were submerged in that hovering grey.

She stirred; her cold lips melted to send a whisper floating:

> 'Never was night so tedious but it knew
> The last watch out and saw the dawning too . . .'

BOOK TWO
(1701–1707)

CHAPTER ONE

'Il n'y a plus de Pyrénées!'

LOUIS OF FRANCE had yielded to temptation. The major portion of the Spanish Empire, rejected by Leopold of Austria, was his for the taking. The 'gallant loser', 'the great gentleman' who had pledged his word to England's King in the terms of a Treaty, retracted. He may have reasoned that Leopold had been given his chance of acceptance. If he refused the prize offered, and demanded the whole or nothing of Spain, he must face the consequences of his greed and his stupidity. The moderation, wisdom, foresightedness of Louis waned before the dazzling prospect of a future in which he saw himself returned in all the glory of 'Le Roi Soleil'.

He made his first startling move of aggression when he seized the Dutch barriers to the Spanish Netherlands, and waited for reprisals from that 'upstart princeling of Orange'; his friend no longer, his foe declared.

But William, not yet disposed to come to grips with France, bided his time and summoned his forces in Holland, and sent Marlborough to command them.

In September 1701 James II died, and Louis, watching Marlborough's silent armies massed on the plains of the Netherlands, brought the European crisis to a head with his master-stroke of insolence when, at Versailles, he proclaimed and crowned the outcast Prince of Wales, King James III of England.

The fat was in the fire, but the fire did not blaze although the whole of Britain had been roused to boiling pitch at this audacious provocation on the part of Louis to expedite the now inevitable war. Yet while the Tory majority in the Commons still hoped to keep the peace—if peace could be kept with honour—the Whigs were loud in their demand for immediate revenge. William's bluff, however, was not to be called, nor he precipitated into a life and death conflict. He must go warily before he launched his desperate

4*

last venture, already formulated in the proposed terms of the Grand Alliance between England, Austria and Holland: an armed alliance that would hold at bay, suppress, and vanquish for ever the growing might of France and Spain.

All through the summer of 1701 he had played for time and temporized, and even when the news that the French had occupied Belgium resounded through the country with fresh shock, William withheld the final declaration that would fling Britain and her Allies into war.

And while he waited, the King watched the mustering of his troops gathered from Land's End to John o' Groats, from the vine-clad banks of the Danube, from the toy villages of his beloved Holland. Marlborough would lead them—Marlborough to whom he handed now the torch of war, the hazards of a future, battle-wrought, invincible; victorious.

The curtain was about to be run up on the greatest military drama of all time. He, the King, must live to see the first Act through, if not the Grand Finale. And behind him, non-committal, cool, ever ready to advise, stood Robert Harley, 'man of mystery', and Speaker of the House.

*　　*　　*

An expectant hush hung over the Palace of St. James's. In her Green Closet sat the heiress of England with her dear 'Mrs. Freeman' asleep on the couch, and her dear George asleep and snoring in the adjoining room.

The poor King! She wished she had never called him 'Caliban'. She wished she had been kinder; and if it were not for George, who would so greatly miss her, she wished it were she and not her Cousin William who . . . And to think that a fall from his horse, and he the finest rider in the Kingdom, should have brought so swift an end to one who for years had been dying . . . A molehill. His horse had stumbled and put his foot in a molehill, and half the Town and all the Jacobites, so Mrs. Freeman reported, were toasting 'The Little Gentleman in Black Velvet', the mole whose purblind workings in the earth looked to kill the King they had named 'Usurper'. And now, with her, all England waited for the news that she so greatly dreaded, but she must not shrink from that high destiny to which she had been called by the will of God, and against her own. Yet, if Gloucester had lived how she would have welcomed—with due respect to the dying— the sovereignty that one day would have been his.

She was calm, placid, frightened, though none, not even George, must suspect her of fear. Voicelessly she prayed, and furtively she wept: not even Mrs. Freeman must see her tears.

She glanced at the couch where Mrs. Freeman, after not very much persuasion, had consented to rest. Anne herself had placed the cushion for Mrs. Freeman's head and covered her with her own gold-embroidered satin bedspread, had kissed and bidden her: "Sleep, my dear Mrs. Freeman, if you can."

Her dear Mrs. Freeman apparently could, and almost as soundly as George.

On a side table at Anne's elbow stood an empty cup. Her throat was parched, her tongue tasted of lemons, she longed for another drink of 'cold tea', but she would not disturb Mrs. Freeman. Where was Danvers?

She called fretfully: "Danvers!" And from a screened corner at the far end of the room emerged a slight figure in grey. For two hours she had stood there unnoticed.

"Your Highness," she rose from the curtsy, and lowering her eyes, said: "Mrs. Danvers sent me to relieve her. She was taken with a megrim, Madam."

"Poor Danvers," murmured the Princess. "Who are . . . You are . . . ?"

"Hill, Madam."

"Hill. To be sure! You are so soft and quiet in your movements, one hardly sees you when you are about. . . . Hill?"

She spoke in whispers, and in whispers was answered.

"Your Highness?"

Anne lifted the cup.

"I would like some more cold tea."

"Cold, Madam?"

The Princess glanced aside.

"My orders, Hill."

"Must, Madam, be obeyed." The lowered eyes were lifted. "But may I beg Your Highness to consider a cup of . . . hot tea?"

A faint flush appeared in the pallid cheeks of the Princess.

"Hot? You mean . . . 'hot?"

"Madam, bohea, taken hot, is, I believe, most refreshing."

"I never drink hot tea. 'Tis bad for the digestion."

"Madam, my mother used to say . . ."

"Your mother, Hill? Is your mother alive?"

"No, Madam." The white lids drooped again. "I have been an orphan these four years."

"Poor child. Yes, I recollect. Lady Marlborough told me. What used your mother to say?"

"That bohea, hot, is the best possible correction for any disorder of the stomach, Madam."

"Indeed? My stomach is often disordered—and swollen. 'Tis very swollen now. Go then and bring me a cup of hot tea, but"—Anne gave a hasty look at the recumbent Mrs. Freeman, and laid a conspiratorial finger to her lips—"I need not tell you to go softly, Hill. I think you must be shod in velvet."

And watching Hill's gentle exit she smiled to herself. What a pleasant little creature to have about the place! So quiet in her movements and such a soothing voice. Strange that she had not, until this moment, been aware of Mrs. Hill as an entity; yet she must have been attached to the Household for quite a while, surely, employed to relieve the Women of the Bedchamber. Was she not some obscure relative of Mrs. Freeman? And how characteristic of dear Freeman's generous warm heart to have placed the girl here at the Palace! Yes, certainly, a dutiful willing young person.

"Your Highness's bohea."

"Ah, Hill, I did not hear you come in. Thank you, child."

Anne gratefully sipped. The warm fragrant tea just not *too* hot, was very soothing, and dispelled at once that nasty sour taste of 'cold tea'.

"Have you put milk in this, Hill?"

"No, Madam, cream. Will Your Highness take another cup?"

"No, thank you, Hill. . . . Cream. Yes, I like it with cream."

Again Her Highness looked towards the couch where Mrs. Freeman, flushed with sleep, her mouth a little open and her jaw a little dropped, was making whistling, rattling noises in her nose.

"Poor soul, she's tired out. And so must you be, Hill."

"No, Your Highness, I am never tired."

"You are young," Anne sighed. "What o'clock is it?"

"A quarter after three, Madam."

"Such a long, long night."

As Hill retired with the empty cup to her corner Anne's eyes followed her, and in that same hushed voice she asked: "Have you been standing there behind that screen all this time?"

"Yes, Madam."

"You mustn't stand. You must sit. Bring forward that stool and sit here."

The plump hand waved a gracious invitation. A candle guttered in its socket and dropped grease. Mrs. Hill snuffed it, and then without a sound opened a drawer in a bureau and took from it something small. At first idly, then with more interest, the Princess observed her while she lighted and burned a pastille

which she held daintily between her fingers, and waved to and
fro in the air to disperse the acrid odour of dead wax.

"That is a pleasant smell, Hill. What is it?"

"Amber, Your Highness. 'Tis a novelty I saw on sale in the
New Exchange."

"And you bought it? For me?"

"Yes, Madam." Abigail curtsied. "If Your Highness will excuse
the liberty."

"Liberty? But it was most thoughtful of you, Hill."

"A pleasure, Madam."

The Princess smiled approval, and leaning back in her chair
closed her eyes.

Mrs. Hill sat. Her eyes did not close. Of what was she thinking
as she crouched on the stool at Her Highness's feet, her gaze
unwinkingly fixed on the penduous, middle-aged face? Of all
the slights, the disdain, the rebuffs she had encountered and endured from those above her, and in particular from Mrs. Danvers
who took her cue from the one supreme of all the Princess's attendants? And why, for the hundredth time, she may have asked
herself, if Cousin Sarah was at such pains to show that she dis-
liked, despised her poor relation, had she offered her this golden
opportunity? To relieve her of her too redundant duties? *That*
had been admitted. She had been glad enough to leave behind a
deputy when, last year, she had accompanied Lord Marlborough
to the Hague to be at his side for the signing of the famous Treaty
that had made England, Austria, and Holland joint Allies in the
pending war.

Mrs. Danvers, however, had taken exception to Mrs. Hill's
lieutenancy in Mrs. Freeman's absence. Had not Mrs. Danvers
the prior right to serve Her Highness? A right which she intended
to maintain against any newcomer. Abigail had been relegated,
by Mrs. Danvers' agency, to the least significance, as Abigail
would not readily forget. . . . But Mrs. Freeman, on her return
to Court, had made it known to Mrs. Danvers and to others, that
her cousin, Mistress Hill, was not to be put down: she was, in fact,
to be raised up, acknowledged Under Woman of the Bedchamber.

Her ladyship had been pleased to compliment her on a marked
improvement in her manners. "You were such a shy, gauche,
forlorn little object when I first took pity on you. I am happy to
see you are gaining self-confidence."

"It is your great kindness, madam, that gives me confidence."

"Well, well, we will only hope you do me credit. You are
civil-spoken and you certainly know how to dress." Which since
she had now the wherewithal to buy and to choose her own gowns,

she certainly did, and was unstinting in her gratitude for her lady's patronage. Alice, who for the first few months after the Duke's death had remained at Camden House in no very certain capacity save that of Royal pensioner, had been brought by Cousin Sarah to St. James's as Mrs. Abrahal's assistant.

And now, with Jack who was page to Prince George, they three were together again under one roof. Yes, indeed, Abigail had much cause to be grateful. What were harsh words, blows, gibes, compared to these tangible benefits? She looked across at the source of her good fortune, and observed that the Lady's position had shifted. Her head hung precariously over the edge of the couch.

Abigail rose and, without waking her ladyship, readjusted the pillows. The candle-light shone on the gold-tinted hair, the exquisite rose and cream of that ever young face, on the long curved lashes that lay like crescent moons upon her cheeks. In repose, bereft of the tumultuous expression that too often marred it, her cousin's beauty smote Abigail with fresh wonder. If only she could always be like this—so peaceful, and so lovely! Were her childish outbursts of rage, her dominance, her arrogance, due to some stray restless spirit that possessed her? At Holywell Abigail had studied something of the ancient contemplative mysteries. Pythagoras believed in the theory of transmigration. Was it possible that the soul, or Psyche, could return to dwell in many oft-repeated human forms, till it attained perfection? Was Cousin Sarah's Psyche still in the most youthful stage of its immortal journey? That would account for much. Or if, mused Abigail, we regard the body as a fortress that imprisons the human spirit, we might believe, with Sir Thomas Browne, that 'Transgressions are epidemical, and that there are certain tempers of the body which match and with an humoral depravity of mind produce certain vitiosities . . .' Perhaps his lordship, who so utterly adored her, saw her as Abigail saw her now: and as she remembered she had seen her for the first time, long ago, as a light rayed down from Heaven. . . .

A snort from the Lady's rose-leaf lips sent Abigail scurrying to her stool; but she did not sit.

A sound below in the courtyard, a scraping of wheels and stamping of hooves, aroused the Princess from her doze.

"Open the curtains," she whispered.

Abigail drew them apart. In the greying light she discerned a clerical portly gentleman descending from a coach. He appeared to be in haste. So soon as his foot touched the flagstones, and scarcely waiting for the door to open to his knock, he bolted in.

But that brief sight of him had sufficed for recognition. On several occasions Abigail had admitted him to the Princess Anne's apartment. Her eyes flew to the sleeping Mrs. Freeman, and betrayed a gleam of triumph before the sandy lashes drooped.

The Princess put a hand to her throat.

"Who is it?"

"The Bishop of Salisbury, Madam.   Shall I . . . ?"   She paused. The Princess, whose face had whitened, nodded.

"Yes. Go, meet him, Hill. Announce him."

And still the Countess slept.

Abigail tiptoed from the room and outside the door collided with a page: her brother Jack.

"What are you doing here?" she hissed. "Why aren't you in bed?"

"I'm waiting on His Highness."

"This is not his door. Go back."

"Not yet. The fun is just beginning."

"Fun! You callous young——" She looked up sharply. "What have you heard?"

"That the Bishop is come, which means the King is—gone!"

"And I," Abigail raised her chin, "am sent to bring the Bishop to the . . . Presence."

"You!" Jack stared. "Why, where's her ladyship?"

"In dreamland. I'll not wake her." She nudged him. "Go away!"

"I shan't. Look! Here is the old porpoise, with Masham."

She sneaked her hands over her bodice, and, with a deft adjustment of its 'modesty tucker', revealed a little more than was meant to be hidden. The Bishop was known to be susceptible, and if she were not pretty, she did, as Cousin Sarah had said, know very well how to dress.

Her lips tilted upward in a shy smile of greeting as the Bishop strode along the corridor on the heels of Mr. Masham. So he too had waited up!

"The Bishop of Salisbury desires audience with the Qu . . . with the Princess," murmured Mr. Masham, whose tactful hesitancy was not lost on Mrs. Hill.

The Bishop hemmed impatience. Abigail bobbed.

"Will your lordship please to follow me?"

Mr. Masham's brows shot up and his lips turned down, but at the slanting glint of those green eyes he bowed and stepped aside for the Bishop to pass.

Disdaining the tall page at Her Highness's door, Mrs. Hill opened it, raised her hand and gestured the Bishop to halt. He puffed out his lips and he frowned; but he halted. She closed the door softly upon him and left him standing on the mat.

Like a swift shadow she crossed the room, flooded now with the rose-torch of the risen sun.

The Prince still snored; Mrs. Freeman still slept; the Princess was on her feet, and very pale.

Abigail curtsied low to the ground and rested there.

"Your Majesty . . ."

She bragged about it afterwards to Jack and Alice. "History will say that the Bishop of Salisbury was the first to announce the King's death to the Queen, but actually 'twas I."

"Why," Alice wished to know, "should history say that the Bishop announced the King's death to the Queen if he didn't?"

"I didn't say he didn't I said I announced it first."

"Then why should he have all the honour?"

"Because he is a most important person, and I," responded Abigail with unconvincing diffidence, "am not. Besides, he is writing a history of his life and calling it a 'History of his Times'."

"How do you know?"

"I know because I know."

"You know," Jack told her bluntly, "because you glue your ear to keyholes."

"One lives," she smiled at him, unabashed, "to learn." And then suddenly she laughed and went on laughing breathlessly. "Oh! 'Twas rich to see her."

"To see?" Alice vacantly inquired. "To see whom?"

"Cousin Sarah—when I called the Bishop in. She didn't know that I'd been sent to fetch him. I think she could have killed herself for having overslept. I'm certain she could have killed me. She leapt from her couch as if she had been bitten, and all tousled as she was, with her bodice unfastened, she bore down on the Bishop like a galleon in full sail."

And up Abigail jumped to give an imitation of the scene with a boldness and vivacity that would have much astonished the ladies of the Bedchamber and good Mr. Masham, and everybody else, not excluding Cousin Sarah, who was acquainted with the bashful little Hill.

" 'My Lord Bishop' "—her reproduction of Mrs. Freeman's voice was inimitable, " 'what do you here?' That took the wind out of his sails and all his pretty speeches went a-hopping. So did he. He tripped over a rug—I always knew that floor was too high polished and that something of the sort would happen one day. He only saved himself from sprawling by a miracle. And then"—spurred by Jack's chuckles, Abigail went on gleefully, "then, my dears, he kicked over a stool. The poor Queen was greatly alarmed. I think she thought the Bishop was demented. Lud! 'Twas the drollest, most comical performance! And there was he, so full of himself and his words and his prayers, sliding and slipping and mumbling and stumbling, till finally he got down on his knees, *pros*trate, to touch the Queen's toe with his forehead. 'Your Majesty.' But I had said it first!"

Three days later all London was saying it, shouting it, as they stood at their windows, in the doorways of their houses, clustered in the sunlight to see their Queen in her coach and her mourning purple, drive through the streets of her capital to Westminster. And there to her Lords and her Commons the sweet, thrilling, surprisingly young voice spoke those few simple unprepared words that raised aloft, and for all time, her royal standard of sincerity and solid worth, for:

'My heart,' she said, 'is entirely English, and I can very sincerely assure you there is not anything you could expect or desire from me which I shall not be ready to do for the happiness and prosperity of England. . . .'

'Entirely English.' That was the message that circled her islands; that was her promise pledged, to serve and to give of her best. While the King, whose heart had never been English but who also had served of his best, lay embalmed in his coffin, unmourned by all save his Dutch Colony at Kensington.

'Our entirely English Queen Anne!'

They toasted her in ale, in good honest English ale. The taverns that exploited Hollands gin did a poor trade. A few among the elders, who had heard their grandfathers speak of the time when *they* were young in the days of another Queen, prophesied a future as glorious as had been Elizabeth's past. The feuds of Whig and Tory were forgotten. Hope blazed anew with the call to arms and, with war declared, the hope of speedy victory; for Marlborough was gone to take command.

* * *

"We have had a delightful rest," said Queen Anne, "but I am glad to be home."

Her Majesty, the Prince Consort, Mr. Masham, Mrs. Danvers, and a discreet selection of attendants, including Abigail Hill, had just returned from a visit to Bath. The Coronation had proved too much for Prince George. The food and the drink, the toasts and the general excitement, had induced in him a severe attack of asthma and in his wife an attack of the gout. The two invalids were thankful to escape to the comparative peace and rusticity of the little grey town on the Avon, where they dutifully drank the waters prescribed by their physicians and pronounced the cure quite marvellous, but:

"I am glad to be home," said Queen Anne. "Pray serve the tea, Mrs. Hill. . . . George? Mr. Masham?" The Prince sat: Mr. Masham sat: and finally Mrs. Hill sat, behind the urn.

It was an intimate company of four that, at the Queen's desire, had gathered round the table in her Green Closet to drink tea. Mrs. Danvers had been granted a week's leave. Lady Marlborough had retired to her country house, and had promoted Abigail in her absence to the position of First Bedchamberwoman to the Queen.

She was 'stupefied, was overwhelmed, would be everlastingly grateful,' thus she had assured her benefactress, 'for the great signal honour bestowed on one so utterly unworthy of it.'

"If you had been unworthy," had been Sarah's blunt reply, "I would not have allowed you to deputize for me." And afford her this opportunity to escape from the demands of Mrs. Morley, which, since her Coronation, had been more than ever excessive. And Sarah, of late, had much to occupy her mind and her attention of greater concern than Mrs. Morley's gout.

Her John was at the wars, and she, like a thousand other wives, waited, feared, longed, prayed for news from the fighting front. She had accompanied him to Margate the day that he embarked to join his forces. Tear-blinded, she had stood on the quay, straining her sight for a last glimpse of the ship that was bearing him away from her, perhaps for ever, till it dipped below the white-crested rim of the horizon.

But she had his letters for her comfort and her daughter Betty's pending marriage for her joy.

It was to superintend the preparations for the wedding that she had returned to Holywell House. Elizabeth, at fifteen, had been wooed and won by young Scrope Egerton, Lord Bridgewater. The courtship was tempestuous and swift. Elizabeth had made it clearly understood that with or without her parents' approval she intended to marry her Scrope. It was entirely a love match, and from Sarah's point of view to be encouraged. Bridgewater had all to his favour; money, good looks, an Earldom, and, moreover he was Master of the Horse to the Prince Consort.

The sentimental Mrs. Morley was delighted. She fully understood a mother's heart. Alas, if only her dear beloved Gloucester had been spared to her! . . . Tears, smiles, blessings, and jewels from Mrs. Morley's coffers were shed on the departing Mrs. Freeman, followed by a letter.

'My Lord Bridgewater being in haste to be married, I cannot any longer delay telling my dear Mrs. Freeman what I intended a great while, that I hope she will now give me leave to do what I had a mind to do when my dear Lady Harriet* was married. Let me speak to Lord Treasurer about it when I see him, that your poor unfortunate faithful Morley may not be any occasion of delay to other peoples' happiness.'

Nothing therefore, in these circumstances, could have been more satisfactory than that Mrs. Hill should be appointed to the Bedchamber. Mrs. Morley did not feel herself so utterly deprived of Mrs. Freeman's loving presence when Mrs. Hill, dear Mrs. Freeman's cousin, was so quietly about her: pouring tea.

Mr. Masham also may have found the change agreeable.

Seated at the walnut-wood round table between the Queen and Prince George, he watched the dainty hands of Mrs. Hill moving like white mice among the cups, adding cream—"And sugar, sir?" she asked of Mr. Masham, having served the Prince with two large spoonfuls, and the Queen with three.

Due justice having been done to the dishes of ratafia cakes and caraway biscuits and rusks, Mrs. Hill locked away the gold tea-caddy and possessed herself of the key which hung on a thin silver chain round her neck and was slipped, for safe keeping, in the hidden valley of her breasts. Whereupon Mr. Masham blushed to the ears and felt exceeding discomfort. And when the footmen had carried out the trays and the Queen had been settled in her chair with her feet on a stool and her King Charles's spaniel on her lap; and when the Prince had removed his great bulk to a sofa and put up his legs on a cushion, the Queen smilingly commanded her attendant: "Play a piece on the harpsichord, Hill."

Hill played a piece on the harpsichord. The Prince woke from his doze to exclaim: "Charmingk! Very good! Brava, bravissima! Does she not play very—where is my snush-box, Masham?"

Mr. Masham, who had been about to agree with fervour that Mrs. Hill played very charmingly indeed, started up from his seat and hovered anxiously over the Prince, while His Highness dug in all his pockets till he finally produced the snuff-box from under the pillow.

"Est-il possible! I have laid on it, and not a grain spilt! The lid is quite closed. I am wheezing bad to-day."

* Henrietta Churchill.

"Are you sure that red snuff the poor King used to take for his asthma is not too strong for you, George?" the Queen asked with wifely concern.

"No, it is goodt snush. It sooths my wheeze."

The Prince took snuff. Mr. Masham returned, bowing, to his seat. The Queen said: "George, I think you have not heard Hill sing. Pray, Hill, sing something."

Abigail got up, curtsied, sat down again, and sang very sweetly this 'something':

> 'Melodious songstress! Cry'd ye swain,
> To shades, to shades less happy go,
> Or if thou wilt with me remain,
> Forbear, forbear thy tuneful woe.
> While in thy loving arms I lie,
> To song, to song I am not free,
> On thy soft bosom when I die,
> I dis . . . cord find in thee.'

Whatever discord may have been found, it was certainly not in that melodious songstress nor her song, which brought tears of emotion to the Queen's eyes, a sparkle to Mr. Masham's, and loud applause from the Prince, who declared:

"Your little Hill, my dear, has an uncommon good voice. Capital! Why have we not heard you singk before? Why have you hid your light under bushels, Hill?"

"Because," the smiling Queen answered for her, "she is too bashful. It was only by chance that I happened to hear her. I came into the Bedchamber one day and found the door ajar and such pretty little sounds drifting through it that I confess I listened for quite several minutes before I was seen. Didn't I, Hill?"

"Yes, Your Majesty." The downcast lids were never so modestly lowered. "I would not have dared had I known that . . ."

"Pimpimpim!" The Queen playfully wagged her finger. "We were enchanted. Such a very tuneful little voice. Is it not, Mr. Masham?"

"O, positively yes, Your Majesty, indeed! I have seldom heard, save at the Opera——" And Mr. Masham, in a sweat, subsided.

"Sing again, Hill, if you please."

Hill sang again, and, at the Queen's request, again; while the Prince alternately dozed, wheezed, snored, and woke from his slumbers to say: "Brava! Encore! Bravissima!" And watching Mrs. Hill's hands moving up and down the keyboard very daintily, while her pink lips formed harmonious O's and Ah's, Mr. Masham began to fidget and reflect upon that tantalizing glimpse of the key sliding down between her . . . Well, but what a place to keep it. And agad, what a skin! White as milk. And those devilish eyes that seldom looked at you directly, but when they did . . . Why, blister me! decided Mr. Masham, what a plaguey, provocative, agreeable little baggage to . . .

A scratch at the door interrupted these pleasing conjectures and brought Mr. Masham, a trifle shamefaced, to his feet. Mrs. Hill paused in the middle of a shake and fixed her green eyes on the disturbed Mr. Masham.

"Come," said the Queen.

A page entered.

"Your Majesty, Lord Godolphin is in the Ante-room."

"Lord Godolphin! Good Heavens!" The Queen raised her hand to her mouth. "I had forgot I had an audience with my Lord Treasurer. No, George, do not leave me. Yes, Mr. Masham, you may go. And you, Hill. I have so *much* enjoyed your playing and your songs. Bring the Lord Treasurer in."

"Pray, Lord Godolphin, be seated."

She was distantly gracious, unsmiling. He noted the absence of the familiar 'Montgomery', bestowed upon him as a mark of her esteem. It was one of her childish fancies, never outgrown, to indulge in pet names for her friends; but why she should have dubbed him 'Montgomery' he had never known, nor did he very much care. What he did know, however, and to the cost of his patience, was that these first few months of her reign had proved her the deuce of a tough proposition to tackle. Her Stuart obstinacy allied to her doting infatuation for that oafish clod, her husband, had rendered a hundredfold more difficult his unwelcome task of having to inform her that Parliament had decided against the title of 'King Consort' for Prince George. He had left Marlborough to deal with the still more preposterous suggestion that the Prince should command the Allied Forces. Marlborough had wisely referred the ultimatum to the Dutch, and had probably tipped a hint to Heinsius, who had, thank God, firmly vetoed a proposal which, if followed, would have brought the war to a speedy and disastrous end with the collapse of the Allies.

To mitigate the Prince's disappointment the Queen had made him Lord High Admiral of the Fleet. In that capacity, as a figurehead adorned in cocked hat, gold lace and splendid uniforms, he could review squadrons to his heart's content and leave their command to Admiral Rooke. But despite this compromise,

Godolphin was aware that the Queen and her Great Dane regarded him as the head and front of these offendings, which, to judge by the scowl on the Prince's face and the absent look upon Her Majesty's, still, most decidedly, rankled.

Fixing his slightly bulbous eyes upon his sovereign, and in the fruity catarrhal voice of a man who eats, drinks and lives too indulgently, Godolphin spoke.

"Madam, am I to understand from Your Majesty's latest communication that you are quite determined to restore the practice of touching for the King's Evil?"

"If, my lord, you mean that we desire to use the gift of healing with which we are endowed by Almighty God, we most emphatically do."

The defiant look of those bovine eyes, together with the Royal plural never before used by the Queen in conversation with 'Mr. Montgomery', gave him further indication of his fall from grace.

Squaring his pugilistic jaw, Godolphin reconnoitred.

"Madam, I am Your Majesty's servant, whose privilege it is to honour and obey Your Majesty's commands."

She inclined her head and stroked her dog, and stared at him.

"But it is also my duty," he carefully continued, "to advise."

She lifted the spaniel to her shoulder. It's moist black nose nuzzled her cheek. She cooed at it: "Diddle, diddle pimpimpim," and said: "We refuse to be advised on so sacred a subject, my lord. We have been endowed with the miraculous gift of healing——"

She has acquired this goddamned repetitive trick, the Lord Treasurer savagely reflected, from her George. Once she gets a notion in her simple head she'll go on and on like a parrot, until from very weariness you give it her. There lies her strength if she but knew it. She *may* know it.

"——which," the Queen continued, in cool gentle tones, "is God's legacy to the Anointed Heir of Edward the Confessor. We wish it to be made known that we intend to revive this holy ritual that has been in abeyance since the accession of the late King, who was *not* a direct descendant of the Saint. I *am* a descendant, and I intend to perform those God-given miracles which are my divine right. So if you will be good enough, my lord, to make the necessary arrangements and place at our disposal a sum of Angel Gold——"

The spaniel wriggled from her arms, jumped down and pattered to the door.

"Hill!" The Queen raised her voice and called again. "Hi—ill!"

From an inner chamber emerged a young person in grey. The Queen pointed. "The dog. He is asking to go out."

The young person curtsied, tenderly lifted the spaniel, and carried him away. The Queen turned to Lord Godolphin with a frigid smile. "Forgive the interruption, my lord. You were saying——?"

He was not saying, he was thinking: And where do you suppose I am to find your 'Angel Gold'? Under a gooseberry bush? God's fish, Madam, I've a war to finance which is costing me hundreds of thousands a day, and you talk of Angel Gold! But: "Your Majesty," he declared, "it shall be done." And he goggled an eye at the Prince Consort, who was taking snuff and no part at all in the discussion.

"I am happy to see Your Highness so greatly improved in health."

"I am not," mumbled the Prince, "improved in health."

His large good-natured face showed every indication of the sulks. He had it firmly fixed that Godolphin and Marlborough between them had deliberately quashed his command of the Allies, and offered him instead the nominal title—he had no illusions about that—of Lord High Admiral of the Fleet. But he was not such a fool, whatever they might think of him, as to believe he would ever be allowed to take any more than the most passive part in naval warfare. And here was Lord Treasurer telling him his health was much improved, when all the doctors knew that his asthma had become distressingly acute since he had been deprived of his command.

"No, it is not improved," the Prince Consort repeated sourly. "I am wheezing bad to-day."

The Lord Treasurer expressed profound concern.

"His Highness and I too," said the Queen, "have been greatly disturbed by recent events—and disappointments."

This barbed implication having ricocheted harmlessly from its impermeable target, the Queen launched a decisive attack.

"It is my earnest desire to pay tribute to the service of Lord Marlborough and his military genius. I wish him to have"—she glanced at the Prince, who nodded encouragement till all his chins shook—"to have bestowed on him the title of 'Duke', and an income of five thousand a year for life, and to his heirs hereafter."

S'truth! Only by the supremest effort did Godolphin restrain the escape of that unministerial ejaculation. A dukedom certainly —if she were bent upon it—would cost nothing, but five thousand a year for life *and* hereafter! Sliding a look at the Prince, Godolphin was pleasurably surprised to see the scowl had returned to his face. So that had shocked George too! His support in the Lords might sway the issue if he dared voice public disagreement to his wife's demands; which was unlikely.

Godolphin sucked in his full, pock-marked cheeks and rolled an eye from one large presence to the other.

"I will put Your Majesty's decision," he said, "before the House."

"Surely, my lord, since we have advised you of our decision, there is no necessity to put this question to the House? I myself will write to Lord Malborough and acquaint him of our intention, which is also our earnest desire."

Crossing his knee, Godolphin clenched a veinous fist upon it.

"I suggest, Madam, as a point of pure formality, that the House should be advised."

"But it is a *per*sonal, not a Governmental honour that I wish to bestow."

Godolphin bowed.

"I knew"—her smile was that of a gratified child—"I *knew* my Lord Treasurer would support me in a matter that is so dear to my heart. I wish it fully understood that it is my desire——"

Say it again! inwardly groaned the Lord Treasurer.

She said it again—"my *earnest* desire to encourage all who concur faithfully in my service, whether they be Whig or Tory, but I won't be tied to one or other. I have my own views, though party politics"—from a silver box on a table beside her the Queen took a sugared almond—"party politics I do confess to be my bugbear." And popping the comfit in her mouth she licked her thumb.

"All our bugbears, Madam." Goldolphin got upon his feet. "When we are at war we should strive to be impartial."

"I am always impartial." She held out her hand. He bent over it. "You will arrange then for the Angel Gold and for the five thousand a year for Mrs. Free—for," she hastily corrected, "Lord Marlborough."

"My love!" burst out the silent Prince, "that is too much. I think it is too generous. I realize it is the promptingks of your most kind and generous heart, but it is too much."

"Too much? You said," queried the Queen in a tone of stupefaction, "you said, 'too *much*'? George!" A world of reproach was in those ringing tones, and in the wide grieved eyes she turned upon her scarlet spouse. Godolphin smothered a grin. "You, my dear Mr. Montgomery," her voice, bereft of former chill, and her return to the endearing name, promoted him her ally against this deplorable desertion of her better self. Her George! "Do *you*, my dear Mr. Montgomery, think it too much?"

"Madam, it is not for me," Godolphin hedged, "to criticize or question Your Majesty's bounty." Leave that, he silently commented, to the House. A fine clutter it'll make.

"You hear, dearest, what Lord Godolphin says." She shot a look of triumph at the now deflated George. "He entirely agrees, and so will you, my love, when you come to consider more carefully my proposition. I think that is all, dear Mr. Montgomery. No! There *is* one more thing, a very small matter, that I have forgot to mention. I want five thousand pounds for Lady Elizabeth Churchill's wedding-gift. But that I can take from the Privy Purse . . . May I offer you a comfit, my good lord?"

Declining a comfit, Godolphin backed, bowing, to the door. In his coach he drove straight from the Palace to Pontack's in Abchurch Lane, the most fashionable ordinary in town. He found the room crowded and humming with talk, foggy with tobacco smoke, and almost every table occupied.

Looking neither to right nor left, he pushed his bull-necked way between groups of periwigged beaux, and recently commissioned young officers swaggering in the novelty of gold-laced and scarlet uniforms. One among a cluster of heated Tories, who at the Lord Treasurer's approach had ceased their argument to stand respectfully aside for him to pass, indicated a vacant table at the upper end of the room.

Godolphin took possession of a seat and called for wine. The air, which apparently had never been renewed by ventilation, was oppressive. His steinkerk, damp with sweat, clung with a throttling sensation to his throat. As he fiddled with the fastening to loosen it, he received the pressure of a hand upon his shoulder and in his ear the murmur of a rhyme:

'Will my good lord join me in a wise debate
While he adjusts his cravat and reforms the State?'

Swinging round on his rump, Godolphin goggled up at the impassive countenance of Harley.

"Pize take you!" exclaimed the Lord Treasurer testily. "Why do you come creeping at me like the ghost in Hamlet, with your everlasting jingles?"

"I was not aware that the ghost in Hamlet was addicted to the jingles," the smiling Harley lowered himself into a chair and signalled to a drawer, "though I perceive my lord is in the jangles. What have you ordered?"

"Sewer-water," muttered Godolphin. "The nearest approach to liquor you can get in this house."

Harley regarded him with some amusement.

"May the devil disparage my parts if you're not in the deuce of a pet. Here, drawer! A magnum of Frontiniac. We shall not have much more of good French wine in future, so let us make the best of it now."

"I'm drinking Burgundy," growled Godolphin.

"So I see. I advise you pour it down and spew it up. Frontiniac will revive you."

"By the stink of your breath," remarked the Lord Treasurer acidly, "it has not revived *you*. I judge you've been at it, as usual, all day."

"What? I?" Harley spread his charming hands in an exaggerated gesture. "My dear fellow, here's calumny—a gross unmitigated libel. What has Anna Regina said to provoke her 'dear Mr. Montgomery'?"

"Provoke!" snarled Godolphin. " 'Pon life and honour, I'd have seen myself pickled in brine had I known what I would be faced with under a petticoat government."

"Pickled in brine, resign, resign," chanted Harley.

Godolphin glowered.

"That's a bloody, vexing, goddamned trick you've learned yourself, Robin. Curb it, or use it on your Grub Street gutter spies and not on me."

Harley cocked an amiable eyebrow.

"You're right about the trick and wrong about its source. It does not emanate from Grub Street, but from hard by the Haymarket—from Monsieur Foubert's Academy to be precise, where I went to school and where we learned, besides riding, fencing, dancing, handling arms and mathematics, the construing of bawdy French verse into English. I could repeat to you——"

"I'd rather you didn't," rasped Godolphin.

"The French! Ah, the French!" Harley affectedly sighed. " 'Tis a grievous sorrow to my mind that we are at war with a nation so devoted to literature, the arts, and by Bacchus! to good wine. Try this. You won't? I will."

He poured a brimming goblet and drained it at a draught, flicked invisible snuff from his sleeve, and said pleasantly: "I hear your colt won the Three Thousand Guinea stakes at Newmarket yesterday. Are you suffering the natural result of jubilation? Is that why you are crabbed?"

Godolphin ground his molars, then exploded: "You can't *talk* to her! She gives you that cow's look of hers, chewing the cud over and over, and which now proves to be no less than——"

"The offer of a dukedom," Harley gently interposed, "to 'Mr. Freeman'."

Godolphin's eyes were bolting.

"God's beard! But you're a feret. How d'you know that?"

Harley sipped and smiled again, and answered nothing.

"You know too much," resumed Godolphin surlily. "I'm inclined to believe that what the Whigs say of you is not all Party venom."

"I have the gift of second sight—and healing," murmured Harley.

" 'S'death and deuce!" roared Godolphin. "You'd have been burned for a warlock fifty years ago. Yes, 'tis a gift you have in all conscience, though whence it comes I would not care to guess. Do you read thoughts—or sink your pride and purse to pay your agents? 'Tis a dirty, low, intriguing way you take, my friend, but I'll wager it will lead you to *my* place in the long run. Isn't that what you're aiming for, Robin?"

If Godolphin's tone was cordial, the look on his face was not. Harley returned it, steadily.

"My aim is your aim too, Godolphin. To serve our country and our Queen—but not our Queen's familiars. In that one point we differ. We don't see alike in our friendships. If you're unseated as Lord Treasurer 'twill be the Marlboroughs who, in their long run, will pull you down. But you have your loyalties and I have mine. Each to his tastes—and beliefs."

"Yes." Godolphin rubbed his nose. "Your loyalty's a Royalty —why, here, pox me, if your pest of a rhyming is not infectious and I've caught it! I've heard," he twirled the stem of his glass, looking down, "that they call you a Jack."

"Of all trades?" Harley's lips parted to show his fine teeth. "Come, let's not quibble. Unburden, unburden. What more than a duchy is Mrs. Morley asking for her Freeman?"

"Hah!" Godolphin uttered a sound like a crow and smacked his thick jaws upon it. "So there's something you haven't picked out of the laystalls—or black magic."

"Picked? Pooh! You credit me with wizardry, or worse, while I can plead guilty to nothing more particular than the slick-working mind of an attorney. Deduction is simple. What's the dukedom going to cost?"

"Five thousand a year for his life," returned Godolphin glumly, "and to his heirs—hereafter."

"Five! Phew!" Harley's hooded eyes narrowed. "Not five?"

Godolphin grinned at him.

"The 'mystery man' is taken by surprise? Zounds! And so was I. She don't ask me for much, hey? With an army to clothe and feed and ammunition to find—and then *this*!"

" 'Tis the most outrageous demand," agreed Harley in his engaging drawl, "but not so much as might have been appropriated by the Mistress of the Robes who holds the Privy Purse. Thank your stars she hasn't asked for more!"

"No." Godolphin, frowning, shook his head. "You wrong her, Harley. Sarah has had no hand in this. She knows nothing of it yet, and I am convinced that, for her part, she'll urge Marlborough to refuse the strawberry leaves."

"And take the straw?" Harley tilted the bottle. "You're wrong. You're utterly and fatuously wrong. The matter with you is that you judge men and women by the same high standards as you judge your Newmarket winners. Human flesh is not horse-flesh nor is it half so pure, neither in its breeding nor in those natural and honourable instincts that go to make a race-horse. You've staked your all on the Marlboroughs. You've married your son to their daughter, and they twist you——" he negligently clasped his fingers round his glass and smiled, "and they twist you."

Godolphin sipped, grimacing.

"You're a vindictive beast, Robin. I'd not like to be on your opposite side."

"I have no opposite side," he said blandly.

"This," Godolphin grunted, pushing aside his half empty flagon, "is a plaguey abominable wine."

"I told you, take the Frontiniac. What do you propose to do about the Freemans? You can't give 'em five thousand a year. The country would rise to a man and bawl you down. Marlborough's popularity doesn't yet extend beyond the limits of his armies."

" 'M. Maybe." Godolphin, frowning, ran his tongue around his teeth. "I know I've the deuce and all to face when I put it to the House, but I'll have to. If I don't——"

"If you don't," added Harley to his pause, "Mrs. Freeman and the Queen will have you out, and 'Dismal' Nottingham in."

"Nottingham!" Godolphin protruded a derisive lip. "Not he."

"No? D'you think he'll be content to stand for ever on the second rung as Secretary of State?"

"He's not Secretary yet."

"But he will be very soon. Who else if not——?"

"Not you." Godolphin flashed a grin at him. "I find you too valuable a Speaker."

"I might be," admitted Harley, returning him a gentle smile, "were I allowed to speak . . . Come on! Unbend your brow. Here's young St. John approaching with his eyes on stalks. That's a lad worth watching, but I'd as soon trust him," he lowered his voice and said, scarcely moving his lips, "as I'd trust a pet panther. Nor is he, come to think on't, unlike a panther in his movements. Very feline—but unfeelin'."

Godolphin groaned. "A plague upon your punning!"

Harley laughed and hooked a finger at a drawer.

"Bring a magnum of the same and take away this poison you've served to his lordship. Hah, Harry! Our squire of dames. You look more exquisite than ever . . . I never see you twice in the same suit. I wish I could afford your tailor. I'm rusty and fusty and dusty——"

"—and drunk," put in Godolphin sourly.

"You malign me," smiled Harley, "I am never drunk. I'm at my best in my cups. I thrive on the bottle. Here goes and no heel-taps!"

He drank deep again, and sat back in his chair. His eyes were unclouded, the whites very clear, his skin fresh as a girl's. He took snuff and slid the box across the table to Godolphin.

"My lord, Mr. Harley." The young gentleman, in a suit of corbeau-coloured velvet and a rakish cocked hat that he deferentially removed as he stood waiting for the invitation to join his superiors, was a very young gentleman indeed.

Possessed of more than his share of good looks, he had besides more than his share of good sense. The brightest star in the brilliant constellation of younger Higher Tories he was an ardent Jacobite, and he did not care if the world—and the Queen—should know it. Stealing a glance at the empty seat beside Godolphin, he was answered by a curt nod from Lord Treasurer.

"Sit down, St. John. I'm going."

"What! So soon?" protested Harley.

"Yes. I'm dining with my son Rialton and his wife."

Godolphin got up, gave a significant look at the empty flagons in front of his Speaker, a fatherly pat to St. John's broad shoulder, and moved with cumbrous dignity away.

"There goes an ass in a lion's skin," remarked St. John, gazing after him. "Sink me if I can see him anywhere but in a stable with a straw in his mouth, or on Newmarket Heath training fillies. And talking of fillies"—he leaned forward confidentially—"there's a young piece at the Palace, I'm told, with a face as plain as an egg, but a body that would tempt a cod to rise. And she's that rarity—a virgin."

Harley regarded him with cold disfavour.

"You disgust me."

St. John sniggered.

"I had forgot you despise all recreation that is not to be found in the pages of a book or in the contents of a bottle. For my part, I frankly own there is no pleasure so good as good wenching. Which reminds me——"

"May we," suggested Harley, "dispense with reminiscences? If it be the tale of the housemaid I have heard it."

"It is not the tale of the housemaid, although I'll allow 'twas the most jovial, happy little housemaid that ever I—but that's a private matter which your asceticism could not understand, and for which I pity you. I was about to ask if there is any truth in this talk that's all around the town, to do with the Cadiz expedition."

Harley presented the eager inquiring face with a specially caustic look.

"What has the Cadiz expedition to do with your particular hobby?"

"Only this," returned the irrepressible St. John. "That all of Clubland is saying our troops have lately joined with the Dutch in an attack on the churches at Rota, plundering, looting the town, and burning——"

"If you've had the smell of the smoke," Harley interrupted, "there must have been a fire."

"No, agad! But if 'tis indeed a fact——" the boy flushed with anger, "then 'tis a foul, dastardly blot upon the honour of our men and Britain's name. I've heard they forced their way into a convent and ravaged the nuns."

"Yes, you would have heard that," smiled Harley. "All wars are barbarous, and some of war's secrets are shameful; yet the lust of the fight brings out the highest, and seldom the lowest, in human nature. Best forget that incident and remember only the men who died their soldiers' deaths."

St. John blinked. When Harley was not mocking, he decided, he could be as prosy dull as any starch-nosed Dissenter.

"Well, but what do you presume will be the retort of the French to such a sacrilege? They'll not take to it kindly, or forget it."

"They cannot lay it nor can we, to Marlborough's account."

"No"—St. John called for a glass and added as he poured the wine—"unfortunately."

"Such observations," remarked Harley taking snuff, "are better kept to yourself."

"For this present I agree, but the time will come when I'll voice my views at the top of my lungs, though my head be brought to the block for it! You know my life's aim, Robin?"

"I know," said Harley carefully, "that you brag too loud of your likes and dislikes—and of your affections. Play with the Jills as much as you please, but keep your hands off the Jacks."

St. John received this veiled advice from the man upon whose political skill he consciously modelled himself and his future career, with an impudent lift of his eyebrows.

"Why was Lord Treasurer glum?" he asked coolly, turning the trend of *that* lecture.

"He said the wine was sour."

St. John let out a voluminous sigh.

"For so straight a gentleman you are uncommon crooked. I thought it might be the belly-ache. He's had a stomach-full of my Occasional Conformity Pie—too raw. D'you think he'll cook it before he serves it to the Lords?"

But what Harley thought remained unsaid, for at that moment the room was thrown into an uproar by the sound of a drum and fife band, a shouting and a singing and a mighty tramping outside in the street. The groups of officers surged to the door; the painted beaux, giggling and twittering, fluttered after them to peep and point.

"The Volunteers!" cried St. John as, excited as any, he leapt to his feet and rushed out.

Only Harley and a company of dice-throwers absorbed in their play remained seated, while the song that called to arms the youth of Britain was yelled and brayed to the marching steps of the newly joined recruits.

'*Over* the hills and *over* the main,
To *Fland*ers, Portu*gal*, and Spain,
Queen *Anne* commands and we *obey*,
Over the hills and *far* away. . . .'

It was midnight when Harley left Pontack's. Some rain had fallen to make a quagmire of the narrow street, but he had not far to walk to Leicester Fields, and he needed air.

Avoiding the urgent offers of escort from a huddle of link boys posted at the door, he took the right of the cobbled way with a contemptuous grin for a drunken fop who clung reeling in his vomit to the wall. A coach lumbered by and spattered Harley from top to toe with slush. Cursing roundly he removed his hat which was new, flicked a handkerchief over the mud-blotted gold lace, and tucked it under his arm for its protection

A withered crone, raking on all fours in the gutter for edible items among a heap of decomposed fish-heads, rotten vegetables and a dead cat, rose up to whine at him for alms as she pulled aside her rags to expose her chancrous breasts. With a pucker of his nose at the stink of her, he flung a coin. She grabbed it as it rolled, croaked fulsome thanks and blessings, and shuffled off to the nearest gin-house.

Although late for street traffic, the night was young for the varied entertainments that would now go on till morning in the clubs and taverns, brothels of the town; or in those less known but more exclusive haunts that offered to the old and jaded their secret epicurean delights.

A girl with a pitifully fresh young face laid her finger-tips caressingly on Harley's cuff, and pointing her tongue at him between her painted lips, she whispered.

He shook her hand away and hastened on, while his innate prudery shuddered at the obscenities she shouted after him. He must see to it when he should come to power, that the night life of London be cleansed of these ruttish marauders.

Tilting his uncovered head he gazed up at the fragrant sky, where one lone ice-blue star winked from its perch above a chimney-pot. And as he stood an instant, pleasuring that boundless remote serenity tented above the city's stifling lusts, its creeping forms that came and went from God alone could tell what unplumbed dregs of crime and poverty, he mused upon life's inconsistencies. That girl, aged young enough to be his daughter: that shrivelled drab who might have been a mother—his mother, but for the accident of birth—were equally at one with him, working in their own ways and in the ultimate conflict for survival—to what end? Carnal or sacerdotal? To save or be saved? To live or to let live? O, but 'tis a world, he mused, of shiftless unrealities and villainous corruptions, take it how or where you will. We preach of God and murder Him in the same breath. We are constant to our laws to save our skins, but not our souls. Is there a pin to choose between that rag-picker digging in the dung like a pariah bitch, or myself who dig my way through a cesspool of political lies and insincerities that I may feed on the plums I pull out o' the garbage? What am I but a scavenger too? . . . A laugh, not mirthful, escaped him; and staring heavenward he felt again that touch upon his arm and turned with an oath, unuttered.

"Mr. Harley."

No trollop this, no woman, but a man, whom, in the outflung orange flare of a lanthorn guarding an open drain, he dimly recognized: a hawk-faced, shabby individual with grey keen eyes and a mole on the left side of his mouth. He accosted him with jocular familiarity.

"Star-gazing, sir? You follow the longer way above, and I, the *shortest way* below—with the Dissenters. They'll be stiff when they read what I have written." He chuckled. "So will I. But I think I have here what you want, if you'll give me what *I* want."

Harley narrowed his eyes.

"How much?"

"Enough for a square meal and a bottle o' the best, Mr. Robin —Robin—Robinson—by God!" He slapped his thigh in a moment of exuberance, immediately hushed. "I've got it," he muttered. "At last I have got it! 'Tis strange, inconsequent, and unpredictable how these sudden inspirations alight upon my shoulder like a fairy. Or a witch. Queer, queer, prodigious queer. For look you how I sit all day and half the night in my hide-hole tracing patterns with a quill on my paper, and not a word to cherish until now. Sir, you have given me my title. I'll begin, although it will not be completed for years. It belongs to my future, when you and your works"—he bowed profusely—"are my past."

Harley's face expressed some wonder and small patience.

"What, sirrah, is this rigmarole?"

"An idea, a symbol, a parable, a story for youth, a story for age, a story of adventure, of uncharted seas, of exploration. Wait, you wait! 'Tis here." He tapped his forehead. "I'm chocked with it. I'm blocked with it. I'm pregnant, and pray God when I've delivered I shall not have to go a-begging or sink myself to *this*."

And into Harley's hands he slid a pamphlet.

Before his fingers closed on it, Harley shot a look around his shoulder and breathed thankfulness to see the street a void. But the thought bore at him uneasily: a pawky uncouth fellow. Was he wise to use him when he knew so little of him?

"Your name?" he asked coldly. "I cannot for the moment recollect——"

"Ohoa!" The thin lips wriggled humorously. "You don't know it yet, but you will, O, yes, you will. For this present meantime call me . . . Friday."

And slinking back into the dark he disappeared.

* * *

'Here's *for*ty shillings *on* the drum
For *those* as volun*teers* do come . . .'

5

"Your deal, Mr. Masham."

The Prince Consort scooped up the cards, handed them to his gentleman and beamed at the pile of gold on the baize at his elbow. Mr. Masham dealt. The pile of gold at *his* elbow had diminished to three pieces. It certainly did not pay to play—with Royalty. He had given the game to his Prince once too often. Last night he had lost twenty-five guineas, to-night forty. Sixty-five down the drain, and his diamond pin up the spout. He gathered his cards and played the knave of hearts. The Prince triumphantly played the King.

"Here goes my Lord Shrewsbury. Do you know they are calling Shrewsbury 'King of Hearts'? Your luck is out to-night, Masham, but—unlucky at cards," the Prince chortled slyly, "lucky in love, hey?"

Mr. Masham reddened and put down the ace.

The Prince pushed out his underlip. "I spoke too soon. Not so unlucky." He turned to the page behind his chair. "Fill up the glasses."

The glasses were filled. The Prince gulped deep, Mr. Masham took a sip. The game went on and the page went out.

In the ante-room adjoining the Prince's apartment he stood at the closed window with his nose pressed to the pane and his eyes fixed on the raggle-taggle column marching down St. James's Street towards the Palace. Some were in uniform, some in rags, some in periwigs, satin, plush; some wore aprons, some wore smocks, but every one of them bawled the rousing song that for a year had dragged the hearts of Englishmen, that they must up and follow it for Marlborough and the Queen.

From manor house, from ale-house, from prison-cell and ploughshare, from St. Giles's stews to the Clubs of St. James's, recruits fell into line to fight the French.

'Come *on* then boys and . . .'

Jack opened the casement a stealthy inch. They were advancing nearer. He could see them tramping along, four abreast. Their voices roared up at him,

> '. . . *you* shall see
> We *every* one shall *Cap*tains be,
> To *whore* and *rant* as well as *they*
> When over the hills and *far* away.'

Wider and wider the casement swung; Jack was head and

shoulders out of it with a redness in his sight and a burning in his ears.

> 'The *constables* they *search* about
> To *find* such brisk young *fel*lows out.
> Then *let's* be volunteers I *say* . . .'

"Page! Hill! Page!" boomed the voice of the Prince. "What is this cold air cuttingk at me like a knife? Have you a window open?"

Jack softly closed it, drew a deep breath, and walked into the room with his chin up and his shoulders square.

The game was done, and the Prince glumly counting out twenty guineas to the smiling Mr. Masham.

"Sir, may it please Your Highness to give me leave to speak with you?"

"Hey? What?" The Prince looked up and Jack looked down. His lashes were damp, his cheeks very bright, his voice tense and quick.

"I beg leave to tender Your Highness my resignation from to-morrow an it please Your Highness."

The Prince Consort's mouth fell open; Jack shut his. Mr. Masham gave a gentle cough and began to build a card-house.

"Est-il possible!" The Prince broke a stupefied hush. "You ask to resign—to resign your post as my page. Are you mad? How? Why? What for do you want to go?"

"I want to go for a soldier, Sir."

"A soldier!" The Prince jerked his head. "You want to go for a soldier?" He muttered something inaudible and repeated it loud. "So do I."

Mr. Masham let fall a card and stooped to pick it up.

"So do I," said the Prince, and the faded blue eyes moistened. "And so would my boy have wished to go. He would have been younger yet than you." The Prince cleared his throat of some obstruction. "You said to-morrow. To-morrow? . . . But that is ridiculous. You cannot go to-morrow. You cannot run off like that to join the ranks."

"Sir," a small muscle crisped in Jack's set jaw. "I can."

"I've no doubt you can." The Prince's flabby cheeks expanded. "But you won't."

"Your Highness." It was Mr. Masham who surprisingly said: "If I might suggest, as a soldier once myself, I think Mr. Hill is just the type of officer the Duke is asking for."

The Prince shook his head violently.

"It is not for Marlborough to ask. It is for the Queen to ask—and to decide."

"Sir! If you"—panted Jack—"if Your Highness would speak to Her Majesty for me——"

"No." The Prince heaved his huge body out of his chair. His emphatic chins quivered. "I will not speak to the Queen for you, Mr. Hill. You must speak to the Queen for yourself."

And clapping his hand on Jack's shoulder he marched him solemnly out of the room.

There was no prouder lad in Britain than young Ensign John Hill when, some few weeks later, in his brand new scarlet uniform he boarded a ship to go over the sea, and away.

CHAPTER TWO

"My heart grieves for the poor Duchess. May God comfort her. I too have known the same heartbreak in the loss of my one beloved son."

The Queen's tears fell on the scarf-fringe she was plaiting. Mrs. Danvers sympathetically sniffed.

"It has been such a terrible shock to me," sighed the Queen. "My own angel boy was always so attached to Lord Churchill—Lord Blandford, as he now is—was, I should say. It is unbelievable that he has gone. What a ruthless disease is the smallpox. My poor sister, the late Queen, died of it. Where is Mrs. Hill?"

Mrs. Danvers, who was successfully summoning a sob, checked it to answer in a tone as dry as her eyes:

"In the garden, Your Majesty—with Mr. Masham."

"Send Mrs. Hill to me. You may leave us, Danvers."

Mrs. Danvers curtsied and left. Her head was high and the rising colour on her cheek-bones clashed with the recent carmine application of the hare's foot. She was met by Mrs. Abrahal in the gallery, and beckoning her to a window, she hysterically pointed. "The *vice*-viceroy," she hissed, "is to be sent in, and *I* am sent out. Look!"

Mrs. Abrahal looked.

The February day was fair and mild with a beading of buds upon the trees, crocuses upon the lawn, snowdrops peering under the box-hedge, and Mrs. Hill in a dove-grey gown seated on a circular stone bench.

Beside her sat Mr. Masham; his hands, held stiffly at arms' length, were wrapped in the rose-coloured wool Mrs. Hill was deftly winding.

Mrs. Abrahal pursed her lips. Mrs. Danvers tittered.

"I vow and declare I have not the heart to shatter such an intimate, affecting little scene. . . . Page!" Raising her voice, Mrs. Danvers clapped her hands.

Ensign Hill's successor, Peter Bathurst, detached himself from a window-seat and came leisurely forward.

"Go down to the garden," commanded Mrs. Danvers, "and tell Mrs. Hill that Her Majesty desires her attendance."

Mrs. Danvers had not taken kindly to Mrs. Hill's advancement in the Bedchamber, with her songs at the harpsichord and her 'pretty taste' for music. For until the arrival of Hill there has been none but 'my dear Danvers' who could so efficiently rub chalk-stones from the fingers of the Queen; nor was that so surprising, for Mrs. Danvers had been rubbing chalk-stones from those fingers these ten years; had poulticed, bandaged, blistered the Royal feet for almost twice that length of time. Was it not Danvers who had assisted in the flight of the Princess Anne from the Palace to the house of the Duchess of Somerset during the Revolution? And who but Danvers had laid upon the nuptial bed, on the Princess Anne's marriage night, the exquisitely embroidered wedding shift? Who but Danvers had been told that there was not, nor never *could* be, so gentle, tender, kind, affectionate a nurse—until the advent of a certain mealy-mouthed, freckled-faced, bread-and-butter 'Miss'?

But now it was: "Danvers, do not press so hard upon my joints. They are sensitive. Hill uses oil when she rubs. Pray go gently." Or it would be:

"Danvers, when you snuff the candles you should burn those nice-smelling pastilles that Mrs. Hill buys in the Exchange." Or:

"No, Danvers, *not* Hungary water for my handkerchiefs. Every second person is scented with Hungary water. Mrs. Hill has discovered such a delicious perfume—in that crystal flask, Danvers, labelled 'Eau sans pareil'."

It was Hill this, Hill that, Hill does or Hill doesn't, and almost always, Danvers don't: and now, "Send Hill to me."

What for? To mourn upon her shoulder? To weep in chorus for the death of Marlborough's son?

" 'Tis a shocking sad calamity to befall the poor Duke and Duchess," said Mrs. Abrahal, wet-eyed. "He was the heir."

"God's will be done," intoned Mrs. Danvers. "Others are

suffering similar losses every day of their lives. What of the lads who are being slaughtered on the fighting front? He might have been there."

Mrs. Abrahal offered a mild reproof. "He would have been there—the poor young man—if the Duchess had not held him back from joining his father. She was only acting as any mother would to save her son."

"We would not have much chance of winning the war," retorted Mrs. Danvers, "if every mother tried to save her son." And leaning closer to the window, she inconsequently added: "See her now, the baggage, winding wool!"

And very daintily she wound it, over and under, round and round the hands of Mr. Masham, that tilted up and dipped to her quick movements as if they were dancing a jig.

The pale sunlight on her capless head touched the silken sandy hair with gleams of copper. Mr. Masham's glance roved from the whiteness of her throat to the modest curve of the down-pointed bodice defining her supple waist; and Mr. Masham's ears turned hot. He was embarrassed to hear himself breathe.

"Have you," he asked hurriedly, "had news from your brother of late?"

She lifted her pale lids; he caught a glint of green and the sound of a sigh before those lids were lowered.

"No, sir, I have had no news this great while. In his last letter he told me he had joined the Forces on the Maas. There has been some heavy fighting in that quarter, I fear."

"And if I know anything of him," Mr. Masham said with better intent than tact, "he will have been in the thick of it."

"O, sir, no! . . . I mean, O, yes!" She stayed a strand of wool upon his thumb and raised wide startled eyes to his. "I am sure, knowing Jack, that he will, and I," her words trembled, "am so dreadfully anxious."

With an inward groan for his clumsiness Mr. Masham hastened to amend it.

" 'Twas unpardonable in me, atrocious, idiotic, to make such a remark—but 'pon honour, Mrs. Hill, I think, am sure—I can more or less vouch for the safety of your brother. I have a friend, a Colonel Parke, who is the Duke's aide-de-camp, and I have asked him to keep a watch on Mr. Hill and his movements and—— Pardon me!" Mr. Masham dipped his hands again, as the winding, with a pretty show of palpitations, was resumed.

"I have asked Colonel Parke," continued Mr. Masham resolutely, "to keep in touch with Mr. Hill's senior officers as far as may be possible, and to apprise me of any mishap. I trust, madam, you will not believe me presumptuous."

"Presumptuous! O, sir"—Mr. Hill's sister dropped her ball of wool to clasp her hands—"it is most kind, most thoughtful in you to interest yourself on my—on our behalf. I am immeasurably grateful."

"Pray, Mrs. Hill," Mr. Masham dived to retrieve the rolling ball, and came up more hot than ever, "pray do not," he entreated, "be grateful. You put me to shame, Mr. Hill is so young and so ardent, I feel for him almost as if he were my son."

Mrs. Hill's remarkably even small teeth became visible.

"Not your son, sir. You——" she hesitated, and began to wind wool so fast that Mr. Masham had all to do to keep pace with her.

"My"—said Mr. Masham frantically—"my brother, would you mean? Could I think—dare I say——?"

"Sir, but surely!" And all he could see in Mrs. Hill's face was the most simple amaze. "You could easily pass for Jack's brother. You too," she whispered it, "are very young."

"I am five-and-twenty. Do you think that very young?"

"Yes, sir, for a man. You know the French have a saying," there was no holding her eyes for a second; down they went, " 'A woman may be as old as she looks; a man is old when he ceases . . . to look.' La, Mr. Masham, my wool! 'Tis all a-tangle."

"A thousand apologies! What a lamentable mess. Allow me."

He fumbled with the knotted threads. Her laugh trilled out. "Why, sir, you are all thumbs. Allow *me*."

With a twist here and a pull there she attempted to relieve Mr. Masham's hands of their encumbrance. Their fingers met; and then their eyes. Hers were screwed against the sun; and in his was a twinkle.

"And what, madam, shall I allow you? A provocative wit? The way you have of unexpected laughter, seldom heard within the walls of this godforsaken Palace? Shall I allow that since you came to us the days that used to be so long are all too short? Or that not an hour passes when I'm boxed up with the Prince but I do not count the minutes when I will see you—pouring tea —or hear you singing at the harpsichord? Shall I allow that you tempt and tantalize me beyond endurance, that you've bewitched me utterly, and the deuce alone knows why, for you never give a look in my direction save to make some use of me—as holding wool! Yes, I *will* say so!" cried he to her startled interruption, "and I'll say more—I'll say——"

But what he then had been about to say was surely not:

"Hell's torment! Who comes here?"

A page came there.

"Mrs. Hill, Her Majesty desires your attendance."

"I thank you, Mr. Bathurst . . . Mr. Masham," his hands were still enmeshed, "I must ask you if you will, untie yourself."

And gathering her petticoats she tripped across the flagstones and in and out the flower-beds. He, dizzy, watched her go.

Young Peter Bathurst giggled.

"Shall I untie you, sir?"

"No," said Mr. Masham dreamily, "you can't."

"You sent for me, Madam?"

"Yes, Hill." The Queen blew her nose, gave a last dab to her eyes and said: "Take quill and paper and write a letter for me. My hands are very swollen to-day. Grief always affects my joints. Everything swells. My knees feel like cannon-balls."

"Shall I rub your knees, Madam?"

"Presently. But write this letter first."

Abigail sat at the bureau, trimmed a quill, and wrote to the Queen's dictation.

'*From Mrs. Morley to Mrs. Freeman.*

'May Christ Jesus comfort and support you. It would have been a great satisfaction to your poor unfortunate faithful Morley if you would have given me leave to come to you at St. Albans, for the unfortunate ought to come to the unfortunate, but since you will not have me . . .'

"She will not have me," the Queen's voice dissolved in another gush of tears. "I sent a message entreating her to let me go. She has shut herself up with her grief. How well I understand her sufferings. Where was I?"

" 'But since you will not have me', Madam."

"Ah, yes . . . 'since you will not have me I must content myself as well as I can till I have the happiness of seeing you'."

"This is the most dreadful letter," sobbed the Queen, "that I have ever had to write. No, don't put that in . . . Go on. 'God bless and comfort my dear Mrs. Freeman, and be assured I will live and die always sincerely your . . .' "

The Queen broke off again to blow her nose. "Poor soul. Poor bereaved parents. What a melancholy coincidence that she and I should both suffer the same loss of an only beloved son. But mine was an only child. . . . Give me a clean handkerchief, Hill. This is wet through."

A clean handkerchief was supplied. Abigail resumed her seat and poised her quill.

"I do not know what else I *can* say. I may add something when I re-write it, for 'tis no compliment to send a letter such as this in any other hand but mine."

And having wept herself dry, the Queen made an effort to rise from her couch and sank back with a whimper of pain. "My knees!"

Abigail leaned over her, whispering: "Madam, do not attempt to walk till I have bathed them. May I attend Your Majesty here?"

The Queen nodded, forcing a smile.

Abigail went silently out and returned with two pages carrying a steaming silver basin, towels, cloths, bandages, unguents. In a brisk undertone she gave her orders. "Spread a towel and place the bowl upon it. One of you guard the door, and let no one in on any pretext whatever. Her Majesty does not wish to be disturbed."

*　　　*　　　*

Persistent in her refusal of condolence from the Queen or from anyone else, the Duchess of Marlborough remained in retreat at Windsor Lodge. This, at her express desire for a country house other than Holywell, Mrs. Morley had graciously conferred on Mrs. Freeman, together with the Rangership of Windsor Park. Emerging only to haunt the cloisters of the Castle, the distracted mother nursed her grief till it was feared she would lose her reason. She had indeed declared her intention of renouncing her attendance on the Queen since she, perforce, 'must bow to no other throne', she told her weeping daughters, 'but the throne of sorrow at whose feet I must for ever sit.'

She did not sit there long.

The Occasional Conformity Bill introduced into the Commons by that remarkable boy, Harry St. John, had been thrown out by the Upper House with a Whig majority led by Lords Somers and Wharton. This defeat decided the Higher Tories to elect four new peers to strengthen their support in the Lords.

Shaken from her stupor of mourning at the news, the Duchess hurried post-haste to Godolphin. In a tempest of rage, and calling on God to witness this perfidy, this underhand false practice in creating peers without consulting her, she finally flung down her ultimatum.

'She would not show her face again unless she received Lord Treasurer's promise that her dear friend John Hervey* should be raised to the peerage to represent the Whigs.'

* Father of 'Lord Fanny', satirized by Pope.

For notwithstanding that Godolphin and Marlborough led the Tories, Sarah remained firm to her convictions in support of the opposite camp. Godolphin gave in. The Queen gave in. Mr. Hervey was created Baron Hervey. Mrs. Freeman threw herself in gratitude at Mrs. Morley's feet with tears, smiles, sobs, vows of lasting friendship, love and reconciliation. Mrs. Morley drank 'cold tea' and thanked God to see her broken-hearted Freeman in such good part restored. All was right with the world—and Mrs. Freeman.

But not so with the Bedchamber-women.

If life at Court in the Duchess's absence had been noticeably peaceful, since her return it had been greatly the reverse. A few hours after the resumption of her duties as Groom of the Stole and Mistress of the Robes, she had the Household topsy-turvy, Mrs. Danvers in a huff, and Mrs. Hill on the carpet with a mop.

"Six filthy spaniels piddling on the floor. Six!" stormed the Duchess. "Why six? When I left there were only two."

"The bitch has had a litter, madam," Abigail ventured.

"Then Danvers should have had them drowned."

"The Queen would not have them drowned, your Grace," said Danvers, cringing. "Her Majesty likes to see them play."

"Play! On that valuable carpet! They've made a kennel of the Bedchamber. It stinks."

The Duchess next turned her attention to the Queen's wardrobe, ransacked drawers and cupboards and declared there were moth in the furs.

"A fine to-do! This ermine—these sables—devoured! They must be taken away to be treated."

"*And* they will never come back," caustically commented Danvers as she watched from a window the procession of pages bearing tippets, muffs, stoles, cloaks to the Duchess's chaise. "If there's moth in the sables there's a flea in her ear."

Mrs. Danvers was never loath to vent her grievances, of which not the least were Mrs. Freeman's highty-tighty ways, on the unobtrusive silent Mrs. Hill.

Mrs. Freeman also had her grievances. She was indeed beset with them. So soon as one had been satisfactorily settled came another, and this she brought to Mrs. Morley and lifted up her voice for all the Queen's ladies and Abigail Hill, mopping in the Bedchamber, to hear.

It was incredible, disgraceful, the most prodigious abominable slight upon her state and dignity, that Parliament should have refused Mrs. Morley's gracious request to bestow upon Mr.

Freeman an income worthy of his dukedom. Surely Mrs. Morley was aware that Mrs. Freeman had been unwilling to accept so great an honour——

"Indeed yes," came the placatory answer. "Only by the utmost persuasion did I induce Mrs. Freeman to——"

"And why, Madam, should I be forced to accept so high a title when my husband's income is so miserably low? It has always been the Royal custom when an honour is conferred, to add a substantial sum to support it."

"I offered you," the Queen attempted to remind her, "two thousand pounds a year from the Privy Purse as compensation for——"

"Two thousand! Lord, Madam, what is two thousand when our raised circumstances call for more than twenty times that amount? And considering that I hold the Privy Purse, what a noise would have been raised had I dived into it! 'Twas incumbent on my duty, to say nothing of my pride, to refuse Mrs. Morley's misplaced endeavours to atone for this insult with which you and Parliament think fit to present us."

To the listener in the next room who had tiptoed to the keyhole, the Queen's inaudible reply indicated that Her Majesty was on the verge of tears. Abigail bit her lip and reddened in a flare of indignation. How monstrous to torment the poor lady in this fashion! Dared she, on some pretext or other, interrupt? She dared not. The Queen was speaking.

"If Mrs. Freeman would reconsider her decision and take what was but a portion of her right——"

"My right!" The Duchess gave vent to rageful laughter. "I am no mendicant, Madam, to pocket donations doled out in con-solatory measure. Why, even the late King, close-fisted though he was, rewarded his servants less grudgingly than you. But I do not blame Mrs. Morley for her weakness. I pity you. In this short while of your reign you look to be no more than a puppet on the throne. . . . Why, Madam, what else can I think when I return from an absence so grievously enforced, to find Mrs. Morley has been grossly imposed upon? I say she *has* been imposed upon by Parliament in this fantastical creation of Tory peers. Why did you not consult *me*? Because you knew I would have dissuaded you from such marked Party preference."

The Queen's low-voiced answer was drowned in another volley from the Duchess.

"Lord, Madam, yes—I say it *must* be so! There are evil in-fluences at work that gnaw like rats at your kingdom's very vitals. I warn you, Madam, if you turn from my advice, these malicious agents—and I could name a few,—who sit high in office, will dispose of you as they disposed of your father."

Again the Queen's reply was hampered by her sobs.

"Tears," the Duchess stated scornfully, "were ever Mrs. Morley's refuge. . . . No! I will not retract one word. 'Tis evident that you and Lord Treasurer have put heads together to humiliate me and my husband with an offer of a miserable pittance that would scarce serve to keep us in a sty."

"Pray, Mrs. Freeman, consider——"

"Consider, consider! Fiddle-de-dee!"

It might have astonished Mrs. Danvers and the Duchess, and every other lady, or gentleman, acquainted with the humble mild-mannered Mrs. Hill, to see the glitter in her eyes and the rush of colour in her cheeks as she laid a determined hand on the door-knob and heard the Queen brokenly say: "I beg Mrs. Freeman to control herself. Do I deserve these unjust, unkind thoughts?"

"Only you and your God can tell you that," came the answer, awfully, as Abigail in quite a little passion flung open the door preparatory to enter, and was pushed back by the exit of the Duchess.

"I left you cleaning the carpet. Go back to your work."

"The carpet is cleaned, your Grace."

"Send Danvers to Her Majesty."

Sweeping Abigail aside, the Duchess sat down at a table on which reposed, among a pile of the Queen's correspondence, a pair of the Queen's gloves. She took up an envelope, broke the seal, and ignoring Abigail's presence began to read the contents of the letter.

Abigail silently went out, but not to send for Danvers. Leaving the Bedchamber by the gallery door, she returned to the Queen's room by the main entrance.

"Did Your Majesty ring?"

"No. Yes . . . I was about to do so. My head is aching cruelly, Hill."

"Will Your Majesty lie down on the day-bed and let me bathe your temples?"

The Queen reclined. Abigail laid cool fingers to that creased, throbbing brow; and as the Queen gazed up at the plain freckled little face compassionately bent above her own, saw the unspoken sympathy in those green eyes, not downcast now but steady, clear, her own eyes brimmed again. "You are so young," she murmured, "so young . . to be so kind. Young people as a rule are very heedless. I too was heedless, shamefully heedless, when as a girl I deserted my poor beloved father. But I have been justly punished for my sin in the loss of my angel boy.''

And turning her face to the pillow, the Queen sobbed unre-strainedly.

Abigail moved away and went to a bureau where, in a secret drawer, she hid the salves, perfumes, essences that she bought and paid for out of her pocket-money. In another drawer she kept a bundle of muslin cloths with which she applied the lotions. The Queen's shoulders shook with the spasmodic jerking of her breath. Her eyes were closed, her hair dishevelled, her sallow cheeks flushed and burning. Abigail knelt beside her.

"Madam . . . Dear Madam, pray do not grieve so bitterly. I have sometimes thought that those who have known the dregs of grief are strangely privileged. 'Tis as if such trials were sent to test our faith, our strength. Your Majesty, God never sends us sorrow too great for us to bear.''

At this hesitant soft utterance the Queen lifted her head from the pillow, and stared up at the speaker with a look in which wonderment was mingled with appeal.

"You think that? How wise above your years you are . . . Strength.'' The Queen gazed at the ceiling; her lips moved voicelessly as if she were repeating a lesson, then: "Strength,'' she whispered. "Yes, I *will* have strength. Child, you comfort me.'' She caught Abigail's hand in hers and held it close. "Such a kind gentle little hand . . . Yes, bathe my poor head, Hill, with that nice-smelling stuff you use.''

And after half an hour's treatment the Queen pronounced herself miraculously better. "You have magic in your fingers, Hill. I am quite rested now. I would like to take the air. We will walk in the park. Fetch my cloak and gloves.''

When Abigail returned to the Bedchamber, leaving the com-municating door ajar, she was surprised to find the Duchess still seated at the table, reading letters. Her Grace looked up.

"What do you want?''

"The Queen's cloak, madam . . . and her gloves.''

They were on her Grace's hands.

"Her gloves! Good God!'' The Duchess tore them off. "I must have put them on in a moment of abstraction. Do you think I would wish to wear gloves that had been on the hands of that odious woman? Here, take them!''

Abigail took them and went out, closing the door behind her. The Queen had risen from her day-bed and was standing, ashen-faced.

"Your Majesty's cloak and . . . gloves.''

"No." The Queen's head, slowly moving from side to side, was pitifully reminiscent of some poor bewildered beast's that has been battered by a brutal herdsman's stick. "I will not go out . . . I have changed my mind," said the Queen in a thick strangled voice; and again, "I have changed my mind."

CHAPTER THREE

THROUGHOUT the spring and summer of the year 1703 the gossips of the Court chewed a tasty piece of scandal. The Queen and the Duchess were not so sweet together as they had been! None knew whence arose this talk, or why Her Majesty had lately shown some interest in the Opera, which hitherto she had seldom cared to patronize. The Duchess, however, who was still in mourning for her son, did not, that season, grace with her presence the Theatre Royal, Drury Lane; save once.

On that occasion her Grace was attended by a slight young girl who could not be a daughter, for she had nothing of the handsome Churchill looks; nothing indeed to recommend her save her youth and a remarkably white pair of shoulders.

Quizzing-glasses were raised, eyes levelled. Whispers floated: "Who? Who is she?"

While the versatile Mr. Leveridge, who played the leading rôle in 'The Island Princess'—which he also had written and composed—thundered *basso profundo* to the gallery, the boxes watched the Duchess. With gracious nods and smiles to acquaintances, a wave of her fan to Lord Godolphin seated between his son and her daughter Henrietta, with kisses wafted from her finger-tips to favoured friends, her Grace of Marlborough in her flower-decked enclosure attracted a great deal more attention than did Mr. Leveridge, in tawdry tinsel, on the stage.

"Quite a family gathering," observed the elegant, languid St. John to Harley, with a look across at the box in which sat the Duchess's daughter Anne, whose husband had recently succeeded to his father's earldom of Sunderland. "But who's the little piece she is parading?"

Harley's hooded eyes surveyed, indifferently, the 'little piece', and returned to the sonorous Mr. Leveridge.

"Not displeasing," murmured St. John with his glass up to his eye. "Haven't the French a name for that elusive type—'belle laide'? We English think too much of skin-deep beauty, which to me suggests the obvious—the merely horizontal. I remember when I was in Paris——"

"Best forget what you remember when you were in Paris," Harley interposed. "If your adventures began in the alcove they look to finish in the melting-pot." And cupping his chin in his hand to hide his lips, he asked: "Have you had any news of that miniature yet?"

St. John let fall his quizzing-glass. "God's life, sir! Give me time. It is a matter that requires the carefullest negotiation. As you know, I have despatched a courier."

"You'll need a couple."

"I'll send another if this one don't come back. Ten to one he won't. 'Tis now six weeks since he set out, and the last I heard from him, a month ago, he wrote that he'd been forced to take a cross-country route via Belgium under fire . . . Lord! How this fellow bawls. Can you sit out this act? I can't."

Harley's narrowed glance, skirting the lower tier of boxes, came to rest on the lace-bordered edge of a fan that concealed all of its owner's face save a pair of uplifted green eyes.

Harley smiled.

"I can."

"The man bellows like a bull," complained St. John. "And talking of bulls reminds me——"

"Were we talking of bulls?"

"We were—or as near as dammit—discussing heifers. I'm vastly intrigued with this fallow-pied who is stalled with our prize-winning cow."

But the buzz of conversation from the more exclusive seats was not permitted to continue. There were yells of 'Silence!' 'Silence there!' 'Hold your clack!' from the gallery and pit; and high above the bass of Mr. Leveridge, a voice seemingly as if it issued through a trumpet, declared that it had 'paid to hear the singing and not you!'

"What politeness one finds among the lower orders," muttered St. John, skilfully dodging an orange that whizzed past his head. Harley caught and hurled it back whence it had come, which gesture occasioned loud derisive hoots, and cries of 'Shame!'; while in one supreme last effort that looked to split his lungs, Mr. Leveridge received a thunder of applause intermingled with boos and cat-calls from the gallery, some gentle clapping from the boxes, a shower of rose-leaves from the Duchess, and potatoes and a cabbage from the pit.

"A lamentable singer," said Sarah, leaning from her box to throw kisses at the flattered Mr. Leveridge. "Bravo! Bravissimo!

Magnificent! Prodigious! . . . Execrable," she added aside to her companion. "He acts upon me like a clyster. Let us go."

The honours were now divided, with a balance in her favour, between the exit of the Duchess and the re-entrance of the star, who, in a desperate attempt to direct the acclamation to himself, stepped forward to the foot-floats and expanded his diaphragm in ready compliance to the not very ardent requests for an encore.

"You are right," said Harley. "We cannot sit this out. We'll sup at White's."

In the foyer they came face to face with the Duchess and her young attendant. The lavish bows of the gentlemen were received with a remote inclination of the Duchess's head, and looking not at, but through Harley as if he were a window, she walked down the steps to the door.

The young lady, following to lift her Grace's train from the dust, curtsied with admirable modesty and a flutter of her eyelids, as St. John, hand on heart, bowed again and pointedly, to her.

And the smiling Harley chanted low:

> " 'I want a little babye
> As pretty one as may be,
> And now I think again
> I want a toy . . . from Spain.' "

He prodded the ogling St. John in the ribs: "And if you give me the chance I want that *face* from *France*. . . ."

*   *   *

The appearance of the Duchess at the Opera with Abigail Hill aroused some speculation in Court circles. What was her Grace's motive in thus exhibiting her humble relative for all the world to see?

Mrs. Danvers had the answer. Mrs. Danvers vouched for it and passed it on to Mrs. Abrahal, whence it came to Alice Hill.

She, swollen with this latest tit-bit, shared it with her sister.

"Ridiculous! I never heard such folly," was Abigail's verdict. "Why should the Queen object to the Duchess giving me an evening's entertainment?"

"That's the point." Alice mysteriously nodded. "Why? Shall I tell you?"

She sat herself upon a stool and launched into a tale of which Abigail made but little sense. How that the Duchess, well aware that Her Majesty was not of late disposed to be so friendly as she had been heretofore, was using Abigail as a foil to intrigue her.

Abigail lifted her eyes from her tambour-frame to say: "I don't understand. Intrigue whom?"

"The Queen, of course. 'Tis clear that Mrs. Morley resents this sudden interest Mrs. Freeman is taking in her poor relation." Alice giggled. "But not on Cousin Sarah's account. Oh, dear no! 'Tis you whom the Queen is striving to save from corruption. I've seen the letter she wrote to her Freeman, which was left lying on the floor of the privy—and Danvers found and read it, and copied it before she gave it back."

"Aha!" Abigail wrinkled her nose. "So 'tis Danvers who has served the tabbies with their cats' meat. I might have known as much."

"Whatever you may think of Danvers," persisted Alice, "she hasn't wit enough to have invented such a letter."

"For heaven's sake, *what* letter?"

"I'm telling you! The Queen's letter to the Duchess, in which she hopes Mrs. Freeman will not frequent the Opera with Mrs. Hill, and that she—Mrs. Freeman—'will have a care of engaging herself too much in *your* company, which is a thing that grows upon you.'"

"Grows!" Abigail murmured; and she carefully sorted silks. "Danvers has indeed surpassed herself in her romancing. 'A thing that grows upon you'—like a fungus. I don't believe a word of it. How provoking! I've run out of green thread. I shall have to go to the Exchange to-day for more."

Alice got up from her stool and stood before her stolidly.

"You had best believe it. Why should Danvers, who is so spitefully disposed, repeat anything to your advantage if it were not true?"

"I can't see how likening me to a fungus is to my advantage."

"I didn't say 'fungus'. You said it. Oh, yes! That's the way. Make mock of me. You always have, you always will, but you can mock me now till you're blue in the face. What I'm telling you," said Alice earnestly, "I saw in black and white."

"In Danvers' black and white?"

"There you go again! Abbie, pray believe me and take heed. I'd burst my stays with pride in myself if it were said of me."

"I can see nothing in what you've said," objected Abigail mildly, "to make me burst *my* stays."

"Well, what of this?" Alice came portentously nearer. "The Queen in her letter begs the Duchess to have as little to do with 'That Enchantress'—meaning you—'as possible.' Now then!"

And having got that out, Alice anxiously awaited the effect, which disappointed.

Abigail shook with laughter, at first silent, then audible, then high.

"Enchantress!" she crowed. " 'Tis too rich! *Me*! Enchantr—lud! I'd ha' given a fortune to have seen the Duch—and Danv—their *faces*—when they——*grows* upon you! Gro—oh!" She held her sides.

Her paroxysms were infectious. Alice too began to laugh until the pair of them were helpless. Alice wiped her eyes.

"Yes, I know 'tis the drollest—you! Enchantress!"

"I can only think," gasped Abigail, "of those two, Mrs. Mor—— Mrs. Freem—— quarrelling over *me*! Can't you hear her? 'Lord, Madam! Do you begrudge that shuffling miserable poor little wretch a night out? Are you jealous, Madam? Lord, Madam! Yes, you are. You do. You are. I say it *must* be so!' Oh, God, I've a stitch . . . But why, if it's true, which I shall never believe, did the Queen bring herself to write it?"

Why indeed?

The answer to that question has never yet been solved. Did Anne, in that strange letter, attempt for the first time in her life to dissemble, fearing to lose the one creature at her Court on whom she had learned to rely and to trust, as, in the secret places of her heart, she had never trusted the woman whose dazzling beauty and imperious will had dominated her emotional existence? Or was it a last attempt to rekindle the fires of a springtime friendship from the wintered ashes of a lost illusion?

The Duchess may have asked herself some questions such as these, or she may not have asked one. She may have been provoked, outraged, astonished, or she may have laughed, as Abigail laughed again, recalling it, when half an hour later she was carried in a chair to the Exchange.

But although amused and a little inflated, she also was faintly alarmed. She had unwittingly attracted some ominous attention to herself. Where would it end? She knew that she had enemies among the women of the Household; that the Queen's constant demand for her attendance had caused malicious comment. She knew that when the Queen insisted on her presence at the tea-table with the Prince and Mr. Masham, she was ringed around with jealousy. This being so then, was the letter a mere fabrication on the part of Danvers to make mischief? But surely Danvers, as Alice had said, would never have risen to such heights of envious fancy as to think of, or describe, her as 'Enchantress'?

She could find no solution to the riddle of that letter from the Queen, which, had it indeed been written to the Duchess, might well bring an end to her sojourn in high places and return her to the lowly life of lady's maid. If so she must be philosophic and accept the destiny to which she was most suited.

But from these commendable arguments she derived but little comfort. She did not want to be a lady's maid. She had been a lady's maid quite long enough. She would be a lady's maid no longer. Were she thrown out of office she could put herself and her wits to better use than waiting on a pack of women. She would have to find a husband, or, if not, some kindly gentleman who would take pity on an unprotected orphan and allow her to keep house for him . . . Meantime, why fear the future? For the present she was placed, and very highly placed, as a Woman of the Chamber to the Queen.

Having thus decided and made her own simple purchases, and bought an expensive flask of Bergamot water to which the Queen was partial, and for which Abigail paid—with the inward reflection that she would hang herself before she paid for any more—she returned, very hot, to her chair.

The July sun poured from a brazen sky on baking cobbles, on houses that seemed to shimmer in a white transparency of heat, on windows that looked to be filled with peering heads, on streets that appeared to be uncommonly crowded with pedestrians, and every kind of vehicle bound in an eastward direction.

So great was the press of traffic that the chairmen, unable to go forward or turn back, were held up in the middle of the Strand.

"Why," asked Abigail, "what's amiss? Where are all those people going?"

"To the pillory, madam, at Temple Bar."

"Then you must go down a side alley to the river. I will take the wherry-boat."

But since all the ways to the river were thronged it would be better, the chairmen advised, to follow the crowd and return by a circuit of the Strand to St. James's.

"Do so then."

The sedan that bore upon its panels the Royal coat of arms, and the attendants in their Royal liveries, commanded respect from all persons in their immediate vicinity. Even the draymen, waggoners, hackney-coach drivers, squeezed their horses nearer to the posts at the approach of the Royal chair. Drawing aside the curtains that obscured her from the curious, Abigail, not displeased to find she was a focus of attention, offered condescending smiles and a gratuitous view of herself to the jostling, swaying, bobbing mass of sight-seers who regarded her, rightly or wrongly, as one of the sights.

"Make way—make way for her ladyship!" was the gratifying comment of a fellow pushing a barrow of melons.

"Move aside, you lousy dog—or I'll roll out your gizzard!" roared a sweating carter, with a flick of his whip in the face of a vendor of fish that swarmed with flies and stank to heaven.

The violent retort of the fishmonger in suitable Billingsgate, to the effect that the carter had been spewed up and not born and was pimp to his own mother, was interrupted by a scream of delight from a young seamstress with a bandbox on her arm.

"See her! She comes from the Palace. See the sign o' the Lion and the Unicorn! Look at her fine kincob gown and silver lace—half an ell deep!"

"Ay! An' look at the patches on her face to hide her pimples!" cried a saucy orange girl.

"They be'nt pimples, they be freckles," was the answer, which Abigail affected not to hear.

"Whoa! Come up you misbegotten son of a crab—what for are ye walkin' sideways?" demanded the driver of a donkey-cart; while a showman from Bartholomew Fair yelled through his trumpet: "At Hartshorn Inn at Pye Corner will be seen a calf with six legs and a topknot, and a blackamoor who swallows a sword and vomits it up whole. Also a woman with a beard and three breasts!"

The babel of noise and laughter resultant on this declaration, was now increased by the cries of apprentices who dashed from shop doorways to fight among themselves for a first sale of their merchandise to the lady from the Palace; and suddenly above that roaring dim and the incessant monotone of a noseless man who cried: 'The latest bloody new from Flanders', Abigail was dismayed to recognize one voice.

"Och, crucify me if 'tisn't Mrs. Hill!"

A hired chair had halted not two feet away from her own, and in it, nodding, rosily beaming, with a smile that exposed every tooth in her head, sat Mrs. South.

A swift glance into the uncurtained interior of Mrs. South's sedan gave shuddering revelation of a plucked goose, a basket of mackerel, some flagons of wine, and a cheese. It was evident Mrs. South had been to market.

Horror crept in between a second and a second while Abigail unenthusiastically returned:

"Of all persons in the world—to see you here in London."

She hoped that guarded greeting would satisfy the wooden-visaged lackeys that this boisterous lady was the merest acquaintance.

"And of all persons in the world," replied Mrs. South at the top of her lungs, "to see *you* seated in a Royal chair, so grand and all! I've heard of your rise—up—up—up. But what goes up has to come down—see-saw! Ha-ha!"

These observations were accompanied by much cackling, eye-winking, and winey drifts of breath, scarcely less overpowering than the stench of a verminous tumbling dwarf who had wedged himself in the narrow space between the chairs.

"And to think we are met again together on this happy chance!" familiarly continued Mrs. South. "Do you mind our evenings in my room with a bottle o' the best after you had put the Old Sausage to bed? Those were the days when you couldn't say Bo to a goose. I've a fine fat goose here by the way—would you like to come along o' me and share it?" And without waiting for an answer, Mrs. South ran on: "D'ye remember Virginia, the ape? She's dead, poor soul, but the old lady's still quick and lively. She's had a dozen maids since you left. And now I've left, and ole Zack—ye remember him? He's left. We've all left, and *she's* left with none but her old rip, and he's as randy after the petticoats as ever he——"

"I think," cried Abigail wildly, "the press is not so heavy here. We can break—Drury! Can you not break through?"

But the chairmen had scarcely advanced a step when she was again shattered to hear: "Sure we can break through. We're all going the same way—to the pillory. Move up, ye scrag o' mutton!"

This to the foremost of her carriers who was, in truth, inordinately lean. Once more the face of Mrs. South was brought alongside Abigail's.

"Hey! Mrs. Hill! Mrs. HILL!"

Abigail shrank back against the padded upholstery and closed her eyes in resignation. The whole of London now must know her name. "Mrs. *Hill*!" More nods, smiles, beckonings, chuckles. "Sure an' all 'tis a rare show we're after seeing. I take it you've come with the rest of us to watch that whoreson dissenting putt with his head in the collar. Ah! He has his true deserts, the rat! Would ye believe he could have hoaxed the High Fliers with the publication of his wicked pamphlet. Have ye read it?"

Abigail had not read it, nor had she the haziest notion to whom or to what Mrs. South alluded. Nor was she any the wiser when Mrs. South produced some printed sheets of paper and waved them in the air.

"Here 'tis—the scurvey rogue! His 'Shortest Way with the Dissenters' that he hoped would confound the Tories and the

Church, but they clapped him into Newgate for his villainy. They did so. And I'll see him rot or I'm a Dutchman. I've a prime wet fish along o' me with which to clout the dirty pimp if I get near enough."

And diving into the recesses of her piscatorial lair, Mrs. South drew forth a highly unsavoury dab.

With a murderous desire for Mrs. South's immediate extinction, Abigail closed, in haste, the chair-curtains; but although she could no longer see that shaming exhitition, she could still hear those penetrating accents, and the applause, laughter, hisses, boos, occasioned by the lady's spritely argument.

"Still an' all, you folk, the fellow has flown in the teeth o' the wind, ye can't deny . . . Sure, I'm for fair justice, but not for foul means. He tricked the Tories, I'm telling you . . . Yes, you over there with the carbuncle on your nose . . . What's that? Courage? Honesty? God save us! Where's the honour in playing old Harry with sacred matters? . . . Och, divil a bit of it! He did so, the pawky Low Church jerry sneak. Hey, you! Go steady, skeleton! You'll have me in the gutter. Mind yourself—mind *out*!" until at last the voice of Mrs. South was drowned in a roaring and a shouting, the clatter and stamp of feet, and multitudinous cries of:

"Daniel! Long live Daniel! A health to our . . ."

Stealthily Abigail drew aside a corner of the curtain. From her elevation above the heads of the crowd she could see the pillory as her chairmen skirted it, and the hawk-faced victim, who despite the wooden bar that gripped his neck, could still smile down upon the people that had come to mock and stayed to cheer.

The platform and the steps leading up to it were strewn with flowers. Garlands draped the supporting poles; some stray petals had fallen on the prisoner's head. Women wept, girls pelted him with roses, men, kneeling, drank to him in ale, saluted him with pewter tankards of wine. The swords of the mounted guards flashed wicked gleams of sunlight as they charged down upon the mob, momentarily scattered, to return in massed hysteria and with shouts of:

". . . 'Foe! Defoe! God bless you, Daniel Defoe!"

"Hey! Mrs. Hill! Mrs. *Hi-ill*!"

Abigail peeped, to see Mrs. South brandishing her fish in preparatory assault.

"They're praying to um, the poor worms!" cried Mrs. South. "Sure, he has them all bewitched, may he burn for't. A plague upon you, sirrahs! The devil and his works are in this place. Here, ye son of a bitch, ye wry-mouthed wart-hog—you! Take this!"

Something slimy, white and stinking, flew past the window of Abigail's chair and fell harmlessly short of the pillory steps among the roses.

The sun blazed down on the prisoner's uncovered head. Girls were throwing flowers to disperse the cloud of flies that buzzed around his sweat-begrimed face. The warders forced back those who held their tankards up for him to drink. His blackened tongue came out to lick his swollen lips; his forehead was red and scarred with insect bites; his hands, in that wooden vice, were stiff and bloodless as the hands of the dead, but still he smiled while his keen twinkling eyes surveyed the crowd who toasted him, drank health to him who was half mad with thirst.

Abigail was mad with indignation. She forgot her state, her dignity, herself. She dragged aside the curtains to cry: "Shame! Shame on you, the poor man! You guards there, give him water!" But none heard her pleas save Mrs. South.

"Water? I'd drown him in ut! Why pity the dog at all, and you a High Flying Tory? Where are your principles? Where your faith, that you turn tail to fall a-weeping for a foul wretch that has held up to scorn and derision your Established Church? The traitor. Glory be to God! See him, how he grins. Ay, you scrawny whelp, you should be grinning up there on a pike, had I my way."

Following the direction of Mrs. South's pointing finger, Abigail saw a row of green and grisly faces rotting on the gates of Temple Bar. She hid her eyes.

"That should be his end, and 'twill be his yet for his sins or I'm a——"

"Drury!" In a last desperate appeal Abigail leaned out to tap the leading chairman's shoulder. "Pray go forward."

"Sure," Mrs. South agreed, "we'll all go forward now. I'm bound for Sir Andrew Fountaine's. I'm his housekeeper," she volunteered to Abigail's hastily drawn curtains. "He's a grand gentleman. A High Flyer with the best o' them—in more ways than one! And now we've met again, Mrs. Hill—hi! Mrs. *Hill*, where are ye? I said, now we've met once more we'll meet aplenty. I'll be glad to see you any time if you'll call upon me at Sir Andrew Fountaine's house in Leicester Fields. And I'll find you, I have no doubt, in style at Saint J——"

"Drury!" urged Abigail frenziedly, "Go *on*!"

If Defoe had been hailed by the rabble as a hero, Mrs. Hill on her own showing was a heroine. To an audience composed of Alice, Mrs. Abrahal and Mr. Masham, she dilated on her intervention in the prisoner's behalf. At the same time she was at pains to make it clear that she held no brief for his disgraceful conduct in writing that scurrilous pamphlet—which, it must be confessed, Mrs. Hill had never read. But having recovered from the shock of her embarrassing encounter in the Strand with Mrs. South, she had been induced to accept that lady's pressing and repeated invitations to call upon her at Sir Andrew Fountaine's house. For, notwithstanding Mrs. South's exuberant exterior, she possessed a ready fund of information in political affairs and a curious collection of acquaintances.

To one of these, a Mrs. Manley, Abigail had been presented. Her name, as she afterwards recounted to her sister, described her very well. It might indeed have been assumed to suit her person. She wrote books, it seemed, and drank a deal, and had a bawdy humour and was indeed alarmingly emphatic.

"I am aware that in this pamphlet," Mrs. Hill informed her listeners, "Defoe purports to uphold the High Church Party while he mocks them, tongue in cheek. 'Tis an inexcusable, most shocking hoax on the part of a Dissenter, to parody the Tories in their own words. Think of their humiliation and disgust to discover how this anonymous champion of their beliefs had so scurvily tricked them."

And this she had from Mesdames South and Manley, and repeated it direct, with expurgations.

Mr. Masham was exceedingly impressed. There appeared to be no end to Mrs. Hill's accomplishments. Not only could she sing like a lark and play the harpsichord divinely, but she took an interest in current events which, for a lady of her tender years, he judged to be exceptional. He seized an early opportunity to tell her so.

"Madam, I am bound to say," he said it in the garden where Mrs. Hill, whom he had followed, was out with the morning dew to gather roses for the Queen's Green Closet, "you surprise me."

"La, sir!" She snipped a bud—"and why should I surprise you?"

"Your intellect, your charm—all your qualities," floundered Mrs. Masham, "are extraordinary, in particular when combined with extreme youth."

"Why, sir, I am not young." Her eyes, turned for a brief moment full upon him, were larger than he ever had supposed. "I am," said Mrs. Hill with the suspicion of a simper, "growing old. I'm three months short of twenty . . ."

"The merest child," murmured Mr. Masham.

"Ah, sir," she sighed, "my childhood was clouded by my

parents' death that left me penniless and orphaned, unprotected, to care for my young brother and sister."

This half whispered confidence, that gave so touching a glimpse of her earlier environment, on which Mr. Masham had often speculated, roused all his chivalry and still more admiration. To think that such delicate shoulders should have borne the responsibility of motherhood—no, no! He reddened hotly—not motherhood, but the *cares* of motherhood—was most affecting.

"I did not know," said Mr. Masham, greatly moved, "that you had suffered such adversity and loss. Your courage, madam, in overcoming your misfortune is all the more to your credit."

She received this tribute with a deprecatory smile and a turn of the head as if to hide a tear.

He struggled on.

"I cannot bear to believe—I was utterly confounded—when you told me of your horrible experience—held up in the crowds around the pillory. You must promise me you will never again venture out unattended."

"But, sir, I was not unattended. The chairmen——"

"You should have had a female attendant—or a—or someone who would wait upon you, guard you—as would I, if you would call upon me at any time"—he stammered—"anywhere you wish to go."

She plucked a crimson rose and rapturously sniffed while she composed herself to tell him, " 'Tis too kind of you to make the offer. What an exquisite perfume. Smell this, Mr. Masham."

She held it to his nose; and he, who had already lost his heart, grabbed at her hand to lose his head.

"Kind?" he babbled. "Kind? To offer you so paltry, so small a thing as my escort—my attendance on your missions, would give me inexpressible delight. If I dared I'd offer more. I would give my——"

"Oh!" A faint shriek from Mrs. Hill brought these incoherencies to an abrupt conclusion. He gazed at her while she, terror-stricken, gazed at something else; but not at him.

"What is it?" he demanded with pardonable brusquerie.

"A caterpillar! A horrid crawly caterpillar—I touched it with my finger. There it is. Look! Oh! the creature!"

Mr. Masham stooped to peer. He saw no caterpillar.

"Oh, lud! I vow 'twas on this rose." She shook and cast it from her. Nothing fell. "Or maybe 'tis on my gown. Can you see it on my gown, sir?" She revolved with her petticoats swung wide for his inspection. "Or my neck?" She bent to expose the snowy nape.

Mr. Masham's glance reverted to her hair and rested—as she came round again to face him—on her lips. Against the cream of her skin they looked as red as the rose at her feet. And Mr. Masham staggeringly said:

"By God! I'd like to bite you."

"Sir!" Her eyes were wide at him again. "Are you demented?"

"Yes," cried Mr. Masham in a heat, "I am. If to be demented is to think of you all day and dream of you at night—fantastically—as no sane man should dream and keep his reason. Lord knows what witch's spell you've put upon me, madam, but I find you as vexatious as a tick!"

Now this was not at all what he had meant to say when he followed Mrs. Hill into the garden; but having so far forgot himself he forgot himself still farther, and regardless of the basket, pulled her to him, dived his head, and violently kissed her on the mouth. She struggled. Her face was scalding; his was white.

"Sir! Mr. Masham! For heaven's sake——" The basket dropped. She fought him like a kitten, claws out, to fasten in his wrist, and leave there three scarlet crescents. That pulled her up.

Shamed, mortified, and staring at those tell-tale marks that edged the lace of his cuff, she asked him: "Have I hurt you?"

"Mortally."

But she could have sworn that he was laughing for all he looked so glum.

"You had best suck it," she said hurriedly. "I didn't mean to make you bleed."

"What? Suck away this gentle token? Never. I hope it scars me."

She glared at him. His ill-timed jocularity she found to be a great deal more offensive than his previous assault.

"I have," she said with virulence, "been bitterly insulted."

"Is it an insult to tell you I admire you—to show that I desire you? I was about to say——"

"Don't say it! If you must behave like a lunatic I beg you to remember we can be seen from every window in the house."

This was a slight exaggeration. They were well screened from view of any window save those above the stables, by a box-hedge.

"Give me," she curtly demanded, "my basket."

He picked up the basket, gathered the fallen roses, placed them in it, and then took one and stuck it in his coat.

"For a memento," he told her, cool, as a moment before he had been hot. "I know I've nothing much to offer save my heart, my life, my name. All are yours if you will take them. If you won't——" he shrugged, then smiled; not his courtier's automatic smile, but a boy's, dubious, questioning, with something in it charmful, and for the first time in their acquaintance she observed he had good teeth; the first time perhaps that she had noticed any feature in his face at all.

"If you won't," said Mr. Masham, "I will not importune you but I warn you I am going to try again."

He gave her the basket with a bow. She dropped a curtsy and lowered her eyes; nor did she lift them as he stepped back to watch her shadow glide behind her in the grass.

CHAPTER FOUR

It may be assumed that Abigail was more flattered than disturbed by Mr. Masham's declaration which, to do her justice, she divulged to no one—not even Alice. If she deliberately had led him on to let him down, she did at least respect his sentiments sufficiently to keep them to herself. Yet when she recalled his singular behaviour in the garden, she was bound to admit that despite his impassioned offer of heart and hand and name he had seemed prepared to accept a refusal. "All are yours if you will take them —if you won't I'll try again."

And if he tried again, would she take him? The question was debatable, for if she saw herself installed in some airy castle with a nebulous companion of noble mien and fashionable bearing, he certainly did not resemble Samuel Masham. She had only lately learned his Christian name, which she allowed was an improvement on the name with which he had been willing to endow her. Could she go through life as Mrs. Masham?

No.

His name, however, was a lesser disadvantage. Mr. Masham, as the eighth son of a baronet with no prospect of succeeding to the title, appeared to be, not only on his own admission but from tactical inquiry on her part, nothing of a match for a young lady with little more to recommend her than her wits. And these she kept about her and of these she made good use, since she had no mamma to establish her position, and by unflagging chase and indefatigable effort to secure for her an eligible husband.

Her opinion of herself had become somewhat enlarged since Alice's report of the Queen's letter to the Duchess. For if the Queen of England had indeed described her as 'Enchantress', and appeared resentful, one might almost believe jealous, of the interest taken by her favourite in humble Mrs. Hill, it was evident she had made her presence felt, not only in the Bedchamber but out of it.

Her head began to swell; ambition soared. Her cloud castle multiplied to many mansions. She, the mistress of them, wore a coronet; the master took his orders at her bidding and rose, on her advice, to heights supreme: Lord Treasurer for his beginning and a dukedom for his end. She believed herself to be a fitting mate for such a one; but not for Mr. Masham.

It was, she decided, unfortunate that the Prince Consort had of late discovered her good qualities as nurse, and, when the Queen could spare her, demanded her attention to his gout, while his pages held the basin and Mr. Masham held the cloths, and Mrs. Hill knelt to bathe the princely feet and receive pats upon her head in commendation.

Yet despite the chance afforded by propinquity, Mr. Masham appeared to be in no great haste to 'try again'. To be sure, he was as ever full of courtliness, bows, smiles, darting up to open doors and always at the Prince's elbow; but not often now at hers.

He had quite recovered, she assured herself, from his temporary madness, and was pleased to know his heart had not been broken, scarcely bruised. She would not have wished to see him pining, inconsolable. He seemed in fact prepared to be consoled—and with one Mistress Forester, a Maid of Honour.

Queen Anne's Maids of Honour, unlike those who attended Elizabeth, her august predecessor, were not called to wait upon Her Majesty at morning, noon and night. Their appointments were indeed more nominal than active. Mrs. Forester was, however, an exception. In her youth the Queen had been an ardent horsewoman and follower of stag-hounds, but her obesity in latter years had prevented her from taking more than a spectator's part in the hunt. From her chaise in Windsor Park the Queen had admired the fearless riding of Mrs. Forester, who was always first of the ladies in the field. Mrs. Forester possessed a great knowledge of horses and did, in fact, give the Queen more 'tips' than did ever 'dear Mr. Montgomery', who was inclined to keep what he knew to himself. With the Prince and Mr. Masham, the Queen frequently attended the races at Newmarket, and on these occasions was accompanied by Mrs. Forester.

Now Mrs. Hill had never been within fifty miles of a racecourse nor had she sat a horse since she was six—in the days before her poor papa lost all his money. It was therefore certainly provoking when Mr. Masham asked her, in the most casual manner conceivable, if she cared to ride in the Ring in Hyde Park, to have to refuse on the plea of the megrims. She had subsequently to suffer the mortification of watching, from her window at Kensington Palace, a riding party composed of Mr. Masham, Mrs. Forester, the Ladies Rialton and Sunderland, and a number of young people of both sexes, whose names she did not know and who would never have known hers, set out on a morning in September.

She pressed her nose to the pane till its pink tip whitened. She had a good view of Mrs. Forester, and decided her to be a bouncing tomrig of a girl with a bust like the dome of St. Paul's. Still, no question, Mrs. Forester was seen to best advantage in the saddle. Her gipsy dark hair fell in curls to her shoulders from under a rakish cocked hat. Her close-fitting habit of hunter's green velvet drew marked attention to her curves. Mr. Masham spurred his horse to gain her side. He, in prune-coloured cloth, white buckskins and—Mrs. Hill sneeringly declared—a new pair of calves, as I live!—leaned his head towards the giggling Mrs. Forester in a very intimate and confidential manner. What could he be saying to make her squawk so loud that she looked to be falling from her saddle? No hope of that. She had far too good a seat.

Abigail watched the cavalcade trot over the scorched tawny grass, under low-hanging branches of trees in their earliest glory of autumn, with here and there a flash of rowanberry scarlet piercing the golden green. Their high gay voices shook the mellowed stillness and floated up in laughing chorus to the window.

And, as she turned from it, Abigail, sighting herself in a wall-mirror, looked closer, critically to compare her meagre proportions with those of the robust Maid of Honour. Who but a dolt—or a Masham—she ruthlessly considered, would wish to take *you* for a wife? On the other hand, why should Mrs. Forester wish to take Mr. Masham for a husband? She felt a trifle responsible for Mr. Masham's rebound in Mrs. Forester's direction. She could only hope that Mrs. Forester would be persuaded to accept him should he bring himself to 'try again' with her. And with all my heart, said Mrs. Hill, I wish her joy of him!

But there was no joy in the grimace she bestowed on her reflection as she backed from the mirror at the peal of a bell: the bell of the Queen's apartment.

Flinging open the door she peeped over the balusters of the landing. In the gallery below a group of boys were playing marbles. Effacing from her countenance all signs of ill-humour, she tripped down the stairs and approached the pages meekly.

"Gentlemen, pray excuse my interruption, but I am called to

the Queen's presence. Mr. Bathurst, may I trouble you to bring the basin?"

"She don't want the basin," disgracefully piped young Peter Bathurst, "she wants her pimpimpim, her tooty-pooty Mrs. Hill."

There were titters.

Abigail held herself in dignity.

"If you please, Mr. Bathurst, you will not speak of Her Majesty in that disrespectful fashion."

This rebuke was received with derisive hoots, and the information from one of the Boscawen brothers that: "She's in audience with Mr. Speaker. I showed him in. You'll have to show him out."

Restraining a desire to inflict violence on the ears of Mr. Boscawen, who, she would have sworn, had poked his tongue at her retreating back, Abigail walked sedately to the door of the Queen's room. There she knocked, was bidden 'Come', and entered.

The Queen was sitting near the window, facing a gentleman who rose to his feet as Mrs. Hill rose from the bob.

Her heart fluttered at her ribs in an instant's charged expectancy as he bowed low to the Queen, and again, but not so low, to her.

"You have much eased my mind, Mr. Harley. I have been greatly distressed at these continued heats and broils over the Occasional Conformity Act. It is most shocking that the Whig Dissenters should have dared raise protest against the Bill which has been introduced for the protection of the Church. Even my faithful Tories dispute among themselves in opposition to my most cherished projects. I am all at sea." The Queen wagged her head till her high fontange slipped. Abigail unobtrusively stepped forward to adjust it and stood behind the Queen's chair.

"Thank you, Hill. . . . You must bring me every latest news from the House, Mr. Harley. It is always our pleasure to receive you."

"Your Majesty does me too much honour. . . . Your Majesty's servant."

He backed to the door. The Queen beckoned.

"Hill, have the goodness to conduct Mr. Harley——" She waved a gracious introduction. "Mr. Harley—Mrs. Hill of the Bedchamber."

The door closed upon their exit.

Five, ten minutes passed, and Hill had not returned. The Queen lifted her spaniel to her knee and crooned to it, stroking its silken ears. She looked at the door, at the clock. Fifteen

minutes. . . . She rose from her chair and with her slow un-
wieldy gait moved to the bell-rope and was about to pull it when
Abigail glided in.

"Madam, I crave Your Majesty's indulgence."

"You have been gone an unconscionable time."

The Queen was vexed.

"Your Majesty . . ." She crossed the room, she knelt. Her
uplifted eyes were shining: "Madam, forgive me. Mr. Harley . . ."

"What has Mr. Harley to do with you?"

The Queen stared down, her momentary petulance forgotten,
her interest intrigued.

"Good heavens, Hill! I have never seen you flustered."

Very flustered, glowing, and, for once regardless of her place to
stammer: "Madam . . . Mr. Harley is my kinsman. I did not
know. I believed my sister and my brothers were destitute of
relatives, save her Grace of Marlborough. And now . . . Madam,
Mr. Harley is my cousin, own cousin to my father. Your Majesty, this means so much to me!"

But just how much to her, and to those higher powers who held
the Queen in thrall, how much indeed to the whole complex
divergence of two great political parties, she could not have foreseen. She knew only that the stigma of her obscure paternal
origin had been dispelled. No longer now would she be branded
Sarah Marlborough's 'poor relation'—'a domestic servant, rescued
from a garret, taken from a broom.' Henceforth she was the kinswoman acknowledged and of close blood to him who stood in
rising favour with the Queen: to him on whom the eyes of an unruly Government were turned in doubtful, hopeful, envious
anticipation of his new appointment, which they whispered would
be . . . Secretary of State.

It was then no chance likeness she had seen in him to that lost
image of her father, but proof established beyond all contradic-
tion, though Alice, admittedly, was not so eager to accept this
new discovery of cousinship with quite the same delight as did her
sister.

"For if," she argued, "he is our father's cousin once removed,
he is a very distant relative to us."

"I might have known," was Abigail's withering reply, "that
you would not appreciate or understand the immense advantage
this relationship may be, no matter *how* distant, to us. He is the
most powerful man in the Government to-day."

The Duchess, however, showed more interest than did the

apathetic Alice in this latest revelation which linked the Hills with Harley. But while Sarah now maintained that she had always known of some vague relationship between them on the paternal side, Abigail was urgently entreated to ignore it. The name of Harley, the Duchess declared, was anathema to her and to all right thinking persons. Harley was a toad, a snake, a rat, a venomous reptile (the zoological appellations were inexhaustible). He drank like a fish; he worked like a mole in the dark. He would stab his best friend in the back. She adjured Abigail to have nothing to do with that poisonous Beast, who had obviously launched this sudden claim of cousinship to suit his own foul ends, not hers.

"Remember," the Duchess added in conclusion, "that you have one relative on whom you may rely and trust—one closer, too, in kinship, than that Animal. I knew his mother, Abigail Stevens, a shrinking sly-faced woman with a large red nose. Now I come to think on't, you must resemble her. I believe she was your father's cousin. I never knew him, thank God, I only know he was a Low Church Anabaptist and that Harley's family were Presbyterian. Low life, all of them. *His* father fought with the Roundheads. Be on your guard, my girl. Harley's a skunk."

Abigail thanked the Duchess for the warning, which served only to increase her regard for Mr. Harley. Since their first meeting in the presence of the Queen they had met again, and often. For while controversy in the House still raged round the burning question of Occasional Conformity, Harley paid frequent visits to Her Majesty and sat with her in audience for hours. The Queen delighted in his company. She found him most diverting. His talk was not entirely of politics. He told her anecdotes that made her laugh. 'Mr. Montgomery' had never made her laugh, and invariably left her in the dumps with his gloomy prophecies of war prolonged, despite the fact that Portugal had lately joined the Allies, which would speed the means to victory, of which Mr. Harley declared himself to be most optimistic, providing always that the Duke . . .

He had the greatest esteem and affection for the Duke, but it did appear, as Mr. Harley so clearly explained, that 'dear Mr. Freeman' looked to bestride the whole of Europe with his armies. If a mere woman with no knowledge whatsoever of warfare dare voice an opinion, it would have been more advisable had the Duke, as Mr. Harley suggested, concentrated on *one* quarter *first*, before attempting to conquer fresh fields. Had he conquered fresh fields? Since Bonn there had been no news of a spectacular advance . . . . Still, the Queen entirely agreed with Mr. Harley that the Duke was the most brilliant, wise, intrepid General the world had ever known. But besides their mutual admiration of the Duke, Mr. Harley brought her in touch with her people in a way no other statesman ever had done, or maybe had ever thought to do. Mr. Harley knew what was being said in clubs and coffee-houses, in the streets. He had told her—and how delightful to know it—that the common folk called her 'Good Queen Anne.'

Mr. Harley had said that a Queen Regnant roused the chivalry, the most gallant best in every man who served her—as witness the 'golden age' of Elizabeth's reign. Mr. Harley spoke of bees; he likened her to the Queen Bee, the life essence, the Source and Mother of the Hive. If Mr. Harley made her laugh he also made her cry. It was so touching to think of herself as a Bee. The Queen Bee. The Mother of her People. 'Good Queen Anne.'

On another occasion Mr. Harley brought to her notice the sad case of Mr. Defoe, who had been pilloried for having ridiculed the Higher Tories, and, what was more shocking, the Church.

But when Mr. Harley explained that Mr. Defoe had written nothing which had not already been said by Dr. Sacheverell and other divines in scarcely less exaggerated sermons, the Queen was ready to believe the poor man had paid dearly for his transgression. Secretary Lord Nottingham had been almost *too* severe. Did Mr. Harley—in strictest confidence—think that Lord Nottingham was perhaps a little too *harsh* in his outlook, to occupy so prominent a position as Secretary of State?

Thus pressed, Mr. Harley did, with grave reluctance, admit that Lord Nottingham had been a little harsh: uncompromising rather, in his judgment; but Her Majesty must remember his lordship was in a difficult position. Defoe had grievously offended and had been punished for his sin.

"And is he still in prison?"

Yes, he was still in prison.

"Poor creature. . . . Is he married?"

He was married and the father of a family.

The heart-rending picture Mr. Harley presented of Defoe's wife and seven children starving of Defoe's financial loss—it seemed he had owned a brick and tile factory at Tilbury which, since his imprisonment, had fallen into decay—drew tears of compassion from the Queen.

"His poor wife and children! I will offer a sum from the Privy Purse for their relief."

"Madam, your munificence unmans me."

Mr. Harley bowed his head.

The Queen raised hers.

"If my people regard me as their Mother, and," she lingered on the words, "their Good Queen Anne, I must uphold my reputation . . . I am still somewhat anxious with regard to Lord Nottingham's conduct in this matter. My Secretary of State must be above reproach, and above all must he be just. Mr. Harley, may I trouble you to pull the bell?"

Mr. Harley pulled the bell which was answered by Mrs. Hill. She, having removed her ear from the keyhole in the adjoining room, allowed a judicious interval to elapse before she entered.

"Order tea, Hill. And ratafee cakes. Mr. Harley, will you stay and drink a dish of tea?"

If the Queen was charmed with Mr. Harley, her handmaiden was enraptured. He had a way of speaking in his slow lazy voice that seemed to hide a laugh in every word. He had a way of glancing at her sideways, drawing her eyes to his in a delicious intimate conspiracy that filled her with exquisite confusions. She studied furtively his face as if to imprint it on her consciousness, as if indeed each glimpse of it might be the first, or last. She treasured every fleeting contact and magnified them in her privacy, read into his most trivial speeches, the careless touch of his lips as he bent to her hand in politest farewell, a thousand words unuttered. She dwelled upon his first revelation of their kinship.

"Was your father Francis Hill?" . . . His mother's cousin. He had told her he remembered having seen her father in his youth. He was supposed somewhat to resemble him. Did she observe a likeness?

Did she not?

She confessed how on the night of the Century Ball she had singled him out from every one of that assembly. The likeness had been startling.

"But I do not recall you among the guests," he had said.

"I was not among the guests, sir. My sister and I were watching from the gallery. I was not in attendance at the Palace then. I was maid to the Duchess of Marlborough."

At that he had looked at her kindly.

"And now you are Maid-in-Waiting to the Queen. Abigail . . ." his voice made music of the word. "My mother's name was Abigail too."

The weeks sped by and time sped on, but for her the days were narrowed to the hours of his coming; and when he left the Presence Chamber time stood still.

She did not see herself ridiculous, she did not know herself in love; nor, when she searched among her store of cherished moments to steal some slender hope from a word too lightly dropped, a look that lingered, could she find an anchorage for foolish dreams. Yet in these elusive contacts she was encouraged to believe him not entirely indifferent. True, there could be but slightest opportunity of any private conversation save that afforded in their walks along the gallery to the head of the stairs, where a footman waited to conduct him down. Yet while she rehearsed in silence what she would have said to make him feel her not unworthy of their kinship: to make him know that she could meet him on his plane, converse with him on matters besides politics: that she read books, Shakespeare, philosophy, the poets, could quote Sir Thomas Browne and the famous speech from Hamlet, she was dumb: raw, uncouth, unschooled, unscholarly, before so great a scholar.

And then one day, a late November day of high wind and fitful rain when the afternoon was closing in with shadows, her chance came: but not to air her knowledge. He wanted something more from her than that.

The gallery—she saw him look around his shoulder to make sure—was temporarily deserted. The pages were at their dinners; she should have been at hers. He walked over to a deep embrasured window-seat and called her to him.

"Look," pointing to the sky, "do you see that hurrying, hag-ridden belt of cloud in the west? 'Tis chased by the devil of a breeze. I think I never saw a sky so full of wind at this season of the year." He spoke in his slow, even voice, not looking at her. "Sit down," said Harley, "Sit."

She sat, gazing up at him.

"Why do I never meet you at Court functions?"

As he asked that, he bent his head till his face was on a level with her own. Seen at such close quarters and in that dim half-light, she noticed that the pupils of his heavy-lidded eyes were rimmed with grey and had somewhere in their depths a glint of gold.

"I do not attend Court functions, sir. I am not a Lady-in-Waiting, nor a Maid of Honour. I am only a Bedchamber-woman."

"Do you dress the Queen?"

"No, sir. The Queen has her dressers."

"But you are constantly in attendance?"

She nodded.

"To sing and play and pour the tea? Don't serve it to her 'cold'. You know they've dubbed her 'Brandy Nan'. Dirt sticks. I've had a taste of it."

His wine-flavoured breath fanned her cheek. She guessed he

had been drinking: and as if he had divined that thought he straightened up and smiled.

"No, I am not in my cups, little cousin, and you must keep the Queen from hers. We want to save and use her wits for what they're worth, which is less in her whole bulk than I find in this one small finger."

He took her hand and held it an instant in his palm and let it go.

Her little body quivered in a conflict of emotion. His touch was sheer enchantment, but his words outraged her loyalty. She flung at him a hot defence.

"I'll thank you in the Queen's name not to bring such dirt to me. I'll not listen to it. I have never——" She paused, blushing crimson.

"Never listened to it?" he suavely supplemented. "Although 'tis common talk? I applaud your allegiance and am, believe me, heart and soul with you in that. We must protect the Queen."

But his too glib apology did not decrease her apprehension. Surely it was unwise, unstatesmanlike, to repeat to her—a lesser servant of the Houshold—such slander? Could the Duchess have some reason in her loathing of this man? He was looking past her now, and at the sky. In the west, between the stripped park trees, a dull orange flare lit the edges of that leaden cloud with a fringe of fire. The brittle leaves, torn from the waving branches, spun in the dance of the wind. And while he watched the fall of dusk, Abigail watched him. Framed in the formal periwig, his high dome-shaped forehead had the smooth lustre of marble. His mobile mouth, his hands, were womanish, but the clear line of his jaw, his square cleft chin, showed strength of will and purpose. His eyes, under the drooping lids, were hard and bright as an eagle's, ruthless, guarded. No, this man could never stoop to shoddy tricks . . . unless to gain his ends.

"And what," he asked, still sky-gazing, "do you make of my face that you study it so piercingly? What do you read there? Am I readable?"

"No, sir. You are enigmatic."

He directed his eyes to hers again and held them.

"You should know, for you and I are of one kin, and if I am right in my conjecture, of one mind. You too, are enigmatic to some, but not to me. Although you have the air of a nonentity, you have acquired a self-discipline that is remarkable in one so young. That, however, is the advantage of learning the way of life in a harsh school. I know something of your early youth and the difficulties to which you were subjected—and which you have surmounted. You knew what it meant to starve when I, and other of your fine relatives, were stuffed full as Michaelmas geese with the fat o' the land. You knew the threadbare ugliness of poverty when we others walked in silk. All that was to your credit and lifts you from the common rut of womankind—or such womankind as it is my lot and my misfortune to meet. Of *your* misfortune I have but lately learned, and I commend you for your courage."

But there was nothing in his glance that offered commendation: no warmth in his one-toned voice as he made this cool statement of facts. He paused to take snuff and continued:

"You have assumed the mask of a tame mouse, and you wear it well. You profess, for your purpose, timidity. I, for my purpose, quiddity. But you may lift your mask. To me."

Decidedly, thought Abigail, he is the worse for drink. She half rose from her seat and was pushed gently back.

"Sit. There's none to see or hear us." He folded his arms; his eyes returned to the sky. For a minute or two he gazed at it as if he had forgotten her existence. Then: "God," he murmured, "still remains the greatest artist, the greatest colourist of all. Others have attempted to surpass Him. Leonardo almost touched Him, but he did not paint skies . . . Yes, once, in his Gioconda, where she sits, rock-girdled, with a faint graceful light behind her. You have something of her look. You are much with the Queen?"

This abrupt conclusion to his soliloquy was accompanied by another pinch of snuff. He still gazed, not at her, but at the sky.

"Yes, sir, when . . ."

"Don't address me as 'sir'. We are cousins. You were saying?"

"When I am called to tend her feet and wash Her Majesty and——"

"Very intimate." His long nose twitched. "On these occasions does she talk to you!"

"Yes . . . Yes, she does, s . . ."

"My name is Robert."

She had nothing to say to that.

"Well?" He slipped a smile, looking down at her. "And of what does Her Majesty talk?"

She knitted her forehead. She could not recall a word of what Her Majesty had talked.

"Does she ever speak of her son?"

"Yes . . . She has sometimes spoken of her son."

"Of her father?"

"Once or twice."

He was drawing her eyes to his again; hers widened. He laughed softly.

"Very green. Whoever calls you plain deserves to be struck blind . . . Her father. Is she full of woe when she mentions him?"

Abigail nodded; her lips were dry. She moistened them with the tip of her tongue.

"Don't do that," said Harley, brusquely.

"Do what, sir?"

"You know very well what. Save your tricks for others more susceptible than I. We were speaking of her father. She is remorseful?"

Abigail was silent.

"We take it then," said Harley, "that she *is* remorseful. You need not fear my questions for I ask you none that you cannot, or should not, answer. My interest is in the nation's interest, and the Queen's. Does she speak of her brother?"

"Not to me, sir."

He lowered his voice.

"Listen carefully. You will receive in a week's, or a month's time—I cannot exactly tell you when—a packet by the post. Inside it you will find another packet, sealed, and addressed to the Queen. You will give her that packet, but you will not know how or whence it came. Do you understand?"

She caught her breath.

"You are asking me . . . ?"

"To commit no wrong. To right a wrong, we hope. I believe you to be trustworthy."

"For the Queen, sir, yes. But . . . this packet?"

"Give it to her. Be with her when she opens it and report all to me."

"Sir!" She put her hand to her throat. "The Queen will wish to know how I came by the packet. All letters are brought to her by Mr. Kirk, one of the Grooms of the Chamber, or by her page."

"I am not concerned with Mr. Kirk or the page, or how they respectively distribute Her Majesty's post. I am concerned only that you deliver this one particular packet into the Queen's hand. In private. Here comes a servant . . . How the sky darkens. The wind is rising to a gale. Most unusual for November."

She rose with a weakness in her knees and a faintness at her heart that drained her face of colour. He watched her covertly and said without moving his lips:

"Don't look so scared."

The footman was lighting the candles in their sconces; another followed to draw the curtains at the windows. Harley bowed. "My duty, little cousin."

She curtsied, bade the footman: "Conduct Mr. Harley to his chaise." And stood to watch his tall spare figure pass along the corridor, until he reached the staircase. Then she fled. She felt, suddenly, dreadfully sick.

And that same night the Storm crashed over England, the like of which before or since has never been experienced this side of the Equator.

With a breaking of the waters that churned the seas to frenzy and overflowed the Thames flooding Westminster Hall, the gale sobbed, roared, shrieked, as if in some abortive labour of the elements, wreaking its vengeful fury on ships, on houses, hovels, on the Palace of the Queen, on every obstacle that barred its way.

Buildings collapsed; leaden roofs were ripped off and rolled up as if they had been sheets of parchment. Church spires, beaten from their steeples, bent like pins in the blast. Tiles fell and bricks, on cobbled streets empty of any living creature save night-stalking cats, tossed and sent spinning in that howling whirl of death. Fragments of wood, masonry, the wreckage of Thames wherry-boats, flying glass, cocked hats, sheep, a blacksmith's anvil, the wheels of coaches caught along the highway, a horse knocked senseless, scraps of bedding, petticoats, rags and tags of inanimate objects were given brief resistless life or resurrection, to dance in the thunder of the winds. The fear-stricken cowered in cupboards, cellars, under tables, in firm belief that dawn would bring their Judgment Day. And when the hurricane had reached its awful climax the Queen, who throughout the night had shown remarkable courage, stood at the window with her Consort in his nightgown at her side, and wept to see the great oaks in St. James's Park torn like weeds from their roots and crash to earth.

"My good brave trees, planted there by Cardinal Wolsey. My Uncle Charles was said to have loved those trees . . ." She summoned her attendants. The prince called his gentlemen. The Queen, for once, waived her rigid observance of etiquette that forbade any man to appear in her presence without a periwig, and sent a quaking page to knock at the doors of the equerries and tell them Her Majesty would not object to their wearing tie-wigs or their natural hair.

The Bedchamber was filled with Ladies and Gentlemen-in-Waiting, Maids of Honour, Pages of the Backstairs, all in various stages of undress, and, all fired by the Queen's example, hiding panic under a ceaseless cacophony of inane remarks. The Queen bade them play at cards and keep well away from the windows, but she refused to move from hers. The Prince was reminded of a similar tempest when he had served in the navy of his father, King of Denmark, at which his wife with unwonted sharpness contradicted: "Nonsense, George. That is quite impossible, for there has never been known anything like this. Where is Mrs. Hill? Page? Mr. Masham, be so good as to find Mrs. Hill and tell her I will take a dish of chocolate. George, you will take chocolate?"

George said he would take wine.

Mr. Masham, in dressing-gown, no stockings and a tie-wig, passed his Prince's command to a page, who in his turn passed it to a servant.

But where was Mrs. Hill?

Mrs. Hill, with her sister, was in the gallery kneeling on a window-seat, gazing out at the convulsion that had transformed the tranquil park into a seething black inferno. She saw the shattered grey cloud-shapes scurrying across the moonless sky. She saw the tortured trees keel over and sink, riven, groaning as if in protest to their pain. And Alice, secretly terrified, outwardly calm, almost lost her senses when to add to her fears Abigail murmured:

"I have the strangest feeling that this frightful thing is a kind of prophecy. A warning."

"Warning? Of what? Lord save us! Look at that."

She ducked as a tile shot past the rattling casement. "Abbie! Stand back. If that had hit the window you'd have been killed."

"I feel," said Abigail, staring out at the screaming dark, "I feel as if this will be seen again in some other form, some other time. Do you hear the whirr of gigantic wings beating down upon us?" Her voice was thin and high, unlike her own.

"You're crazed," panted Alice. "I can hear nothing but the boom of the wind. I can't hear myself speak."

"I hear . . . I see . . ." A meteoric light grazed the writhing blackness, and for one split second illumined Abigail's face with an unearthly radiance. "I see London, and those that will live after us enduring this again . . . Only it will be more terrible."

"It couldn't be more terrible. God's sakes, Abbie! Don't talk so." Alice cast a fearful glance along the shadowed corridor. "You tempt the devil."

"It could be much more terrible. This is nature at cross purposes with the Almighty. Suppose it were *not* nature? Suppose it were some evil force? Suppose it were all the evil of mankind concentrated in . . ."

She passed her hands across her eyes and shivered. "A grey goose walked over my grave. I thought I saw, but now I can no

longer see. I had the queerest feeling, as if I were outside . . .
outside my*self*. I saw Things, winged monsters, godless, horrible,
dropping balls of fire from the skies. Their sound was worse than
thunder, worse than the fall of trees. Worse than . . .''

"Abbie! Don't be so frightening. You talk like a witch. What
do you mean, 'outside yourself'?''

"Nothing. That's how the soothsayers make their fortunes.
'Tis easy as pie."

But Alice was not to be convinced by this return to norm.
"Abbie, you didn't truly see monsters, did you?"

"I heard them, and I saw them with this little third eye of mine
that sits in the middle of my forehead and is only visible to me and
God. I heard Jupiter roaring to his satellites because the incle-
ment weather has caused his corns to shoot. 'A star danced' . . .
Do you remember Beatrice? 'And I was born.' "

"You're possessed," gasped Alice. "Stop this wild talk."

"I can't!" She flung wide her arms and laughed in reckless gay
abandon. "The howl of the wind makes me brave—and mad.
I'd like to run with the storm and fight in it, lie in it, be wrapped in
it and carried up, up, up in its savage arms and tossed on the horns
of the moon."

"There isn't a moon to-night," objected Alice. "And you are
certain sure mad—or play-acting."

"Was it to-day?" Abigail pressed closer to the window. "Was
it only to-day that I watched the wind, a little small wind, chasing
a huge tigerish cloud over there in the West? Was it to-day he
said——"

"He? Who? Mercy me, how strange you are!"

"Yes. I'm strange. I *am* strange! I am not one, but two persons. I always knew that. And now, when all of you are scrabbling
and hiding in your holes, I am exalted. I am——"

"Mrs. Hill!"

The sparkle in her small elfish face vanished as she turned it
blankly in the direction of a voice that unmistakably was Mr.
Masham's. He came hurrying along the gallery. Alice found his
presence immensely reassuring; for Abigail it was a tiresome
intrusion. She stood waiting for him to gain her side. She noted
his dressing-gown clutched around him, his tie-wig, his stocking-
less legs, and she decided swiftly she had done him an injustice.
His calves *were* his own, and muscular enough in all conscience.
She suppressed a giggle. He was obviously embarrassed by his
negligent attire, and deeply conscious of his naked legs.

"Do you know if a footman has gone to fetch the Queen's
chocolate, Mrs. Hill?"

6*

"No, Mr. Masham. I was not aware that Her Majesty desired chocolate."

He made an impatient gesture. "The Staff are all terrified out of their wits. Pray allow me, madam, to give the order to the servants. I beg you not to venture downstairs. One of the chimneys in the new wing has fallen. Another may fall at any moment."

Mr. Masham hastened on.

"He's in a great state about you," Alice tittered. "But not about me, oh, dear no! The roof may drop on my head and crush me to death for all he or any other gentleman would care. But *you* must be protected. *You* must not go downstairs to fetch the chocolate lest you be blown away, you little, poor, dainty creature. I wish he'd heard you just now, talking like a wanton, of rolling and running and lying out there in the arms of the—— Lord alive! What's that?"

A terrific concussion rocked the gallery, followed by a cataclysmic fall of stone and bricks. Alice, whimpering with fright, flung herself on the floor. Plaster dropped from the ceiling, and somewhere below was heard the sound of a woman's shriek.

"O, God! What is it?" quavered Alice.

"Nothing that has hurt *us*, anyhow," said Abigail. "Get up. We'll go to the Bedchamber. If we're to be killed we might as well die in good company."

At the door of the Queen's Ante-room she told Alice: "Go in. I have to wait for the chocolate."

Her momentary exultation had now vanished. She thought she could detect in the bluster of the storm a shrill despairing note, as if the full force of its violence had been depleted by that last impetuous shock. And as dawn struggled up into the east, the wind's velocity had spent itself, exhausted.

She was relieved at last to see Mr. Masham approach her, attended by a white-faced footman carrying the chocolate on a salver.

Abigail took it from him.

"What was that particularly awful noise awhile since, Mr. Masham?"

Part of the battlements in the west wing, he said, had been blown down.

"Is anyone hurt?"

"A kitchenmaid, I fear, has been injured."

She did not know that his delay had been caused by his attempt to save the maid who had been struck by a falling beam; or that when he opened the door to bow her in with his customary smile, the blood from a wound, caused by a jagged piece of glass embedded in his shoulder, was trickling down the arm he hid behind him.

* * *

The nine days' wonder of the Storm endured with intermittent lapses of ferocity for almost that same length of time before it passed, amid the ruins of far-reaching devastation.

Mrs. South, whom Abigail visited at the end of that fateful week, had ghoulishly picked from the bones of disaster the most harrowing tales to tell in which romanticism flourished among scattered grains of truth.

Eddystone Lighthouse and all its occupants, including Mr. Winstanley who had built it, had been swept away.

"Ah, the poor creatures! No boat could cross those seas to aid them. And in the morning the rock was bare as the palm of your hand, and the Lighthouse gone, Lord have mercy on their souls! And the Bishop of Bath and Wells—killed dead as a stone, he was, by the fall of a chimney-stack as he lay bedded with his wife. And you may believe it or not, but as I stood at my window above I saw a ship, all sails furled, riding the sky like as it were on the ocean, wrenched from its moorings in the Thames. Such a sight may I never behold again. 'Tis a miracle how any of us lived through it, at all!"

It would appear that Mrs. South had been vouchsafed, by special dispensation, sights more horrible, more blood-curdling than any other citizen had been privileged to witness. She had seen a coffin, torn from a graveyard, go reeling like a drunkard on the wind and land, to disgorge a mouldering corpse stripped naked of its shroud, upon the roof-top opposite.

She had seen, and would swear to it, the Old One himself perched on yonder steeple frisking his forked tail and spewing hell-fire from his mouth in blasphemious defiance of the saints. Ah, the divil and all his company from below were battering at God's own Door that night. 'Twas all the blessed St. Peter himself could do to keep 'em on t'other side the Gate. . . . "And what now of your doings at the Palace, Mrs. Hill?" Mrs. South inquired when imagination waned. "Do you ever hear aught o' the King?"

"The King? What King, madam?" asked the simple Mrs. Hill.

"There's only one King for me," rejoined Mrs. South, "and you know right well who 'tis. King James III over the water. We'll drink to him."

They drank.

"Sure, it should be the aim and purpose of each one of us who serve him," Mrs. South with due solemnity continued, "to save this country from the Hanoverian succession There's talk now of bringing over that old besom the Electress Sophia, who swears she'll live to wear the Crown of England on her head before she dies—and her so far removed from it as niece to King Charles the Martyr himself, *and* in her dotage, begar! And if she don't live to inherit the Kingdom, those pelf-licking Whigs have sworn to put her son George Lewis on the throne, and him no more than a sausage-eating German! Now, will ye tell me, Mrs. Hill, if you have ever been presented, in the grand life ye lead up there beyond, to one o' the name of Saint John?"

"I have heard tell of Mr. St. John," Abigail guardedly replied. Mrs. South nodded.

"Ah! The brave lad that he is! The heart and soul o' the Jacks. His is a name to remember, believe me."

Mrs. Hill did believe her, and widened her eyes and her ears. St. John. A name to remember. Yes, she *had* heard of him from Sarah Marlborough, who held him in almost as great abhorrence as she did Mr. Harley. That he—Cousin Robert—should have chosen her for confidante had greatly enhanced Abigail's belief in herself. If she had no beauty to offer the gentlemen, it was evident she had something else, or something more, that made it worth their while to seek her company. Mr. Masham, she must own, had not of late sought much of it; and Mr. Harley had not visited the Palace since the Storm, but he would come: certain surely he would come.

The packet, however, did not.

While in daily expectation she awaited its delivery, she racked her brains to know on what feasible excuse she could hand it in private to the Queen.

On this problem Abigail brooded to worry herself sick when she returned in her chair to the Palace after her visit to Mrs. South.

The streets, littered with bricks, slates, broken glass, twisted iron, sheets of lead, the debris of fallen walls and shattered windows, looked as though they had suffered an eruption or bombardment. A general air of gloom pervaded the city, reflected in the faces of the many who had suffered the loss of their homes: or the bewildered incredulity of grief in the faces of the few who had suffered the loss of their kin. Around the Palace gates a cluster of sight-seers had gathered to snatch a glimpse of the shorn battlements in the new wing, deriving some vicarious satisfaction in the knowledge that even the Queen's house had not escaped. Workmen, toiling amid the rubble, were collecting barrow loads of fallen bricks and tile-sherds. As Abigail alighted at the entrance to the apartments of the Household, she saw Mr. Kirk, Groom of the Chamber, handing the day's post to a page for distribution. Letters at all times were a rarity, and that one of the three delivered should be for Mrs. Hill was remarkable enough to arouse the curiosity of Mr. Kirk.

He, a chinless young gentleman with a deplorable stammer that embarrassed others more than himself, had obtained his appointment at the Palace only because he had served the Duke of Gloucester.

"A lerlerletter for you, Mrs. Hill." He weighed it in his hand. "It feels mermore sersolid than perpaper. A perperpresent from your berbrother in Flerflanders maybe."

"I cannot tell, Mr. Kirk, till I open it. And my brother is not now in Flanders . . ." Nor could she tell him it came from Jack, since he knew perfectly well it did not as it bore the inland post-mark of twopence, the price of delivery within a radius of eighty miles.

"Are the serserstreets serstill in deperplorable condition?" persevered Mr. Kirk, in evident hope that she would open the letter at once.

"Yes."

"It lerlooks like rain."

"Yes."

"I tertrust your cahcorrespondent has no bad news to cahconvey?"

"I trust not indeed, Mr. Kirk."

And she left him.

Now it would be all over the Palace that she had received a 'sersolid' letter—from whom? Her heart beat fast as she broke the seal to find inside a facsimile of the packet addressed to her: but this was addressed to Her Majesty. And how to hand it, as instructed, 'in private' to the Queen, she did not know; for she would certainly have to explain how she had come by it. She must wait her opportunity and take her chance.

The packet, though bulky, was small enough to conceal beneath her bodice under a fichu of muslin; and although her bust looked to be somewhat enlarged, none would notice that, if she arranged the muslin so and pulled it *so*, and let it fall *so*. . . . And feeling as if between her breasts she hid an asp, she made her way to the Queen's Green Closet.

"Did Your Majesty ring?"

The Queen was seated at her table reading her letters alone.

Her chance was offered more readily than she had dared to hope.

"No, Hill, I did not ring." The Queen frowned over the sheets of paper in her hand. "The war news grows ever more distressing. The Duke seems to make no headway at all. I dreadfully fear we are at a deadlock with the French."

"The Storm, Madam," Abigail suggested, "may have impeded the advance."

"The Storm did not attack the Continent, and we have had no encouragement to hope for victory within the year . . . Hill, what in the world are you doing?"

While the Queen was speaking, Hill had advanced and dropped on all fours to crawl under the table. She emerged and stood upright, very flushed, to curtsy.

"I entreat Your Majesty's pardon. I saw this on the floor, Madam. It must have fallen."

"Thank you, Hill." The Queen's swollen fingers fumbled with the seal. "It breaks my nails. Open it for me."

For the fraction of a second Abigail hesitated; controlling the hurry of her breath, she took the packet, broke the seal and drew from the paper wrapping something small, encased in velvet.

Silently she passed it to the Queen, and stood with lowered eyes and in a tremble, then:

"Dear God! What is it? *Who* is it?" she heard. "Hill, look. Look!"

Hill looked.

In the Queen's palm lay the exquisitely painted miniature of a pale oval face, the eyes languorous, almond-shaped; the lips full and parted in a half smile, the chin dimpled, the hair dark and curling to the shoulders: a young boy's face.

"It is . . . it must be!" The Queen's whisper was caught back on a sob. "See, Hill, the writing on the back."

And Hill saw, written in a pointed careful hand:

'To Her most gracious Majesty, Queen of Great Britain and Ireland, my beloved sister Anne from James Francis Edward.'

"Queen of . . . O, my dear, my dearest!" The clumsy shoulders heaved; tears brimmed over and splashed on that gentle pictured face. "My brother! Of what have I deprived you? My father's son. . . . His heir."

The Queen bowed her head on her outstretched arms; and with an ache in her throat and a mist in her eyes, Abigail stole quietly away.

CHAPTER FIVE

The milkmaids were holding festival around the maypole in the Strand. Decked in tinsel, ribbons, gewgaws, with pyramids of silver plate borrowed from willing customers and piled high with fruit and flowers on their heads, they danced, sang, gambolled from door to door followed by pipers, fiddlers, and all the lads of the town.

The stress and storm of winter, a capricious spring of snow, rain, hail, the bitter news of war, were forgotten on that blue and golden morning of May Day. The city rang with laughter, the cobbles with the patter of young feet. Old folk who watched rubbed a moisture from their eyes—and dust into them, kicked up by the clatter of the dance—as they remembered some such other morning when they too had partnered a girl, or engarlanded, had been partnered by a boy, roped in hawthorn, waving branches, shouting, singing, frolicking. . . . From Cheapside to Charing Cross and back again along the Strand they danced from sunrise and would dance until sundown, holding up the city's traffic. Not a soul objected. Waggoners, chairmen, hackney-coach drivers, postilions and outriders of the rich, the donkey-carts and barrows of the poor, alike were drawn into the merry whirligig, good-humouredly lined up against the horse-posts to let the milk-maids have their day.

The fun had reached its gladdest height when a coach and six came lumbering past Charing Cross and halted there. Its occupant, Lord Treasurer, was not amused, and in a hurry.

He stuck his head out of the window to frown at a footman: "Tell him to get on. We're two hours behind time, thanks to these fandangos——" encountered in all the villages from Newmarket along the Queen's Highway.

He had left the posting-inn at Stevenage before cockcrow; he had breakfasted on mutton collops, underdone, and on eel-pie, overdone, and had all but swallowed a snail in his beer. The inn-servants were out dancing with the girls and the Jacks-in-the-Green, neglecting their duties, a pox on 'em! And as his lordship now sat glowering upon that happy throng—much have *they* to joy for, he reflected grimly. Yet he might have wished himself as care-free, young, as any butcher's boy or raw apprentice. He might have wished himself in any place but his.

He had enjoyed a few days' respite from the strain of leadership

at the close of the April session to see his colt, his pride, his
Arabian Knight, run to win at Newmarket the Hundred Guineas
Gold Plate presented by Prince George. To see him win. He
couldn't lose. Everyone had said he couldn't lose. Tregonwell
Frampton, 'Father of the Turf', keeper of the Queen's horses, had
said he couldn't lose. And he *had* lost—with his owner's shirt on
him, the devil. That alone was bad enough to turn his stomach
without this filthy taste of sour beer and snails, of all obnoxious
goddamned—ouch!

Godolphin retched.

These incessant feuds, disputes, dissensions in the House had
been brought to a head when the Occasional Conformity Bill—
St. John's pet lamb turned pet tiger—had been thrown out in the
autumn by the Lords: the Whig Lords, the wry Godolphin
recollected, led by that greasy bumble-headed Bishop Burnet and
twelve votes. If Godolphin had had his way he would have seen
the bloody Bill buried in Thames mud before he would have
dragged it up again, but it would *have* to be dragged up again.
That young game-cock would never let it rest. What a clutter!
And now the Queen, forsooth, was offering (for the benefit of the
poor clergy) her whole revenue from the First Fruits and the
Tenth, that ancient tax levied by the Crown on Church livings.
The 'poor clergy' . . . Hum! Doubtless a noble sacrifice, if it
were not certain the Lord Treasurer would, soon or late, be called
upon to make good the deficit. And to cause the vexed Godolphin
further itch, here was 'Dismal' Nottingham laying down his
challenge that unless the Ministry were cleared of Whigs he would
resign. Well, let him go and good riddance to him. 'Twas a scurvy
trick to run whining behind his Chief's back to the Queen, who,
since her High Tory views and 'Dismal's' marched together, might
have weakened. But he had adopted a dictatorial tone and
Godolphin remembered what 'Dismal' did not, that a Stuart
could be coaxed though never driven. Nottingham had laid the
seal on his resignation with the froth of his own spittle.

"Fippence for the Maypole, m'lord. God bless yer honour!
Here's rare young 'riginal sin, fine as fippence for ye!"

A girl jumped on to the step of the Lord Treasurer's stationary
coach, to shove through the open window her rosy laughing face.
Godolphin averted his, swore silently, and dug in his pocket for
a coin.

"Take it—get out! Go away!"

"Lord love your honour!" She was head and shoulders at
him, clawing at his arms, tipping off his cocked hat to plant a
kiss on his chin.

"Praise be to ye, m'lord. Make it fippence more—and cheap at the price—and all the luck in the world to your honour."

"Go!" snarled Godolphin.

She sprang off the step, pulling a saucy face at the footmen perched behind, to put Godolphin in a fuss. Those fellows up there would never have done grinning!

"Drive on," he shouted, "can't you?"

And as the coach, leaving the sounds of revelry behind it, pursued its way towards the Palace, Godolphin pursued his interrupted thoughts . . . Mmm. Harley would step up as Nottingham stepped down, that was certain. And why not? Why should he, Godolphin, niggle and naggle and pick imaginary flaws in Harley's political integrity? Why did he mistrust him, whom, outside Westminster Hall, he regarded as his friend?

Because . . . Godolphin's grim smile reappeared, because Harley is the friend of no man, unless it were that conceited popinjay, St. John. Those two were thick as thieves together. Set a thief to catch a thief! And St. John was a Jacobite.

He had never got to the bottom of that dirty business up in Scotland at the end of last year, instigated by Lord Lovat with the fantastical notion of raising a Highland rebellion to bring over the pretended Prince of Wales. Harley had shown a strange reluctance to disclose particulars of that conspiracy. The Queen, too, had been uncommonly obstructive. True, she had latterly been full of moans and hints and conscience pricks about her brother. And why of a sudden should she, who had been the first to dub him 'the Pretender', be taken with the fantods over *him* and now she would never call him anything but 'Prince', 'her father's son', and all the rest of it? She had even gone so far as to admit he should be King. Well, come to that, so he should. Humha!

Godolphin cleared his throat of phlegm and spat. What with this dust, and the draughts sniffing down chimneys and under the door of the miserable bedroom he had occupied last night, his palate felt dry as a lime-kiln. He had a tickling in his nose. That meant a cold. He had a tendency to colds.

Taking from his vest pocket a tiny gold-framed mirror, too small to see more than one quarter of his face, Godolphin stuck out and examined his tongue. It was furred. No wonder, after all the filth he had swallowed; and now that milk-maid wench had given him a flea.

He scratched, sneezed, goggled at the red plush upholstery. A fine to-do! To take a flea and a cold to the Queen . . . But he was thinking neither of colds nor of fleas when his coach, driving into the courtyard of the Palace, passed Harley and St. John driving out.

"How good of you to come, dear Mr. Montgomery."

The Queen received him with gush, offered him tea, and called Sarah's cousin to serve it.

Godolphin stared. Sarah's cousin—*and* Harley's cousin it would seem. And since when had Harley claimed relationship with this whey-faced little person who stood in servile attendance behind the Queen's chair?

"I intend to build and present to the Prince," said the Queen when tea had been consumed and carried out, "an Orangery at Kensington. It will be so pleasant to sit there on summer evenings. I hope, my lord, your splendid horse—what is its name?"

"Arabian Knight," muttered Godolphin.

"Ah, yes. Did he win the Gold Plate?"

"No, Madam. He lost."

"How unfortunate. News travels slow. Yes, an Orangery," beamed Anne, "with trellised walls and windows looking out on to the garden. Don't you think that Sir Christopher Wren . . . ?"

Yes, Godolphin thought that Sir Christopher Wren . . . And subsided in the fidgets. He had a burning in his nose, shivers in his back, and an ache behind his eyes. Sure sign of a rheum or worse. Let's get to business for God's sake, he urged voicelessly, and don't blab to me of Orangeries. Wren. A nice expense!

"Your Majesty. I exceedingly regret Lord Nottingham's suggested resignation."

"Do you?" The Queen took a comfit from a dish on the table at her side. "To my mind 'tis the only possible thing he could have done." She popped the comfit in her mouth and scrunched. "His lordship is so *very* ministerial. He laid down the law to me. I won't be dictated to."

She selected a piece of candied orange peel and bade Hill pass the dish to his lordship.

His gorge rose.

"I thank Your Majesty, but my doctor," he fabricated hastily, "has forbidden me to eat of comfits. Any kind of sugarmeats, I understand, encourages the gout."

"Does it?" The Queen's fingers hovered above the silver dish that Hill, returning, had presented to her. "*My* doctor—Dr. Arbuthnot—has never told me that. I know sweets are supposed to be fattening, but still"—she smiled up at her demure attendant— "I hardly eat enough of them, do I, Hill, to make me any fatter than I am." She nibbled. "Now with regard to Lord Nottingham. I do confess I object to be treated by my Ministers as if I were a recalcitrant child."

"Madam!" Stifling a sneeze, Godolphin exhibited shock.

"Yes," the munching Queen nodded. "If his lordship had not threatened to resign I would have been compelled to have ordered him to do so."

"Quite, Madam, quite," mumbled Godolphin.

"He actually told me I must choose between the Tories and the Whigs and abide by my choice. Was not that impertinent?"

"Most impertinent, Madam. Has Your Majesty considered a successor to Lord Nottingham?"

"I had considered"—the Queen stooped to lift her spaniel to her knee and fed it with the last of the marchpane. "I *had* considered Mr. Harley."

Godolphin drew a handkerchief from his cuff and mopped his streaming nose. He felt hot.

"Do you not agree, my lord, that there is positively no one else? And I had thought also that Mr. St. John, who is so handsome and such a brilliant speaker—although I confess I have not yet had the opportunity of hearing him, but I will—I thought that he should be our Secretary of War."

Godolphin sneezed.

"Dear Mr. Montgomery, I trust you have not taken cold upon your journey. I know," resumed the Queen "that Mr. St. John is very young, but I do feel that youth should be given its chance. After all, young shoulders are sometimes more fitted to bear the burden of responsibility than old."

Touché! Godolphin hid a grin behind his handkerchief. The Queen's glance came to rest, with faint disapproval, on Lord Treasurer's creased travelling suit, on some dust that had collected on his shoes; on his steinkerk, slightly soiled, on his disordered periwig. In fact, his whole appearance was nothing so spruce as etiquette demanded, and which the Queen relentlessly enforced.

"I see, my lord," no mistaking now a marked reproof, "that you have not changed from your coaching dress."

"Madam." Godolphin rose and clumsily bowed. "I have but this morning arrived in Town, having hastened here all speed at Your Majesty's request. I judged—and beg forgiveness if I judged wrongly—that affairs of State are of more importance than the state of my attire."

An astonished flush crept into those sallow cheeks, but the Godolphin stood his ground. He knew that she would take from no man, not even from Marlborough, what she would take from him.

She reared her head; her lips opened to speak, said nothing.

Lord Nottingham's dictatorial challenge had lost him his appoint-ment as Secretary of State; and now Lord Treasurer, with dirt on his shoes and blowing his nose, dared to rebuke her. Still, if the poor man had a cold . . .

"You had best go home to bed, my lord," the Queen suggested frigidly. "Allow me to send my good Dr. Arbuthnot to attend you. He is a most able physician and a true"—she emphasized the 'true'—"Tory".

Godolphin bowed again above the two swollen fingers extended. The Queen, who could never be displeased with her Montgomery for more than a minute at a time, relented at the touch of his bulbous lips.

"You know, my dear Mr. Montgomery, I am always grateful for, and dependent on the guidance and devotion of you and the dear Freemans. We four must never part. I wrote that to Mr. Freeman. 'We four,' I wrote, 'must *never* part till Death mows us down with his impartial hand . . .' Pray go to bed, my lord, and nurse your cold. Affairs of State," for all her kind concern, it rankled, "are less important than the health of him who leads us."

Godolphin left in worse humour than when he had arrived. What had she on her mind to speak of parting? 'We four . . . Till Death mows us down.' Despite her cow-like gentleness, he had always known she could be canny. She got that from Edward Hyde. She was not his granddaughter for nothing. Harley! So Harley had stolen a march on him and pushed that youngster for-ward too. For what purpose? He would have given much to have known how he had insinuated himself into such high grace . . . Mr. Secretary Harley.

But there was positively, and he must admit it, no one else.

"If my Lord Treasurer had not been in such haste to go, which is just as well for he was sneezing and may pass his cold to me, I would," Her Majesty told Mrs. Hill, "have shown him the . . ."

She exchanged with her attendant a long confidential look. None save Mrs. Hill and perhaps one other, knew of the minia-ture the Queen kept hidden in a secret drawer of her bureau.

"But," the Queen sighed and stroked her spaniel, "he might not have approved. He might have started tiresome inquiries. Mr. Montgomery has never acknowledged the Prince as my brother. It seems so cruel, unjust, that I and my nearest, dearest of kin, must not correspond or even meet. But as Mr. Harley said . . ."

It was as well for Lord Treasurer's peace of mind that he could not know it would be henceforth, 'as Mr. Harley said.'

CHAPTER SIX

THE summer months dragged on with days of airless heat, suspense, anxiety, for those who awaited news from the fighting front. The Queen with her Prince and her ladies left for Windsor. The Duchess remained at St. Albans and read and re-read the letters that trickled through to her from John. They gave her little cheer, and less hope of victory that year. He was 'extremely out of heart . . . uneasy, but he loved her at this minute better than he ever had before.'

While his tenderness moved her to tears, she was practical. Wars could not be won on love alone. Did he think to dispel doubt by these repeated protestations, as of an adolescent ensign to his sweetheart? If only she were with him! She had toyed with the idea of joining him when he had left again in the spring for the Hague. 'What you propose, as to coming over, I should be extremely pleased with, although I should not be able to see you often . . .' he had written with heaven knows what misgivings lest she should take him at his word. 'Your letter transported me, but . . .'

There was always a 'but'. And then, more decisively: 'You will see by my first letter as well as by this that what you desire is impossible, for I am going up into Germany.'

And now she could follow him only in thought and in prayer.

In May he wrote to her from Kühlseggen, and to Lord Treasurer from Bonn; and now he was at Braubach. He gave no hint of a success. And in June he was at Weinheim—'in a house of the Elector Palatine that has a prospect over the finest country that is possible to be seen.'

From his chamber window he could gaze out upon the sloping terraced valley of the Rhine, on the dimpling waters of the Neckar, and away in the clear cobalt distance, half hidden in that richly verdured hill-land, he could see the towns of Heidelberg and Mannheim. 'But I would be much better pleased with the prospect of St. Albans, which is not very famous for seeing far.'

Sick at heart and sick of waiting, Sarah took herself, but not her fears, to the Queen, and was amazed to find her cousin Abigail had come to Windsor, and without consulting her! The Queen explained that Danvers had applied for leave of absence.

"Danvers applies too often for leave of absence," snapped Sarah.

Her nerves were frayed to breaking-point. She had all to do to keep her temper down and her smiles up while she sat plaiting fringes with the Queen, who chatted of nothing, played with her spaniels, and munched sweets as if the fear of defeat and the Sun King's arrogance, shining resplendent amid Allied pessimism, did not exist; as if the Fate of Britain were not balanced on the scales of precarious endeavour.

In July the general gloom was temporarily dispersed by the victory of Schellenberg. Sarah took heart, the Queen took tea, served 'cold', in celebration.

Mrs. Morley's apparent indifference to the general uneasiness had deceived Mrs. Freeman, and indeed all her ladies save one, into thinking Her Majesty too stupid to know or too callous to care how grave was the present situation. Mrs. Hill was not deceived. In the privacy of the Queen's Bedchamber had been revealed to her alone a glimpse of the Queen's agonized suspense, and a burst of unwontedly regal indignation when the report reached her how that Louis, confident of his success, had given a sumptuous banquet to 'the King and Queen of England . . .' The Queen of England—her stepmother, Mary of Modena, and the King, her half-brother, James!

The miniature was brought from its hiding-hole. The young face gazed up at her from the palm of her hand.

"He would never have wished to promote himself King in my place. The mouth is weak, the eyes so like . . . so like my father's. Yes, weak. You know that it was I, to my shame, Hill, who named him 'Pretender'. He shall not be King while I live, but afterwards . . . He is a Stuart. George Lewis of Hanover, what is he?"

So would she ramble on while Abigail, bent above her sewing, held her peace. More than ever now, in these weeks of uncertainty, did the Queen require her attendance. Mrs. Danvers and the other ladies deemed it wiser not to query the position held by Mrs. Abigail Hill. The support of two such powerful relatives as Her Grace of Marlborough and the Secretary of State had endowed her with the right to elevation. They ceased openly to question it, while whispers flew: Mrs. Hill would yet be raised above herself, above them all and . . . above one other!

The wish may have mothered the thought, since not a woman among them had not suffered from the tongue of Viceroy Sarah.

But those whispers died, dispersed, as when sudden sun breaks through a fog, in the dazzling triumph that hailed Marlborough, saviour, conqueror, hero. The long awaited news came in a hurried pencil scrawl torn from a page of a note-book. He had

written it while still in the saddle and on the slaughter-field amid
the dead and dying; and he gave it to his aide-de-camp to carry
to his wife.

The Queen received Colonel Parke in her closet overlooking
the terrace at Windsor. He had ridden seven days and seven
nights across Europe to bring her the news.

"A letter, Madam . . ." He was out of breath, dishevelled,
travel-stained. He wore no wig, but etiquette for once went disregarded. "A letter, Madam, from His Grace of Marlborough to
the Duchess, who bade me bring it to Your Majesty."

She did not, in this greatest moment of her reign, query the
Duke's want of tact or respect in sending that message to his wife
to pass on to the Queen of England; but as her hand, for a second,
rested on her heart her face closed; then she took the crumpled
paper, and she read:

'I have not time to say more than to beg of you to present
my humble duty to the Queen and to let Her Majesty know that
her Army has had a glorious victory. M. Tallard and two other
Generals are in my coach. and I am following the rest. The
bearer, my aide-de-camp, Colonel Parke, will give Her Majesty
an account of what has passed. I shall do it in a day or two by
another, more at large.'

Not since the battle of Agincourt was a victory acclaimed with
such turbulent rapture. For days, for weeks, the capital and every
town and village rang the nation-wide tumult in peals of joy-bells.
Steeples rocked. Beacons flared on hill-tops. Guns thundered
their salutes, and at night the shouting beflagged streets blazed
their gay illumination of coloured lanthorns, bonfires, and rockets
shooting snake-like to the sky. Cellars were emptied of wine and
beer to fill the drinking-cups. Scarce a man in all the land stayed
sober.

Accompanied by her Guards and Grenadiers, watched by a
myriad cheering spectators seated on scaffolding, crowding windows hung with blue cloth, tapestries, white and scarlet streamers,
the Queen and her Consort drove to St. Paul's to give thanks for
the glory of Blenheim.

Yet even amid the general rejoicing there was trouble, signs of
Party rancour, criticism led by the Higher Tories. Marlborough
had exceeded his power, had deserted the Dutch, imperilled the
future with his uncertain enterprise . . . Uncertain! howled the
Whigs, with all of Britain save the Jacobites huzzaing at every

mention of his name? A dig here at the debonair St. John, who throughout the clamour in the House had sat with his legs outstretched before him admiring the buckles on his shoes. True enough, concurred the extremists of the High Church Party, true enough . . . The concession was not without grudge. They then brought forward more grievance. Why had no honour been paid to the gallant Admiral Sir George Rooke, who had stormed and taken the Rock of Gibraltar? Which of the two would stand through immortality as a landmark of Britain's greatness? The Mediterranean fortress that would endure for all time, or a battle that had slaughtered the flower of British youth and had not yet won the war?

These High Flying views aroused a further noise. At such a time no man worth his salt or blood would listen to such sacrilege. The Queen's Ministry was tottering, and those of the 'Faithful' stood on tenterhooks to see their Hanoverian satellites turn towards the Electress Sophia and her son, George Lewis, in support of the Protestant Party. It was said the old lady had become so inflated with the promise of England's Crown, to which if she lived, she must succeed, that she could hardly wait to come over and snatch it from the head of its wearer. She was old but more healthy than Anne, and more virile. She would hang on to life till the throne was hers to pass on to her son and her grandson, who by every right should be naturalized English and created a Royal Duke. This suggestion was promoted by the Hanoverian Tories.

"The Tories!" The Queen was most dreadfully shocked. "The Tories, mark you, Mr. Harley. Only think! I could better understand this preposterous idea had it emanated from the Whigs—but the Tories!"

"Madam, 'tis but a storm in a teacup." And over the rim of his, Harley reassuringly smiled.

'One of the most delightful traits in Mr. Harley's character,' she had confided to his cousin, Abigail, 'is his manner of making light of gravest matters. Lord Treasurer is always so glum. He depresses me. Mr. Harley is my ray of sunshine.'

Her ray of sunshine was now seated at her table, sipping tea and admiring the Dresden. "Such an exquisite design. Your Majesty has an admirable taste. I am a collector—I might say something of a connoisseur—of china."

"Indeed? And are you not also a collector of books? I hear you have a remarkable library."

"A modest collection, Madam, but 'twill grow."

"And china! How charming. It would give me great pleasure

to present you with this tea-set . . . Hill, have this Dresden tea-set sent to Mr. Harley."

And when Mr. Harley had sufficiently expressed his humble gratitude at such beneficence, he carefully returned her to the stormy cup in question. "Why does Your Majesty not attend the debates? Your presence would moderate the attacks of all parties."

"Would it?" She was childishly pleased. "I will."

She did, and sat, not on her throne in the House but on a bench near the fire toasting her toes, and heard her poor Mr. Montgomery 'quite brow-beaten'—thus to Mrs. Hill she afterwards described it—'by both the Whigs *and* the Tories.'

The Queen, however, was not so much concerned with Parliament's brawls as with the burning desire to reward Marlborough with some lasting token of her gratitude for his immortal victory. What should it be? A monument? A statue? No, neither of these could be of any substantial benefit to the nation's idol and his heirs. Nothing short of a Palace fit for a King would be Mrs. Morley's gift to her beloved Freemans.

At her own expense—and thus dispose of obstruction from Lord Treasurer and his perpetual croakings—she would raise a memorial to revere in perpetuity the name of Marlborough and Blenheim.

Blenheim Palace.

Sarah was overjoyed and overwhelmed. A Palace! How fortuitous that victory should have come just at this time, when for so long had lurked between herself and Mrs. Morley the shadow of estrangement. Not, certainly, on Sarah's side; nor could she place a finger on any tender spot; nor had she an inkling why her 'poor unfortunate faithful Morley' had been of late so unaccountable, constrained, and sometimes chilly in her manner.

For example, Mrs. Morley had offered no thanks to Mrs. Freeman when one morning she returned from the New Exchange with a pair of perfumed gloves—too large, as she afterwards discovered for herself—and had begged the Queen accept them. Mrs. Morley's demeanour at that moment had been odd. She had taken them, certainly, looked at them, sniffed at them, laid them aside and said absently: "Oh . . ."

Well!

One might have asked oneself (but didn't) why so churlish? Embroidered gloves of Spanish leather, sweetly-scented (and they cost a guinea) were worth something, surely, more than 'Oh? . . .' However, let that pass for a whim and forget it. All was as it should be now, and as it ever had been, with Mrs. Morley full of gratitude and Palaces.

A hundred were designed between the two in talk, but nothing tangible. Mrs. Morley was determined on a moat: battlements, peep-holes, turrets, a feudal frontage. No. Mrs. Freeman abhorred sham and ostentation. She desired something modest, or as modest as might be compatible with : 'Beauty, Magnificence, Duration.'

To whom should be given the honour of designing it? The Queen's Comptroller of Works must, of course, be consulted.

He, a young man who wrote plays—of all things!—and had run, unsuccessfully, a theatre in the Haymarket in partnership with Congreve, was the son of a Cheshire sugar-baker, and had already made his mark in architecture with the building of Castle Howard for Lord Carlisle.

To this handsome, dashing, witty young gentleman, John Vanbrugh, was given the honour of building the Palace. Plans were submitted: a model erected and placed in the gallery at Kensington for the Queen's consideration. Mrs. Morley was ecstatic. Mrs. Freeman dubious. She considered it too vast, too ornate, too this, too that, unsuitable, impracticable, not at all what she herself had visualized. Never mind, get on with it and finish it before the war was over, so that the Duke could return in triumph to his home. . . .

In this frenzy of idolatry it must be confessed that Mrs. Morley had overlooked her promised gift of an Orangery to her Consort. But now, in the rôle of Queen Bee, she could work miracles.

Blenheim took several years to build; the Orangery but a few months. In June, to celebrate its completion, the Queen gave a banquet, followed by a musical soirée. To the latter entertainment Abigail was graciously invited. "None who waits on me," the Queen had said, "must be left out."

Nor were they.

Mrs. Abrahal, Mrs. Wanley, who since the Duke of Gloucester's death had been retained in some obscure household capacity, the dressers, and even Alice Hill, the second Royal Starcher, received an invitation.

For days before the great event the sisters talked of nothing else but the gowns they would wear. Visits to mercers, seamstresses and mantua-makers occupied every minute of their spare time. Abigail chose a dress of ivory brocade with a tiny gold leaf pattern over a quilted petticoat of amber satin. Alice decided on puce.

"To give me colour," she explained at Abigail's protest. "I'm pale as dough."

"But you can rouge. You'll look like your great-aunt."

"I haven't got a great-aunt. Puce," said Alice obstinately, "with a black and silver fringe to tone it down—as Madame Thing suggested—and a striped black and silver petticoat, which is the latest fashion."

Abigail had no more to say. If Alice wished to make a guy of herself, that was her affair. Both were in the flutters, breathless with excitement, palpitating, nervous, as they helped each other dress on that June evening.

Alice, who from idleness and good food had grown fatter, begged Abigail not to lace her 'so cruel tight'. She could not endure the agony.

"You must endure it. Hold yourself in."

Alice held herself in and turned the colour of her gown with the effort.

When at last they were ready, their hair entwined with crystal beads, "which none could guess are not real diamonds," mistakenly said Alice, Abigail as a final touch dabbed perfume behind her ears and on the tip of her tongue, much to Alice's astonishment: "Why do you do that?" she asked, and: "Why do you suppose?" was the tart reply, "to smell nice, naturally."

"Unnaturally, you mean. And what a place to put it—on your tongue!"

In the dainty garden-room, enthroned on gilded chairs backed either side by myrtles, oranges, and every variety of exotic plant in tubs, the stout and beaming hostess and her Consort received the Hills with as much warmth and cordiality as if they too had been ladies of high rank. "Instead of only us," said Alice, very gratified. It was her first formal presentation to the Queen.

The more favoured guests who had attended the banquet were assembled in the music-room to hear the Court lyrist, Tom D'Urfey, sing his latest ballad, " 'Twas within a mile of Edinboro' Town."

The Duchess, with her four beautiful daughters, Lady Rialton, Lady Sunderland, Lady Bridgewater, and Lady Monthermer— Mary, her youngest, had recently married Lord Montague's heir, and had received from the Queen the same substantial wedding portion as that bestowed upon her sisters—were the recognized guests of honour.

Seated in the front row immediately beneath the platform, the girls whispered and giggled behind their fans, while their mother, in her splendid robes and glittering with jewels, accepted homage, applauded Mr. D'Urfey, welcomed the Queen's guests as if they were her own, and was, indeed, the focus of all eyes. Her daughters' four husbands with other less significant persons, were grouped in attitudes along the walls and appeared to be bored to extinction.

Keeping close to Abigail's side, Alice was complaining: "We don't know a soul here but those nose-in-air Churchills. We are nobodies. The Duchess hasn't seen us—and she won't want to."

"I'll pinch you," threatened Abigail, while she kept her smile fixed, "if you don't shut your mouth."

Alice shut it.

The long windows open to the summer night, gave glimpses of a pastoral scene, which a few years later might have been recalled by Watteau. Against a tangled background of dim trees Court ladies in hooped petticoats, head-dresses of feathers, lace, and silver gauze, accompanied by their periwigged cavaliers, strolled through the dusky gardens. Slender voices and decorous laughter mingled with the sound of music to wake the sleeping birds. The brilliant colours of their costumes as they passed, were revealed in momentary flashes from candle-light within. Along the flagged walks rose-trees wound and twisted over trellises; flowers in porcelain pots subdued with fragrance the not so sweet pervading smell of perspiration.

D'Urfey twanged his harpsichord and sang again, this time in Italian.

Abigail gave a glance around. Her quick eye searched the company to find one missing. Would he come? He surely must have been invited.

"Mrs. Hill."

She turned; her limited smile widened in automatic greeting. His exaggerated bow, hand to heart and nose to knees, was, she scathingly considered, too absurd. One would think he had not seen her for a year. Critically she surveyed him. His suit of flesh-pink satin profusely embroidered, his stockings, white with silver clocks, his flaxen furbelow—all were quite impeccable, and must, she thought, have cost his whole year's salary.

"Mr. Masham." She curtsied, extending finger-tips. He bent above them, straightened his back, turned to Alice, bowed to her, and suggested refreshment.

Alice brightened.

To the sisters with equal partiality, he offered his escort and an arm, and led them to a small inner room adorned with Corinthian pillars, friezes, girandoles, and niches containing statues. Here, grouped round a walnut table were discovered Mesdames Danvers, Abrahal and Wanley; and near the service entrance, tactfully placed behind a screen of bay trees, were seated the Queen's dressers to whom the Hills, with one accord, offered barest recognition.

Mr. Masham, having found a table for his ladies, ordered a choice of edibles to make Alice's eyes bulge in anticipation of calves' brain patties with asparagus; neats' tongues in aspic; strawberries steeped in brandy, citron tarts and muscadines washed down with Rhenish wine.

To these delicacies Alice earnestly applied herself, while Abigail nibbled frosted violets. Mr. Masham, after attempting an assortment of conversational preludes to be answered with monosyllabic inattention, lapsed into silence and observed her, of a sudden, all a-sparkle. Her eyes, obstinately lowered, lifted, widened. Her mouth broke into tremulous smiles.

Was this stimulation caused by something he had said? His last remark, concerning a revival of 'Camilla' at the Queen's Theatre in the Haymarket, in which the chief rôle was to be performed—'or rather sung, by Signor Guiseppe Cassani from Italy—have you seen it, madam?' had been answered perfunctorily.

"What? I have . . . No."

And here she was, half risen from her chair, her fan unfurled to look over its edge and away from him. The next moment she had resumed her poise, to pick with dainty fingers at the dish of comfits on the table. Murmuring, "How warm it is!" she vigorously fanned herself and began again to nibble violets. Then, casting a look at the fall of lace and batiste at his neck, fastened with a diamond pin of purest water, she said in a tone of the liveliest interest:

"I do entirely agree. Sir Christopher Wren has indeed performed wonders. Those girandoles!"

Mr. Masham experienced discomfort. The name of Wren, to his knowledge, had not passed his lips. For one moment he asked himself—could she possibly be deaf? If so, she had most successfully disguised her affliction from him, and from everybody else. But deaf or not she was delicious in her unexpected animation.

She raised her head to hold his eyes with hers. The black dilated pupils drowned the green and reflected him—his face, his flesh pink satin shoulders, diminished to a fairy's size. Amazing!

He forgot her sister, scrunching bon-bons happily beside him; he forgot the watchful stare of Mesdames Danvers, Abrahal and Wanley. He forgot his situation; he forgot his manners—everything: remembered only that the urge was on him now to 'try again.'

"I have never," blurted Mr. Masham, "seen you so radiant as

you appear to-night. 'Pon honour, madam, your gown is prodigious becoming."

But it was not at her gown that he gazed. At the corner of her
mouth she had set a heart-shaped patch, and just below her left
eye was another. She placed a brandied strawberry between her
parted lips that were no less red and ripe and tasty . . . Could he
taste them! Mr. Masham broke into a sweat and heard her say
low, softly:

"Nor have I ever before observed that you carry a dimple,
round as a farthing, in your chin. I wonder what that signifies.
They say——"

But what 'they' said of dimples on chins or any other parts,
Mr. Masham was not destined to know. From some reeling
seventh heaven he descended to the depths of abysmal misery and
hate.

"Good evening, little cousin. I hoped to find you here."

The colour that had leapt to her cheeks at his approach, lingered
like a pale sunset as Harley bowed above her hand and turned with
negligent grace to her sister.

"Cousin Alice."

"Sir."

Gobbling the last crumb of a sugared almond, Alice got up to
curtsy.

Intimate indeed is this relationship, reflected Mr. Masham with
excusable contumely. The fact that Mistress Alice, who had been
kept heretofore in the background, was also addressed as 'cousin',
indicated a familiarity with these sisters, or with one of them, that
had not, it seemed, bred contempt.

"Ah, Masham," Harley's careless drawl and the smile that
went with it swept Mr. Masham's smile from his face. "I hear
your elder brother," said the Secretary suavely, "intends to stand
at the next Election. You should follow his example. We need
men of your calibre in the House."

"I have other occupation, sir," retorted Mr. Masham, "and
little time to spare from it to bestow on such absorbing matters,
that are best left to those more suited to strategy than I. Madam,"
he bowed to Abigail, whose fan was raised again to eye level,
"with your permission." And he turned. "Mistress Alice, may I
conduct you to the garden to watch the illuminations?"

"Illuminations?" Alice echoed rapturously. "Are there to be
fireworks?"

Mr. Masham thought so. If Mistress Alice would care to see—
and take the air with him?

Mistress Alice greatly cared to see—and take the air with him.

"Shall we also take the air? There are no fireworks," said Harley, "save those," he stooped to retrieve from the floor Abigail's fan that had dropped, "which you have kindled."

"I, sir?" She was all innocence; wide-eyed.

"Yes, you. But," Harley tendered her the fan and hummed casually the words of D'Urfey's song. " 'Since that his fate,' " he misquoted, " 'intends his amity shall be no dearer, still let him kiss . . . and be friends while you sigh, may he never come nearer . . .' And now, let us walk in the garden."

Three pairs of eyes, hostile, envious, forbearing, watched them pass.

"See," tittered Mrs. Danvers, "how he plays her like a trout upon a hook."

"Well, but if she's his cousin," ventured Mrs. Abrahal, "he is entitled to show her some attention, which is more than others do whom I could name who are closer kin to her than he."

"Cousin! Kin! He's as much her cousin as the cat's." Mrs. Wanley was in full agreement with and sympathy for Mrs. Danvers' criticism, since Mrs. Hill had been of late overweeningly high-crested for such small fry as she professed to be. "Whoever heard her mention him as her relation when she first came to Court? Would she not have boasted round to everyone had she known of it? She didn't—until he chose to tell her, and for his own purpose I'll be bound. Not hers."

"Her relation he may be," Mrs. Danvers hinted darkly, "and more than you may think to look for—above-board."

"Or bed," supplemented the jovial Mrs. Wanley.

Mrs. Danvers received this intimation with delight. "But not in the Bedchamber I'm thinking!"

"And *I'm* thinking," broke in Mrs. Abrahal, uncommonly red in the face, "that if the poor girl's hooked she's to be less blamed than pitied."

"Pitied! Pah!" Mrs. Danvers retorted briskly. "She's diddled you as she diddles the Queen. What of those flagons of wine she wheedled from Mr. Lowe at Windsor when you lay so shattery one would have thought you dying if one hadn't known your vapours were due to your time of life? Beware of her kind intentions, Mrs. Abrahal. I'd as lief trust a rattlesnake as her."

Meanwhile, in the star-silvered garden, the object of these airy explosions walked sedately. Harley slackened his step to her pace, grazing the grass without sound as might the feet of the dead . . . And at that thought a chill cloud brushed her happiness like a breath on glass, as swiftly fading. Just that extramundane quality of his, that subjectiveness, was, she considered, his charm's elusive secret which divided him from others, from all men.

Superimposed on the pellucid dark the jewelled gleam of promenaders lent a vivacious impermanence to tree shadows, flung, black as a witch's cloak, across the lawn. The trick-light of flambeaux ranged along the terrace, brought to emerald metallic life the moon-dusted leaves of box and privet. And suddenly from some near bough, a nightingale sang. Voices were hushed, laughter hesitated, fell to silence. The air trembled in consuming solitary passion downpoured, to ravish and submerge all consciousness beyond the wonder of pure sound. It stopped, and the interrupted flow of talk flitted through the night— "Like bats," murmured Harley, "flapping blind idiot wings in some virginal pearl-grey room." Then, before she could take breath from that, "There's a story in Boccaccio's Decamerone of a nightingale. Do you read Italian?"

She did not.

"A pity. A Frenchman named Le Macon made a mutilated translation. It is said that Savonarola burned the Decamerone in the Piazza della Signoria in Florence before he was himself committed to the flames in that same place—which, however, is improbable, since Shakespeare derived certain of his plays from the tales of Boccaccio."

She could find nothing to say. Her joy in him transcended the polite veneers of conversation. It was for her enough to hear the tone of his temperate cool words rather than their meaning. He told her of his library, his rare editions. He was possessed, he said, of the collector's curse which resembled that of the miser's: the one hoarded coin, he hoarded books, treasure of more worth to him than wealth or honour, human values, human loves. "Some day I will show you my books."

Some day . . . He offered books to be shown uncertainly 'some day'. His library, where was it? At Frampton Castle, his family seat in Herefordshire, or at his London house? She did not know, for he had never told her where he lived. She had heard he had been married and that his wife had died. What more did she know of him? Nothing, beyond his baffling paralogisms that disclosed, withheld, or gave her as little of himself as he might give to a personal tame mouse fed with cheese from his hand . . . A shiver of inward laughter shook her, caught back at his startlingly inconsequent remark:

"I agree that those who court folly should wear a dunce's cap. The grass is damp and your slippers are thin. Here is an arbour. Will you sit awhile?"

A rustic bench hemmed by imponderable walls received them. Sly moonfingers probed warily through chinks. A crazy window, cobweb-veiled, overlooked the privet-hedge of King William's garden. The brooding panoply of night seemed to be alive with unseen flying things and sounds, not human; the hoot of an owl, the pursuit and capture of some small hunted fugitive from field or distant meadow, the muffled death-cry of the killed, the piercing melancholy triumph of the killer: primeval savagery stalking that shiftless carnival parade revealed in silver-gold chaos of moon and torchlight.

She heard Harley hum a tuneless tune and halt on an abrupt unfinished note; and in that urgent pause she found her voice. It was dry, her tongue clove to her palate, but she must break this bursting tension, this unbearable agonizing intimacy of his shoulder touching hers.

"You spoke of folly . . . Whose?"

"Not mine." He smiled dimly. "And not yours."

"You said," she managed to articulate, "court . . . Who would wish to court folly?"

His moon-rayed eyes found hers and held them.

"Who would wish to court wisdom when a fool in his folly is wise?"

She clenched her hands till her nails pierced her palms.

"I cannot," she said distinctly, "understand you. Why will you distort words to make no sense? Must you . . . Why must you torment me?"

She had not meant to say that, and her lips sagged with the shock of it while the blood surged in her ears. She recalled stray threads of conversation, insignificant enough and yet compelling, that emerged from other moments, unforgotten. He had said once —when was it? Yesterday, a week, a month ago? She had lost count of time. 'You and I must not compete. We must conjoin. Your blanched elusive spirit holds unlooked-for possibilities.' And again, 'The artifice of dalliance is not for us. It is inadequate. I ask more of you than your ungiven body . . .' And now, unbelievably, with a savour of wine in the breath of his words:

"If I torment you am I not prolonging my own torment? There is between us—surely you must recognize it—a curious link, a strange invisible cord that binds we two together. I have the quaintest notion that if we are finally to part, if I take my way of life and you take yours, one or both of us will bleed internally. Eternally." He cupped her chin in his hand. She saw his eyes again, down-gazing, contemplative, before hers closed beneath the careful exploration of his lips. But even as she fused and

7

flamed and, unresisting, sank, she was chilled to bemused exasperation. If a star could kiss, so was his touch, as cool and unsurrendered.

"My little nymph," his whisper taunted her too eager yielded mouth, "are you so greedy? This is moon-madness. I am twice your age, and you tempt me to adventure like a boy. I think I never was a boy, as you have never been . . . a woman." And then he put her from him and was upon his feet, alert and listening. He had heard what she had not: a step upon the path behind the privet.

"Come," his fingers trapped her arm to raise her up. Resuming his polite evasive mask, " 'Tis a pity," he said, "that you do not read Italian. Your father was something of a scholar, I believe."

And taking her hand in his, he led her from that place.

She did not see what Harley saw, the hesitant confusion of one who had emerged, a solid shadow, from the deeper shadows of the hedge; the moon's gleam on flaxen furbelow, on livid knuckles clapped to the jewelled hilt of a trifling dress-sword. She did not see, for sight was blinded and senses drugged against her will, her reason, duty; against her better self.

It was midnight and the candles, dying in their crystal lustres, were swathed in shrouds of wax; the guests departing, Prince George yawning, the Queen retiring.

"Hill? Where is Hill?"

The Duchess and her daughters had already left. The few who remained were uncomfortably aware that they should have followed her Grace's example; the Queen tiredly accepted rhapsodic obeisances, gratitude, farewells.

"Mr. Masham." He hurried to her side. "Where is Mrs. Hill? She should be in attendance."

"Mrs. Hill is in the garden, Your Majesty," submitted Mrs Danvers. "She went out with Mr. Harley an hour ago, Madam."

"Then will you have the goodness, Mr. Masham, to go and find Mrs. Hill and tell her we wish to go to bed?"

But Mr. Masham was so long gone upon his search that Mrs Danvers, although not officially on duty, attended Her Majesty to bed.

In the connubial heavily curtained fourposter, the Queen turned from her right side to her left and poked at an umbrageous mound beneath the coverlet.

"George."

From deep amorphous glades embowered in gentle obscurity, from the dawn of a dream to do with a carp, a mottled peculiar carp that rose from a pond to gape at him and eject from its mouth a flagon of wine, the Prince jerked open his eyes, gave a startled snort, and lifted his head from the pillow.

"Who? . . . Est-il possible?"

"George, are you asleep?"

"Na! Not now."

"It was a most successful evening, I think. Don't you?"

"Very. Yah. I have ate too much of stewed carp. The onionss repeat to me. Tell Centlivre not to cook so much with onionss."

"Garlic, dear, not onions."

"Garlic. Onionss. It is the same. I have the belly-ache."

"My darling!" The Queen's hand surveyed her spouse's lower more intimate regions. "Yes, you are very distended. I will ring for a page to bring you the warming-pan."

"It is too hot a night for a warming-pan. I am already too hot. I will take a liquorish powder before breakfast. I have not been relieved since two days."

"George! Dr. Arbuthnot must give you a clyster."

"We will wait, isn't it? If the powder does not . . . then perhaps. Now shall we sleep?"

"Certainly. But first let me ask you this. Did you not think it rather odd that Hill, who is always so punctilious in her attendance, should have to be fetched?"

"Fetched? When? How 'fetched'?"

"Well, George, *fetched*. I had to send Mr. Masham to find her. Danvers said she was walking in the garden with Mr. Harley for an hour."

"Danvers is a gossip," said the Prince profoundly. "I will not have a clyster. Liquorish powder."

"Yes, dear. You shall. To-morrow. For an hour, George. I dote on Mr. Harley, but I wonder that he pays so little heed to the conventions as to take that girl walking in the garden for an hour."

"I am thirsty." The Prince sucked his teeth. "I have a prodigious thirst."

"There should be barley-water beside you. Let me——"

"No. Do not be disturbed. I can reach."

The Prince hoisted himself up and leaned out of bed to fumble for the tinder-box on the top of the commode. Having lighted a candle, he poured a drink from a carafe into a glass, gulped it at a draught and deeply belched.

"That is better. Red wine does not march with onionss."

"Blow out the candle, George."

He blew out the candle.

"George."

"Yah? Yip!" There was another deeper belch, then, "Ah—eh—yah!" And the Prince snuggled down and pulled the covers to his chin.

"George, did you not think Hill looked more than usually peaked to-night? I am sure she is not well."

An indistinguishable sound issued from the pillow.

"I have decided to promote Hill's sister to the Bedchamber to relieve Hill of some of her duties. She has never, to my knowledge, taken leave of absence. It is time she did so. I will send her on a long vacation. Don't you agree?"

There was no answer. And presently:

"George." Again the Queen poked beneath the counterpane to whisper: "Don't snore, dear." And then louder, "George! Don't *snore*!"

CHAPTER SEVEN

ALICE's promotion to the Bedchamber in order that Abigail should enjoy the long vacation on which the Queen insisted, was received with some misgivings by the younger Mrs. Hill.

"I shall never be able to take your place. I'm clumsy and awkward. I know I shall drop those horrid little handleless cups. And what am I to say to her if she asks for 'cold' tea? Am I to give it her?"

"Certainly not. You know Dr. Arbuthnot has forbidden 'cold' tea. All you have to do is to serve it hot and strong, but you mustn't let anyone else infuse it. You must keep the key of the tea-caddy always about your person. Don't let Danvers or the Duchess know where it is."

"I see," said Alice, glum. "And what now of singing? The Queen makes you sing to her. I can't sing. My voice is about as tuneful as a crow's and I only know one piece to play on the harpsichord—'Met I with a Jolly Palmer'. Why does she want to give you a holiday all on a sudden like this?"

"She says I'm looking peaked."

"You always look peaked. Where will you go for your holiday?"

"I don't have to go anywhere. I can stay in the Palace and read and loll and be lazy to my heart's content if I wish, but Dr. Arbuthnot says——"

"Dr. Arbuthnot? Did you consult him?"

"I didn't. The Queen did, on my behalf. She made him examine me when he called this morning to give the Prince a clyster."

"Lord, Abbie!" Alice expressed some faint alarm. "I didn't know you were ill."

"I'm not ill. I'm only sickeningly tired. I've had too many years of waiting upon women, of perpetual genuflexions. My knees are growing corns and the whole of me feels like a drum——" Abigail's voice quivered on a wave of suppressed hysteria—"a *drum* so tight drawn it only needs a special beating to—to burst open."

"Well, I declare!" ejaculated Alice. "And you so calm and self-contained. Who'd have thought it?"

"Yes, who? Who'd have thought that I, the stick, the stone, the maid of all works, has any heart or feeling? Any blood? That's what's wrong with me—too little blood, according to the doctor. I'm to drink physic—black slimy stuff that tastes of iron, to give me blood."

"You're not going to die, are you?" gasped Alice.

"O, God!" Abigail began to laugh and went on laughing till she cried. "If I do, you'll be the death of me. No, I'm not going to die. At least . . . not yet."

"I'll wager there's some," was Alice's ambiguous reply, "who'd wish you would."

"I have no doubt of that." She glanced at her sister's placid moon-round face and smiled thinly. "Come, out with it. What have you heard?"

"Nothing much." Then, because Alice was incapable of prevarication when Abigail looked at her in that particular dragging way of hers which made her feel as if—though not remarkable for sensibility, the unsought notion took Alice by surprise—as if she were a pool containing something drowned, she added uncomfortably; "The same old talk. That you're wheedling yourself into the Queen's affections to oust the Viceroy, and that you're Harley's——"

"Yes, I know. You needn't say it," Abigail interrupted, with her smile fixed.

"'Tool' is what they said. Abbie, don't stare like that! Why should you mind? I wish," exclaimed Alice with unparalleled heat, "he had never come into your life."

Abigail extinguished her smile.

"He? Who?"

"You know very well who. He has as much heart for you as a hawk has for a weasel." And having rid herself of that immense admission, Alice walked to the window that overlooked the court-yard of St. James's. "There's your substance," she stated surlily, "but you can't see him for your shadow."

Abigail stiffened.

"May I ask again to whom or to what you allude?"

"To him." Alice pointed. "Sidling along and very mumpish. He's always mumpish these days, poor gentleman. And there's something else I've heard." She swung round. "He's off to the wars."

Abigail's head went up with a jerk.

" 'Tisn't true!"

"I tell you it is. If you hadn't been so eaten up with Some-body, you would have known what's common knowledge."

"How should I have known? He has never mentioned it to me."

"And I don't suppose he will. He's man enough not to care to dance to your tune when it's played to another. You've ridiculed him, mocked him, made him eat dust——"

"Dust unto dust," murmured Abigail. "I've eaten dust too in my time."

She came and stood by Alice, looking down at Mr. Masham, who was running an expert hand over the legs and hocks of a horse brought for his inspection. His voice drifted up through the open window.

"It don't carry enough weight for what I want and it's too old."

As he turned away his eyes lifted. The girls hurriedly with-drew.

"I told you so," Alice said provokingly. "He's buying a war-horse."

"All luck to him I'm sure," was Abigail's indifferent rejoinder. "I wonder the Prince allows him to go."

It had needed some persuasion. The Prince had at first refused.

"I cannot replace you, Masham, but Marlborough can. He has a thousand men ready waitingk to follow him and I have only you, my friend. I do not care for any other equerry to be so close my friend."

Mr. Masham was touched but unshaken. He said he had fought in the last war as a boy, and now as a man he could not see others older than himself go to *this* war while he stayed behind.

The Prince lifted his great head. "And do you think *I* like to stay behind? I too have offered my service to my Queen and country, but my service is refused. My health will not permit me to—how is it?—strut? in an Admiral's uniform. Do you think I like to look me in the face and say, 'Good man! You stay behind and eat and drink of plenty and play at cards,' when my boy, had he lived, would have——" The wheezing voice cracked. A large red hand came out to wring his gentleman's. "Na! I will not hold you back. It must not be said that George of Denmark has held back a soldier from the war while men are so badly wanted. You must go and—God be with you."

Mr. Masham knelt.

"Na! No, no! You are a soldier now—one of the Queen's soldiers. You shall not kneel to me, who is not a soldier." And as he stooped to raise the blushing Masham, the Prince drew from his pocket a gold snuff-box encrusted with diamonds. "Take this as a token of remembrance—my remembrance. Wear it always against your heart. It is heavy. Who know? It may save you"— the Prince gave him a watery smile—"from a bullet. Your place will wait for you, Masham. Come back soon. And safe."

That was the Prince's unofficial farewell. The Queen undisguisedly wept.

"We, the Prince and I, will miss you sadly. This cruel war! Pray God protect you, Colonel Masham."

He had left his regiment with the rank of Captain. He rejoined it promoted, at Her Majesty's command.

That was her gift to him.

He spent a week at his parents' house and returned on the eve of his departure. He did not seek to take his leave of Mrs. Hill. She sought him in his chambers.

She brought Alice with her to conciliate propriety, and found him supervising his valet's packing of his baggage. He was in tie-wig and uniform which she thought became him vastly, and told him so.

His smile was a failure.

"I am honoured, ladies, to receive you, but must beg you to accept my apologies for this disorder." He indicated the yawning valise filled with shirts, jackboots, nightshifts. His sword lay on the table.

"I could not let you go," Abigail braced herself to say, "without wishing you Godspeed."

"I take it more than kindly, madam."

He stood stiffly at attention, while his eyes roamed the room, as if to recall to his memory some forgotten item. Her presence, it was evident, impeded his arrangements; and flushing, embarrassed, she gave him her hand. He bent over it formally and bowed again to Alice, who blurted:

"Sir, if you should meet our brother——"

He produced that shadow of his smile.

"I hope to meet your brother, Mistress Alice, at headquarters. I understand he is now one of his Grace's aides-de-camp. Can I take him a message?"

"Our love," said Abigail softly.

"Your love," he automatically repeated, but still he looked at Alice.

"Our united love, sir, if you please," she said. "God save you, Colonel Masham."

He went with them to the door and bowed them out.

In silence they walked the length of the gallery and stood aside at the head of the staircase for someone to pass, cloaked, hooded, in a hurry. She barely glanced at the Hills, who watched her stride with mannish steps along the corridor, searching the names on the doors.

"Who is she?" Alice asked.

"Mrs. Forester of course."

"Why 'of course'?"

"She means to marry him."

"I don't believe it. Unless," Alice said obscurely, "he may be forced to marry *her*. There's a brazen minx she is to visit him alone! Why wasn't she at the Queen's soirée last June with the other Maids of Honour?"

"Because she had the smallpox," Abigail answered briefly, and proceeded down the stairs.

"And if she hadn't had the smallpox," said Alice at her heels, " 'tis likely Mr. Masham would have been better occupied than to go sneaking after you. 'Twould serve you right if that bouncing Jane *does* marry him. And if he gets killed out there," she added grimly, "you'll have only yourself to blame."

So Colonel Masham left St. James's to join the life and death struggle of war; and none in the Palace missed him save the Queen and the Queen's Consort.

He was replaced by Mr. Kirk, second Groom of the Chamber, and to console himself for the absence of his favourite equerry, Prince George resumed his hobby of carpentering, discarded since the death of his son. He built a model man-of-war and sailed it on Rosamond's Pond in St. James's Park, watched by Mr. Kirk and a group of giggling pages. And so engrossed was the Prince upon his latest occupation that he could rarely be persuaded to attend when Mr. Secretary Harley called on the Queen to condole, advise, and listen sympathetically to her complaints of:

"This Whig Junto, Mr. Harley. I find Lord Somers' speeches inexpressibly tedious. He sends me to sleep. Lord Halifax is the best of them. I have a tender spot for *him*. He wrote such charm-

ing verses for me on my wedding day. But Lord Sunderland——"
The Queen suppressed a shudder and glanced fondly at her spaniel
bitch, nursed on the Secretary's knee. "She likes you, Mr. Harley.
She is most cautious of caresses from stranger as a rule. Come
sweetheart, pimpimpim! They lose their coats at this season of
the year. She will cover you in hairs. Come to mother, darling.
Pray don't let her annoy you, Mr. Harley."

"She doesn't annoy me, Madam. I love dogs."

"So do I." Their mutual affection for dogs was yet another
bond between them. " 'Tis a Stuart characteristic to love dogs.
Minette's pedigree goes back to the famous strain bred by my
Uncle, King Charles. We were speaking of Lord——?"

"Sunderland, Madam."

"Yes, Sunderland. The Duchess tells me he is brilliant. If so, he
obscures his light beneath an unfortunate manner. He professes
to have no respect for Princes. That is not to say, I hope, he has
no respect for me?"

The Queen paused. Mr. Harley was smiling blandly at
Minette.

"And then——" The Queen unknit her brow, following his
smile, "And then there is Lord Orford. The Prince refuses to
speak to him—and I certainly will not receive him at Court after
he has dared to criticize the Prince's command of the Navy. And
as for Lord Wharton—did he not write the words of that disgraceful song, 'Lillibulero'?"

"Did he, Madam?"

Mr. Harley evinced, successfully, amaze.

The Queen nodded her head.

"So I am told. He was supposed to be a great debauchee in
his youth. Have you heard, Mr. Harley, that . . ."

Yes, Mr. Harley had heard.

The exchange of confidences, wittily expressed by Mr. Harley,
made the Queen laugh till she blushed.

"Really, Mr. Harley, I can't believe—I *must* not believe—such
naughtiness. My Ministers are——"

"Not angels, Madam." He added, to her still blushful hesitation, "nor are we always Ministers . . . of grace. We are but
human."

"Fie!" She wagged a roguish finger; and from his veiled look,
that seemed to hold within it something more than homage due to
Royalty, she looked away and dimpled, in the tremors. Mr.
Harley was so droll and . . . *very* human.

It might have dismayed the Duchess if she had known of those
intimate gatherings round the tea-table in the Queen's Green

Closet, followed by the strains of Purcell played so sweetly on the harpsichord by Mrs. Hill, returned from her vacation still 'peaked' and more than ever silent; or had she known of the talk that ranged from King's Charles's spaniels to Hanover and the problem of succession; or that the Queen's chief medical adviser, Dr. Arbuthnot, was frequently invited to complete the quartet, and was, besides a most able physician, an ardent Jacobite.

But the Duchess did not know. She was entirely preoccupied with the building of Blenheim, and quarrelling with Mr. Vanbrugh, who refused to do as he was told or as she wished, and must for ever contradict her orders and go rushing up to London vowing never to return. He always did. He was not disposed to forfeit the vast sum he had demanded for his work.

And could she but have known, the building of Blenheim may in part have contributed to those many factors in the Duchess's disarmament against that secret insidious attack which, when it came, found her so completely unprepared, and shattered her whole life and its foundations.

Yet her life upon its surface had never been more radiant, its foundations more secure. Her husband, the great Duke, was again the nation's darling. Repeated victories had put fresh heart into the Allies to turn the enemy in his tracks and press him back upon the Netherlands. Once more a courier rode hell for leather through war-racked territory to kneel at the feet of the Queen with the news of the Duke's latest triumph, the battle of Ramillies. Again in town and capital the streets were one continuous illumination; again the beacons flared, again the drive through cheering joyous crowds to give thanks at St. Paul's. And then anxiety renewed, and repeated murmurs of dissatisfaction. The war was costing far too much. Hostilities in Flanders were at a deadlock. The Duchess, the Tories' butt and censure, had been openly accused of undue interference in political affairs, and for her coercion of Godolphin and her husband to the Whigs.

It was about this time that the Queen suffered that astonishing bombardment of abusive letters from 'Mrs. Freeman', in which she accuses 'Mrs. Morley' of 'indifference and contempt, which does not so much surprise me as to hear my Lord Treasurer say you have complained of me to him . . .'

Mrs. Morley may have had her reasons for disguising her complaints. She had been given of late too strong a dose of Mrs. Freeman's vehemence when crossed.

And the tide of hostilities rose between the two opposing factors, both in and out of Parliament. Not since the Civil War had the nation stood so ruthlessly divided. Even the sisters Hill held private arguments together. Abigail accused Alice of undue moderation.

"You're half-hearted. You should declare yourself for one side or the other."

"I'd sooner be half-hearted," was Alice's reply, "than declare myself a Jack."

Abigail pinkened.

"When have I declared myself a Jack?"

Alice pondered, to say positively: "I judge your preference by your associates. I am surprised you can tolerate that foul-mouthed gin-drinking old Irish bawd and her Jacobite songs. And as for that evil Mrs. Manley and her poisonous pen——"

"Mrs. Manley is a writer of high intelligence," broke in Abigail hotly, "and a powerful supporter of the Cause."

"What Cause? The Cause of underhand intrigue and a promoter of all this political hubbub? I don't know what you hope to gain by dabbling in dirt, or——" Alice paused and asked significantly, "don't you know you're being used?"

Abigail turned from pink to white.

"Used? What do you mean by 'used'?"

"What do you think I mean? I'm not *quite* a fool if you are. And if you go on the way you're going you'll find yourself in gaol —if not in worser case, my girl."

At which stupefying transmutation from Alice's habitual placidity to depths of dark insinuation, Abigail flushed again while she collected, ineffectually, her forces.

"I'll thank you for your warning—clear as mud."

"There's no mud in my eye, at any rate," said Alice; and having given Abigail time to swallow that, she added with unconcerned irrelevance, "What gowns shall we wear to-night?"

"To-night?" Abigail queried blankly. "Wear?"

"Have you forgot we are to dine with the Doctor?"

She had forgotten, having much else on her mind and a letter from the Duchess on her person. This, purloined from the Queen's correspondence, would be shown, when opportunity arose, to him who held her as he held the Queen, in thrall.

"Yes. What gowns *shall* we wear?"

So it was amity restored again with talk of gowns; but that startling revelation of Alice's profundity was a shattering experience, a flagrant transgression of the code that all their lives had nominated Abigail the leader, Alice the led. And now a wholly unsuspected personality had uprisen to confound her with Delphic and sinister augury . . . Mud in her eye! What next! What next?

Mrs. Arbuthnot, the doctor's wife, a thin hen-faced woman with faintly surprised eyebrows and a perpetually apologetic air, had never yet accustomed herself to the prominent position her husband occupied as medical adviser to the Queen. A chance service rendered to Prince George when he had cut his finger to the bone while carpentering, had brought the doctor to Her Majesty's notice. She delighted in his blunt out-spokenness, his Scottish accent, his breezy, sometimes playful, manner of address—"Hearken to me, my leddy. If ye'll no' do as ye're bid and tak' the physic I prescribe for ye, I'll have to give your Queenship what I give my daughters when they refuse their porridge."

"And what may that be, Doctor?"

"Brimstone and treacle, Ma'am. Part penance and part purge."

And he was the only one of the Court physicians who knew how to treat that recurrent trouble in the Queen's eyes from which her son Gloucester had suffered, and with which in later years she too had been afflicted. Dr. Arbuthnot came daily to apply a feather dipped in sweet oil to the dry caked lids; and afterwards he would sit and chat with her and give her, as did dear Mr. Harley, the news of the Town. In all Anne's experience of doctors, he was not only the most entertaining, most versatile and witty, but the one physician whose visits she enjoyed. That he might always be available at shortest notice, she had allotted him a suite of rooms in St. James's Palace.

Mrs. Arbuthnot, shunned by the ladies of the Court who were prepared to receive the Queen's doctor but not the doctor's wife, was grateful to the young Hills for their polite acceptance of her invitations to tea, dinner, cards; for their gratifying interest in her small-talk and her children; and for the fact that despite their high family connections, they, like herself, were not 'received'.

The dinner to which on that evening in the late spring of 1707 Abigail and Alice were invited, was an intimate affair attended by no other ladies and three gentlemen: Harley, St. John, and one Matthew Prior, a recent acquaintance of the doctor. "And how to feed them," lamented his wife, "I do not know, for they drink so much—and Mr. St. John is so grand, and as for this Mr. Priam——"

"Prior, my dear, Prior," the doctor corrected. "A poet, a Master of Arts, of amative pursuits and of diplomacy. The two distinctions often march together. He was, besides, Secretary to Lord Portland's Embassy in Paris under the late King William. And now ye can go dress yourself in your best, and put a patch on your chin where ye carry a pimple, for ye've come out in a spring rash like the suet-pudding my good mother used to call 'Spotted

Dog'. As for food for these rare fellows, give them red meat and red wine with some body to't. Stick to red dishes and I'll be satisfied, and so will they—and dinna fash yourself."

But Mrs. Arbuthnot continued to 'fash' herself thoughout the excellent meal she had provided, and which, in slavish obedience to her husband's command, consisted mainly of underdone sirloin of beef, supplemented by red speckled trout, a lobster, jellied prawns, rhubarb tarts spiced with cinnamon, red currant pie, and red wine.

Seated next the lordly St. John, Alice was so captivated by his handsome looks, his eloquence, and the attention which, between courses, he lavished upon her, that she lost for once her appetite for food. And when the circulation of claret had been succeeded by port, and the talk among the gentlemen had become more general and boisterous, she sank into a stupor of speechless admiration, spellbound, beatific.

Prior was ragefully attacking Godolphin.

"The fellow's so utterly sunk in his stables he can't smell the Augean filth from ours. If it were not for the Queen's—and her Viceroy's—fatuosity, he'd have been out and you in, Harley, at the last reshuffle."

"Nay now, Matt," Arbuthnot's lean hatchet-face smilingly broadened, while his cool professional eye noted the high flush on Prior's prominent cheek-bones, "I'll tolerate no Party personalities nor disfavour at my board. Fill up your glasses, lads. Maggie, bring out the Stilton. We've a fine prime Stilton cheese here, sirs. Douse it with the Porto, Mag, and let it soak. A plague on these French wines! Give me the wine of Portugal for preference. And take that to yourself, Robin. Port won't touch your gizzard, but this French vinegar will rot your guts. Maybe I'm prejudiced, but the duty we pay on it since the war is not worth the . . . richt, sir! Claret if ye prefer it. Maggie! Hand round the claret to Mr. Harley. A grand wife that," the doctor added in a loud aside. It was evident his preference for port had markedly increased his good humour. "She has that rarest quality in women—a short tongue and a long memory. I told that good lass o' mine—'Prepare a dinner, Mag, and make it red——' and see now how red it is—as red as her face, poor worrm. Come sit ye down, Maggie, and drink a wee drop an ye can stomach it . . . Mrs. Hill, Mrs. Alice, a wee drop o' the Porto? Nay, lassies, it won't harm ye. 'Twill put some colour in your cheeks. I never did see such a pair o' pale sisters. Porto for you, Matt? How's the cough?"

Prior shrugged his slender shoulders.

"I still cough despite your blisterings, and I sweat like a pig at night."

The doctor glanced at him shrewdly and nodded.

"Ye should take a diplomatic post in Spain for choice, and when this pest of war is over I'll be sending ye there for a lengthy vacation. Ye require the sun in your blood, as do we all. But we're a hardy race, we Britons. We need to be, in this fog-bound plague pit of a climate—a race o' bulldogs and John Bulls."

"John Bulls?" queried Harley, alert.

"Ay, 'tis a notion o' me own which will more substantially materialize when I have found time to exchange the surgeon's knife for the author's pen. I intend to exemplify, in moderate satire, the British characteristics which, take it how ye will, are in the bulldog. A grand beast that. He's thorough, he's loyal, and he's obstinate. Should he find a delinquent he'll punish him fairly. He'll catch on with his teeth and he'll ne'er let go. So should his master follow his example. A courtly life is no life for a man, tripping hither and thither on high red heels, suffocating in a periwig and stinking o' musk and amber——" the doctor bestowed an amiable grimace on St. John, who was flicking snuff from his cravat with a lace-edged handkerchief. "Let him join that honest band of brave lads who circle Britain and are bred from the rich earth, born of good yeomen stock, as was I in Kincardineshire. And now, friends," the doctor jovially concluded, "a toast. *The* toast!"

The men stood, the women remained seated while the toast was drunk in silence with a spectacular finale from St. John, who dashed his empty glass to the floor and ground his heel upon it.

Mrs. Arbuthnot gave a startled gasp.

"No other toast," cried St. John, "shall be drunk from that glass. I beg forgiveness for the breakage, madam," said he, bowing to his hostess.

"'Tis of no consequence, sir," Mrs. Arbuthnot untruthfully assured him.

"Indeed," St. John said carelessly, "it is. I will send you a new set of glass goblets."

"I beg you, sir . . . No. I . . ."

But Mrs. Arbuthnot's feeble remonstrance was loudly interrupted by her husband.

"Never refuse a gift, Mag! By all means, Harry, send the goblets, and ye can break 'em again in the same good cause."

"Yesterday," said Prior to no one in particular as the laughter subsided, for the gentlemen had now reached that convivial stage when laughter flows as easily as words, "yesterday I ran across a fellow at the Cock in Threadneedle Street. He was pencilling verses on his tablets and drinking brandy punch. 'Sir,' says he, accosting me, 'I perceive you are a poet.' "

"Now," murmured Harley in Abigail's ear, "he is off on his Pegasus-winged hobby. If he'd stick to his pen and forsake politics he'd leave some memory more than his coughin' when he goes to his coffin."

"Lord, lord!" Abigail turned her eyes ceilingward, and pointedly sighed.

"I agree," grinned Harley. " 'Tis a direful habit to pun—and to pun poorly. Pass the wine."

This peremptory command was not, she perceived, addressed to her, but to his host, who after refilling his own glass and Prior's, complied with the utmost good humour.

" 'So,' said I," continued Prior, undeterred by the murmur of talk around the table, " 'How do you know that I follow your Muse, young man?' 'Why, sir,' says he, ' 'tis writ in letters of fire on your forehead.' 'Come then,' says I, 'give me your verses and I'll give you my honest criticism of them.' 'Faith, sir,' quoth he, 'there's no honest criticism to be found in poet to poet, nor in your professed critic neither, being cursed as he is with a kind of special malignity that exudes from his sick humorous condition— and not humorous mark you in the sense of wit, but of distemper, that turns him to snarl at your syntax and discard your quaint conceits of rhyme in favour of unintelligible explication. Then, sir,' says this young gentleman while he sipped sourly at his punch with which I could see he was not on the best of terms, 'when his first poetic stammering is tossed proudly from his quill to find favour from those readers who care more for rousing verse than for all your dithyrambics, your classical odes, your scarifying satires, or what have you else of academic pickings, then, sir, before the ink is dry upon the page, your disgruntled critic will be on your heels to flay you because you are paid in fair coin for having tickled the tenderest parts of public fancy. Is this poetic justice?' asks my particular young poet. 'No, 'tis not. 'Tis catch-penny,' yowl the catchpennies who cannot themselves earn one honest groat in good verse-making, nor in their own bad prose!"

"And who is your particular young poet, Matt?" asked Harley as Prior paused to belch.

"He gave me his name. 'Tis Gay."

"A gay name?" quered St. John, patting an open yawn.

"No, Gay. John Gay. Yet his nomenclature belies him. He is anything but 'gay.' " Prior's voice began to trip. "He's suffering his labour pains an's not yet delivered of his firs' born. I was, however, impelled t'impress upon my young bragga—braggadocio thishstirring fact—that no cr'ative artist, writer, poet, poetaster nor polit'cal philanderer, but must approach his life's work with humility. How many times have I been told by third-rate mediocrities, swollen with the fat of their importance: 'See now, I have here a most excellent tragical, comical, philosophical something of wonder, my own life story in three volumes, unexampled of its kind. 'Tis no hardship, but a simple thing to write a book.' Holy Heaven!" Prior banged his fist on the table to make the glasses jump, "if they could know the heart-yearning drudgery and blood-sweat, the black sullen rage of 'spair tha' goes to make one small poem—these ig'rant unschooled putts would not talk so glib of books and penmanship, but would go bang. So rot their bowels!" He belched again, and rather green about the gills, got up from his chair and bowed extensively to the ladies.

"With you p'mission, graces, I mus' leave you before I am dis. . . graced."

And he lurched, swaying, from the room.

"Poor Mr. Prior, he is sadly affected," murmured Mrs. Arbuthnot, and catching Abigail's eye, she asked diffidently, "Would it please you to withdraw, Mrs. Hill?"

It pleased her greatly to withdraw.

"Mr. Prior is so delicately constituted," Mrs. Arbuthnot volunteered, when they had retired to the adjoining parlour, "he is more easily overcome than other gentlemen of hardier disposition. The Doctor tells me he is the son of a joiner—or is it a footman? I forget which. But I have no objection to that. I come of humble stock myself. Not highly born, like you, Mrs. Hill, who are so close related to the Duchess and Mr. Harley." Her timid hen's eyes wavered to the door. "I hope, Mr. Priam—Prior, I should say—will not become unconscious. The last time—which was the first time he dined here—he lay in the hall for an hour, and the Doctor had finally to hold him up by his ankles with his head in a tub to pour the wine out of him. The Doctor insisted I provide red meat and red wine, although, Mrs. Hill, I had my private doubts of it."

As Mrs. Hill had hers.

When presently the survivors of the feast rejoined the ladies, Abigail was called upon to sing. And having obliged and been vociferously applauded, her host suggested a game of bassett.

Harley begged to be excused. St. John accepted Alice as his partner, "which leaves my choice," declared the genial Arbuthnot, "between my wife and you, Mistress Abigail—unless you prefer to take a hand later?"

She did prefer to take a hand later.

The Arbuthnots followed the fashion of early dinner, and although they had sat at table throughout the afternoon, twilight had not yet spread its bridge of dusk across the day.

Harley strolled to the window overlooking the park and motioned Abigail to his side. Unlatching the casement, he leaned out for air, on which was borne the scent of sun-filled hay and clover fields. On the whitening sheen of Rosamond's Pond waterfowl rested undisturbed by the familiar saunterings of fashionable folk.

"Shall we join them?" suggested Harley; and at her doubtful look in the direction of the card-players he smiled.

"Do not fear to offend propriety . . . Madam," approaching his hostess he asked, "have I your permission to escort my little cousin to the Mall while your game proceeds? Your good man tells me I sit too much and should walk more. I am willing enough to take his advice, but unwilling to walk alone. I promise to return Mistress Abigail to your charge within this next half hour."

And then he bent his head to peer at the flustered lady's cards, spread fanwise in her hand.

" 'Tis always a safer policy to hold your heart," he said, "and play the knave."

"Nay now, Robin!" cried the doctor, "I'll not have you play my wife's game to Harry's disadvantage. This is a match of skill between him and myself, for the ladies, God bless 'em, know no more of the cards than which is their fronts and their backs. Your deal, Mistress Alice. Away wi' ye, Rob, ye distract me and mine. . . . Hey, Maggie, hold up your cards! Ye give your game away, girl. Hold 'em up."

Abigail sped to her room to replace her satin slippers with walking shoes. Having covered her light dress with a dark cloak, she rejoined Harley at the side entrance to the Mall.

"But why," he murmured, "the vizard?"

Her eyes shone greenly through the slits in the velvet mask she held before her face.

"I might be recognized."

"And if so, what then? Do you think you will be branded wanton for honouring your cousin with your company? Come, shed your fears and enjoy with me this marvellous fair evening."

The sun had spent itself in one last pouring radiance that lingered on the tree-tops massed in fullest leaf against a saffron-tinted sky. And now, as day marched nightward, so did the belles in fly-caps, flounced petticoats, laced aprons, hoops and patches, give place to the more modestly attired young seamstresses, milliners and serving-maids. The beaux in their square-tailed satin coats with absurd little hats a-top of their wigs, escorted their ladies to the waiting chairs and coaches, and returned to out-rival the 'prentice lads, office clerks, and valets dressed to kill in their masters' leavings.

Courting couples sat on benches, full of sighs and giggles; or mutely entwined against some sheltering hedge, stood oblivious to everything beyond themselves. Disbanded officers in rusty uniforms leered and ogled the girls, evading the more subtle advances of prowling professionals. For what they might, with luck, be offered free of charge they were not prepared to pay. Others, with pockets better lined, succumbed to invitation and were walked off to make a night of it in the brothels of Old Drury.

As they emerged from the Palace gate, Harley clasped his right hand over Abigail's as it lay in the crook of his arm. He felt her shiver.

"Are you cold?"

"No."

She was torn between consuming happiness and the blurred shame of her surrender to his touch that tormented to prolong, but never to appease, her urge and ache for him. In that lay his power. O, she knew it, as, in his epicurean discrimination, so did he. . . . What now did he want of her, ask from her?

She was soon to know.

"The letter of which you spoke—you have brought it?"

"Yes."

Her feet dragged in the grass. He guided her to a seat, islanded in solitude beside the osiers that fringed the water's edge.

"Let me see it. No, you had best read it to me. The light is fading and your eyes are younger than mine."

"You can read it for yourself."

They spoke in whispers, although there was none within sight or sound. She lifted her petticoat and drew from its pocket a folded paper. He took and scanned it, holding it close to his eyes.

" 'Tis plaguey long. I can't read the whole of this in the dusk. I'll have to take it home with me."

"No, you can't. I must return it, now, to-night, before she misses it." She peered over his arm. "I can prompt you if you cannot see the words—I should know it by heart. I've read it aloud every day for a week! The doctor won't let her read any-thing—not even letters—while her eyes are bad."

"But this," Harley ejaculated softly, "is a masterpiece of inso-lence. Does Sarah think by such abusive hammering to gain her ends? You know why it has been written?"

Abigail shook her head.

"To me it makes no sense. I only know it hurts the poor dear to that extent she has come almost to enjoy the pain it gives her. I have begged her to destroy it."

"Destroy it? My good child, never! 'Tis a weapon to hold and to keep. You must watch that the Queen holds it." And passing an arm under her cloak to clasp her waist, he drew her to him while in silence, together, they read:

'*From Mrs. Freeman to Mrs. Morley:*

'Can flatteries in so short a time have such power? Can you think it safer to take advice from those you have little or no experience of than from those who have raised your glory higher than was ever expected? . . . There is no perfection in this world, and whoever will be honest, does one in Mrs. Morley's service more than in venturing a hundred lives for her, and if I had as many I could freely hazard them all to convince her (though I am used as I don't care to repeat) that she never had a more faithful servant. For nothing sits so heavy on the heart as to be thought wrong by Mrs. Morley, who I have made the best return to that any mortal ever did, and what I have done has rarely been seen but upon a stage . . .'

"That is so certain," Harley said in chuckling parenthesis.

'. . . most people liking better to do themselves good than really to serve another, but I have more satisfaction in losing Mrs. Morley's favour upon *that* principle than any mercenary courtier ever had in the greatest riches that has ever——'

"Poh!" Again Harley interrupted himself to exclaim, "here's naught but the most illiterate blather, and serves me nothing but to point the further evidence that she is determined to force upon the Queen a Marlburian family Junto. She has been yelping at her these six months to promote Sunderland as Secretary."

"But you," Abigail said, "are Secretary. Will you allow yourself to be deposed for him?"

"My dear, surely you know that nominally there must be two of us? Hedges is to be put down and Sunderland put up. Your admirable relative will batter the Queen with her ram of a son-in-law until for very weariness she will give in. Agad, I like the naïve reference to 'mercenary courtiers'. That, coming from the Freeman, is sublime. She has evidently overlooked the mere trifling sum of ninety thousand pounds of public money she has appropriated to herself and the Duke. . . . Keep this. It may be useful. . . . See," he added musingly as she returned the letter to its hiding-place, "how time sifts the gold from the dross. Both my father and my grandfather were Roundheads, and here am I, fighting the backwash of Cromwellian hypocrisy with which the Whigs have built their sand-house of dissension. I thank you, child, for your vigilance." He gave a cautious glance around before he bent to brush her cheek with his cool lips. "It is the fate of some to move silently behind the scenes of critical affairs, unrecognized and unacknowledged, but none the less influential in the sequence of events that go to the making of history. Such a one—who knows?—are you. We are faced to-day with an unexampled division of parties and the Government is a door that swings open both ways."

"A door——" she lifted her love-warmed face to his—"of which you hold the key."

He stroked back a stray lock of hair from her forehead.

"Yes. The door opens, when I will it, on my side that you and I may work together, as do all things in God's sight, for good."

The last liquid gold had drained from the tree-tops and from the tender rose-tinted clouds above. Shadows lengthened to pursue the twilight and enclose them in its secrecy.

For good? . . . Her heart narrowed. Were these stealthy ways through which he led her to the boundaries of passion's promise unfulfilled, for good? Then, as his arms held her closer and more tenderly, doubt fled.

No word passed between them. He had never spoken, he would never speak of love in these moments of love's mockery, of slow, adventurous caresses that roused her to a gentle torment of frustration, a pulsing surge and throb of senses frayed, uneased, to melt on a whimpering sigh.

His eyes gazed down at her where she lay limp and slackened in his arms, her shamed face hidden in the shelter of his sleeve.

"I never want to possess you." His words, soft, calculated, fluttered over her nape, where the dishevelled curls had parted.

"I want never to possess you more than in this quintessence of desire, exquisitely delayed." He got upon his feet, stretched his hands and raised her. "I leave others, less selective, to their petty probing lusts that once satisfied are at once discarded. But your equivocal virginity is immensely more alluring than the voluptuous offerings of——"

"Stop! I can't—I *can't*——" She hushed the scream in her voice to say with controlled calm, "I cannot endure these post-mortems. I am become your creature. With you I die my little deaths. Is not that enough? Why must you resurrect me? If you will not—do not——" She faltered, then went on resolutely, "if you do not want me as a man should want his woman, *any* woman, then leave me, at least, my illusions."

"Come, come." He took her hand in his. "What a sensitive mouse it is. Would you have me pleasure myself with you as I might were you *any* woman? I set you higher. I refuse to rape you, if that's what you are asking."

"O, God!" She halted and came close to him. Seen in the gathering dusk, her face was pinched and livid. Raising her fists, she clenched them to beat upon his chest with impotent puny blows.

"I hate—I hate you——" She unfisted her hands and let them fall to her sides, saying wearily: "And I hate myself for the thing that you have made me. A thing that creeps to your arms in hiding, and always in darkness. Have you no heart for me? Am I——" she swallowed her words. No. She could not sink to this self-degradation, could not whine for more than these furtive ephemeral joys she so hungrily snatched, as a begging spaniel grabs at a tit-bit. She repressed a shudder. She must accept what he gave, unquestioning, as she accepted him for what he was. . . . But what was he?

He walked on. She watched his graceful figure move across the grass. Now she had disgusted him, had wallowed in self-pity, had become loathsome in her sight and his. He turned, came back to her and held her face between his hands. Her hood had fallen from her hair and hung on her shoulders by its loosened ribbon.

With careful precision he adjusted it, and lowering his lips to her forehead said softly, "How it loves to flagellate itself. How truly feminine! Even while it indulges its dainty appetite it must decry its need and sink to self-induced abasement. There is no shame in hunger, sweet. The shame lies in over-eating, in which the best of us are apt to indulge. There are, however, obstacles which you seem to disregard. I cannot have you, as, dare I dwell on it, I might want to have you."

"Why not?" She caught at his wrist and shook it frenziedly. "Why not, when I would give you all—all of me? Not in marriage. I am not asking you for marriage, but to end this misery of love-play that taunts my womanhood. I can't—I cannot endure——" Tears drenched her eyes; she widened them and shook her head as if to shake those tears away, but they brimmed over and rolled down her cheeks. Her hood had fallen back again. She looked very young, forlorn, and lost.

"Like a hurt child," he murmured with rare tenderness, "asking for its broken toy to be made whole. I wouldn't have you otherwise than as you are, my little sweet."

"But I," she flung back at him, "would have you otherwise. I would. I would be glad and proud if you professed for me those same petty lusts you despise. Your way is not my way of . . ." Her lips trembled. "I cannot call it love. You make me feel as if I were not as other women. Or is it . . . that you are not as other men?"

To this he made no immediate answer, but again to take her hand and lead her on.

"Let us hurry. We will be missed and our hostess in a pother. I think the time," he said clearly, "is come to end our 'love-play' as you so charmingly call it. I forget when I am with you that I am old enough to be your father. If I had known you ten years ago——" He was suddenly, and for the first time in his life, at a loss for words. The girl's white patient face, swept clear of that first wild gust of emotion, was like a ravished windflower, devoured—he savoured the notion grimly—by a slug.

"But ten years ago," he continued in his unslurred even tones, "you were scarce out of your nursery, and I was widowed and married again. You must come to my house and meet my wife."

There was a moment's silence; then, high and shrill as the call of the water-fowl circling the pond, she echoed him:

"Your *wife*?"

"But surely. . . . How dark it grows. The moon is not yet risen. Your hood is off again. Let me tie it." And as if indeed she were his daughter, he knotted its ribbons under her chin and pulled her cloak more snugly round her shoulders.

"I did not know," she said, dry-mouthed, "that you had been twice married."

"Did you not?" he answered lightly. "I always thought you did."

"No. Foolishly, I . . . didn't."

Her knees sagged under her as she walked, as if each step must put her down. Shrinkingly she raised her mask before her face to shield it from the inquisitive stare of a stroller in the Mall. "Why do you not bring your wife to Court? I would——" to herself her voice was unpardonable: a timorous panting bleat. "I would have been happy to have met her."

His hand sought hers beneath her cloak.

"How needlessly you suffer! I beg you to believe I had not the least idea you were unaware of my marriage." He spoke sincerely, gazing down at her with troubled eyes. "Would I have been so utterly a brute as to misguide you wilfully? You see——" the mesmeric touch of his fingers holding hers lulled her to a dazed acceptance of his words, "I have never regarded marriage in its possessive sense of a joined feather-bed existence. The Greeks understood so well the difference between the woman who is essentially a wife and she who is essentially hetaera."

"The Greeks may"—she loosed her bitten underlip with an ooze of blood on it—"they may have understood, but I do not. What do you mean by 'hetaera'?"

She heard his whispered laugh.

"You are always so deliciously receptive. Even now, when you believe yourself deserted, shattered, your eager searching mind must question what and why. . . . The hetaera was the most exquisite cultural facet of all that is feminine in woman. She whom the Greeks loved; but they married the others and bred from them. The hetaeræ were, in all probability, epicene—half girl, half Ganymedes, as, I think, are you—in your superior intelligence—to that of the average female. If I had my way, I would never let you out of my sight. I would keep you in a casket, my hetaera. As it is——" he shrugged and opened the gate in the garden wall.

"As it is," she finished for him bitterly, "I still have, it seems, my uses—in your sight. Are you not coming in with me?"

"No. I have a slight emotional conflict to discuss with myself and . . . myself. Good-night, little lover." He crushed her hand in his and let it go. "You *are* my little lover, very dear to me. And very gentle."

She watched him walk unhurriedly away. She watched till the dark enwrapped him; then she turned and closed, carefully, the gate.

BOOK THREE
(1707–1714)

CHAPTER ONE

MRS. DANVERS, in a state of nervous tension, hovered about her table, fingering the china, rearranging the dishes of ratafia and angel cakes, with one eye on the clock and another on the tea-urn. Would she come or would she not?

Mrs. Danvers had been at pains to impress upon the lady that she had a matter of greatest importance to divulge, a matter which she deemed it her bounden duty to deliver in privacy and strictest confidence.

Her Grace's curiosity was piqued. Her Grace had sent a note to say she would attend on Mrs. Danvers at four of the clock.

As the clock chimed the hour Mrs. Danvers gave a quick survey of the circular room to see that no last touch had been forgotten, that the bowls of early dahlias and late roses were displayed to their most colourful advantage on tables, window-sills, and tall-boys: that her page was in attendance at the door; that the curtains were drawn sufficiently to cool the low-ceiled room, yet leave enough of sunlight to penetrate the darker corners. Although Mrs. Danvers' suite at Windsor Castle was not remarkable for space, being small and stuffy and situated in a tower, its windows overlooked the Great Park with a view of grassland, forest trees and a glimpse of the river winding through fields of ripening corn.

A scratch at the door sent Mrs. Danvers in a hurry to her chair behind the urn.

"Come."

The door was flung wide to admit a scrubby page almost completely hidden by a sweeping advance of petticoats and floating scarves. The visitor paused upon the threshold. From under her right arm, raised to allow her hand to rest on the jewelled top of her high ebony cane, a childish pipe impressively announced:

"Her Grace the Duchess of Marlborough!"

"Your Grace." Mrs. Danvers billowed to the ground. "This is indeed an honour."

"You were so mighty mysterious with your singular request," said the Duchess, stepping clear of the page to hand him her cane, "that I had no other choice but to comply."

Mrs. Danvers bridled. Singular indeed! Her Grace was determined, it seemed, to let Mrs. Danvers know that her request had been not only out of order but a liberty, and that the Duchess's compliance was less gracious than reluctant. All this was conveyed in the tone of her Grace's remark and in the flounce of her hissing silks as she rustled to the table and sat in the chair Mrs. Danvers obsequiously placed.

Flinging back her scarf and producing her fan, the Duchess waved it to and fro before her face.

"Your room is like an oven, Danvers. 'Tis prodigious hot to-day. Have the goodness to open a window."

Mrs. Danvers had the goodness to open a window. And as the two faced each other across the polished table, Mrs. Danvers rendered tactical apology.

"Madam, I would not for the world have encroached upon your valuable time if I had not——" her words ran down in an affronted silence. Her Grace's inattention was wholly unconcealed; her gaze fixed upon the silver tea-tray, heavily emblazoned with the Royal Arms.

She pointed. "That! How do you come by that?"

"That, madam?"

"The tray," snapped the Duchess. "Her Majesty's tray."

Mrs. Danvers reared her head; her high fontange quivered with the restraint she put upon herself to answer mildly:

"Her Majesty, madam, gave this tray to me as a token of her gratitude for my thirtieth year in her Majesty's service."

"Thirty *years*?" cried the Duchess in tones of lively disbelief. "You have not served Her Majesty for thirty years. If so you must be a female Methuselah, for you were no chicken when you first came to the Cockpit."

Mrs. Danvers simpered, hiding wrath.

"I was but a girl, the merest child, madam, as your Grace may possibly remember, when I——"

"La, Danvers! How could I possibly remember when you must be twice my age?"

Danvers let that pass. She was not disposed to enter into argument relative to the respective ages of the Duchess and herself. The interview was not shaping at all as she had planned. But if, she silently commented while she poured the tea, you think that I don't know you'll not see forty-nine again, my lady, you're mistaken. You've been razing off *your* years ever since the late

Queen died, and at your rate of reckoning you should be in second childhood by now.

"Does your Grace take sugar?" fawningly inquired Mrs. Danvers.

"Yes, *and* cream."

The Duchess divested herself of her gold-embroidered gloves. Mrs. Danvers rose to take them from her. . . . Gloves? Was there not some story hawked about to do with gloves? The Queen's gloves. And this pair, as she lived, she could swear had been worn by Her Majesty last May Day on the occasion of a Thanksgiving at St. Paul's for the success of the Union with Scotland. Well, well! And she can talk of tea-trays, come by honest service! She, who don't mind what she picks from the Queen's wardrobe, nor the Privy Purse neither. But Mrs. Danvers still retained her smile.

Sugar and cream were supplied, ratafia and angel cake refused. The Duchess must care, she confessed, for her figure. . . . And you need to, said Mrs. Danvers, but she did not say it aloud. What she did say was:

"Lud, madam, you're a sylph! Such curves, such exquisite proportions—can I not tempt you to a slice? The smallest——?"

"No. Let's hear what you have to say, for I've little time to waste."

If the Duchess had had more time to waste she might have raised the query as to how Mrs. Danvers came to be wearing the Queen's gown. She made a mental memorandum to investigate that and other matters at a future date. The Queen was far too generous in the distribution of her property. To the certain knowledge of the Mistress of the Robes that purple brocade and primrose satin petticoat had been worn by the Queen only once; and now it was worn by Mrs. Danvers. And an odious guy she looked in it, too!

"Well," said the Duchess, "I am waiting."

"Madam," with inward glee and outward diffidence, Mrs. Danvers prepared her visitor for the supreme announcement. "Has your Grace observed of late a certain boldness, a—how shall I put it?—an air, that might almost be termed arrogance, in the demeanour of Mrs.—hem—of Mrs. Hill?"

"Mrs. Hill?" The Duchess set down her cup to frown upon the question. "Boldness? Arrogance? No. I cannot say I have observed it, Danvers."

That answer, which admitted nothing yet did not deny the possibility of arrogance or boldness on the part of Mrs. Hill, encouraged Mrs. Danvers to proceed.

"Your Grace," said Mrs. Danvers with careful hesitation, "could not be expected to observe an untoward familiarity in one so close of kin to you."

She paused to sip bohea, and thus fortified appeared to brim with greater tidings. For Mrs. Danvers had not spent the better part of her life at Court without learning something of diplomacy.

"The manner of which I—of which we all complain, madam, is addressed exclusively to us," Mrs. Danvers gave a genteel cough behind her hand, "who are her colleagues of the Bedchamber."

The Duchess stretched to the dish of ratafia cakes.

"I cannot," she said, "resist temptation. They look delicious."

"Madam," Mrs. Danvers passed the dish, "they *are* delicious."

The Duchess took and crumbed a cake between her fingers, conveyed a morsel to her mouth and swallowed it before, upon reflection, she replied:

"If Mrs. Hill has caused offence either in the Bedchamber or out of it, she must be called to account irrespective of her kinship to me. In what way has she offended?"

Mrs. Danvers fixed her eyes on the Duchess's magnificent bosom where reposed a ducal coronet in diamonds and rubies.

"Madam——" But thus invited, Mrs. Danvers seemed unwilling to reveal herself; for this was Mrs. Dancers' pinnacle of triumph, her reward for a surfeit of humble pie, forcibly fed to her along the years from this very hand that held her best porcelain. Those beautiful sulky lips that were sipping tea from Mrs. Danvers' cup had poured mouthfuls of spleen and tyrannical abuse on Mrs. Danvers. She had suffered. She had writhed, had sunk herself in abject non-resistance, awaiting this, her moment.

It had come.

Seated deferentially behind the urn, malicious and moustached, gaunt with decades of servile repression, the austere Danvers was about to taste the exquisite fruits of revenge.

Yes, said Mrs. Danvers, you who flaunt a coronet upon your bosom and the Crown—in your dreams—on your head; you, who twist the Queen round your thumb as you twist her rings round your finger—you, who have bestrode us as a witch bestrides her besom—and there's witch's blood in you, they say, on your dam's side: you, who set yourself as high, or higher, than the angels may yet wish yourself in my low station for I've nothing to lose, and you, my fine madam, will likely lose all. Not only your pride but your place!

She did not, however, voice her exultation; nor with the fruit at her lips, did she snatch at it. She dallied.

"Madam, I am loath to tell you what I think your Grace should know—unless you do already know that which has been held so fast a secret?"

To this tentative preliminary the Duchess offered no reply, save to scourge the hesitating Danvers with a look.

"A secret," continued Mrs. Danvers, "that has leaked out, and of which, with exception of one—or two," a world of meaning was conveyed in that stressed pause, "more favoured, I am the sole possessor."

"Lord, Danvers!" broke forth the Duchess, "how you love to beat about the bush. What is this secret that appears so mightily to have impressed you? I'll warrant it will prove to be false as a dicer's oath. Come on, woman, out with it. I can't sit here all day."

"Why, madam," Mrs. Danvers licked her lips, "do you remember when—um—Colonel Masham was returned in May on sick leave?"

"Masham? Sick leave? Well?"

The Duchess's toe began to beat a tattoo on the carpet.

"Yes, madam, when he, poor gentleman, was wounded in the leg."

"Not so badly wounded," rasped the Duchess, "and not so lame neither, that he couldn't hobble round the garden on a stick."

"With Mrs. Hill," said Danvers, widening her smile.

"And if he did—what of it?"

"Yes, madam, what of it?" Mrs. Danvers ducked her head. Her eyes were now upturned to show the under whites of them; her voice shook with suppressed excitement. "Yes, madam," she repeated, "what of it? You may remember too, that Mrs. Hill's brother returned with Colonel Masham, also wounded—in the arm. As gallant a pair of soldiers as ever I did see, maimed in their country's service, and——"

"What, may I ask," her goaded Grace interrupted, "has this nonsensical farrago to do with me—or you? As for that rumbustious, good-for-nothing Mr. Hill, he can be shot in both arms for all the loss to the Army he'd be. The Duke reports him an undisciplined young dare-devil who fights like a pole-cat and drags his men with him into every sort of danger."

"The young gentleman has now rejoined his regiment," murmured Mrs. Danvers, "but he was present at the ceremony too."

"Ceremony?" The Duchess turned pale. "For God's sake, woman, if you've anything to say—*say* it!"

And Mrs. Danvers stood, and bent, and said it, to share in whispers with the Duchess the hoarded contents of her cornucopia.

The Duchess sat in arctic silence. Then: "I don't believe it. I don't *believe* it," she mechanically repeated. "If you are lying I'll——" a spark of her numbed rage flew up, "I'll discharge you from office to-morrow!"

"Madam, would I lie about so serious a matter?" cooed Mrs. Danvers. "Would I risk my situation——"

"I'll see you and your situation damned in hell before I will believe it!"

"But, madam, only think." Mrs. Danvers' appetite had not yet been surfeited: there were still some pickings to be sampled, tasted, spewed. "Think back awhile. Has not that person ingratiated herself by her sly trickery into Her Majesty's favour, ever since you first brought her to Court?"

"Yes," agreed the Duchess with avidity, "she has!"

"And if 'twere not for your Grace's beneficence she'd still be a domestic servant, sweeping, dusting——"

"Yes!"

"Why, madam, all the time that you've been occupied with the building of Blenheim she has sat in your place."

"My *place*?" screamed the Duchess.

"Madam," said Danvers tearfully, "it grieves me sore to mention it, but only think what perfidy, what evil she has perpetrated——"

The Duchess sprang up to pace the room, biting at her nails.

Mrs. Danvers followed her.

"And then her songs, madam, her mimicry. She even mimics you."

The Duchess halted.

"Me!"

"I've heard the Queen herself rock with laughter, madam——"

"Never!" shrieked the Duchess.

Mrs. Danvers checked hysteria.

"She and Mr. Harley sit closeted with the Queen for hours. Even the Prince is not allowed—te-he—to interrupt their sessions. Did your Grace know that?"

"Yes . . . No!"

"The Queen has made a pet of her," Mrs. Danvers purred in her Grace's boiling ear. "Even the pages remark on it."

The Duchess moaned.

"She's anybody's quarry," smiled Danvers, "easy come, easy go, your Grace. She was seen walking on a night this spring with Mr. Harley in the Mall, and the paint on her mouth had come off on his cravat."

"No!"

"Yes!"

"The dirty little whoring jade! I'll have her gaoled."

"I don't see," the glutted Danvers said, "how your Grace can gaol her for walking with her cousin."

"I can! I will! I'll have her in the stocks for all the town to jeer at. And, if what you tell me of her latest secret doings be proven, then——"

"Madam, I can vouch for it. My page reported faithfully what he had witnessed."

"Bring him in. I'll question him."

The scared page was brought in and cross-examined; but despite his awe and terror of the Duchess, his answers corroborated Mrs. Danvers' tale.

It was monstrous, apocalyptic, unbelievable . . . And true!

When the Duchess left the happy Mrs. Danvers, she straightway took herself to Mrs. Hill. To say she burst open the door is to underestimate her entrance. If a cyclone had crashed upon the startled Abigail it could not have created more disturbance. The lady's drifting scarves knocked down a bowl of flowers on the table; the sweep of her petticoats overturned a chair. She trod on the shocked cat to send it flying. She seized her cousin's slender wrist and held it in a vice, to demand, with no apology for her intrusion: "What is this I hear? Danvers tells me you are married!"

The indignant rush of colour to Abigail's face fled, leaving it ghostly white.

"Can you deny it?" yelled the Duchess. "*Can* you?"

In silence Abigail extricated herself from the lady's grasp to retreat behind the table. Her pale lips unclosed upon a whisper. "No, madam, I cannot."

"You——" the Duchess bared her superb teeth and lunged. Abigail was thankful for the table. "You dare to tell me you are married—and to *him*!"

"Yes, madam."

"You have *married* him?" Her Grace, with unimaginable violence, repeated. "You have married that smiling, bowing, furbelowed fool?"

Raising her chin, Abigail answered in a voice of frozen calm:

"If you allude to the gallant officer and gentleman whose wife I am proud to be—yes, I have married Colonel Masham."

"Good God!"

The Duchess put out her hand to grope for the overturned chair, found nothing, and tottered to the sofa.

It would have joyed Mrs. Danvers to have seen the tender rose fade from the Duchess's cheeks, leaving two less tender patches of rouge on the shell-like skin: to see that majestic woman for once deprived of speech to combat this calamity, while Mrs. Colonel Masham, from her vantage-post behind the table, returned the lady's baneful look with one unruffled, cool as a summer sea.

Momentarily robbed of her belief in herself and her absolute seigneurity, the Duchess sank her pride to save her face.

"I am well aware that my guardianship of you and yours ceased in the sense of all legal right to authority when you came of age, but——"

"Madam," was Mrs. Masham's meek, respectful interruption, "I am not aware that you have ever had any legal right to authority or guardianship over me and mine, other than your boundless charity—for which we are most gratefully beholden."

Yes, her tone was respectful and meek, but the purport of that gentle utterance, insignificant although upon the surface it appeared, was a challenge, cataclysmic, epoch-making.

The Duchess received it with ominous quiet, while in growing horror she surveyed the puny speck who dared even this so mild opposition to autocracy. Yet the skies did not fall, nor did the earth open to swallow the offender who unflinchingly and brazenly confessed that without advice from, or consultation with her benefactress, she was married. And secretly. To Masham.

Waves of shocked vibrations beat upon the Duchess as she floundered in a labyrinth of wild and repetitive conjecture. Married! Slinking off, and secretly! Why? In the name of all un-holiness—*why*? Why had she not announced her betrothal? If she wished to withhold the news of her intention from the world, why did she not at least have the courtesy to confide in her nearest relative: her patron? What ulterior, malevolent motive lay behind the stealth that had prompted her to spring this hideous surprise upon the one person who, by every law of decency, priority, should have been advised of it? Had she not befriended this miserable chit when she was friendless, fed her when she starved, clothed her when she went in tatters, given her a home, and raised her from the gutter to the Court? And now, this maggot she had nourished repaid her manifold philanthropies with traitorous deceit. But why? Why? . . . Ah!

The Duchess kindled as the lightning solution flashed upon her. "I see it all!" Her ebullience was demoniacal. " 'Tis plain as the nose on your face."

"What, madam, do you see?" Abigail asked with no expression more apparent than a gentle thirst for knowledge.

"The reason why you kept your marriage secret from me and from everyone else, save your father confessor—or whatever worse he may be. 'Twas *he* who prompted you to your dirty scheming, I'll be bound."

The Duchess ran an experienced eye over Abigail's childish figure. Her glance lowered to the trim waist from whence the petticoat was gathered into full silken folds over a whale-boned hoop; and the Duchess nodded gloatingly. "Aha! You follow the latest fashion. A convenient fashion indeed. The hoop!"

"The hoop, your Grace?"

"Yes, the hoop. It hides a mort of what is not convenient to show. And lucky 'tis for you, my girl, that this newest fashion is discreet. Why, you mealy-mouthed fornicating strumpet——" and as the Duchess menacingly leapt from the couch Abigail backed to the window that gave exit to the terrace. "Oh, no you don't!" The Duchess darted round the table. "You don't leave this room until I've dragged the truth from you. Come on! You can't gull me. Was I born yesterday? though I'll say it's a near miracle your child wasn't!"

Abigail gasped.

"Madam, what——?"

"Yes, madam, what?" mimicked the Duchess. "Vermin! You can't play the innocent to me. I'm not your Masham—the poor dupe. I'll take my oath there's more hid beneath your petticoats than *he* has ever put there for all he'll preen himself that he's the father of your——"

"Good life!"

This low-voiced interruption was followed by an indignant broadside that swept away with it the last remnants of compliance and docility. Here was no shrinking, humble self-effacing hand-maid—indeed, no maid at all, but a matron, the equal in wifely knowledge to her whom now in open enmity she faced.

"Madam, I cannot pass your insults without protest. I demand instant apology."

"I'll see myself and you in hell before I——"

The Duchess choked.

"Then, madam——" in Abigail's eyes a green flame flickered dangerously, "I am obliged to request that you repeat your offensive accusations before a witness." She made a move towards the bell-rope. "I will call my husband. You will repeat to him what you have said to me."

"I'll repeat it," shrieked the Duchess, "to the housetops!"

"At your peril, madam. For years I have suffered uncomplainingly your slights, your gibes, your disparagement of my unworthy origin which—let it now be said—is compatible with yours, since we both spring from the same grandfather. You sent my mother from you with a pittance of ten pounds, although you must have known that she was dying. We were left in poverty, neglected, till for very shame you were forced to acknowledge our existence, and you have boasted ever since of your charity to me and mine till I have thought myself the lowest cur to accept the crumbs you so grudgingly scattered. But now," the inexorable young voice rose to strike with all the force of long pent grievance at the castigated Duchess, who stood aghast, agape, dumbfounded in the face of this incalculable mutiny, "now," said Mrs. Masham rapidly and clear, "I am no longer undefended, at your mercy. You have hurled at me an accusation that is not only slanderous but an impeachment on my chastity and married state. You will retract your words, or I will take this matter further—to the Queen!"

The Duchess found her voice. It was a croak; hoarse, petrified.

"You've run mad. You've lost your senses. If I was mistaken——"

"You *are* mistaken, madam. Mistaken in your judgment of me. Greatly," said Abigail on a meaningful pause, "mistaken. Will you give me the apology that is my right, or must I——" she made another move toward the bell. The Duchess dashed after her. Their eyes met. Shattered, dazed, the Duchess blustered, hiding panic.

"Lord, child! What a pother over nothing. You should know by now that I'm outspoken. What's on my tongue must out on my lung."

Abigail inclined her head.

"I accept your apology, madam, if such it is. But your insults I can never forget."

The Duchess paled. There was that in the girl's transformation from an indecisive weakling to an entity unrecognizable in its unafraid and confident directness which appalled. The magnitude of the elaborate deception wrought upon her, shrank beneath this heaped horror of defiance. The fighting spirit of the Duchess was for the moment quelled while ingratiatingly she temporized.

"Then all's right between us, yes? For I forgive *you* the wrong you have done me in keeping your marriage secret. But why——" she attempted rough persuasion, "why did you not tell me? I would have been delighted to have sponsored——"

"Madam," Abigail cut her short, "I admit I may have been at fault in that I did not let you know of my intention. But, believe me, I was not so underhand in my designs as fearful of your Grace's interference."

"Interference!" The Duchess blazed again. "You can say that to me—to *me*, whose only interference on your behalf has been to raise you from the dust. Heavenly powers! What monstrous perversion of good into evil. The treachery of it—the treachery!"

"No, madam," Abigail's eyelids sank, "not treachery. Tact."

With one supreme last effort to cloak herself in the ragged remnants of her dignity: "Does the Queen," demanded the Duchess, "know of this?"

"I believe the Bedchamber women," was the evasive reply, "may have acquainted Her Majesty with rumours which," the slight hesitation was significant, "have now reached your Grace's ears."

'She hoped by this answer', thus the Duchess's own version of that interview,* 'to divert any further examination into the matter. But I went presently to the Queen and asked her why she had not been so kind as to tell me of my cousin's marriage . . . All the answer I could obtain from Her Majesty was this, "I have a hundred times bid Masham tell you, and she would not."

'The conduct both of the Queen and of Mrs. Masham convinced me that there was some mystery in the affair, and thereupon I set myself to inquire as particularly as I could into it. And in less than a week's time I discovered that my cousin was become an *absolute favourite*; that the *Queen herself* was present at her marriage in Dr. Arbuthnot's lodgings, at which time Her Majesty had called for a round sum out of the Privy Purse; that Mrs. Masham *came often to the Queen when the Prince was asleep*, and was generally two hours every day *in private with her*. And I likewise then discovered, beyond all dispute, Mr. Harley's correspondence and interest at Court by means of this woman.

'I was struck with astonishment at such an instance of ingratitude and should not have *believed* if there had been any room left for *doubting*'.

There was no room left for doubting. Not only had the Queen attended the ceremony, but, unknown to the Duchess, had presented the bride with three thousand pounds as a wedding gift.

While the Court titillated with amazed excitement, the Duchess

* *Conduct:* Sarah, Duchess of Marlborough. The italics are Sarah's.

sat in solitude and raged. For the first time in her life she was
forced to acknowledge the catastrophic, immense humiliation of a
rival for the favour of the Queen. A rival! And one, whom
least of all the world she had considered a possible successor to
her unchallenged sway upon the Queen's affections. A bitter blow
to be dealt by the child she had fostered; the girl who owed to
Sarah Marlborough that Royal opportunity which, with serpen-
tine low cunning, had been seized to supplant her.

Abigail Hill! . . . That meek, cringing little creature, whom
from the heights of her vast superiority she had condescended to
exploit. 'That Enchantress', of whom the Queen, in one of her
rare moments of insight, had obscurely warned her and had perceived what Sarah unsuspiciously had not, that this female Machia-
velli would worm her evil way between them to their mutual undoing.

Shreds of unlikely evidence, culled from the most trivial occur-
rences, were served to the ex-Viceroy by gleeful tattlers who delighted in her imminent decline.

She bombarded the Queen with letters and reproaches. She discharged volleys of fury on paper to her John. She harried Mrs.
Masham up and down the Palace. She hid herself in doorways
to pounce upon her as she passed. The Court was one huge snig-
ger. Abigail wisely kept out of her way and maintained an
inimical silence to Sarah's repeated requests for an interview in
which she would have 'something of import to tell—that must be
told.'

Finally, and in despair, she laid a stronger bait.

'*September* 23, 1707.

'Since the conversation I had with you at your lodgings,
several things have happened to confirm me in what I was
hard to believe, that you have made returns *very unsuitable* to
what I might have expected. I always speak my mind so plainly
that I should have told you so myself if I had had the opportunity which I had hoped for. But being now so near parting, I
think this way of letting you know it is like to be the least uneasy to you as well as to

Your humble servant,
S. Marlborough.'

She waited the whole day for a reply. . . . 'But this could
not be had so soon, it being necessary to consult with her *great
director* in so great a matter. At length, however, an answer was

sent after me, the whole frame and style of which showed it to be the genuine product of an artful man [Harley] who knew perfectly well the management of such an affair.'

'Windsor. *September* 24, 1707.

'Your letter surprises me no less than it afflicts me, because it lays a most heavy charge upon me of an ungrateful behaviour to your Grace. Her Majesty was pleased to tell me that you was still angry with me for not acquainting you with my marriage. I did believe, after so generous a pardon, your Grace would think no more of that. I am very confident by the expression of your letter that somebody has told some malicious lie of me to your Grace, from which it is impossible for me to vindicate myself till I know the crime I am accused of. I am sure, madam, your goodness cannot deny what the meanest may ask of the greatest; I mean justice, to know my accuser. Without that, all friendship must be at the mercy of every malicious liar, as they are who have so barbarously and unjustly brought me under your displeasure, the greatest unhappiness that could befall me . . . As my affliction is very great you will, I hope, in compassion, let me hear from you, and believe me what I really am,

> Madam,
> Your Grace's most humble
> and faithful servant,
> A. Hill.'*

One might suggest that Sarah's comparatively temperate appeal for an interview to clear the air scarcely justified Abigail's innocent and injured protestations: or it may be that Sarah has withheld from her memoirs more provocative material. She certainly had cause enough for grievance. One can hold no brief for Abigail's conduct in concealing from her nearest relative the greatest event of her life, but Sarah was mistaken in thinking Harley had prompted her in the writing of that letter. He had no hand in it, yet he may have been an indirect contributor to Abigail's clandestine marriage.

She was ardent, young, and for all her studied sophistries, immensely inexperienced; and with the blind and touching confidence of youth had ignored the possibility of disillusionment. Harley's ruthless pursuit had discovered latent deeps enclosed within her fiercely chaste defences. Under his skilful mastery, she

---

* For some time after her marriage Mrs. Masham retained her maiden name in all her correspondence.

unfolded, was bewitched, bedrugged, had rendered him her citadel to storm—and he retreated.

The anguish of that cool rebuff had laid her low. She wished to die. She prayed to die. She would have eaten, willingly, rat-poison. In her shocked recoil she turned loathsome to herself, rejected, wanton, loving . . . and unloved.

Lacerated by the knowledge that she had given him her heart to fritter and her imagination to possess, she had withdrawn herself from further contact, any sight of him, since that memorable evening in the Park.

She burned when she recalled those bitter moments of his whimsical denial to her blatant, quivering appeal. She had whined to him, had all but grovelled; wept.

Her nights were one long misery of sleeplessness, and resurrections of unkissed kisses, the echo of his words. 'How it loves to flagellate itself. . . . There is no shame in hunger, sweet. The shame lies in over-eating. . . . There are obstacles.'

His wife.

O thrice besotted idiot not to have known, have guessed.

She smothered her groans in the pillow, bedewed it with her tears. Did she, crass fool, have thought, then, to have married him? As if he, from his pinnacle, would stoop to her! And in the night she rose and lit the candles at her dressing-glass and mercilessly surveyed her unflattering reflection. Plain, thin, freckled, peaked. . . . She had snatched her nightcap from her head and let her hair fall, long and straight as rain, about her shoulders to her knees. He had never seen her hair loose, hanging long like this. He would never see it, never touch it now; never draw it through his fingers and wind it round her throat. If she could lie upon his doorstep, strangled in her hair! . . . And then she laughed loud, shrill, to scare herself, and snuffed the candles, snivelling; and crept back to her tossed bed.

Such nights showed in her face, grown narrower, more pale, and more pinched, with shadows like faint bruises underneath her eyes. She could hide her pallor with judicious application of the hare's foot, but she could not hide those mauve rings round her eyes.

How to avoid him on his visits to the Queen was her next problem. She pleaded sick. She invented a green bile. Discarding the hare's foot, she sought Dr. Arbuthnot's advice. He prescribed a nauseating physic to be taken before meals. The Queen was sympathetic and gave her leave of absence. She rid herself of the physic by pouring it down the privy. She wished she could so easily have rid herself of love. . . .

Two weeks later Jack arrived, and with him Colonel Masham. Both had been wounded in the battle of Almanza. Jack carried his arm in a sling. The Colonel limped. Jack was a Captain now, and grown so high Abigail had to crane her neck to see his face. His sisters fluttered round him, bathing his arm with compassionate tears and Dr. Arbuthnot's lotion. The bullet, clumsily extracted by an Army surgeon, had severed an artery to cause a gangrene that refused to heal. His Commanding Officer had sent him home on sick leave. Colonel Masham was in scarcely better case. He had received a sabre stroke that gashed his knee to splinters.

They had each received a decoration 'For Valour' from the Queen, pinned with tears of pride and pity on their chests, while the Prince from his couch applauded and Mrs. Hill poulticed his foot.

The Prince had, of late, grown alarmingly stouter. He was crippled with gout and constitutionally weakened from frequent attacks of cardiac asthma. His ruddy complexion had paled; but his ailments did not deter him from drinking the healths of 'our two heroes'.

The Prince's repetitive enthusiasm for the two 'heroes' reduced them to sheepish embarrassment.

"Est-il possible!" the Prince had emotionally declared. "To think that my two gentlemen, the one my page, the other my equerry, should meet together in this so bloody battle! Yes, you are veritable heroes. The Queen has heard from Lord Galway that your gallantries were most conspicuous. . . . How that you saved both the other's life, not? Two English against twenty-four French, hand-to-hand fighting. . . . Thank you, Mrs. Hill. That is better. Very much better. I am not a wounded hero, but my foot gives me as great pain as if I was. I must lie on my couch with my feet on a pillow and I cannot go to the wars. I have to fight by—how you say it?—proxy. See now what a good nurse I have, Masham. She must attend your wound. Hill, you shall bathe the Colonel's wound. His man cannot bathe it so well as you. . . . Na! Masham, I insist."

The Colonel, looking all ways at once and deeply flushed, had protested that his knee was on the mend, and that he would not for the world put Mrs. Hill to any such inconvenience.

"But, sir, it is no inconvenience," Mrs. Hill had meekly dared to contradict. "It will be my pleasure."

So supervised by the Royal invalid, and with gracious assistance from the Queen who held the bandages, Mrs. Hill had knelt at the feet of Colonel Masham to sponge and tend him, very much against his will.

For if this thrice daily performance was Mrs. Hill's 'pleasure', it may, or may not, have been the Colonel's. The pain of his knee was as naught to the pain of his heart, which, still faithful, had been sorely bruised. He thought it broken. It seemed unlikely he would ever 'try again'.

And yet . . .

Colonel Masham had not reckoned with those implacable compulsions which, with equal stern impartiality, decide the loves of mice—and men. No pricking of the thumbs, no premonition, warned him that all he asked of life was at his knees when, on a summer's morning Abigail dressed his wound, and the Queen's Consort slept upon his couch. Yes, the Queen's Consort slept; and sleeping, did his kindly spirit hover like some heavy unseen chaperone to witness, between winey snores, a miracle?

Engrossed upon her task she bent her head; and Masham too bent his till his lips rested on her hair. The movement was involuntary. He did not know—how could he?—that the first primeval cause had, in that one moment of eternity, decided his own fate and Mrs. Hill's. Nor did he know that the mere atavistic instinct of self-preservation had induced her to exert her most persuasive powers to drag from him his long-belated avowal. Yet thus it was and neither guessed they had been urged to act, as individually they did, by the same microcosmic energy that superintends the meeting and the parting of amoebae. They did not know, for neither Mrs. Hill nor Colonel Masham was aware of the existence of amoebae. They knew no more than the existence of themselves.

Hah! The Prince snorted. He had a taste in his mouth of roast pig, a tongue full of sawdust, a head full of whispers. . . .

"I am pressed beyond my strength, beyond, maybe, my true regard for you which dares to doubt. I ask, entreat . . ."

Hey? What? Ach! The Prince hawked, smacked his lips with a clucking sound and swallowed: slept again, to blunder in upon and steal a secret.

Did that cumbrous astral presence discern in the tracery of lines at the corners of the Colonel's eyes, and in the furrows deep carved each side his mouth, the marks of a man who had come to grips with life and death? A man who may have learned, as had Mrs. Hill, that this predestined human ritual cannot be en-glamoured in gauzy tissues of illusion; that youth's perplexities, youth's crises and suspenses, its impossible desires, dissolve as vapour in the critical harsh light of reason?

". . . Is your heart engaged and given? If it is not—can I hope? I return soon to the fighting front, healed, thanks to your ministrations—healed of this, but not of the hurt I carry with me. Always."

She was reprieved.

For in that moment of her revelation she must surely have divined that here was surcease from restless longings after contraband delights; from conscience-seared and disenchanted self-reproach.

"No, my heart is not engaged." Her eyes shone as she had answered him, "but it is given . . . now."

And on an impulse, shaken from her as swift and softly as a leaf is shaken from the branch, she had laid her cheek, and then her lips, to his bared knee.

Ouch! A prolonged gurgling snore returned the Prince's errant counterpart to its earthly residence. He woke in time to see enough to make him nod his head in smiling approval; then he tactfully had turned, to snore again.

It was at Masham's insistence that the marriage should take place without delay: at hers that their intention be kept secret. Her arguments against her cousin's interference had been plausible enough, but both had agreed that the Queen and the Prince must be told.

The Queen had expressed herself delighted. Nothing, she declared, would have given her more joy than 'this most happy news, which,' she slyly added, 'she had long ago foreseen.'

The Prince had waxed, with much nodding and eye-winking, sentimental. He, it seemed, could keep a secret too.

The carefully laid wedding plans of Mrs. Hill, in collaboration with the Queen and the Queen's doctor, had gone apace. Mrs. Arbuthnot, who could not be relied upon to hold her tongue, had been despatched to the country when her husband conveniently found her to be suffering from a semi-tertian fever.

And had it not been for one unlucky chance the marriage would, in her own time, have been announced by Mrs. Masham, the Duchess reconciled, and Danvers deprived of her triumph. But who could have guessed, least of all Mrs. Danvers, that her page, sent with a message to one of the Queen's dressers, would have met with the doctor's page upon the way?

By him and, to Mrs. Danvers' scrubby messenger, was imparted some news of mysterious doings in Dr. Arbuthnot's rooms; of tables laid as for a feast, with bottles of champagne and a cake that towered high with sugar icing; of the doctor's orders to his servants that he was not at home to visitors save those whom he himself would admit: that the cook, the footman, and the maids had been given a day's outing, and the page a sixpenny piece to go to Bartholomew's Fair. All of this had wakened curiosity in Dr. Arbuthnot's page, who preferred to hang about and watch the comings and goings within and without his master's door.

From his post behind a pillar he had seen Colonel Masham arrive with Captain Hill, followed by a chaplain in white sleeves, and by Mrs. Hill and her sister in white satin, all of whom were admitted by the doctor in a fuss. And there was one other besides, who must have entered by the chimney, for the doctor's page had not seen her—or him, arrive. The sex was indeterminate, since only a back view of this person's shape, veiled, bulky, hooded, cloaked, had been perceptible. But there was no mistaking what those two pages, at the keyhole, saw and heard.

'I, Samuel, take thee, Abigail . . .'

The giggling urchins pinched each other's bottoms. What a peepshow! As good as any to be seen at Bartholomew's Fair: as good, or even better, than a hanging.

And when, in excuse for his long dalliance and to avoid the threatened birch, Mrs. Danvers' page recounted what the keyhole had revealed, he received, to his surprise, a stick of marchpane.

CHAPTER TWO

LORD GODOLPHIN, mother-naked, reclined on a couch in the cooling room of the Hummums. His face expressed profound disgust, his body a gentle aftermath of perspiration. Dr. Garth, the fellow Sarah swore by, for his Whiggery, Godolphin guessed, rather than his skill, had ordered sweat-baths for his gravel. It was his first experience of this revolting treatment, and he vowed that it would surely be his last.

Resignedly he submitted his oily carcass to the operations of the rubber, who having curried his flesh with a horse-hair gauntlet, and what Godolphin thought to be unnecessary vigour, proceeded to grease him with a concoction of aromatic gum.

"Here!" protested his lordship, "What the pox is this stink you're using on me?"

The glib assurance that it was a marvellous refreshing unguent obtained from the excreta of the civet, did not greatly comfort the Lord Treasurer.

"D'you mean it's made of cat's dirt?"

"The smallest ingredient, my lord, from which all the sweetest essences are compounded. Will your lordship allow me to roll you over?"

His lordship, grunting disapproval, was rolled over.

The rubber, a young man with a purposeless chin, an open-throated shirt, the shortest of breeches, no stockings and very soft hands, proceeded soothingly to anoint his lordship's parboiled backside.

Damme, conjectured the discomposed Godolphin, if this smooth-spoken fellow is not one of these Tom-essences himself!

"And now, if your lordship will be pleased to turn again——"

His lordship was very pleased to turn again. His vast abdomen did not comfortably support his sprawling weight. "Haven't ye done?" he demanded. "I've had enough of your mauling and pinching."

"Near upon done, my lord. You've sweated lovely."

"And I'm sweating still. Let be, let be! You're squeezing out my guts. Not content with melting me like butter in a stew-pan, ye needs must grease me top to toe as if I were a haunch of pork ready for the basting." He sucked his tongue. "I'm thirsty."

"Will your lordship take a nipperkin of cordial?"

"What kind o' cordial?" asked Godolphin with suspicion.

"Eastern honey syrup, my lord. 'Tis mightily sweet and refreshing."

"Syrup? God's life, no! If you don't supply wine in this inferno, go tell my footman—he's outside with my coach—to fetch me a bottle from a tavern. White and cool. And cover me, will you? I can't lie here stark nude."

He was covered.

Left to himself, the Lord Treasurer, with increased alarm, surveyed his vast rotundity, now discreetly swathed in a towel. After all that dubbing and rubbing and loss of juice—and he must have shed a gallon—his redundant flesh did not appear much to have dwindled. He looked indeed, and felt so too, as if he were considerably swelled. Like enough he'd have an apoplexy as a result of these unnatural activities.

From the cooling-room, devoid of door, he could watch other victims undergoing the miseries of the third and last equinoctial oven he had quitted. Propped panting against the walls oozing rivulets of grime and sweat, their feet protected from the excessive heat of the freestone floor with wooden sabots provided for that purpose, they diligently stewed.

Godolphin eyed their agonies with a complacent grin. One elderly fop, whose head, bereft of his wig, was hairless as a billiard ball, whose rouged wrinkles dripped a rosy dew, prayed in piteous gasps for a mouthful of air. At which appeal an attendant opened the one very narrow window about half an inch, amid a storm of complaints from the less debilitated, and in particular from one lobster-red young gentleman whose voice Godolphin recognized before he saw his face.

Harry St. John! Godolphin twitched his bulbous nose. Trust him to be in the heat o' the fashion.

"No, faith!" loudly expostulated St. John. "I'm just beginning to sizzle. Sir Andrew must roast with us or be taken out."

The collapsed sufferer, who by this time had slid to the floor, shot up again with a howl as his bare buttocks came in contact with the baking stones. Whereupon the attendant hauled him up, carried him to a cistern of steaming water and plunged him into it.

The re-entry of the rubber with a bottle of Rhenish wine obscured Godolphin's immediate interest in Sir Andrew Fountaine's immersion.

Hoisted into a sitting posture with a pillow at his back, the Lord Treasurer thankfully refreshed himself. He had just poured his second glass when he was interrupted by St. John with his loins sparsely draped, and the rest of him coloured bright pink.

"Let me die! I did not know you were a frequenter of these torrid zones, my lord," said St. John, languishing.

"I'm not," growled Godolphin. "One visit's enough for me."

St. John ruefully regarded his navel. "But not for me. 'Twill take a month of sizzling to reduce *my* paunch."

"You oughtn't to have a paunch at your age."

Readjusting his towel which had slipped, and with a contumelious glance at his uninvited guest, Godolphin bade him dourly: "Best call that mincing fellow there to bring another glass."

Another glass was brought, the wine gratefully accepted by the now completely naked Secretary-at-War, who having stripped off his loin cloth, spread it on the stones and sat.

Godolphin eyed him with repugnance. There was no end to this young stallion's sauciness. To accost him in his privacy was bad enough; but to sit before him in a state of nature, and begad! to drain the bottle dry as well, was worse.

"A likeable wine, my lord," remarked St. John agreeably. Godolphin looked at him again with multiplied aversion.

"They haven't smothered *you* with cat's pomatum. I've been smeared and pounded to a pulp."

"You don't appear to be a pulp. I've never seen your lordship in such buoyant health. A glass of wine, sir?"

Godolphin hitched his towel higher.

"I think it's time I dressed."

"No, no—not yet. You must allow at least a couple of hours in which to cool and rest yourself. What's all this I hear," St. John continued, unperturbed by Lord Treasurer's scowl, "of a rumpus to do with the Duchess and a chambermaid?"

"The Duchess and a chambermaid?" echoed Godolphin with unease.

"Why, yes." And St. John seductively smiled. Without his periwig, his hair damp and curling, his cheeks full and ripe as pippins, he had the appearance of an overgrown cherub. "Has not your lordship heard that the Duchess has turned rampant because one of the Queen's dressers, or Bedwomen—or whatever, who is a humble relation of her Grace's, has married herself to Masham?"

Godolphin shied.

"So I understand. A very suitable match."

"Very suitable," agreed the bland St. John. "Only it seems the Duchess has a notion that the young lady has supplanted her in the Queen's affections."

"Pshaw!" snorted Godolphin, "how could she?"

"That is what we are all wondering. How? She is also"—St. John held his re-filled glass to the light and squinted at its brimming amber—"she is also a cousin of Harley's."

"Oh?"

"My lord." St. John emptied his glass and set it carefully on the floor beside him. Raising his knees, he clasped them. "I am loath to pay the smallest heed to Court cackle, but in this case I think the cacklers do not err in their suggestion that the chambermaid is like to cause trouble. Yes." St. John quelled Godolphin's impatient attempt at denial with emphatic repetition. "Trouble. It seems her Grace has righteous cause to feel herself aggrieved, since the Queen who was in Mrs. Masham's confidence, which the Duchess was not, attended the marriage and presented the bride with a handsome dowry from the Privy Purse. But your lordship must surely know this."

His lordship did not now deny it. He lay mum.

"The Queen," proceeded St. John, smiling down at his polished knees, "is, I am told, absolutely infatuated with the charms of Mrs. Masham. Yes, she has undoubted charm, which is not to be confused with beauty of form or feature. She is freckled, plain, too small, and her nose is too big. But withal she has an indefinable peculiar attraction. She is magnetic in the same way that the Frenchwomen——"

"Be damned to her charms!" exploded Godolphin. "What have you heard?"

St. John dropped his bantering tone.

"That unless you can appease the Duchess you may be faced with a serious repercussion from her frenzy. She is beside herself. She pesters the Duke with letters demanding that he sends in his resignation as alternative to the Masham's dismissal. He thought at first—as would you and I or any other reasonable person—that the wranglings in the Bedchamber could not affect the trend of Parliamentary affairs——"

"Nor can they!" Godolphin raspingly cut in. "Odso, Harry! You're as bad as any city hussif with your gossip."

"I have it," St. John doggedly persisted, "on authoritative information, that a fuse had been set to what appeared to be a heap of frippery—a fuse which looks to light a bonfire. I call upon you, my lord, to bring a hose and douse it. 'Twill be a powerful burning to quench, but you're the only soul alive to whom her Grace will listen."

"And from where—or from whom——" Godolphin sardonically inquired, "have you gleaned this authoritative information? Do you resort to Harley's tricks, and pay your town-trash spies to dig in Grub Street gutters for their garbage? Gah! I gave you credit for a cleaner taste. Your palate has suffered a surfeit of bawdy-house hodge-podge."

St. John flushed angrily.

"You mistake, my lord. I do not eat dirt, nor do I employ spies—other than those of my own sense and sight—in the course of my investigations. I adjure you, sir, take heed of what I tell you, gleaned neither from the gutter nor the bawdy-house, but from the lobby of Westminster House. There's a Party crisis pending, and believe me, what I say, it hangs upon the balance of a pendulum that swings in the Queen's Bedchamber. A pendulum that may swing you—an you let it swing so far—right out of office." And rising, St. John re-draped himself. "I crave your lordship's pardon if I appear presumptuous in warning you, my Chief, of this danger, but I regard it as my duty to do so . . . An unpleasant duty and a duty done." His bewitching smile reappeared. "I trust your lordship will benefit in due course from your steaming. Shall I see you at Pontack's later?"

"No," Godolphin goggled up at him, "you won't. I'm going to Newmarket to-night."

But he did not go to Newmarket that night. More perturbed by St. John's insinuations that he cared to admit, he drove home to find a coach at the door and the Duchess on his doorstep.

"I have been back and forth three times," she complained. "Where have you been?"

"Attending an undress rehearsal," Godolphin grinned awry, "for my first appearance in the nether world."

She stared.

"I don't know what you mean."

"I've been," he explained, "to the Hummums—which is hell."

"Oh, the sweating-baths."

She preceded him into the house.

"Well, Sarah?"

Apprehensively he offered her a seat. She refused it. Unfastening her cloak, she threw it aside. Her beauty was, as ever, disconcerting. There had been a time when he had believed himself in love with her, but had long known that he loved his fillies more. A horse, God bless it, couldn't talk: and Sarah could. And how she talked! She had a flail in her tongue to lash him with abuse and accusations.

Did he wish to see himself deposed in a Tory Cabinet controlled by Harley? Did he not know what was brayed in every tavern, every club, that the new female element in the Bedchamber had enticed, not only Harley to her arms, but the Queen? Was he so absorbed in his nags that he couldn't see how he rode for a fall? Did he not know that Harley and his paramour, who had married herself to save her face—or her bastard's—were driving the Whigs out and the Tories in? "And not the Whigs only," shouted Sarah, "but you with them! Lord, man, don't you know that your jockey, Harley, has pulled your horse and rides that fallow mare of his to win? Yes, ecod! He's backed the winner for a certainty."

Her ranting cracked on a storm of tears. She laughed, scolded, sobbed, tore her handkerchief to shreds, imploring Godolphin to go to the Queen and demand that Mrs. Masham should be instantly dismissed.

"John agrees with me that she must be dismissed!"

"My dear Sarah," objected the harrowed Godolphin, "it is impossible that so insignificant a person—a chambermaid—can cause any material disturbance."

But this intervention to make her see reason served only to make her see red.

"Insignificant! Good God alive! So insignificant is she that she has obtained the Queen's ear and hangs on her bosom while she beckons Harley to her side. Her influence is absolute, and the Queen has turned against me to that extent she won't *sit* in my presence, but stands and looks through me as if I were a pane of glass! And when I"—her lips writhed to another burst of laughter—"and when I asked Mrs. Morley why this abomination, this low creature, should persistently avoid me, despite all my efforts

to mend the breach between us, Mrs. Morley's answer was—
' 'Tis very natural for Mrs. Masham to be afraid to come to me
when she saw I was angry with her.' And that—that——" Like
blown dust devils in a sandstorm, Sarah's rage overswept her, cast
her down. She staggered to a sofa and bowed her head on her
hands. Her voice struggled through her rending sobs. "And
she said that—that Masham was 'very much in the right'—in the
right—against *me*!"

She was up and at him again with her hands on his shoulders,
her lovely ravaged face, wet with tears, raised entreatingly, to his.
"So much in the right that she—that evil bitch!—will persuade
the Queen to throw me out and you out and John out, and Sunderland out and every*one* of us out——"

There was no placating her. She was past all reason, all reserve,
and half-demented.

He managed to be rid of her at last, with the assurance that he
would advise the Queen to dismiss Mrs. Masham from office.
"And Harley," sobbed Sarah. "You must promise me, Sidney,
for your sake—for all our sakes—to be rid of him. *He* is the first
danger. She is only his instrument, his mouthpiece."

"Yes, my dear. Yes."

He handed her into her coach and watched her drive away.
Whew! What a woman. What a scene. How had John put up
with years of this? No wonder he was loath to end the war and
return to fiercer bombardment at home.

He felt battered, ill, and was still sweating from that goddamned treatment when he went to bed, but not to sleep. He
worried himself sick. First St. John with his hints, and now Sarah
in her tantrums. While he could discredit her exaggeration of
injuries received, he could sympathize with the cause that had
provoked them. Secure in her belief that she held the Queen in
the palm of her hand, it must have been a calamitous blow to find
herself mistaken, if not, as she believed, supplanted. And by that
sly little puss! . . . But why this uproar re-arisen against the
Masham? Her marriage, or so Godolphin understood, had been
accepted by Sarah, and its secrecy condoned.

He might well have asked himself the cause of Sarah's most
recent eruption, which was not revealed to him, nor, at that time,
to anyone else. But here we have it, in those embittered memoirs
where so much gall is mingled with the ink.

We know that Sarah had written, while at Windsor, for an
interview, with which request Abigail had appeared unwilling to
comply, for:

'I was every day in expectation of hearing from Mrs. Masham, who I supposed would now endeavour to clear up what had created so much uneasiness between us. But to my great surprise I was twelve days under the same roof with her at St. James's before I had so much as any message from her: when at last she came I began to tell her that it was very plain the Queen was much changed towards me, and that I could not attribute this to anything but her secret management; that she had been frequently with Her Majesty in private and that the very attempt to cover this by artifice from such a friend as I had been to her was alone a very ill sign, and enough to prove a bad purpose at bottom.

'To this she gravely answered that she was sure the Queen, who had loved me extremely, *would always be very kind to me*!'

Kind! The Queen, who '*had* loved her extremely', would always be '*kind*' to her. And this from Abigail Hill.

On Sarah's own showing she was so stunned by that remark, which, if unintentionally insolent was distinctly maladroit, that she was deprived for some minutes of speech. . . . 'To see a woman whom I had raised out of the dust put on such a superior air and to hear her assure me, by way of consolation, that the Queen would be always *very kind to me*!' . . .

The affront was past all bearing, all power of credence. Yet, not even now, when the chasm had opened at Sarah Marlborough's feet, did she perceive it. Still blinded by her unshaken confidence in herself and her dictatorship, she fell.

It is beyond belief that one so inconsiderable as Abigail Hill could have brought about a tourney in which the champions of two great political parties were involved in a life and death contest: that one so little could achieve, unknowingly, so much. Yet thus it was, and the struggle for supremacy that began in the Queen's Bedchamber was continued on Parliament's tilting ground. But she who had flung down the gauntlet in the form of a few ill-chosen words was the creature of circumstance rather than design.

While the nation watched with bated breath that bitter clash of arms between the Churchillian factor on the one side and Harley and the Queen on the other, Abigail went about her small concerns and wrote her wifely letters to her husband at the wars.

She thought of him a great deal, prayed dutifully for his safe return. She offered thanks to God for her timely deliverance from premeditated sin. She believed herself wholly undeserving of so good a husband. She had endured the disappointing consummation of their marriage vows with customary patience and docility, and had lain awake long after he, exhausted, slept, to wonder: Was it for *this* that she had grovelled so imploringly to Harley?

Turned over on his side, her husband snored: not loudly, but enough. He had been tender and by no means inexperienced. She could not complain. She was wrongful to complain. She had married without love a man who deeply loved her, a man who was worth, she told herself, a dozen Harleys. But that did not ease the hurt in her body, nor the numb ache in her heart.

The Queen, whose insurable romanticism had delighted in a secret marriage that just a little savoured of elopement, had allotted the bridal pair a suite of rooms adjoining hers and the Prince's. There the bridegroom was encouraged, by Royal consent, to visit his wife unobserved.

In August they had accompanied the Queen and the Prince to Windsor, and a week after their return to St. James's, Colonel Masham rejoined his regiment in Flanders.

During that brief honeymoon, Abigail's life had seemed to pause and her memory to vanish. She could not afterwards recall one moment that had sharpened its edge on her mind. Even her agonized endurance of his connubial transports was dimmed in the resigned acceptance of her marital duty.

But the night before he left for the front she was weeping in his arms.

"I wish—I wish you need not go. I'll not be happy till I know you're safe with me again."

She meant it. He was her rock, her haven of defence against that weaker self that had so basely failed her. He kissed her wet eyelids.

"I'll come back, my darling. The war will soon be over, and then . . ."

They talked of their future together till dawn. She was, as ever, acquiescent. Yes, she too hoped they would have children. Yes, she would delight in a home of her own, and would be most happy to resign office if the Queen would allow her to do so, and live in the country. . . . Yes, most certainly she loved him. Would she have married him if she had not loved him?

"But I think," he, with wistful urgency, had told her, "that you are not *in* love. There's a mighty difference, sweet. Some day, God willing, I'll win you. . . ." He had almost won her then, and would have spared himself and her much uncertainty and future misconception if, at that moment, he had not widely yawned and said:

"Those confounded birds have started now. I ought to get some sleep. I've a heavy day before me."

And while he slept she stole from his side to rummage in his drawers for woollen mittens and over-socks for him to wear against the chill of a winter campaign. And these she packed in his valise along with some mutton-pies she had ordered for his journey. She hoped he would not be sea-sick, but just in case, she placed as antidote a cordial recommended by Dr. Arbuthnot. Then she returned to the bed and bent over him, smoothing back his tousled hair.

"It is time for you to dress."

And time for him to go.

She may have had good reason in keeping her manœuvres a secret from Sarah, but if she had hoped to spring a like surprise on Harley she was baulked. He had been informed of her intention, he airily assured her, from his good friend Arbuthnot, who had pledged him to silence. He had wished her his most sincere felicitations and presented her with a wedding gift—a handsomely bound volume of the Collected Works of Shakespeare.

Since when she had evaded him, which she found not difficult to do while the ailing Prince demanded her constant attention as sick-nurse. But this deliberate avoidance could not be maintained for long. Shortly after Christmas an unexpected and dramatic incident aroused a nation-wide scandal, which, fanned by Whig hostility, fastened dangerous supicion on the Secretary of State.

Harley's personal clerk, a fellow named Gregg, had obtained the keys of a safe where secret State papers were stored, and had sold his pilfered information to the French. Discovery was followed by immediate arrest and a formal charge before the Privy Council of High Treason.

Committed to Newgate under sentence of death, he was finally brought to the gallows. Yet despite his fervent protestations of his master's innocence, which Gregg maintained to the end with his head in the noose, the enemies of Harley were determined to follow this opportune scent of suspicion. The Secretary's methods of espionage in the cause of his party were common knowledge, and Gregg had been his confidential clerk. The case looked black for him whom the Whigs had named 'Robin the Trickster': for him who had proved so treacherous a friend to Marlborough and Godolphin, when he had ranged himself on the side of the Queen, in his underhand attempts to overthrow the Government by his artful pursuit of the Queen's Abigail. It would need but a shred more of evidence now to pack him in the tumbril in the wake of his confederate, and set him dancing on the air at Tyburn Hill!

In coffee-house and tavern the odds for and against his life outwagered lesser bets. Men laid their guineas, some their shirts, on the axe as opposed to the gallows. Heated argument arose upon that point. The Secretary of State, even though a proven traitor, could not hang. His head would roll from the block on Tower Green and not swing in a hempen collar. Blows were struck, swords drawn in his defence by the youthful Tories of St. James, while more mud slung to settle on his intimacy with the Queen's Bedchamber-woman. The feminine interest could not be ignored. It was known that he had gained the Queen's ear through the lips of Mrs. Masham.

"Lips!" crowed the blades of the Kit-Cat Club, famed meeting-place of the Whigs. "Be damned to her lips! Harley's stooped lower to lift himself up—on the highway to Lord Treasurer."

"The hymen-way, you mean!"

It was an age of woeful punning, but they couldn't let that pass. The perpetrator had been forced to eat his words in a revolting and indescribable concoction.

Meanwhile the Junto led by Sarah, the Duke, and Godolphin, had urged an ultimatum on the Queen: her choice between the resignation of Marlborough or Harley. The Duke, indeed, in stronger terms than he had ever before addressed to the Sovereign of England, had written: 'That in view of the treacherous proceedings of Mr. Secretary Harley, no consideration can make me serve any longer with that man.'

The Queen was distracted. Marlborough! Her beloved 'Mr. Freeman'. . . . How could she let him go? True, he had threatened resignation many times before, but she had never dared to take him at his word. And if she *did* take him at his word, what then? Although no other man alive could replace him as Commander-in-Chief of her armies, as a Minister of the Crown he was by no means indispensable. Was ever a woman in so awful a dilemma? Was ever Sovereign so beset with the disputes of an unruly, and—to herself she could confess it—incompetent Government?

She paced her Green Closet, she gnawed at her thumb, she rang for her handmaiden. "Masham, I am due now to attend a Council meeting, and must listen to their tirades against poor Mr. Harley whom I know to be guiltless. I must make decisions— O, God! How can I make decisions when every other man—and now the Duke—is at my throat?"

"Madam!" ejaculated Abigail, shocked.

" 'Tis so indeed, child. A pack of wolves, whose howls of 'resignation' deafen my ears till I sicken to the sound of them. . . . How do you find the Prince to-day?"

"Nicely, Madam. His Highness has eaten a hearty breakfast."

"Did he take his barley-water?"

"Yes, Madam. And he was able to walk without his stick to the commode."

The Queen pressed her hand. "How thankful I should be for your devotion. There is none in this world would do for His Highness the things you do for him so sweetly."

Abigail curtsied.

"So I may serve His Highness, Madam, in ever so small a way to ease his suffering, I am content."

The Queen gave her a fearful smile.

"Dear child . . . You are my sole comfort in these troublous times. *Such* a little prop."

And with an arm round the shoulder of her little prop, the Queen passed through the open door to the adjoining room.

Raised upright for easier breathing on his pillows, the Prince slept. His wife faltered an anxious query: "That blue look round his lips——?"

"Is not necessarily a symptom for alarm, Madam. His Highness's pulse is much steadier."

"Thank God for that. And thank God for you, my dear. . . ."

*   *   *

The hue and cry raised against Harley, dubbed by his rivals 'The Fox', was elatedly renewed, with Marlborough and Godolphin now declared joint masters of the Whig hounds. What though no concrete evidence had come to light? He had left a stinking trail to be followed for a kill! The man Gregg had been in his employ, had obtained access to the Secretary's bureau. How? If the Secretary of State was so careless as to leave his keys lying about for an enemy agent to seize, then he could be committed on a charge of criminal negligence and arraigned as accessory after the fact, which was nothing short of Treason.

In Justice to the State and the office he held, Harley must be brought before the Council and examined; and the hopeful cry that rose in Westminster Hall was heard in the Palace of St. James's.

"Harley's head is falling! It has fallen . . . on the block!"

It was heard, with fainting heart, by Mrs. Masham. There

could be no avoidance of him now. A few days after that meeting of the Cabinet, attended by the Queen and from which Marlborough and Godolphin had been conspicuously absent, he was summoned to an audience and Abigail bidden to remain.

"I cannot," the Queen agitatedly told her, "face poor Mr. Harley alone. I am horrified at this most dreadful charge against him. But of course the accusation is fantastical. I and all who are acquainted with him know him to be innocent—the soul of honour. I would as soon accuse my own husband of Treason as my Secretary of State."

And as he entered, calm, poised, debonair as ever, to bow with easy grace before his Queen, Abigail felt those charmed tentacles of his attraction reach out for and possess her once again. What use to fight against the slow cobra-magic of this man? She stood transfixed, her eyes, hiding beneath her downcast lids, drawn reluctantly to his as they skimmed her mouth, her body, in the ghost-touch of a caress. She felt herself held, taken. . . . O, God! Not again. . . . But even as that prayer leapt, unspoken, to her lips, she knew she was his utterly, to serve for good or ill: and to obey.

The Queen leaned forward from her great chair.

"My dear Mr. Harley, pray be seated. What can I say on this most shocking subject, beyond my earnest assurance, which I am willing to repeat in Parliament, that I know you to be as guiltless as I, or Mrs. Masham here, of this monstrous accusation."

He knelt to kiss her outstretched hand. "I am honoured by Your Majesty's most gracious generosity." He rose and standing said clear-voiced: "Nor is Your Majesty's trust in me misplaced. The charge *is* monstrous, in that it is based on nothing more than the prejudice of those who seek, not my downfall only, but that of the Party which I, in Your Majesty's name, represent."

"Mr. Harley, I am the Queen, and although the Whigs would gag me, I can still speak. They cannot—they *shall* not force you out of office."

"Madam, they have already done so. I am here to tender Your Majesty my resignation."

A low cry broke from the Queen. She sank back in her chair. Abigail took a step forward and was waved aside.

"I refuse to accept your resignation, Mr. Harley."

"Madam, it is in Your Majesty's interests that I beg you to accept the inevitable. A crisis has uprisen resultant upon"—his hooded glance swerved to that small silent figure behind the Queen's chair—"resultant," proceeded Harley with the shadow of a smile, "on this unhappy incident. The man Gregg has confessed his guilt and will pay his penalty."

The Queen shuddered.

"A ghastly penalty. But because he has been man enough to protest *your* innocence, I could find it in my heart to save his life."

"His life, Madam, is forfeit to his treachery, as my resignation is forfeit to my crime."

"Mr. Harley!"

"My crime, Madam," he said quietly, "is that I am guilty of having placed my trust in one so patently unworthy of it. As I believed in myself, so did I believe in the man Gregg. My judgment has been tried and is found wanting."

The Queen beat her hands together. "No, no! I cannot—I will not take your resignation. I could lose Marlborough with less grief than I lose you. Mr. Harley, why will you give such satisfaction to your—to *our*—enemies who have deliberately sought to encompass your downfall by this wicked attempt to couple your name with that of a wretched creature who has betrayed his country and his Queen? Why do you allow them this mean victory?" The Queen's massive chins shook; the ready tears welled up, brimmed over and splashed on her folded hands. "I implore you to see this hateful affair to its triumphant end. Stand firm, Mr. Harley. Stand firm!"

He stood firm, but not on the grounds she had urged. Despite her entreaties she was at last induced to accept his resignation.

Marlborough, summoned to the Presence Chamber, heard the Queen tell him in cool bitter words of her Secretary's decision. "Since his service to us appears to be so obnoxious to you and your wife and your son-in-law, Sunderland, and all the Lords of the Junto, Mr. Harley has retired from that office which, for these last four years, and to our entire and most grateful satisfaction, he has held. We are shocked. We are disgusted at the slanderous calumnies hurled at Mr. Harley. We consider he has behaved with great dignity and courage throughout these abominable proceedings."

It was no longer the easy, warm relationship of a 'Mrs. Morley' and a 'Mr. Freeman'. It was offended Majesty who spoke in the Royal plural, and the voice of a stranger: one who looked upon the dismayed Duke with eyes of stone.

The Queen's support of Harley caused the winning faction some alarm. No hope now of his impeachment, since not the flimsiest evidence against him could be found. He had indeed become the hero of the Tories, and the day: a popular martyr thrown to the spite of the Whigs. Their side must be strengthened and weeded of those who too loyally upheld him.

St. John, Harley's most faithful adherent, had retired with him, to be succeeded by that brilliant young man of destiny, Robert Walpole, as Secretary-of-War: Harley by Henry Boyle, both Whigs and both hot for the Party.

But there still remained one more to be dismissed; one who, wholly unaware that she was the subject of contention outside the Queen's Bedchamber, or indeed within it, was, when not engaged in poulticing the Prince, striving to divert the Queen's harassed mind from the quarrels of her Ministry with songs at the harpsichord . . . Abigail Masham. Masham, *Masham*!

The name was passed from mouth to mouth in a rising and eager crescendo. If, as the Duchess declared, this girl were indeed Harley's mistress and his foil, why then the combination was a menace.

Mrs. Masham, it was plain to all, must go.

CHAPTER THREE

"Est-il possible?"

That faint ejaculation from the parched lips of Prince George hurried Abigail to his bedside.

"Did Your Highness call?"

"No . . . I was dreamingk. Now I wake. I will sit up."

"Yes, Sir. But Your Highness must not lift yourself. Let me . . ."

With the skilled ease of long practice she raised his swollen body and placed pillows at his back. "There! Is Your Highness comfortable?"

"Very comfortable. Now I breathe not so hard. I am better . . . Much better to-day, amn't I?" The bleared patient eyes gazed up at her with a look of mute appeal to twist her heart.

"Yes, Sir, indeed you are," she lied with false cheer. "We shall have you up and about again very soon."

He took her hand and patted it.

"I give you so much trouble, my little Hill. So small you, to lift so big a lump. A born nurse. How did you learn to be so born a nurse?"

"I nursed my mother in her last illness, Sir. And afterwards an invalid lady."

"So. One sees you are experienced, but . . . experience cannot give a kind nature which is yours. Only God . . . can give you that."

The Prince's slow glance searched the room, his eyebrows

asked a question, and interpreting that unvoiced query: "The Queen, Sir," she told him, "is in audience with Lord Treasurer." And as she wiped a frothy dribble from his mouth, the fierce fight for breath began again. Rising from his bedside she pulled the bell-rope. To the page who came to the door she gave a whispered instruction. In a few minutes he returned with a silver basin of steaming water. Into this she poured a few drops of soothing balsam. The Prince's eyes were closed, his face red, his jaw fallen, his ponderous frame shaken with the struggle against that inexorable sense of suffocation.

"This will ease Your Highness."

Covering his head and shoulders with a towel she raised him higher. Supporting him with one arm, she held the basin under his nose that the soothing steam might penetrate those strangled lungs. After some minutes she removed the towel, bathed the wet flaccid face with cooling lotion and readjusted the pillows.

He thanked her feebly. "How good you are to me, my little Masham. You send away my misery so quick. Now I am at ease . . . Will the Queen," panted that feeble voice, "soon come? Why does not the Queen come? They worry her with their idiot talks. Godolphin has turned coat with Marlborough now. I was thinkingk . . . as I lie here, how mad and how . . . weak in their madness they are to kick so big at you, my little Hill. Take no heed . . . of . . . They shout and . . ."

The flush on his face deepened.

"Try not to speak, Sir. Shall I read to Your Highness?"

He nodded. "The one I like . . . most."

She took a massive leather-bound book from his bedside table. Opening it at a page marked by a ribbon of gold, she read:

'The Lord is my Shepherd, I shall not want. He maketh me to lie down in green pastures; He leadeth me beside the still waters . . .'

The painful breathing lessened. The Prince's eyelids closed; and as she returned the book to its place the Queen came in.

Abigail rose with a finger to her lips. The Queen hushed her step. Her face, furrowed with anxiety and mottled with recent tears, lightened.

"Thank God," she whispered, "he can sleep."

"Yes, Madam. His Highness has slept at intervals all the afternoon."

"He is breathing more naturally."

"Yes, Madam. He has only had one short attack."

The Prince's eyelids lifted. A smile wandered up to those dry lips.

"Ah! My Anna! . . . What news has Godolphin?"

"Good news, my darling. Did I waken you?"

"No . . . I am . . . always half awake . . . when you are not here. Tell me what he says."

The Queen looked helplessly at Abigail, who answered with a reassuring nod.

Seating herself on the chair Abigail had vacated, the Queen stroked the large veined hand that rested on the counterpane.

"Lord Treasurer has promised to consider the dismissal of Lord Sunderland. I told him that if Sunderland does anything more to which I must object—and he has done much already—Lord Treasurer shall bring him to make his leg and take his leave."

The Prince chuckled.

"He has done much you have not liked . . . and much I have not liked. I do not forgive Sunderland, nor Somers neither, their attack on me . . . and the . . . Admiralty."

"Yes, darling." The Queen stooped her lips to his forehead. "And that is all the news of any importance. The rest was merely routine. Now I am going to leave you and let you sleep again."

His eyes strained up at her, doubting, searching.

"My heart, I have told you all there is to tell," her voice was soft against his ear. "You must have all the sleep possible, and I disturb you."

"No . . . never. I am happy with you here. Stay with me."

"Yes, my angel."

She stayed there, watching, waiting till his moist hand relaxed in hers, and he passed into the sound unbroken sleep that the comfort of her presence there beside him had induced. Then noiselessly she got up and beckoned Abigail to follow her into the ante-room.

"Leave the door wide so that we can hear when he wakes." And sinking into the chair Abigail had drawn forward, she turned her head to its velvet back and wept without sound.

Light from the grave March sky crept in at the window and fell upon that huddled shape in its incongruous stiff bright silks, and on that twisted face. Her words shuddered through her silent sobs.

"O God! . . . I cannot bear his suffering . . . I can't. Is there any hope, Hill? Is there . . . Is there?"

Her hand groped blindly. Abigail knelt to take and lay her cheek upon it.

"Yes, Madam, every hope. Dr. Arbuthnot is confident that when the warmer weather comes——"

"We'll take him away. Away from here . . . Go see if he is sleeping."

Abigail went to the door.

"Yes, Madam, soundly."

Raising her head, the Queen wiped her red-rimmed eyes.

"I must tell you this quickly. He may wake at any moment . . . Lord Treasurer, Hill . . ." Her poor swelled hands gripped the chair-arm in a vain attempt to control the agitated tremors that overswept her. "I feel to be at the end of my endurance. The end . . ."

Abigail knelt again.

"Madam, my sweet Lady, what is it? Give me your trouble. Tell."

As a mother comforts her hurt child, so did she comfort the Queen. And composing her lips, the Queen answered jerkily:

"Lord Treasurer has brought me dreadful news. Rebellion. In the North. The Jacobites are clamouring to restore my brother. Reports have come from our secret agents at Dunkirk. An attack on the coast of Scotland, led by the French Fleet, is in preparation. My brother is with them. My brother. That boy. My own blood. My own brother. He prepares to strike a blow . . . at me!"

But that blow never came. So soon as the French Fleet was sighted in the Firth of Forth, an English Squadron under Admiral Byng gave chase along the coast from Forfar to Aberdeen. Foul weather and westerly gales had urged the French Commander, Forbin, to attempt a landing at Inverness, ill-timed in a storm of snow, amid raging seas and with the wind against him.

The attempted invasion ended in a rout. The battered Fleet was driven back to Dunkirk with the loss of several ships.

The deposed Harley and his henchman, St. John, fed the Queen, avid for news concerning the safety of her brother, with detailed reports brought by British agents. From St. John the Queen learned how the Prince had borne himself—'like a true Stuart, through and through.' He had stood on deck in the thick of the fight with balls whistling round his head, and had refused to turn back till capture was imminent.

"Thank God he was *not* captured," sobbed the Queen. "The foolish, foolish boy. How could he have embarked on so rash an adventure!"

"It was against the French Commander's wish, Your Majesty, that the Prince accompanied the Fleet. His Royal Highness had only just recovered from the measles."

"The measles!" The Queen smiled through her trickling tears. "A schoolboy's ailment—poor child! And so weakening."

St. John twinkled.

"It did not weaken him, Madam, although the fever had not left him when His Royal Highness set out."

The Queen shook her head. "So foolhardy. He might have infected the whole of his ship."

"I think, Madam," said St. John soberly, "he did."

The Queen sighed. "Poor dear boy. How I wish . . ." She stopped and glanced at Harley, whose upper lip was drawn back on a dry tooth: and at Mrs. Masham, whose white lids fluttered downwards: and at St. John, sipping tea. And on him her moist eyes rested with a frown between them. So absorbed had she been in his tale that she had not till then noticed he had entered her presence in a tie-wig. How very remiss of Mr. St. John! Her mouth had opened to remind him that she did not permit any gentleman to visit her unless in periwig or furbelow, when he spoke again.

"Some English prisoners at Dunkirk, Madam, have described the Prince's return."

"Yes? Tell me." She was all eagerness, her momentary displeasure forgotten. "How did he look? Did they say?"

"Pale, Madam, and tall, with a blue feather in his hat and a star on his cloak."

"Pale, yes," she murmured, "and he would be tall. His . . . our father was tall. If only it were possible for me to see him! If only we could meet."

St. John looked at her steadily.

"That, Madam, might be arranged."

She took fright. She had been told by Mrs. Freeman of St. John's activities on behalf of the Jacobite party. Such hints as these were dangerous. Having gone too far, she hastened to re-retract. Her eyes rested distantly upon his handsome ingenuous face.

"Mr. St. John, this is, we know, an informal visit, but we are bound to remind you of our objection to the wearing of a tie-wig in our presence."

Any other man would have been shame-covered by that chill reprimand; but not so the unblushing St. John.

He rose, and with easy assurance he bowed.

"Madam, I am wrongfully at fault. I crave Your Majesty's pardon. My negligence is inexcusable, and I can offer no excuse—save that of my doctor's advice."

"Your doctor, Mr. St. John?"

"I suffer a slight eruption of the scalp, Madam, and am advised by Dr. Arbuthnot to discard the wearing of a wig in favour of my natural hair. I have ventured, therefore, upon a compromise."

Harley grinned behind his hand. The Queen extended hers.

"In that case," she said graciously, "the fault is ours. We trust you will soon be recovered, Mr. St. John. It is always our pleasure to see you, with or with*out* your wig. Pray bring me all news you may hear of my brother the Prince—" she paused—"of Wales."

"And what," demanded Harley as they left the Palace gates, "do you think you have gained by stuffing her full of James Edward? I was waiting for you to bring up the Election. Why didn't you ram it into her that this invasion scare has paved a clear way for a Whig majority? We want her support, not her sentiment."

"Lord, Lord!" groaned St. John. "Hear him. Is this our wily Robin? Don't you know by this time that Anna Regina's support *is* her sentiment? Touch her on a tender spot and she'll respond as sweetly as a young virgin to a tongue kiss. I've got her now lapping up the juice of James's adventure, and so big with love for him that the Whigs can cry themselves hoarse with their howls of a 'Popish Pretender'. She'll listen, but you may slit me if she'll hear."

Harley's shoulders moved in a shrug.

"You may be right and you may be wrong, but in your cocksure calculations you have overlooked one salient point—and that's Scotland. Don't forget, she's bound heart and soul to the Union, and if it weren't for this damned young ass over the water she'd be hugging the Scots peers instead of hanging them."

"Tush! If I know Anna, she won't hang one man Jack of 'em. I have her as I want her now. Didn't you hear her? 'Prince of Wales'? The first time she's ever called him that."

Harley looked along his nose.

"Is it?"

"Well, isn't it?" St. John halted his step to hitch up his sword-belt which was slipping. "Pize take me if I haven't lost close on a stone of fat in the Hummums! . . . She's the truest Jack of us all, I'm thinking."

"Here," said Harley gently, "is my coach." And while he waited for his footman to open the carriage door he turned to recite the words of a popular song into St. John's discomfited face.

'The Queen has lately lost a part
Of her "entirely English" heart,
For want of which, by way of botch,
She's pieced it up again—with Scotch.'

"Get in," smiled Harley. "We will drive to the Exchange, and buy you another head—of hair."

*   *   *

As Harley had prophesied, the invasion scare brought in a Whig majority at the General Election. Funds had dropped to lowest ebb during the polling period, and incensed electors who might have voted Tory in the hope of a speedy peace, supported the Whig candidates with a renewal of their war cries against the French King and his 'Popish' satellites.

All Tories, high or moderate, were equally suspect of Jacobite intrigue with the 'Pretender'. Sunderland, whose dismissal the Queen had so ardently desired, was returned unopposed with the Queen's pet aversion, Lord Somers, and Godolphin, still in his crumbling office of Lord Treasurer, swinging his weight on the side of the favoured party.

The Duchess was jubilant. The Whigs were in, the Tories out, and Harley's name besmeared with mud, that, despite the Queen's belief in his integrity, still stuck. But the full force of Sarah's batteries were not trained on the fallen Harley. His fangs had been successfully extracted. Her store of ammunition was held in readiness to attack that other still more noxious presence at the bedside of the dying Prince.

Determined to secure the complete extermination of her loathly rival, she held herself in patience until the Election results were declared. Then, finding that her plaints of injury done to herself were sympathetically but not actively received by the Junto, Sarah gave tongue.

Why this shilly-shallying, she wished to know? Having admitted that Masham's influence with the Queen was a danger to them all, why did they not take immediate steps to remove her? Why stand upon the order of her going when they already had decided she must go?

To her dinner-table a select committee was invited to review the situation. Sarah presented them with a collection of offences attributed to Mrs. Masham, and serious enough to have brought her to the gallows if believed. Abigail was accused of indiscriminate association with persons of low calling, and in particular with a woman of pernicious notoriety, a bawdy pamphleteer of the name of Manley, who wrote scurrilous Jacobite articles and —"libels me," declared the Duchess, "in songs of the gutter! That alone proves Masham's diabolic machinations, without any further conclusive evidence that this creature is plotting, not only the collapse of the Government and the promotion of Harley in *your* place," pointing at Godolphin, "but of connivance with the Jacobites—and France!"

The Whig Lords thumbed their chins and took a pinch of salt. They knew their Sarah.

Infuriated by their smiles, she produced her master-shot.

Abigail was in direct communication with the 'Pretender'. A Mrs. Vane, one of the dressers, had come into the room to find the Queen fondly regarding a miniature which she held in her hand. And Masham, leaning over the Queen's chair in an attitude of great familiarity, had been heard to say: "If, Madam, you think it unsafe that you yourself write to His Royal Highness, I will gladly——"

At which point the dresser's entrance had been discovered and the miniature concealed.

"There is no possible doubt *whose* face," persisted Sarah, "the Queen was so 'fondly regarding'. And if you remain wilfully blind to the evil mischief of this woman who sidles up to the Queen with her whispers—she, whose sole aim is to bring about another Revolution, then your blood *and* the Queen's be on your heads!"

Lords Godolphin, Somers, Wharton, hid their grins, but the pug-nosed Sunderland sprang to his feet.

"By God! If what you tell us can be proven we can charge her."

Sarah beamed upon her son-in-law.

"It is proven. Vane is prepared to swear on oath to what she witnessed. Our Cousin Abigail's day, my dear, is done."

Happily for Abigail's comfort, Sarah's thirst for vengeance did not penetrate the walls of the Prince's sick-room, nor of the Council Chamber. The Junto were not disposed to join in the chase of so elusive a scent. Moreover their position was not secure enough for ridicule. To fall upon that mousy little chambermaid and rend her limb from limb simply because Sarah loathed the sight of her, was too much. And if, they subsequently argued, you sift Sarah's high-flown dramatics to the bottom, what would you find? The babbling hearsay of a dresser. You couldn't hang the Queen's woman on that. Godolphin had the last word.

"Your filly's got no kick in her. 'The Trickster's' your man. Watch *him*, and ride him—to hell."

He was bitter. He had always mistrusted Harley. Of all Sarah's tales he believed only one: that Harley would stop at nothing to displace him.

Sarah's guests departed severally. Sunderland, the last to go, offered consolation.

"We'll have her out I promise you."

"Fine promises," snapped Sarah. "She'll have you out first—you fool!"

She slammed the door in his face, and then sat down to write a thunderous letter to John. He would advise her, and aid her offensive against the reptilian Masham.

His answer when it came was disappointing.

'If you have good reason for what you write of the kindness and esteem the Queen has for Mrs. Masham and Mr. Harley, my opinion should be that Lord Treasurer and I shall tell her what is good for her to hear; and if that will not prevail, to be quiet.'

He might as well have told a baffled tigress to be quiet. That tepid response from her John only whetted Sarah's appetite for vengeance and drove her to stalk her quarry with still more furious determination. She ran her to earth at Kensington whence from that same dresser, whose service may have been rewarded with uncommon generosity, she heard of 'the grand apartments in which my cousin Masham received company, and which must have been the same fitted up by King William for his favourite, Keppel, and afterwards allotted by Queen Anne, to *me*.'*

And which had never been occupied by Sarah; but because they communicated with the Prince's apartments, had, since his illness and at the Queen's request, been occupied by Mrs. Masham.

To that quiet Palace of Kensington came Sarah, hot on the track of her prey. Peace fled; and so did Mrs. Masham, to seek cover in the bedroom of the Prince. The Queen was left to meet the Duchess's torrential abuse, overheard by the giggling pages in the galleries and by the quaking Mrs. Masham at the door.

What right had Mrs. Morley, was the high-note of Sarah's plaint, to dispose of Mrs. Freeman's property? These rooms, by Royal consent, were hers, now bestowed without leave of Mrs. Freeman on Mrs. Morley's chambermaid. Such an affront to the Mistress of the Robes and Groom of the Stole was outrageous.

The affront to Majesty appeared to be equally outrageous. It was not the gentle Mrs. Morley but the Sovereign of England who replied, and: 'in a way of speaking,' confesses Sarah, 'that I had never heard her make use of to any one till she came under the practices of Abigail.'

'I am sure Mrs. Masham has none of your rooms, and to say to the contrary is false—and a lie!'

* *Conduct:* Sarah, Duchess of Marlborough.

But Sarah, undaunted in this battle for her 'Rights' pursued the matter further. She called the housemaids and the housekeeper to witness that Mrs. Masham had 'not only done as I suspected, but that she had used a great many little arts in the management of her design.'

The nature of these 'little arts' is not disclosed in the Duchess's account of Abigail's misappropriation of her chambers, from which, by the Duchess, she was forcibly ejected—and into the arms of the Queen.

"Shameful! Disgraceful! Most shocking. There, there." Pats, promises, were offered with condolence. "My *poor* Mrs. Masham. So uncalled for. . . . You shall have other rooms."

The rows in her Palace and the racket in her Parliament were too much for the sorely tried Queen. With her Prince and her 'poor Mrs. Masham' she retired to Windsor: and there, in a lodge at the gates of the park, she nursed her sick husband through the last summer of his life. But the Queen's intention to keep her husband and herself peacefully cloistered in that cottage at Windsor, was by Sarah at once misconstrued.

That viper, Abigail, in conjunction with Harley, had for their own evil purposes persuaded the Queen to bury herself in a hovel. The season was sultry, the Prince panting for breath, 'and that small house, which was hot as an oven, was said to be *cool* because from the Park such persons as Mrs. Masham had a mind to bring to Her Majesty could be let in privately by the garden.' . . .

And in June, to 'that small house', where Anne shared with Abigail the constant nursing of her husband, came the news of Marlborough's victory at Oudenarde.

With the Prince, by then deemed well enough to travel, she drove to London to attend another Thanksgiving Service at St. Paul's.

The Duchess received her, knelt in homage, kissed with rapture that kind forgiving hand. The Duke, by his latest success, had brought all tiresome misunderstandings to an end. Mrs. Morley and Mrs. Freeman were united once again in joy and adulation of their hero.

Mrs. Freeman rose from her knees. Mrs. Morley opened her arms—and her heart.

"Dear God! When will this dreadful bloodshed cease?"

Mrs. Freeman backed from that loving embrace.

"Dreadful! Bloodshed! Lord, Madam, is this how you regard the Duke's magnificent achievement? Is this all the thanks he merits—to be reproached for bloodshed?"

"No, no! Why *will* you misinterpret my most innocent remarks? I was thinking only of my brave soldiers fallen on the battlefield—their stricken wives, their orphans. It has been so long, so very long. Seven years of slaughter, and still no end to it."

Mrs. Freeman took a deep breath. The colour flew to her face, the words to her lips. "I see you have well learned the Tory parrot-cry that Marlborough prolongs the war for his own gain. Madam, I take your imputation not only as an insult to him, but to *me*!"

The Queen closed her eyes.

"If I insult him and you, I insult myself. Such a thought was never in my mind."

"Madam, the thought has been implanted in your mind, and it bears bitter fruit."

The pale Queen raised herself from her great chair and pointed. "Go," she commanded. "Withdraw."

And Mrs. Freeman did withdraw, in something near to fright.

The Queen was dressed in the gowns of State laid out for her by the Mistress of the Robes; but when Mrs. Vane knelt to offer the jewels she turned away.

"Not these," she said. "My pearls."

It had been a long day. The Queen returned from the Thanksgiving Service exhausted. Still in her State robes, she entered the Prince's apartment. Perceiving that he slept, she beckoned Abigail to follow her into the ante-room.

"Masham, I have had a shock. . . ."

There was a strained yet resolved look in her eyes, as if she had been faced with and taken some desperate decision. Her heavy limbs trembled. She sank on to a couch and covered her face.

"I cannot endure these scenes," she said hoarsely. "I can't!" And in a broken, smothered voice she recounted to the kneeling Abigail how that the Duchess, who had sat beside her in the coach, had raged throughout the drive to St. Paul's "because . . . because I did not wear the jewels she had chosen for me. She said I had offered a deliberate slight to her and the Duke by appearing in pearls on this day of rejoicing, instead of my diamonds and rubies. She knows I do not care for rubies, that I much prefer pearls. I always have. . . . All the way along the streets, Masham, while my dear people were cheering, she was scolding . . . shouting." The Queen lifted her drooped head to fumble with the clasp of her cloak. Abigail rose to relieve her of it.

"I was ashamed . . . ashamed for her and for myself. Even as we walked up the steps of the Cathedral she did not cease to accuse me"—the Queen made a brief helpless gesture—"of every kind of imaginary offence that I am supposed to have committed. She has it firmly fixed that I do not sufficiently appreciate the Duke's or her services, and all this she shouted at me—*shouted,* Masham, at the top of her voice. She wouldn't listen when I tried to hush her. Then she began on you. It was you who had persuaded me to wear these——" she twisted the rope of pearls between her fingers. "She wouldn't heed me when I told her you were not in the room while I dressed. She went on and on. I was so sunk in shame of her loud words, so disgusted at her lack of control, that I could only whisper, 'What you say is not true . . . not true.' And then," the Queen pressed her face convulsively to Abigail's shoulder; her body shook with her dry, aching sobs, "then, for all to hear—my entourage, my servants, and those good people gathered on the steps of God's House to see me pass, she said: 'Don't answer me!' She said it twice. She shouted it, Masham. 'Don't *answer* me.' She said it to . . . the Queen."

The loose lips tightened; that wounded bovine look travelled slowly from the listening face at her knee to spend itself in vacancy. She did not see the eager light that shone in those widened green eyes. The Queen did not see, for when she looked again those eyes, the flicker of triumph that lit them, were shuttered beneath their downcast lids.

CHAPTER FOUR

"MADAM," Mrs. Abrahal announced herself with smiles, "Her Grace is in a rare taking because her dinner has not yet been served."

Mrs. Abrahal's companion did not announce herself with smiles. Her demands were voiced in clamour, ear-splitting, imperative, discordant.

"Give her to me, the blessed! Why did you not waken me sooner?"

Mrs. Abrahal approached the bed and deposited her burden. The yells subsided to a low gurgle of content.

Strange that no memory of torture unendurable remained, no grievance, grudge, was stored in the heart of its slave against this creature who, not thirty-six hours before, had fought, struggled, rent its way out of her body.

It was red, crumpled, hideous, greedy, utterly self-centred, yet she who had suffered willing agony and terror for its sake showered upon it a love as fatuous and worshipful as it was unrequited.

Her soul sang. Her baby sucked and, replete, loosed its pull on her nipple and slept.

She gazed adoringly upon the wizened, old little face at her breast, and for the hundredth time in the last three days she whispered: "I'm a mother." Frequent repetition had not staled the novelty of that recent and exalted state of being.

She lifted her daughter's diminutive hand and covered it with kisses. She nibbled its apology for a nose. She lipped the colourless fluff that shaded its scarlet and almost bald head.

"Pure gold," she murmured. "Blue eyes, no freckles, please goodness. You're going to be a beauty. You already *are* a beauty."

She believed it. She was love-blind. She was proud.

"Shall I take her?" suggested Mrs. Abrahal with matronly forbearance.

"No, let me have her. She'll sleep till it's time to feed again."

Mrs. Abrahal went out. Abigail's eyes turned to the window, framing the grey January sky, and a tracery of bare tree-branches that looked as if cut out of black paper stuck in silhouette upon it. Her rooms were those from which her cousin Sarah had ejected her two years before. They were hers again now. The furniture was hers, the curtains of rich brocade, the ornaments; the bed, with its velvet hangings and gold-embroidered counterpane, was hers. Riches were hers and jewels, and much else of more worth than all of these; the Queen's affection for and preference above all others living. The flattery of courtiers and the homage of political leaders who sought her undisputed influence with their Sovereign, was hers. And all this greatness had been thrust upon her with no apparent effort on her part to achieve it!

Her mind went searching back.

Since that day, eighteen months ago, when the Queen had unburdened her heart to her after that fateful Service at St. Paul's, her rise had been as equally inevitable as her cousin's fall. And when a few weeks later the Prince Consort had succumbed to his last asthmatic paroxysm, and the Queen, broken by grief, had retired from public life, she would have none but Abigail and her dogs for company. Day after day, week after week, throughout that winter of the Great Frost, she had sat in the little dark closet in St. James's that had been her husband's work-room. Her desire for solitude had received universal and sympathetic response—with one exception.

She, who had forced an entry into the sick-room of the dying Prince while his wife knelt at his bedside watching that last enfeebled struggle on the threshold of eternity; she, who even in that sacred moment had upbraided the Queen for her 'usage of me, which is such as can scarcely be believed', was not disposed to recognize the grief-bowed widow's mourning isolation.

There had been other forced entries, other heartless, soul-destructive scenes, stoked by jealousy to burning pitch at the sight of Abigail's perpetual presence in that closet, from which Sarah, at the Queen's desire, had been barred. She hammered on the door praying for admittance. It was opened. She burst in—and she drove the Queen out.

Again the Sovereign of England fled to Windsor. Sarah followed. So did other scenes.

The worst of these, which occurred in Abigail's absence when her husband had returned on short leave from the front, was described by Mrs. Danvers who had witnessed it.

"And all the storm arose," Mrs. Danvers had delightedly recounted, "because you had asked the Queen's permission to take six bottles of wine to Mrs. Abrahal when she lay sick of the jaundice." Which the Duchess regarded as another and deliberate infringement of her 'Rights'. It was *her* office, and not that of a chambermaid, to dispense the Queen's bounty to her Household.

When Her Majesty, Danvers said, 'who had appeared to have been quite confounded by this unwarrantable attack', had risen from her chair to leave the room, Her Grace, whisking past her, had set her back against the door and shouted, shockingly: 'Oh no, you don't! You shall not go till you have heard what I've to say!'

The footmen on the stairs and the pages in the galleries also heard what Sarah had to say. 'That is the least favour you can do for me, who has set the Crown on your head and kept it there!'

Even then she had not seen that she had uttered the unutterable: that offended Majesty would not forget nor overlook such insult. She had raged on.

'What is my crime that has wrought so great a change in your attitude to me?'

And the Queen's reply, carried by the listening servants from one end of the Castle to the other, was forensic, decisive: a charge:

'It is certain to me you have nothing at heart but the ruin of poor Mrs. Masham!'

Recalling that loyal defence of herself, which Danvers, peeping from the Ante-room, had been at greatest pains to overhear, 'poor' Mrs. Masham wriggled on her pillows and gleefully kissed her baby's head.

"So poor am I and so poor are you, that you'll have a Queen for godmother, my girl. . . . So put that in your pipe and smoke it!"

It was pleasant to lie lazily in bed during the later stages of convalescence and to receive visitors, many of whom had once ignored or despised her existence.

Ladies-in-Waiting, Grooms of the Chamber, Maids of Honour, equerries, vied with Ministers of State in their choice of costly gifts and warm felicitations to the Favourite. Nor in view of Parliament's pending dissolution, were all those personages who evinced so great an interest in the health of Mrs. Masham and her daughter, Anne, limited to Tories. The Whig Lords of the formidable Junto arrived with flowers, golden rattles, broidered bibs. The Queen paid her private daily visits and presented her namesake with a christening robe, and her namesake's mother with a silver tea and coffee service. Mrs. Danvers, who since Abigail's high ascendancy had buried her hatchet in warmest affection, arrived in lavender plush to pay her respects and admire the baby.

"A cherub come to earth! An angel's countenance! Such beauty of form and feature—such sturdy limbs I have never in my life beheld." Declared Mrs. Danvers as she came in: and to Mrs. Abrahal, as she went out:

"Of all rickety, evil-eyed, misshapen pups, that's one—and the image of *her*!"

Only from the baby's Uncle Jack, who, wounded again at Malplaquet, was now returned with the promised command of the regiment recently vacated by Lord Essex, did Abigail hear the blunt truth.

"Are all newly-born babies as ugly as this?"

"*Ugly?*"

His sisters loudly protested in chorus, then exchanged indulgent glances for the pitiable senselessness of man. And Jack, Abigail marvelled, was now very much of a man. In his spick scarlet uniform, his face still tanned from last summer's campaign, he towered six feet four inches high above her bed, bending gingerly to inspect his sister's prize.

Abigail pushed his face away.

"Don't breathe brandy all over her. Sit down."

Jack sat down and Alice got up.

"I must go. I'm in attendance to-day."

Alice had stoutened, and looked older than her five and twenty years. She was puffy, pale, dyspeptic, and very conscious of her position as sister to the Second Lady in the land. Her total lack of personal ambition, combined with a placid large-heartedness, had earned her many useful friends at Court. She took an immense interest in clothes, always dressed in the height of fashion, and was generous with gifts and hospitality. She had gained quite

a small reputation as a hostess. She kept an excellent cook. Not a
few celebrities sat at her board; and if she mixed her company with
indifference to their politics, it was well-seasoned with a sprinkling
of wit. Those two leading Whig pamphleteers, Joe Addison and
Richard Steele, editor of the *London Gazette*, fraternized in
sprightly wine-doused argument with Prior and Arbuthnot.
Harley came and St. John, but they did not bring their wives.
Prior brought his mistresses, and once he brought a dwarf.

Of all oddities! Shrill-voiced, conceited, and sickly and young,
with wild, strange, beautiful eyes, he out-talked them all. He
gestured and mouthed, discussed Homer and his hitherto one
publication—his 'Pastorale'; criticized Shakespeare, and trod on
the cat. Not until he had left, rather drunk, did she learn from
Arbuthnot his name. It was Pope; unknown to her, but soon
to be known to the world.

As the door closed behind Alice, Abigail turned expectantly to
Jack.

"Well, what of your appointment? Has the Duke agreed to
grant it?"

The look on his face prepared her for his answer:

"Did you believe he would?"

"You don't mean to say he's refused?"

"He has not only refused, but he has left London for St. Albans
with instructions to the Council for a compromise."

A flag of angry colour sprang to Abigail's cheek. She sat up,
clutching her baby. "How *dare* he compromise against the
Queen's desire!"

Jack grinned.

"Your desire, you mean. And he knows it."

"So might I have known it," said Abigail through her teeth.
"But neither he nor his lady can put you down if I decide to put
you up. What excuse does he give for his refusal?"

Jack crisped his long fingers and closed them.

"That I'm too young for a command. His actual words, which
the Queen repeated to me when I was called to audience this
morning, were that he 'could not set up a standard of disaffection
to rally all the discontented officers in the Army.' "

"Discontented! You? There's a swine he is!" cried Abigail
with concentrated fury. "You, who volunteered to join the ranks
when you were scarce sixteen—you didn't ask, discontentedly, for
a commission then. It was given you—by the Queen. And you
have been in every campaign ever since. But I'll wager 'tis not *he*
who denies you your rightful promotion. He's been hounded to
it by that bitch of his, and 'tis not at you neither that she strikes,

but at *me*. She knows I'd give my head to secure you this appointment, and she'll see you don't get it. But you *shall* get it—or it will
be the worse for her—and him! . . . There, there, mother's
life."

The baby had set up a querulous howl. Unfastening her shift,
she offered it sustenance. Jack, embarrassed, looked away, then
got upon his feet to say awkwardly:

"Here, don't put yourself in a state. The Queen has promised
me my Colonelcy, even if I don't have a regiment," and stooping,
he dropped a brief kiss on her forehead. But as he straightened,
she lifted her disengaged hand to draw his face to hers again.

"You'll have more than a regiment," she told him in his ear.
"You'll have a Brigade, my lad."

She had two more visitors that day. The first was Harley.

He came with a basket of flowers, congratulations, and apologies for not having called on her before. He had been immersed,
he said, in this sorry business of Dr. Sacheverell.

"Is it certain he will have to stand his trial?" Abigail asked.
She had followed with keenest interest the result of that sermon,
preached in the previous November at St. Paul's by a forthright,
but till then inconspicuous, clergyman against the 'revolutionary
principles' of the Whig Ministry and the 'perils of false brethren
both in Church and State.'

"As certain," smiled Harley, "as that his trial will bring down
the Whigs and Godolphin. The nation is in an uproar. Nothing
could have been more opportune than that he could have chosen
this particular moment to thunder his 'Church in danger' cry
from the pulpit."

Without turning her head, she looked at him.

"You have not come to talk to me of Sacheverell."

"You read me," he said, "like a book."

"A book"—and she returned his smile—"that is printed very
small."

He waited a second before he said:

"I find it, as I feared, peculiarly painful to see you with a child.
That is why I have so long delayed to offer you my courtesies.
I am not . . . disaffected."

Time was when his thievish look, the measured insincerity of
his caressing voice, would have plucked her strength and dis-
possessed her of her confidence. Were the desperate, irresponsible
loves of youth so fleeting? Or had she walled within the fortress
of her marriage something indestructible, still fiercely poignant,
and alive? She checked her hurried breathing to say, cool:

"Nor did you come to tell me that."

"If I have not"—the smile left his lips—"it is because you know it."

She pressed her child closer in her arms, as if to hold it as a shield against her heart's betrayal.

"Nor is it the Church," proceeded Harley, with speculative calm, "that stands alone in danger. Sacheverell is but one facet of the fight that lies before us. You are the bone between quarrelling dogs."

"I?"

The quick lift of her eyes to his revealed her unspoken relief. Here was something tangible to meet; no undervaults of treacherous emotion to avoid; no resurrected ghosts to be laid.

"Marlborough spurred by Sarah," Harley said, "demands your immediate dismissal."

"Oh, that!" She laughed breathlessly. "Marlborough has been demanding my dismissal for a year."

"But not," he said softly, "before Parliament."

"Parliament!" And watching the compression of her lips and the warmth in her face, Harley averted his own. "When, and from whom did you hear this?"

For answer he took from his vest-pocket a letter. She snatched it from him, her eyes eagerly following the written words as her voiceless lips moved to repeat them.

'Madam,

'By what I hear from London I find Your Majesty is pleased to think that you are in the right in offering Mr. Hill the Earl of Essex's regiment. I beg Your Majesty will be so just to me as not to think that I can be so unreasonable as to be mortified to the degree I am if it did proceed only from this one thing. It must be a prejudice to your service while I have the honour to command the Army, to have men preferred by my professed enemies'—"Me," murmured Abigail,—'to the prejudice of general officers of greater merit and longer service. But this is only one of a great many mortifications I have met with . . .'

"You!" She glanced up at Harley and down again, and continued her silent perusal.

'I beg Your Majesty to reflect what your own people and the rest of the world must think who have been witnesses of the love and zeal and duty with which I have served you, when they shall see, after all I have done, that it is not able to protect me against the malice of a Bedchamber Woman.'

"So now we know!" Her eyes kindled. "He shows his hoof and Sarah shows her teeth!" Contemptuously she flicked aside the letter. It fell to the floor. Harley stooped to recover it. When he looked at her again those queer eyes of hers, so like a cat's, were two shining slits of green in the whiteness of her face.

"I am accused here,"—again she took the letter from him, smoothing out the paper, searching down, "of malice, but he cannot cite one instance in which I have offended. I have never spoken ill of him or her."

And saying that, her little body raised itself in a sudden gust of passion that twitched her voice and returned to Harley's lips his careful smile.

"This," she flashed at him, "sends me into action, armed! If the Queen does not accept Marlborough's challenge, then by the living God I swear—I will!"

Harley became very still.

"So we are bound," he said, "in one purpose. We are bound in this life and beyond it . . . to all purpose. As it was with us in the beginning. As it will be. To the end."

"Madam." The entrance of the midwife shattered that predatory moment. "Dr. Arbuthnot is waiting to see you."

"The doctor . . . you must go." She gave Harley her hand.

Formally bowing, he turned it upwards to his lips and left her with his touch enclosed, re-savoured in the fierce pressure of her palm against her mouth.

But it was not the doctor who in his unseeing haste passed Harley in the corridor. This was a man in a battle-stained uniform, mud-splashed from his jackboots to his tarnished gilt-laced epaulets: a soldier home from the wars. Nor did he knock at the door of the room Harley had quitted. He opened it and paused a moment on the threshold, to say with smiling breathlessness:

"I've rode a thousand miles in the hope I'd get here first. My daughter's beaten me—by seven days!"

*　　　*　　　*

Spring came with a welter of sunshine and a foam of hawthorn in the hedges that lined the rustic ways to town. The public tennis-court hard by the Haymarket was crowded with spectators, and in the fields of Clerkenwell the archers were busy at their practice for the annual display. The wives of city aldermen who visited the New Exchange to see the latest modes offered in the shops of dressmakers and milliners, stayed to buy; and later, decked in gaudy mimicry of Fashion, drove in hackneys to Hyde

Park to watch the gilded chariots, coaches, horsemen, strolling beaux, that daily whirled or promenaded in the Ring.

There too the nosegay women and the orange girls did a roaring trade among the gentlemen who bandied pleasantries, not always of the nicest, as a preliminary to bribe for tastier fruit.

On a day in early June, two gentlewomen of by no means inconspicuous appearance, were seated side by side upon a bench exchanging caustic commentaries on recognized participants in that lively pageant.

The stouter of these ladies, though to be sure both were amply flesh-covered, wore a petticoat of yellow chintz, a prune velvet bodice, a towering cock-feather head-dress, and a smile that stretched to her ears. Her companion, of more stocky build and stoutish countenance, followed no fashion. Her dress of hot blue cloth was severely gold-braided. Her three-cornered hat, set at an angle, topped a periwig of greasy curls. Her short petticoat exposed a pair of gentlemanly russet leather boots. Her right hand, the nails of which were packed with dirt, held a pencil, the other a notebook in which every so often she jotted down a memorandum. The lady in the feather head-dress slanted an eye at the open page and chuckled.

"Sure an' all, Mrs. Manley, you'll be brought to the Queen's Bench on a charge of Scandalum Magnatus if you publish this. But rape me if I can read a word of it."

"I was not aware, Mrs. South, that you were asked to read a word of it."

"Och, blarney! Amn't I here to prompt ye at your bidding?"

"When you're bid." Mrs. Manley made a cross in the margin of her page, and a query, 'Prado'? "Your encyclopædic knowledge," she continued, "is invaluable, diluted. I call on you for fiction. I write fact."

" 'Prado'?" inquired Mrs. South, peering to decipher Mrs. Manley's scrawl. "What may you mean by that?"

"A suggestion, merely, that occurs to me; a synonym, shall we say, for this distinguished venue, where the fair, the foul and the illustrious come to take the dust under pretence of taking the air. Where is the place so proper for admiration as the Prado? Where such hallowed mysteries—and such caustic repartee?"

And Mrs. Manley cocked her twinkling eye at a handsome, elegant, rather plump young gentleman engaged in jocular back-chat with an orange girl. Her face had the bloom of an over-ripe peach, and her voice the sharp twang of Old Dury.

"What, sir, is the time by your watch?"

"Alas, sweetheart, my watch is run down. Will you wind it for me?"

"Lor', sir! How'd I know how to wind it?"

"I'll show you how, though I'll warrant it can give you better time when 'tis standing than other watches may when they are moving."

Her roguish eyes glinted up at him. "Why, sir, I pray you let me see this fine watch, an it please your honour."

"It pleased my honour well enough, but 'tis not for public view."

Mrs. South released a held guffaw. "Hoho! A likely lad!"

Said Mrs. Manley: "Yes, I'm told that young spark St. John times his watch to strike with more advantage, if with less response, in Mrs. Masham's salon, and that he sets it in advance of Mr. Harley's."

Mrs. South drew a breath deep enough to endanger the seams of her bodice.

"Madam, I'll thank you not to disoblige my ears with any slander to the discredit of the innocentest, best, and most proper of women, which"—she sidled hopefully nearer—"I would abhor to believe."

Mrs. Manley grinned and crammed snuff into her nose, saying: "Talk of the devil—here she comes."

Mrs. South's cock-feathers trembled to the lift of her head. Mrs. Manley put up a glass to her eye. Riders snatched off their hats and ceremoniously bowed from the saddle. Pedestrians halted to stare: not at the swaying gilt coach, drawn by six prancing white horses with postilions and footmen in scarlet and gold, but at the small lady inside it.

"I wonder how long *she'll* stay the course," remarked Mrs. Manley, "with the Duchess of Somerset not half a length behind her."

This was news to Mrs. South.

"The Duchess of Somerset?"

" 'Carrots', they call her. The Queen has a fondness for that shade of hair."

"The Duchess of Somerset is it! Lord God!" ejaculated Mrs. South, "you do surprise me."

"Nothing short of murder would surprise you, madam. And here, as I live, comes the other."

Up went her glass. Mrs. South, taken with the flushes, mopped her face and blurted:

"Crucify me if I ever saw the like of that for boldness! She must have the hide of a rhinoceros."

More resplendent, more ornate than the first, was this second equipage drawn by six Flemish mares with two footmen in canary

plush and conical shaped hats perched behind, while four more
ran ahead waving long silver-topped canes to make way for the
Duchess of Marlborough's coach.

Out came Mrs. Manley's notebook. Her little eyes gleamed.
Mrs. South cackled. "Imagine! There's a brazen image if you
like. You'd think she'd never dare show herself, when the towns-
folk have sworn to tear her to pieces in the streets for threatening
to publish"—Mrs. South meaningfully leered—"Her Majesty's
intimate letters. Ah, what did I tell you!"

From among the huddle of fruit-sellers rose a concerted howl of
boos and cat-calls, followed by a pelt of oranges that fell short of the
Duchess's coach and were trampled underfoot by its startled horses.

With superb indifference for this sinister reception, the Duchess
turned vivaciously to address the pock-marked, beetle-browed
gentleman beside her.

"And I'll wager my garters *he'll* not stay the course," said Mrs.
South. "Lord Treasurer looks as yellow as a guinea and as near to
dead man's meat as any I've seen hanging from a gibbet."

Mrs. Manley focused her glass on St. John's broad back, where he
stood among the orange girls. "That chorus," she tritely remarked,
"could not have been better timed with—or with*out*—a watch."

But Mrs. South was still intent upon the Duchess.

"She's no match for that pawky little piece, for which I could
find it in my heart to pity her, begar, seeing as I've had a taste of
her cunning which would not have shamed the serpent who be-
guiled the mother of man. With me own eyes I've seen her playing
tip the toe under the table with Sir George when she was employed
at Chafford House—mark ye—as *my* inferior, to tend the monkey
and empt the slops. Hah! 'Tis a far cry indeed from my Lady
Rivers' chamber-pot to the Queen's Chamber."

Mrs. Manley, having duly noted these observations in her book,
closed it and got up to go.

"Madam, I have been vastly entertained. The tales of your
earlier acquaintance with the Favourite never cease to amuse, and
may prove to be of inestimable value."

"To you," demanded Mrs. South, suddenly alert, "or to me?"

"That remains"—Mrs. Manley expectorated snuff upon the
side-path—"to be seen. I will wish you a very good day."

Mrs. South hoisted herself from her seat, to say coaxingly:

"Sure, you'll not fly to your inkpot without a drop of something
iced to cool ye down? Come, let's find a hackney. I'll drive ye
home, and on the way we'll call at Leicester Fields. Sir Andrew
has laid down a stock of white Florence wine that's pure nectar,
Mrs. Manley, brewed from the spittle o' the gods."

The ladies departed. St. John left his girl with an address in his pocket and a shilling in her hand. The loiterers walked on. Mrs. Masham's coach rolled by again. The Duchess's did not: and all around the Ring tongues were wagging. . . . The Duchess, who had retired to the country after her latest rupture with the Queen, had now returned! Did that mean the cutty-stool? Another quarrel patched? Everyone knew the truth of the last. It had run like a purse through the town, lapped up by the pamphleteers of Grub Street to regurgitate in Tory broadsides and lampoons.

'*Don't answer me!*'

The Duchess had rung her own knell in those unforgettable words, screamed on the steps of 'God's House'.

There had been a lull before the storm. The Queen's Tories believed her too forgiving. The Whigs were all a-snigger in their sleeves. Not a man of them who did not lay their odds on Sarah. Thirty years of friendship, love, surpassing that of lovers, could not be smashed by yet another scene. Mrs. Morley knew her Freeman's temper when the bit was in her mouth: knew too how to ride her on the curb. She'd never bolt!

A divided nation watched that last round between the Queen and the Queen's tyrant, with one small shadowy third standing umpire.

The Whigs had ceased to grin and turned to frown—at Marlborough. His attempt to wrest Abigail from the side of her Sovereign Protectress had ignominiously failed. Their own threats of a Parliamentary address against the Queen's Chambermaid had similarly failed, and would never have been brought if John, urged by Sarah, had not badgered them to bring it: had not written crazy letters to the Queen and then backed out. And, had the Junto forced *that* issue, which they wisely did not do, they would have had all Europe grinning. For the great Marlborough to slam the door of his command upon himself because the Queen refused to give a servant girl her notice, would have been an act of lunacy. Marlborough would do better to stick to his guns than to go lighting squibs in Her Majesty's closet.

But although his attempted firework display had been damped down, the mortal affront to Majesty still smouldered, stoked by that 'bedroom slut' who, it was said, had heaped it with malicious lies, gathered from the Tories—and Harley.

Was it not known that those two, between them, had informed the Queen how that Sir Solomon Medina, a Jewish gentleman, contracted to supply bread to Her Majesty's forces in the Netherlands, had been secretly supplying 'bread' to the Duke's personal 'bin', and to the tune of something over sixty thousand pounds?

The circulation of that dirty story was the Masham's sweet

revenge on the Duke for having first refused her scapegrace brother a regiment, and then for the omission of his name and her husband's in the list of officers presented to Her Majesty for promotion. The Queen, who regarded that as a deliberate affront to her Favourite, had immediately retaliated by raising both Colonels Hill and Masham to the rank of Brigadier.

Yes, Marlborough, the Whigs decided, had bungled shockingly in showing his hand—or the Duchess's—in that matter of regimental honours *not* conferred. But the greatest error he had ever made was in allowing his wife to rampage on the war-path in a final bid to regain the power she had lost, and the love she had hopelessly squandered.

She had humbled herself, had prayed for an interview, to be sternly told by the Queen that 'anything she had to say she must put into writing.' . . . Why then had she not written? She, who wrote reams on all other occasions! But now, having been ordered to write, she would not. Instead, she had followed the Queen's coach to Kensington and sat all day in the gallery, waiting for admittance like a beggar. And not until light faded was the door of the Queen's closet opened. A page ushered her in. She knelt. And the Queen turned her face away.

Why could she not have known then that the hour was not ripe for reconciliation? But Sarah had never been remarkable for tact. And to that cold averted face she had petitioned for a hearing. Finding no response, her temper rose and so did she—to accuse the Queen of 'lending ear to evil persons who had induced her to believe that I have maligned you—I, who would be no more capable of saying such things than of killing my own children!'

This the listeners at key-holes overheard.

Much else was overheard.

The Queen's reply, relentless, curt:

'You desired no answer. You shall have none."

And broken by her wild sobbing, the Duchess's fatal last words: 'Before God, you will suffer for your inhumanity to me!'

Then the door had been flung wide. The listeners scattered. Half frantic, hysterically weeping, her hair in disorder, the Duchess rushed out, down the stairs, through the hall, to her coach.

At an upper window a small freckled face was stealthily pressed to a pane. And a hush, as of death, had descended on the Palace, unstirred by any sound save that of sudden equivocal laughter above, and the grinding of wheels below.

*   *   *

All through the summer of 1710 the hopes of the Tories ran

high. The Duchess, while still retaining her nominal offices of Mistress of the Robes and Keeper of the Purse, had been banished from the Presence, never to return to it again. The spectacular Sacheverell trial, which had resulted in a sentence tantamount to acquittal, had evoked riotous rejoicings throughout the Kingdom. A convulsive mob burned effigies of Low Church Bishops and Dissenters in the streets, to delight the Tories and worry the Whigs. The Queen had openly declared her approval not only of Sacheverell's mountebank sermon in St. Paul's, but her dismay that the Whigs had attacked him, and, through him, herself as the Head of the Church. And as if this were not calamitous enough, their staunchest supporter, the Duchess, must needs have chosen this unpropitious time for her last offensive.

Even the most optimistic realized that a general exodus would likely be followed by a General Election. In Tory Clubs the odds ran even between the imminent dismissal of Marlborough and his son-in-law Sunderland, whose very name the Queen—with that green-eyed 'Enchantress', and Harley, at her elbow—had now come to detest. But everyone knew that the Masham was plotting to bring down the Duke whom she had never forgiven for having denied her young brother his regiment; and what the Masham chose to whisper, the Queen would surely say.

Which of the two then, Sunderland or Marlborough, would go first?

Sunderland went first.

And in July Marlborough was writing agitatedly to Sarah: 'For God's sake be careful of your behaviour, for you are amongst tigers and wolves.' Too late in the day to warn her to be careful. She had already been mauled.

In August the Queen commanded Godolphin to break his Lord Treasurer's White Staff of Office, but not in her presence. She refused to see him, sent no word of regret to her once much loved 'Mr. Montgomery', who for eight years had led her Ministries and who had known her all her life. He did not, however, leave her unrewarded. He retired with a pension of four thousand pounds a year, to lose the whole of it quite happily at Newmarket.

The day Godolphin broke his Staff the Queen received Harley and St. John in audience. They left her reinstated: Harley as Chancellor of her Exchequer, and Harry St. John Secretary of State.

But the Lord High Treasurer's office still stood vacant. Who, ran the current question, would succeed him? The answer to it, seemingly, was locked behind the door of Her Majesty's Bedchamber.

While she who could have spoken did not speak.

CHAPTER FIVE

On a raw January evening of that same year* a singular figure in a nightcap, with his face in a frown and a shawl round his shoulders, sat up in bed in a fireless room writing a letter to a girl.

An impatient spasm nicked the corners of his wide sensitive mouth as he dipped his quill and made a blot and wrote:

'The Whigs now they are fallen are the most malicious toads in the world. I fear people will begin to think nothing thrive: under this new Ministry. In my opinion nothing can save us but a Peace, and I am sure we cannot have such a one as we had hoped, and then the Whigs will bawl what they would have done had they continued in power. I tell the Ministry this as much as I dare, and shall venture to . . .'

A sharp rat-tat at the door preceded the entrance of a skew-eyed grinning fellow with a tray, and the request:

"Would your Reverence be afther having your supper before I go out, or when?"

"Would I be afther!" roared his Reverence. "God A'mighty, Patrick, is this tongue twisting abomination of a phrase the result of my patience in attempting to teach you the rudiments of grammar? Faugh! You stink of the tavern. Are ye drunk again, sirrah?"

"Sure, Mr. Swift, yer honour, I am not," protested Patrick, giving the lie—in his breath—to that utterance which made his master retch. "There's a Mr. Prior below to see you," said he, as with tipsy care he deposited the tray on the bedside table. "Will I bring him up?"

"Yes." Lifting a dish-cover, Swift grimacingly peered at the cindered remains of a couple of chops. "And you can take this down. 'Tis burnt—as you will be hereafter unless ye drown in your own liquor first. You can leave the chocolate."

His man went out and Prior came in with snowflakes nestling on the curls of his full-bottomed wig.

"Hah, Jonathan! In bed so early?"

"I go to bed early to keep myself warm and save fuel."

"So I see," said Prior with chattering teeth and a glance at the empty grate.

* 1710, Old Style Calendar.

273

Ignoring the hint Swift pointed to a chair. "Sit ye down and take a blanket off the bed, if you're cold. I've no wine in the house. What can I offer you? A cup o' chocolate?"

Prior shuddered. "S'lids, no!" And halting a cough, he drew the chair to the bedside and said persuasively: "You may offer me a dose of more fiery waters than wine, my dear. A scratch of your scorching pen as counterblaze to Dicky Steele's latest tattle in *The Tatler*—and to make your fortune if you please."

Swift turned his amazing blue eyes on Prior's narrow face in a sardonic stare before he answered: "Are you sent by Mr. Harley to lease my scorching pen to your Tory guardians of the peace? And talking of peace—if the Tories give it us they may pick my brains bare, and all strength to 'em. Faith!" He sipped noisily, smacking his lips. "*What* a landslide! With what an avalanche of a majority they've been returned. And what a lamentable confession the Whigs have made of *my* ill-usage, hang 'em! But I don't mind. I am already represented to Harley as the discontented cur who whines at the kicks it receives for not being Whiggish enough. And now the Tories drily tell me I may make my fortune 'if I please'. Ph! I don't understand them, or maybe I understand 'em too well. When you're not war-mongering you're whore-mongering. What of this young woman who succeeds the Duchess? The Whigs may thank her for their defeat, I'm told."

"Young woman?" asked Prior, expressing wonder.

"O wise, O excellent young man!" scoffed Swift. "How you political jobbers love to skate on a thin surface. How delicately you describe an intricate curve with an edge to't. 'Tis admirable to watch your tentative approach, your shy retreat, girlish and coy. And is *she* so?" Again his piercing glance swerved to Prior, who threw it back with an amiable smile and no answer.

"Talk flown by your Grub Street sparrows—even to Laracor —gives it she is nimble-witted, and that Harley, who loves no woman, leches after her and climbs on her shoulders, carrying her bag of tricks on his. Ohoa!" Swift shook his capped head, grimly chuckling. "From Chancellor of the Exchequer to Lord High Treasurer is but a step in the dance o' cuckolds—all awry! And may God forgive me for my profanity—that I should lend tongue to such miserable slander!"

"Hashed in a Whig stew at Laracor?" inquired Prior, taking snuff.

"S'blood, man! We have no stews at Laracor, nor Whigs neither, praise be. Yahoo!" yelled Swift, so jeeringly, startlingly loud that Prior's eyebrows gave an upward leap.

Swift laughed. "That's the way it is, ye see! Yahoo! Yahoo!

Ya*hoo*! That word clip-clops in my brain like horses' hoofs upon the highway—to what?"

His face clouded. He sat in brooding melancholy, pinching his chin on which sprouted a two-days' black stubble: "Is it true——" He beckoned Prior closer to ask again, as eager as any old wife for a gossip—"Is it true that the Duchess flung a glass of water in Mrs. Masham's face at an evening affair, a party, a function, a— what-not? Ah, come, Matt, you should know these things, not I, who am naught but a poor devil of a parson from the bogs—and who should know better?"

"I've heard some such tale," said Prior, fiddling with the lid of his snuff-box, "but not here in London. It was carried first to France and then back to me."

"France!" Swift wiped a dewdrop from his nose and nodded. "France *would* hear of that. And who told it to you? The Sun King or his shadow, Torcy? They say you're hand in pocket with both, and all luck to ye if you bring 'em to a peace."

"And who told *you*," smiled Prior, "that I have seen Torcy?"

"Who? Why, those same lilli-lilli-lilli-lilli-lilliburlero sparrows that bring me all the tasty news tied under their little dear wings. If you've not seen Torcy, you will see Torcy. You will, O, yes, you will! Who speaks such good French as our Prior? Who has such pretty manners? Who—'Ods Blood! My head!" He clapped his hands to it. "Here comes my giddiness to curse me." And avoiding Prior's anxious look, he snarled at him: "What more do I understand of your visit? 'Tis not to satisfy my appetite for scandal. Did Harley send you? Did St. John? Say quick what you will, and then go."

"Tiens, mon vieux!" Prior spread his palms in a Frenchified gesture. "How you snap! I came merely to ask you to dine with me at the October Club to-morrow."

"At your cost?" asked Swift cautiously. "Last time I dined out 'twas with Sir Andrew Fountaine, and I had to pay for my own dinner—breast of mutton and shocking bad wine." And turning to beat his pillow till the feathers flew, he lowered his splitting head to say: "If I'm to dig my quill in your October ale and sharpen its point on your wits, 'twill be at my price, not yours. Your October Club is screaming Jack when it's drunk, and Whig when it's sober. And if it be out of liquor to-morrow night I'm not showing my face inside there. The Whigs are threatening to slit my nose for my attack on Marlborough in *The Examiner*."

"And what an attack," murmured Prior, relishing snuff. " 'Tis a miracle you were not impeached for libel."

"Libel? Pooh! I only suggested that the Treasury would do well to watch the hole in its pocket."

"And in the Privy Purse. The Duchess still holds on to its strings, remember. My dear, you can't," said Prior earnestly, "you positively can't go casting accusations right and left like battledores."

"Without a battle?" grinned Swift from his pillow. "I only write the truth. Those two have been lining their nest with public funds for years, and I said——"

"You did! And for God's sake," broke in Prior, "don't say it to-morrow." He got up. "I'll see you at the Club then, at eight o' the clock."

Swift groaned. "Lord, Lord, will ye hear him? Good will on earth and peace towards men, but not for me. I'll be there—with my tongue in my cheek and my pen in my pouch to spill poison. But I'm told the Whig poison sells better. . . . Where's that puppy Patrick? My feet are froze, and I want a warming-pan. Yes, and the Whigs'll be pushing *their* warming-pans in the Electress Sophia's apple-pie bed, to bring George Lewis out of it and over to us before you can say 'Kiss me', unless . . . Patrick!" He reared his head to bellow. "Patrick! *Pa-ah*-trick! ... See? No answer. He's either gone out or laid out. Snuff the candle, Matt. They cost a deal more in this lousy little village of yours than in mine. Uth uth uth uth *uth*! It's mortal cold. Pize take ye! Shut that *door*!"

"But what I really came to tell you," Prior said before he shut it, "is that Marlborough is back again. Sleep well!"

He groped his way down a black unlighted staircase to the street. There was no moon, but the starlit sky reflected a sparkle, as from a myriad glow-worms, on the powdery whiteness below.

Shivering, he hugged himself for warmth, and darted forward to hail a chair as it rounded the corner.

"To Pontack's—and hurry!"

The chairmen hoisted their load and trotted off at a run. Their breath steamed in the crisp air as he paid them and wished them a cheery good-night, caught back on a fit of coughing. He cursed sourly, spat blood, pushed open the door and walked in, blinking in the smoke-hazed light of candles. The room was, as usual, noisily overcrowded, but his quick roving glance at the company did not produce the man he sought. Strolling over to a table of dice-throwers that included Brigadiers Masham and Hill, and the recently appointed Secretary of State, he tapped him on the shoulder.

"Harry, has Robin been here?"

"Yes, and gone. He was asking for you. He may be coming back."

Prior took a seat and watched the game between St. John and Masham, whose pile of gold had dwindled to a couple of guineas and whose last throw threw him out.

"I'm undone." Masham pushed back his chair and got up. "I'll send you a bill for my debt to-morrow, St. John. I've no more cash in hand. I owe you seven hundred I believe."

"Which is but the half," St. John reminded him by way of consolation, "that you took off me last week." And scooping up the dice, he rattled the box again. "Come on, have a heart! This is my lucky night. Don't go, Masham. Crack another bottle and play me for your revenge."

"To-morrow," Masham's smile, which was never far from his face, returned to it, "when I've discharged my debt. Here you!" He called a servant. "Go tell my footman to bring my coach to the door."

He bowed to the seated company, rammed on his hat, plunged his hands in his muff and walked out.

Prior, who had emptied three glasses in rapid succession and felt better, asked St. John: "Is it a fact that Masham is resigning his seat?"

St. John shrugged. "Yes, and God knows why. He was returned with a majority of a thousand for Ilchester. He's not near such a fool as he looks, and he has a following among the army."

"I could tell you why." Jack Hill spun a guinea, clamped it down on the table, and said: "Double or quits, Harry, for my losses. Are you game?"

St. John nodded. "Heads."

Jack uncovered the coin. "And here she is, God bless her! Well, now, what's to do? You've done *me* well enough, damn you! Half my year's pension gone in the flick of a tail."

St. John grabbed his lace-frilled wrist.

"I'll toss you again for the whole of it if you *can* tell me why."

"Why?" Jack was slightly fuddled.

"Masham's resignation," prompted Prior.

"Oh, that! No." Jack pursed his lips. "Ask Abbie. She'll tell you."

"Your sister," said St. John, beckoning a drawer, "never tells me anything. She reserves her confidences for . . . Bring another bottle of the Burgundy."

Jack reddened to his eyebrows and said with the slow deliberation of the unsober: "Careful, St. John. I could call you out for one word more to her name than that."

"Than that?" St. John repeated with over-marked surprise. "Why, Lord save us! How you quack—sharp as a dissenting parson in a brothel."

Jack glowered. St. John laughed.

"See how he is burning for a fight! But I plead guiltless of any provocation to induce it. My sword stays sheathed. Come, lad, a toast with me"—he sprang to his feet and raised his glass—"to her! Come, fellows, a toast! To the Masham—the hope of our side!"

Others heard, turned, and drank, shouting. Prior clinked glasses with St. John. Jack stood and drank, gloomily silent; then he took up the dice-box and dashed the ivory cubes on to the table. They tumbled and bounced with a splintering sound. His face cleared and he broke into laughter, staring with bright insolent eyes at St. John.

"Here, Harry! I'll play you for my command of the Quebec Expedition. Four aces in three. Will you take me?"

St. John nodded.

"Zounds," muttered Prior, "you're rash."

Men, hearing Jack's challenge, pressed closer to watch. Prior ordered more wine. Jack, breathing heavily, threw: the deuce, three cinques and a trey.

"Two more to go," said St. John.

Again the dice rattled and rolled. Two quatres, two sixes, and an ace turned up.

Jack's face whitened; Prior's lengthened. St. John screwed his sagging eyes into focus and stood. Jack clenched his fist on the dice-box and shook it, raising it high above his head. The cubes clattered and fell. The room hushed. Jack closed his eyes, then:

"God's Body!" cried St. John. "The Brigadier's got it. Four aces and—the deuce!"

While future maritime and military tactics were, with ultimate disaster, thus resolved, the other Brigadier was bumping in his coach to Kensington. He had arrived at that stage of the mildly drunk which is happy and not melancholic. Smilingly he gazed through the breath-fogged window to admire the snow-flakes that whirled daintily as dancing girls against the night's dark curtain. The tree-branches, too, so gracefully whitened, were outstretched like the tantalizing arms of little virgins. The thought pleased him, whose fancy did not readily soar to whimsical flights. He knew his limitations which fell far short of his wife's, as he was the first to admit.

Looking back upon his married years, most of which had been

spent on a battlefield charging with lance or sword, or, latterly, banging at the enemy in command of big guns, he realized, with a qualm, that his intimate acquaintance with and knowledge of his wife were next to nothing. True, she slept in his bed and had given him a child, sang to him, played to him, could chatter like a magpie when it pleased her, or keep silent when she chose to please him, a rare asset in a woman: could be witty and amusing, sometimes at his, and often at others' expense: had a care for his purse and managed his money, which was indubitably excellent. But what more did he know of her than this?

Yet all his previous experience of calf-loves, courtships, or the tainted pleasures of the alcove were as naught to the lawful joys with which this charming creature had endowed him. There had been a period of misery, indeed, when he had suffered hell's own torment, having stumbled inadvertently upon her in an arbour and in Mr. Harley's arms; but that was years ago. He had been shattered, and she had laughed at him to make him feel ashamed that he, for one base instant, had stooped to doubt her.

"But, dear heart, he is my cousin. An old cousin." She had encouragingly harped on Harley's age. "More than twice mine. He could be my father. And it was not at all as you so wickedly supposed. He was merely removing a spider from my hair. You know how I am terrified of spiders."

And of caterpillars too. . . . Her explanation was conclusive. He cursed himself again for his monstrous, quite unfounded, cruel suspicion. What a little marvel of a woman to possess! Her gentle artless ways, her sympathy, her sweet endurance of the rebuffs and slights she had suffered at the hands and from the tongue of her dominant cousin, had earned her a just reward to raise her from humblest office at the Court to heights undreamed. . . . And she had raised him with her. He had cause enough to think himself the most blessed and most envied of men. Only last week she had told him he must be prepared to resign his seat in Parliament. "I'll see you better placed," she had mysteriously promised, "as Queen's Cofferer."

He may not have been so overjoyed to hear of this promotion as she had told him sharply, "I could shake you!" And she had made at him, too, as if she would. "There's others who'll be glad enough to jump at such a chance if you don't. So make up your mind—and stop grinning!"

She had left him no choice but to make up his mind and stop grinning, although, as he had ventured to suggest, a renunciation of his seat in the Lower House, won from a Whig, went hard.

"And you're soft," she had sweepingly retorted. "One day you may sit in the Upper House if you leave all to me, and don't teeter."

And that had finished that . . . and his Parliamentary career. And: Pink me! decided Masham, but she's a jewel. What foresight, what strength of purpose marks her every action. He tingled with pride when he recalled how distinguished politicians would hang upon her words. Why, her cousin Sarah hadn't so much sense in her whole body as Abbie in one little toe-nail! And thinking of Sarah, the gallant Brigadier closed his fist upon his knee. He had been told, but not by his wife, of Sarah's fiendish assault at a public dinner held in celebration of the Queen's birthday, which the Queen had not attended, but which Sarah did.

The incident had created a great noise, and had occurred last year while he was at the war. If he had been present he would have . . . But what could he have done, short of tweaking that vixen by the ear or calling out her husband?

The whole town had talked of how the Duchess, with a carafe of water in her hand, had passed by Abigail where she sat with St. John, Harley, the Arbuthnots, and some others in the garden-room at Kensington, and feigning to stumble had splashed the water all over Abbie's gown.*

Why was she carrying a carafe of water? Her excuse, rendered with apologies had been that she was taking it to Lady Sunderland, her daughter, who had swooned. No one had seen Lady Sunderland swoon, nor had believed her mother's tale, with dozens of footmen standing around to fetch and carry for ladies in the vapours. Abigail, poor child, had been drenched, her gown ruined, and she compelled to retire and change it: nor had she appeared again that night.

The Queen, it was said, had heard with the utmost indignation of the 'accident', and even Sarah's own supporters had been greatly incensed that she should have lowered herself and her dignity to take so vulgar and petty a revenge upon her rival. But, reflected Masham, smiling, he would back the Duchess's 'rival' to return those drops of water with a deluge. . . .

In his dressing-room his valet waited to prepare him for the night.

"Has Mrs. Masham gone to bed?"

"Yes, sir, with the headache."

The headache! Her husband was concerned. She suffered too often from these headaches when she would ask him to be so very

---

* This anecdote has been recorded by Voltaire: 'Une jatte d'eau que la Duchesse laissa tomber en sa présence sur la robe de Madame Masham changea la face de l'Europe.'

obliging as to sleep in his dressing-room, because: "Your snores, my love, disturb me."

He was chagrined to know he snored, but not for the world would he disturb her. He must certainly send for Dr. Arbuthnot in the morning. These headaches would have to be treated.

His man poured water into a silver basin, scented it with attar of roses, offered a soap-ball, and stood by while his gentleman washed.

As he handed the towel, the valet said:

"Sir, Mrs. Masham sent a message by her maid to ask if you would kindly sleep in the dressing-room if you came in after ten of the clock."

And it was chiming midnight.

"Very well."

He went to bed.

But Abigail had not gone to hers; nor, we may as well confess it, was she suffering from headache. She appeared indeed to be in best of health.

As the clock struck the hour she moved from her seat by the hearth, looked in the mirror, patted a curl, and unfastening her fichu, she stowed it away in a drawer. The heart-shaped line of her corsage showed to better advantage, she decided, unadorned. Humming a gay little song she went to the window and drew aside the curtain. A coach, silent as a phantom in the snow, was approaching the Palace. She hastened back to her seat at the fire. The minutes ticked by. A smoking log fell to the grate in a shower of sparks; and as she stooped to lift it with the tongs, her personal footman announced:

"Madam, Mr. Harley has arrived and asks to see you on a matter of some urgency."

"Mr. Harley?" She appeared to be greatly astonished. "At this time of night! I was about to retire, but if it is urgent . . ."

"Mr. Harley, madam, says he comes with a message from the Queen."

"Ah! In that case bring him in."

Mr. Harley was brought in. The door closed. She sped to him with eager eyes and hands outstretched. He took them gravely, said no word and let them go. She backed from him, chilled.

"What is it? And why must you choose these unconscionable hours for your visits? If my servants were not well trained and well rewarded for their training, you would have me marked for a . . ." Then, at his smile, she laughed. "Masham is convinced I have a tumour on the brain. This is my fourth headache in two weeks."

"You will have no more headaches now," he said, "and nor will I."

"Tell me," she whispered. "I'm sick of suspense."

His head turned from her but his smile stayed. Seating himself by the fire, he spread his pale long hands to the blaze.

She followed him and knelt on the rug, gazing up. The flurry of her breath and the flush on her face betrayed her excitement, and that confessed suspense which he cruelly seemed determined to prolong.

"Robin, don't torment me! Has the Duke——?"

His sideways look checked her.

"Won't you," he asked pleasantly, "offer me wine? I am cold."

"Truly spoken," she flashed at him. "Corpse-cold, you are! Naught but hell fire could warm you." But she got up to fetch the bottle, filled a glass and passed it, saying as their eyes met, "Drink is no cure for your headache. What of the Duke?"

"Let him puke, let him puke!" chanted Harley.

Her small teeth snapped, and bending closer she significantly sniffed.

"As I thought," she nodded, "you're properly soused. How can you hope to lead a nation if you can't lead yourself?"

"A crucial point," drawled Harley. "Do I lead myself, or am I led?"

He swallowed the wine, staring down at his empty glass, while she resumed her position on the rug and stared at him.

Why, she asked herself hotly, did she submit to this perpetual searing of her pride, her sense, and her enchained morality? . . . Her eyebrows twisted. Morality! Yes. She had avoided any blot or slur on that. From long battling against his guarded defences, she had assumed at last a hard protective shell; a growth, a callous, like a corn upon her soul. She could approach him at his own level without fear of perjuring her spirit or deflowering her flesh, debased, but never wholly ravaged. She had come to her husband immaculate, defeated . . . unconsoled. Yet she had seemed to thrive upon starvation. Was ever woman in such fashion wooed—and in such bitter fashion won?

"Speaking of the Duke," Harley's voice dropped like rain-cool water on the desert of her thoughts, "I have news of him and his errand."

"Yes. I am waiting."

So must she always wait for his cue, a puppet that played a mimic pantomime in wire-pulled delusion.

"The Queen," he said, "has demanded that the Duchess give up the keys of office. She refused. The Queen wrote again to say they must be returned within the week. But surely you know this?"

Her blank look of amazement assured him she did not.

"The Queen has told me nothing."

"The Queen has told me all."

He got up to help himself to more wine, and holding the glass to the prismatic crystal light rayed from the chandelier, "A ruby," he murmured, "imprisoned. Exquisite." He drank; and, in his clipped contained voice that seemed to spurn his words, continued: "Marlborough entreated Her Majesty to consider her decision. He lamented, 'almost in the language of Wolsey'—I quote the Queen—'that he was worn out with age and misfortune.' Her Majesty said, 'If she could have conveniently turned about she must have laughed outright.' Marlborough then begged for a delay in the displacing of Sarah till after the Peace, when they would both retire together. The Queen again insisted. The key must be returned within a week. The Duke fell on his knees and prayed Her Majesty to give him time to prepare the Duchess for this appalling blow. . . . It must have been," mused Harley, "a most affecting scene."

His eyes narrowed in a look of critical appreciatory detachment. That elusive Leonardo quality of hers, so imperceptible to the canaille was, as ever, disturbing, provocative. Her pallor, her uncovered throat brushed by the firelight, had the luminous glow of old canvas. Her corsage, close-moulded to her still adolescent figure, and the absence of garniture, gave the troublous impression that she was half dressed. Her crouched attitude, vaguely penitential, enhanced her nymph-like charm that possessed nothing of beauty, but rather the fragrance of beauty as in the perfume of a hidden rose.

"Well," she asked impatiently, "what then?"

Harley took snuff.

"The Duke, I understand, hastened back to his wife with the Queen's message. Sarah flung the key at his head. It fell at his feet."

Her lips parted.

"How do you know this?"

"All London knows. Sarah's servants, unlike yours, are not well paid. The Duke picked up the key and rushed with it back to St. James's. I have but just come from there. The Queen detained me till eleven. And that is why"—his voice sank—"I have ventured to call at so inconsiderate an hour."

"But," she answered silkily, "you always call at so inconsiderate an hour."

He got up and in his correct restrained way crossed the room to refill his glass, and returned to stand beside her where she sat on the dim-patterned rug, with her petticoats outspread like the petals of some exotic pale flower. The dying logs burnished the carefully curled arrangement of her hair, and the tips of her colourless lashes.

"Beyond forgetting and for all time," he spoke in the words and the tone of a lover, "you are a perpetual enchantment, crocus-limbed, and for ever untouched. I drink to you and your unending youth, and to the nostalgic memory of mine."

He drained his glass and set it down. A tremor shook her body, and, as if released by that involuntary movement, the scent of her flesh—a mingling of musk and violets so entirely her own—assailed him in an intimacy that was almost unbearable. His hands raised her; his arms enfolded her. There was something pagan in the strained pressure of her flanks to his, her stinging kiss, the grip of her small fingers on his arms. Her gown slipped from her shoulders; her breath quickened.

"Do you believe I am insensible," he murmured, "when all my blood cries out for the sweet recompense you offer to my . . . emptiness. Here"—his lips lightly found and left hers, roamed to her bared breast, "and here—lies my reprieve." Then, as her head fell back entreatingly, he put her from him to rearrange her loosened bodice, saying coolly:

"Allow me."

She was fiercely white.

"Why," she whispered, "do I not kill you?"

"You may kill me yet." He took her hand again and held it to his heart. "Feel how it hurries to outrace my strength."

She looked at him scornfully.

"The hurry of your heart is not for me, but for the wine in which your blood is soaked. Leave me now. Only God knows why you came." And moving towards an inner door that opened to a private staircase she pointed. "Take the back way down—which is ever your way. And go."

Harley turned about.

She stood straight as an arrow and so still that only the stir of her breathing showed her to be alive.

"In the irresistible joy and danger of your presence," he said, with no suggestion in his voice of joys endangered or resisted, "I had forgot to tell you the main purpose of my errand. Her Majesty commands that you hold . . . this."

Into her hand he slid a gold key; and without another word or look he went.

CHAPTER SIX

THE air was thick with rumours and the town alive with talk. The Duchess of Marlborough had, at last, been formally dismissed and deprived of all her honours which the Queen had been pleased to divide. Mrs. Masham held first office as Keeper of the Privy Purse, and the Duchess of Somerset was Mistress of the Robes.

Out came the betting books, wagers were laid. "Odds on the 'Carrots' for the favourite. Twenty to one against the Queen's 'Enchantress'!" . . . The Queen, it was said, had transferred her affections again.

In March Swift was writing to his Stella in a state.

'The Ministry is on a very narrow bottom and stands like an isthmus between the Whigs on one side and violent Tories on the other. They are able seamen but the tempest is too great . . . and the Duchess of Somerset a most insinuating woman. I believe they will endeavour to play the same game that has been played against them.'

And three days later:

'O dear, my heart is almost broken. You will hear the thing before this comes to you . . . 'Tis of Mr. Harley being stabbed this afternoon at a Committee of the Council.'

"By a damned fanatical French traitor," fumed St. John, stamping up and down Abigail's salon at St. James's, hot from the scene of the assault. "And *he* received the blow which was aimed at me!"

He persisted in that. The Abbé Guiscard, whose name was as doubtful as his calling, had been all things to all men from a secret agent to a Colonel in the British Army. He had latterly retired with a handsome pension from the Queen, which, when Harley took control of the Exchequer he had promptly reduced. Whereupon the much aggrieved Guiscard had offered his service to Louis, King of France.

"But why," demanded Abigail, "did this Frenchman strike at Harley if he meant to strike at you? Is he cock-eyed? And do keep still, St. John. You make me giddy."

He kept still, while she returned his look of baffled questioning with one of calm amusement.

If St. John had sought to see her wringing hands in vapourish anxiety for the man whose name was linked with hers in a mistakenly intimate connection, she had him toasted.

St. John's face lost its sparkle.

"I had hoped that you had understood. 'Twas *I* who signed the warrant for Guiscard's arrest, *I* who brought him up before the Council on a treasonable charge. I have received proof enough from my agents to hang him and he knew it. His revenge was directed at *me*, not at Harley who happened to be in the way. The fellow came at him with a penknife."

"A penknife!"

She pealed with laughter. St. John glared.

"Even so small a weapon can kill. It would have killed Harley had I not been there to save him. I struck down the fellow's arm and all but struck it off—and then I drove my sword between his ribs. He fell, bleeding like a pig. And," pursued St. John, with staggering complacency, "he had besides my exposition of his crime, another score to settle against me. He has had a child by one of my mistresses, and hoped to charge his unlawful paternity to my account, for which I would have called him out but that I only fight with gentlemen. However, I've done for him now. My blade broke with the thrust I gave him. He was howling blue murder when they carried him off to Newgate. I fear he will not live to face his trial and a traitor's death. He will die of the wound he got from me. Harley collapsed."

"You said"—she restrained a hand from leaping to her heart— "he was unhurt."

"Unhurt in that his wound is not fatal, nor like to be, but his breast-bone is sorely bruised. He is suffering from shock." St. John spitefully grinned. "I called a surgeon who dressed his injury. He lost very little blood and recovered enough to walk from the Council Chamber to his coach. So, madam, will you be so good as to obtain for me an immediate audience with the Queen, that I may inform Her Majesty of this unhappy misadventure. . . ."

There was no holding him. While Harley lay in bed nursing his wound, which although slight had resulted in much pain and some fever, St. John was racing up and down the town and in and out the Palace, busy with his version of the incident.

The Queen had been greatly impressed.

"Mr. St. John's courage and presence of mind," Abigail was surprised to hear, "has saved Mr. Harley from a blow which most certainly would have been fatal if Mr. St. John had not so bravely intervened and taken the full force of the attack intended for poor Mr. Harley."

This was quite another aspect of the case. Lifting the Queen's spaniel puppy to her knee, Abigail bent her face above it. What, she wondered, *now* was St. John's little game?

The Queen's voice answered for her.

"So, my dear Mrs. Masham, I have decided to reward Mr. St. John for his valour. I intend—but this I tell you in the strictest confidence—to raise Mr. St. John to the peerage."

"Yes, Madam? And is Mr. St. John acquainted with Your Majesty's intention?"

"Not yet. I will have to consult Mr. Harley, and . . ." The Queen hesitated. And your 'Carrots' too, Abigail supplemented silently, and God send you do, for *she'll* soon stop that if I don't.

"I think," mused the Queen, "that Mr. St. John deserves some recognition for his noble action. As for dear Mr. Harley, my heart bleeds for him. I must send to inquire. . . . Pimpimpim! Come to mother, darling. Give him to me, Masham. This is quite the best of Minette's litter. All his points are perfect. Such lovely feathering and *such* a black nose. A true-born King Charles, and so clean in his habits. . . . Oh, no! *Not* so clean. All over your gown! Naughty, naughty! I am so sorry, my dear. I hope it won't stain."

" 'Tis no matter, Madam," Abigail mendaciously replied, and depositing the unshamed pup in his mistress's arms, "may I, Madam," she said meekly, "venture a suggestion?"

"But certainly, Masham. You may suggest anything always. You know how I rely on your judgment. . . . Sweet-tweet, diggle, diggle. . . ."

While the Queen crooned at and cuddled the puppy, Abigail rapidly thought: So that boastful braggart St. John had secured himself a plum, unripe, as yet, for plucking. And when it is—she smiled with closed lips—he may find that it lacks juice. For if peerages were going begging, others, too, could beg! Her hidden eyes glinted. To hold Harley in her hand, to lift him up and then to bring him down and let *him* feel the whip-lash, which for years, she, his creature, had endured at his will, would be 'sweet recompense' enough to fill her 'emptiness'.

She knelt.

"Madam, if Your Majesty honours Mr. St. John, is it not likely Mr. Harley may consider himself slighted?"

"Slighted?" The Queen's eyebrows fled upward. "But . . .

how dreadful, Hill, that I should be so thoughtless. Slighted. Yes, and overlooked. It would indeed be inexcusable for me to honour Mr. St. John before dear Mr. Harley."

Abigail bent her head. The Queen put out her swollen hand to stroke it. "My precious little Masham! What would I do without you to prompt me? I am not old, Masham, but I feel old. The burden of my troubles has aged me sadly. I am so forgetful, and Mr. St. John"—a flash of her rare humour gleamed—"is so persuasive."

"Yes, Madam," Abigail stood; her lashes fluttered, "in his own interests, but Mr. Harley's persuasions are in yours."

"How true indeed. They are. He is so wise. He has performed wonders in my service as Chancellor of the Exchequer. His proposed scheme for the launching of this South Sea Company will enrich the Exchequer by thousands of pounds. But I must confess that I don't altogether approve of trading in black slaves— poor things—with Central and South America, although Mr. Harley tells me that the revenue will reap the reward of these sole monopolies, and all stock holders are to be paid a guaranteed interest of six per cent."

"Yes, Madam, and the public debt of ten millions will be assigned to the Company."

The Queen gasped.

"Ten millions! Do we owe so much?"

"Yes, Madam."

The Queen squeezed her arm.

"What a clever dear creature you are! How did you know that? You are quite a little financier. You have already saved the Privy Purse some hundreds. When Mrs. Free—— when the Duchess of Marlborough held office—though I hate to have to say it—I was not permitted a groat to spend on myself, and you have saved me now enough to invest a little sum, if it would be correct for me to do so, in Mr. Harley's South Sea Company. I consider Mr. Harley to be not only a brilliant politician but a financial genius."

From under the arch of her brows the green eyes lifted to pinion the Queen's. "And has Your Majesty also considered that Mr. Harley's service to yourself and the State still remains unrecognized?"

"Unrecognized?" The Queen's vast bosoms heaved; her face reddened; she fumbled for a handkerchief and dabbed. "Unrecognized, Hill?" In moments of stress the Queen still reverted to Mrs. Masham's maiden name. "How do you mean, 'unrecognized'?"

"The place of Lord Treasurer, Madam," said Abigail softly, "has stood vacant since Lord Godolphin's dismissal."

"So it has! And who but Mr. Harley could fill it. . . . Hill!" The Queen rose from the chair. The puppy was placed on a cushion and Abigail enfolded. "Dear child, you are *such* a little guide. Always so right in your judgment. What a Minister you would make! My little *prime* Minister."

Abigail drew a breath, repeating it.

"Prime Minister. Madam, you give history a lead!"

"History, Masham?"

"Lord High Treasurer, Madam, is an old-fashioned term in these changeable times for . . ." she paused and said steadily, "for a changeable office. Your Majesty has lent to that office a new name!"

All London rang with it. The October Club, turned Jacobite drunk, roared in its cups to it. "Harley! Robert Harley, Earl of Oxford and Mortimer, First Lord of the Treasury . . . Prime Minister of England!"*

But one voice among them was muted; one glass among them unraised. One member, only, unnoticed, went out into the cool April night.

"To St. James's Palace!" he bawled to his coachman; and sent in his card at Mrs. Masham's door.

She received him and his grievance with sympathy. She could afford to be kind. St. John's plum still dangled like the fruit of Tantalus above his thirsty mouth. If he wanted his peerage he could have it—at her price.

Before he left her she had named it.

"The Quebec Expedition, St. John. Have you decided who shall take command?"

He stroked his full chin.

"That remains in abeyance while Harley denies me my choice."

"You have made your choice?"

He presented her with his most bewitching smile.

"It was made for me."

She widened her eyes.

"I don't understand."

"Do you not?"

So that reckless young jackass, her brother, had not told her of his lucky throw, which St. John could in one word, wipe out. No debt of honour must involve a Parliamentary crisis. And the

---

* Although Sir Robert Walpole was the first Prime Minister to be officially so called, the term was used, unofficially, in the latter part of Anne's reign.

Commons, headed by Harley, were opposing tooth and nail St. John's nomination. Brigadier Hill could be returned to Flanders, and the danger zone, with no loss to his honour though he lost his life. . . . St. John winced. Uriah! A dirty game to play, and one at which he was no adept. He excelled at fairer sport.

He was watching her with appraisement. Her lips were startlingly red as if blood, at a touch, would spurt from them. The thought was tempting. A string of pearls clasped her throat where a small pulse fluttered. His practised eye searched lower. And suddenly unrestful, he got up.

"You devastate me."

That was a gambit never known to fail. Her flying glance, her breath, quick drawn, persuaded him it had not failed now.

"I am half crazed for you. I've hungered . . ."

She was seized and rocked in a tempest of passion, not entirely assumed. Scalding kisses rained upon her breast, her throat, her mouth, to meet with a response that surprised and urged him to a greater frenzy. Words stammered on his tongue.

"God! God!" He kissed deeper, closer, frantically. "I must have you! I have wanted you for years."

"Yes, yes. I too . . ." Her arms wound and enticed him. The butterfly caress of her lips on his closed eyes was prodigal of tenderest insinuation. Unfastening his shirt, she slid her hands between the flimsy cambric and his heart. "How it hurries . . . to outrace your strength."

Unseen, she smiled wickedly.

He sighed. "O, rare! . . . You have me now. I am yours, and I am ravished!"

He began to believe it. Her very lack of physical beauty held for him a maddening allure. "Care for me," he pleaded. "Ease my torment. Take me."

His eyes opened dizzily. She drew his head to her breast again, whispering: "Leave all to me . . . and Jack."

"Jack!" His head shot up. His mouth, bloated with kissing, loosened. "What in hell has Jack to do with us?"

"He has all to do with us. We can meet at his lodgings."

She took his pouting face between her hands and laid a finger on the cleft in his chin. "You have a dimple here. Your beauty, St. John, is quite terrifying."

He visibly preened.

"You will come to me then? You must," he urged. "You will?"

She left his arms and stood smoothing her hands over her gown; rearranging her hair.

"I will not."

"What!" He sprang up, clutching her shoulders to swing her round. "You can't deny me now."

"Are you," and in her smile was a secret memory, "are you so . . . greedy?"

He stared at her, dismayed.

"Who schooled you in these arts?"

"Arts?" But nothing could have been more artless than her reproachful look. "You forget I am not free."

"Flip-flap! And am I free? Marriage can fetter our souls but not our bodies. Mine, with its heart, is yours. I have a wife. I've had a hundred other women, but not one, I swear, to whom I could give such unalloyed delight as I will give to you. I will drink your sweetness, drain you dry, and make you hunger more."

He had won his most ardent mistress, Mrs. Gumley, with those same words, and he watched the effect of them on this, his latest capture. . . . Was she captured? Her reeling eyes, her panting breath, assured him that she was, completely. His!

She took his hand, pressed it to her mouth, nibbled his finger-tips and led him to the door.

"It kills me," she whispered, "to let you go in this great moment, yet . . . you must."

He was sure of her now. He knew that guilty backward glance. Her husband. Ph! No conquest to filch her from Masham who was born to cuckoldry, but Harley was another pair of horns, though he'd be sworn, whatever had been said of my new Lord Oxford—St. John caught his twisted lip behind a tooth—he had never more than fingle-fangled with a girl in all his life. And how he could have ever brought himself to couch with that pious scarecrow, his good lady, who had convulsed St. John and her company at her table by saying that she knew no Lord but the Lord Jehovah, was a mystery. . . . And here was *this* little mystery, on her toes with her arms about his neck and her voice like honey at his ear.

"Promise me one thing—that my brother shall have his command of the Quebec Expedition, and if Harley should oppose it, you must fight him, St. John. Fight him!"

And he saw her face distorted by something near to hate: or what?

Oho! She had depths undreamed and possibilities immeasurable; but he would take their measure and his fill of her, with any luck.

He swung her clean off her feet with his parting embrace, and went well pleased with himself and his conquest.

He might not have been so pleased with either had he seen the face she pulled at his swaggering back, or heard the words she threw impishly after him:

"Cock-a-doodle-doodle-*boo*!   Wait until your hen crows, chanticleer!"

*   *   ·*

In August the Court moved to Windsor; Mrs. Masham moved from Kensington to Town—'to lie in,' wrote Swift to Stella. 'I never saw her, though her husband is one of our Society [of Brothers]*. God send her a good time. Her death would be a terrible thing. . . .'

Swift's fears, less for the life of Mrs. Masham than for the Tory Ministry that banked upon her favour with the Queen to keep them in and the Whigs out, were not unfounded.

On the night of August 21, from sunset till sundown, Brigadier Masham paced unceasingly the corridor outside his wife's room, closing his ear against the sounds that came from it; a strangled cry, a pitiful low moaning, the hushed tread of the midwife, the doctor's voice, professionally cheerful, and hers, weak: "Can't you give me poppy-juice? I want to be brave, but . . ."

Brave!

Masham walked away.

In her white parlour he sat, waiting. So for twelve tortured hours had he waited, dreading the sight of Arbuthnot's face when he came from the room of birth or . . . A monstrous sense of injustice flared within him. Why should she suffer and not he? Why should any woman go through this agony, forced upon her by her mate, and by him unshared? Why was it so long a time? Their first, a daughter, had been easy, but this? Arbuthnot had told him it might be slow and difficult. His heart shrank. He who had faced death a thousand times and had never known the fear of it, was now crushed by a shaking terror that made of him a craven, repulsive to himself. He went to the window. The curtains were undrawn. Rain had come after weeks of drought, and fell heavily from a black sodden sky. No star pricked the gloom above, no light below. He turned to the table where his servant had set a meal of cold fowl, fruit, wine. Unable to bear the silence or the sight of food, he opened the door that communicated with the nursery where Anne, his daughter, slept. Her mother had brought her from Kensington during these last few days to save herself the journey back and forth—and for her comfort.

The nurse sat sewing by the light of a candle behind a painted

* A Tory Club, rival to the famous Kit-Cat of the Whigs.

screen. At his entrance she came rustling out to curtsy with a question in her eyes.

"No news," said Masham briefly; and tiptoed to the cot.

Rosy with sleep, her gold hair spread on the pillow, Anne breathed softly with lips just parted to show her tiny teeth. Masham's tense face relaxed. He swallowed painfully, and stooping, kissed the dimpled hand outflung on the coverlid. She stirred; he backed, turned, trod on something, bent and picked it up: an absurd rag doll.

Placing it carefully on the counterpane, he went out.

Arbuthnot was in the parlour helping himself to wine. He looked up and holding his glass, came forward.

"Now, laddie, drink this. It'll steady ye."

"Is there . . . ?" Masham moistened his dry lips.

"No change yet. These things take time."

"How is she?"

"As well as can be expected. Sit down, man, and eat a bite."

"Will it be much longer? I heard her ask for poppy-juice."

"We won't give it her."

"Is there any"—Masham took a sip of the claret and braced himself to ask—"any danger?"

"There is always a modicum of danger in these obstinate cases."

"Obstinate?"

Arbuthnot sat at the table.

"The child," he said, "is not lying head foremost, so you must be prepared to wait."

Wait!

He watched Arbuthnot eat a hearty meal, and therefrom derived some comfort. Surely if his patient were in danger a doctor would not eat? He not only ate, he talked: of the Peace negotiations, of the recent death, from smallpox, of the young Emperor Joseph of Austria, son of Leopold. "That," said Arbuthnot, taking the leg of a fowl in his fingers to gnaw, "may alter the whole aspect of Europe. Charles will now become ruler not only of Austria and Spain, but of Italy and the Netherlands, which—if he knows how to use it—will invest him with power greater than that of Louis who is as anxious to come to terms as we are. Nothing could be more opportune. . . . Man, ye look as sickly as a lemon. Let me cut you a bit of this white meat."

"No. If the child does lie normally, is that a——?"

"Now then, now then, I do not discuss my medical cases with laymen. We shall have Peace within the year, of that I'm certain. And God send Her Majesty will live to see it." Selecting a peach from a dish, Arbuthnot bit. Juice poured down his chin and dripped on to his cravat. "The Queen is ailing—with the gout in her stomach and a bee in her cap. You must persuade your good wife, when she's up and about——"

Masham's head jerked. "Why don't you go back to her? I thought I heard a cry."

" 'Twas an owl. They'll fetch me if I'm wanted. She has the best midwife in London, and Mrs. Abrahal to give a hand. An excellent woman that. Ye can't hurry these things. Nature must have her way. My bull-bitch had a worse time than this with her first litter. A bull-bitch is the most difficult of all canines to whelp. Their necks are too short. They can't help themselves. I was up all night with her. My treatise on John Bull, by the way, will be published shortly."

"Oh?"

"Yes." The doctor chuckled. "It should make a stir. I was saying, you must persuade your good wife to keep the Lady 'Carrots' at a respectful distance from the Queen. Swift has his doubts of her, and I have too. She is the Whigs' decoy duck, believe me. And there's a piece of information for you to hand to St. John when you see him."

Masham's face tightened. "I don't see him."

The doctor shot a shrewd glance, and as if deaf to that muttered remark, went on: "I want you to tell him that 'Carrots' has got wind of His Royal Highness's letter to the Queen."

Masham slid into a chair.

"I didn't know the Queen's brother had written her a letter."

"Did ye not now? You're wife's a rare diplomat. Ay!" The doctor admiringly nodded. "So she kept that from ye, did she? And from me, till yesterday. Finish your wine."

He pushed Masham's untouched glass across the polished table. "I was about to say—and you can pass this on to St. John—that the Prince has written asking the Queen to champion his cause. I've seen the letter. Your wife showed it to me. She wished me to take a copy of it in case—— Hahum!" The doctor sputtered, coughed, and drank again.

Masham turned his eyes.

"In case of what?"

"Nay, lad!" Arbuthnot leaned forward to pat Masham's tensed knee. "Dinna fash yerself! All women have fancies at these times. Here's the letter copied. And to-morrow when ye're at the Club——"

"To-morrow?" said Masham, close-lipped. "I may not be at the Club."

"Never fear, ye will. Shall I read it to ye?"

"No."

"It says——" the doctor produced a paper, put spectacles upon his nose and read:

'You may be assured, Madam, that though I can never abandon but with my life my own just right which you know is unalterably settled by the fundamental laws of the land, yet I am more desirous to owe to you than any living soul, the recovery of it. . . .'

"I did not take down the whole, but this," said the doctor, "is of interest and inexpressibly moving. He says: 'I am satisfied, Madam, that if you will be guided by your own inclination you will readily comply with so just and fair a proposal as to prefer your own brother, the last male of your name, to the Electress of Hanover, the remotest relation we have, whose friendship we have no reason to rely on or to be fond of, and who will leave the Government to foreigners of another language, of another interest. . . . In the meantime I am ready to give all security that can be desired to maintain those of the Church of England in all their just rights and——' "

"God alive!" Masham sprang to his feet. "How do you think I can listen to this when my——"

"That's the way." The doctor removed his spectacles and beamed upon him. "Let yourself go. It will relieve ye. And no matter to me whether ye listen or not, here's the letter." He passed it to him. "Take it and read it while ye're waiting. I must return to your wife. Finish the bottle and eat something—do! I'll be back."

So soon as Arbuthnot had gone Masham strode over to the bell and pulled.

"Clear the table."

The footman removed the dishes, left the wine, snuffed and replaced the dying candles. Again Masham went to the window, unlatched it. Rain drifted in. His head felt hot and, strangely, his loins ached. Removing his periwig, he hung it aside. The cool moist air fanned him. Long he stood there, his eyes sightlessly straining and his thoughts adrift. . . . St. John! Why had this canny Scot brought up that name of all names now? Why? He passed his hand over his forehead which was wet. Since when had this creeping suspicion wound its evil way into his heart . . . his home, his life, to lie coiled like some dark snake, spawning amid poison spat from forked tongues? There had been sneers, gossip, tattle enough, unheeded by him in his loyalty and faith. . . . Yes, sweet heaven! Faith. In the smug possessive certainty of the complaisant husband he had lived on faith, was swollen to bursting with it. And even when that painted monkey, Andrew Fountaine, had come up to him tee-heeing at White's with his parlous puns and dirty hints, he had paid no heed. So why recall them now? . . . 'Your brother-in-law's command of the Quebec Force goes hard with Lord Oxford, I hear. St. John has lost no time in making the most of his chances as my lord's deputy.' And then Swift, with his burble and bluster, to hand him a farewell finale. 'St. John and your lady wife between them appear to be settling the affairs of the nation. . . .'

But you couldn't knock the teeth out of the head of a divine whose cloth was his defence, and whose quill picked at live men's reputations like a vulture at dead men's bones—and St. John's reputation was, in all conscience, damned enough. What was that filthy jingle hawked by the gutter-wags before the Commons returned him to office?

> 'From business and the noisy world retired
> Nor vexed by love, nor by ambition fired,
> Gently I wait the call of Charon's boat,
> Still drinking like a fish and— —like a stoat.'

Jack had sailed in April. This was August. Four months. But how long before she had become pregnant were she and St. John between them 'settling the affairs of the nation'?

Masham turned from the window to the dazzle of candle-light within. Her room! Filled with her presence, as she had left it this morning when, with their child in her lap, their little Anne, she had suddenly risen from her chair to say clearly, softly: "Take her to the nursery now. My time is here."

Ominous words, uttered fourteen hours ago; and still she lay struggling to bring forth life, or . . .

A choking sensation came into his throat. He put his hand to his steinkerk, wrenching it free. On the chair where she had sat lay a morsel of lace-edged lawn. He took it up. Her handkerchief, one he had given her, smelling faintly of musk and violets, embroidered in a pinkish pattern. He looked at it more closely. Strawberries! . . . Was there not something said, written, of a handkerchief 'spotted with strawberries'? Othello's gift to Desdemona. A harsh laugh, loud to his ears in the stillness of the room, escaped him. Forgotten words danced in his brain. . . . *'I'll be hanged if some cogging cozening slave, to get some office has not devised this slander.'* And with awful distinctness he heard himself say: "I shall go mad."

The door opened. Mrs. Abrahal stood there, her face agitated, her voice breathless.

"Sir, the doctor bids you come."

His fingers crushed the handkerchief. This then was the end. He had let her go with evil lurking in his thought of her. He had suffered, not for her physical anguish, but for his own biting jealousy. And now . . .

He followed Mrs. Abrahal along the dimly-lit passage to a door. She whispered: "You can go in."

His way was barred. Coatless, with shirt-sleeves rolled to the elbow, the doctor shot out a hand to take his.

"Let me be the first to offer ye my heartiest congratulations! Your wife and son are doing well. She's sleeping. You can have a look, but don't waken her. She's comfortable now, and he— 'pon life, sir, 'tis the living spit of you!"

From somewhere within came a querulous whimper that rose to a lusty howl.

The doctor grinned.

"Your son is being washed and he don't like it." A warning pressure of Masham's rigid arm followed the words: "Go steady, lad. Go steady."

He went steady.

One glance only did he give to the noisy atom squirming on the nurse's lap before he knelt at his wife's bedside as if before a shrine.

White and frail as a tempest-tossed flower she lay there with eyes closed; they opened a very little, wider; and she smiled. Her hand lifted to his face, to his wet eyelids. "Old stupid. . . ." Her whisper, with faint laughter in it, tore through his heart. "You're crying. Don't cry. . . . Go see your son."

CHAPTER SEVEN

For three days it had rained without ceasing, to make of the roads a morass and to empty the pockets of Jonathan Swift in the hire of coach and chair. On the evening of August 22 the weeping clouds parted, pierced by a silvery light.

Swift, who had dined with Lord Oxford, picked his way ankle-deep in mud to save his purse, and passing White's Chocolate House in St. James's Street, was loudly hailed by a smiling gentleman at the window.

"Hey, Brother Jonathan! I have great news for you. Come in!"

Swift, unwillingly, came in.

He had a deal of work in hand, a belly well-lined at Lord Oxford's expense, and the final proofs of his pamphlet '*The Conduct of the Allies*' to correct before going to the printers. But the Brigadier was a member of that fraternal Society to which Swift had been recently elected, and held besides a more important office as Queen's Cofferer and husband of the Favourite.

Taking the seat and refusing the glass of rack-punch offered him by Masham, Swift reluctantly accepted a cup of chocolate, the sickly smell of which pervaded the whole room. At the far end some rowdy drunks were gathered round a roaring fire to quiz the young woman at the counter where stronger beverage than chocolate was dispensed. A silent group of card-players occupied a nearby table, but Masham sat alone.

"We're in need of any news, great or small," said Swift, with a sour look at the steaming bowl of punch and Masham's flushed face above it. "Lord Oxford is as mumpish as a cricket in an icehouse over these brangles between the Lords and Commons and——"

"My wife," attempted Masham, lifting his glass, "has been——"

"And Prior," Swift continued, undeterred by interruption, "is in Paris, baiting Torcy with his Peace terms. God send the French Frog'll swallow them." He sipped his cup and grimacing said: "Enough to turn my stomach after wine. I've had dinner with Lord Oxford." He threw this out for the benefit of those who cared to hear, that the Prime Minister of England sought his company. "And what were ye sayin' of your wife? I wish she'd come back. We need her. That damned Duchess 'Carrots' is winding more than wool when she sits tatting in Her Majesty's Closet. If I had my way I'd have her and Marlborough out of their employments before she turns your good lady and Lord Oxford out of theirs. Trouble's on the boil, and methinks St. John has had some stirring of the brew. I've ventured all my credit with those two Ministers to clear some misunderstanding between them." Masham's wavering smile went out. "Bring back your wife," said Swift bluntly. "She's needed at her post. The 'Carrots' gains ground daily."

"Be hanged to the 'Carrots'! My wife," blurted Masham over his raised glass, "was yesterday delivered of a son! That's my news, sir, if you'll let me tell it."

With suitable congratulatory replies and some hasty calculation, Swift allowed him to tell it. . . . Yesterday. That would mean two weeks if not three, before she could return to the Queen.

"And if it had not been for Dr. Arbuthnot's skill," said Masham solemnly, "I would now have been a widower with a son born dead. However all's well, an' she's well an' he's well, ecod! As fine a boy as ever. . . . Eight pounds at birth, sir! Small wonder he all but killed her. If I tell you, Brother Swift, I had the labour pains myself in my own loins an' . . ."

Perceiving Brother Masham to be a trifle raddled, Swift let him go on till he talked himself out. Then, consulting his watch, he got up.

"You're not to go yet!" cried Masham, ladling punch. "What's your haste? Drink a health to my son. Drawer! Another glass here."

Swift scowled. Wine, chocolate, punch. What a mixture! This'll leave me sickish. And to take his mind off his stomach, "Is it a fact," he asked the effulgent Brigadier, "that the Duchess of Marlborough has presented the Queen with an account over-due for the sum of twenty thousand?"

"Twent——" Masham cautiously blinked. "How the deuce should I know?"

"Who but you should know," retorted Swift. "If your wife keeps you informed as a good wife should, of what may be told, in confidence to her?" And watching the colour deepen in Masham's ruddy face, Swift grinned on one side of his mouth. "Those two between 'em will have cost the Treasury something in the region of a quarter of a million."

"How d'you make it a quarter?" Masham carefully scooped up a floating lemon rind from the punch-bowl and dropped it in his glass. "I hold no brief for either of 'm, but they can't have cost——"

"I said, 'they *will*'," Swift corrected. "Here's this dirty case of those bread contracts with Medina to be sifted to its bottom, which will show a debit on the Exchequer's side and a pretty credit to the Duke's. And there's Blenheim not yet finished, and the price of it not half paid."

"Nor will it be in their life-time. The Queen refuses to give another penny to the building of it now, since Sarah tore the locks off the door and the panels off the walls of her 'partment at St. James's when the Queen turned her out of 'em." Masham chuckled and leaned forward to say with remarkable achievement: "That woman's efferver—vessence and audacity's incromp"—he tried again—" 'sincomparable. The Prince—Prince George, you know —I was hiseck—his equerry—always usessasay 'That woman'll bounce,' he usessasay—'like a ball, however much you throw 'er down.' And there she is," declared the Brigadier, fishing out his snuff-box from his vest-pocket, "planted. Opposite. Within a

hair's fligh'—crow's breat'h—o' the Queen's house. Fearful
liberty, I call it. Snush, sir?" He offered the gold box. "The
Prince gave me that when I went to the war. But talking of Sarah
and her chick——" Masham stopped, smiled, and triumphantly
launched, "her chicaneries, I have heard——"

"And what—hee-hee!—may you have heard?"

Swift glanced up and Masham glanced round.

A simpering spindle-legged gentleman in a girlish golden periwig and painted to the eyebrows, stood behind his chair.

"Why, bless me, Dr. Swift here too! Merry met! May I join
you?"

"By all means," said Masham heartily, "pray do. I have some
'drigious great news for you, Fountaine. We're celebratin'—
Swift and I."

"Not I," Swift contradicted sourly. "How's your health, Sir
Andrew?"

"Bonny," lisped the beau, "but for my asthma and my bad leg
that is swelled to the groin. Mrs. South, my housekeeper, has
clapped a plaster on it, and I"—he waggled his padded hips—"I'm
limping."

"You should walk in slippers then, and not on stilts," rejoined
Swift with a pointed look at Sir Andrew's high red heels. "Take
my seat, sir."

He rose from it and ramming on his shovel-shaped hat, bowed
to his host. "My warmest felicitations to you and your good
lady, sir. Good-night."

"You'll not leave us, Jon'than, without a strip'pup cup,"
protested Masham.

"I am neither in my stirrups, nor," Swift answered sternly,
"in my cups. And here's a motto for you both to take to heart.

> 'Drink a little at a time,
> Put water in your wine,
> Miss your glass when you can,
> And go off the first man.' "

And off he went.

"May the devil corrupt his carcase for a prosy tedious sermonizing ass," quoth Sir Andrew, gazing after him. "He flaunts
his cloth when it suits him, but not to his suit—tee-hee!—of the
ladies. They say he tutors Mistress Vanhomrigh in Greek and
pays court to her in Latin. A young lady of vast accomplishments, and personable too. How is your good wife, Masham?"

Having held himself in patience for that opening, the Brigadier let forth. The glasses clinked. Sir Andrew's tongue was loosened. He too had been dining, but not with Lord Oxford.

"I have just left Mr. St. John and his lady. Poor soul," giggled Sir Andrew, "I pity her."

Masham lowered his glass.

"And why should Mrs. St. John, sir, invite your pity?"

"Why, sir"—a shrug, a simper, a whinnying laugh, accompanied the oblique reply—"a complaisant wife is only less to be pitied than a complaisant husband is to be despised, tee-hee!"

A sharp movement of Masham's elbow splashed the brimming contents of the refilled punch-bowl on to the spidery hands and pink satin breeches of the beau.

"Blister you, Masham!" squealed the vexed Fountaine, snatching out his handkerchief, "you've drenched me."

Sobered and unsmiling, Masham laid a hand on his sword-hilt and stood.

"An unpardonable accident, sir, for which, if you demand a more proper satisfaction than my verbal apology, I will meet you to-morrow morning in Hyde Park."

"Faith, sir!" Fountaine's face beneath the rouge had yellowed. Pop-eyed, he sat shaking in his chair. " 'Tis I who should apologize if I have said aught to offend. I am no swordsman, and I'll not quarrel with you, Masham. No. Your Society of Brothers, so I understand, forbids a fight. If my tongue slipped——"

"Then I advise you, sir, to hold it," interrupted Masham, glaring, "lest it should slip again. For if your pity be challenged, I would pity *you* to see your tongue slit up. Drawer! My count, and this"—he paused—"this gentleman's."

Sir Andrew left off mopping his knees to mop his wet forehead.

"*My* count, sir, I pray you. Drawer, give me the bill." He beckoned. Masham bowed.

"Your count is settled, sir—with me. Good-night."

The incident had passed unnoticed, but Masham's exit did not. The group around the fire watched him go, and turned again with hands to mouths in sniggering asides. Fountaine tripped to join them at the hearth, shrill with indignation.

" 'Pon honour, gentlemen, the Brigadier's as tetchy as a spinster who has naught but her pillow for her comfort, which is all that he has, I'll warrant, to heat *his* bed! He spends his married life between faith, hope, and no charity. He spilt punch on my new breeches, damme, and when I offered to fight him—for 'twas no accident, sir, I'll wager my parts—he sheered off!"

And edging to the fire to dry himself, he gave an interested audience his views concerning Masham's lady—"whose green eyes look to split more than her happy marriage! The party stands divided, gentlemen, upon her word, with Oxford and St. John juggling for first place while she dangles each upon her beaux' string—hee!"

The howls of derision that greeted this pun from the sorriest punster in town, were interrupted by a shriek and a startled leap from Fountaine. "Hey, why! What the devil—what's here?"

A black cat had slunk from its corner and was arching its back against Fountaine's skinny legs. He aimed a kick. "Get out, abomination! A black cat for a witch—two peers for a bitch—tee-hee! St. John disregards the notice-board warning trespassers off Masham's private property! And not so private neither! St. John's angling in deep waters for his earldom, and I'll stake my shirt he'll land it! Come, fellows, lay your odds. Mine's a hundred on—fifty against!"

*   *   *

In the fall of that year the calamitous news of the Quebec Expedition was received in London. The magnificent Armada that had set out—and with what high hopes—to attack the French colonies in Canada, had run into fog and foul weather that drove eight transports on the rocks, drowned eight hundred of Marlborough's picked soldiers and almost as many ships' men.

A Council of War, hastily summoned in Admiral Walker's Flagship, revealed that their remaining supplies would not see their troops and sailors through a winter campaign even should they succeed in landing them safely, which was doubtful. Jack's insistence on taking the risk had been outruled by the Admiral, who hurried home to clear himself leaving Jack with his troops behind him.

Abigail, in firm belief that she alone by her persuasions had secured for Jack his heart's desire, took his defeat not only as a bitter disappointment but as a source of self-reproach. Through her unhappy interference Jack had crowned his young career not with the glory of achievement, but with abortive failure. To cover herself she rounded on St. John with reproaches, accusations. To lay all to a storm was the meanest excuse. He alone was responsible for this appalling fiasco and the ruin of Jack's future. He had sent the expedition into danger unprepared and unprovisioned. He had been too precipitate and, as always, too cocksure. And Jack must now come home the victim of a fruitless errand and of gross misguidance—if indeed he ever *did* come home! Knowing Jack, she believed him more like to blow his brains out or force a landing with his men to certain death among those savage Indians!

St. John let her rail on at him, uninterrupted. Her reproaches, lamentations, were far less insupportable than Oxford's polished gibes and the careful reminder that he from the first had opposed the expedition and Jack Hill's command of it. St. John, however, was not to be drawn into open hostility with his Chief, whose sneers he swallowed while he added their score to his budget for repayment. He knew that he must grind his axe in secret if he wished to gain the upper hand, and his seat in the Upper House.

To this end, therefore, he pursued his siege of Abigail, who appeared now to be not wholly indefensible. Since his first impetuous advance he had indeed made no significant headway. True, the birth of her son had impeded his approach, yet even when she was herself again she had skilfully avoided his manœuvres. His amour propre was piqued; his abundant faith in his own charms a trifle shattered. But, although mortified, he was not inconsolable. His 'hundred other women' were still ready to console.

She bid him to her table, she wined and dined him well, but not once did he dine with her alone. She contrived always that her husband should be present as his host; and even when she called him to her chamber to discuss the all-absorbing topic of her brother and that disastrous expedition, her sister or her maid were with her in the room. If, by this coy resistance, she had thought to heat his ardour more, she might find herself mistaken. And determined, at all costs, to let her know it, St. John forced an entrance.

Her footman informed him that she was at her toilet. The door between her bedroom and the salon stood ajar. Disdaining further parley, St. John flung it wider and walked in.

Her maids—she had two, one to coif and one to gown her—uttered screams of protest and covered her bare shoulders. St. John's bow to her reflection in her dressing-glass was returned with a look of unmitigated venom.

"Who gave you entrance here?"

"Your servant, madam."

"He shall be instantly dismissed."

"And reinstated," said St. John, smiling, "in my service as a reward for the service he has rendered me. Send away your women. I must speak to you in private."

His impudence succeeded where more courtly tactics might have failed. To her maids she gave a whispered order: "Return

here in ten minutes. Guard the outer door. . . . And now, sir,
you may speak to me in private, but"—she stretched an arm as
barricade to his approach—"pray keep your distance."

"I have kept my distance," he said urgently, "too long. I am
past myself and on my knees."

He was. Her laughter rippled.

"If you value your knees, sir, I suggest you rise. My clumsy
maid has spilt the contents of my rouge-pot. She too shall be
dismissed. Your visit, St. John, looks to leave me servantless."

He assumed, in haste, the perpendicular, surveyed his blushing
knee-caps and swore softly.

Abigail offered sweet concern and reparation. "My husband's
valet shall provide you with a fresh pair of hose before you go."
She selected a patch in the shape of a star, stuck it in the middle of
her cheek and turned to face him. Her eyes glittered; her voice
cut the air like a whip. "Button your foil, St. John! Have done
with fencing. I've parried your thrust."

And at his look of unguarded surprise that changed to one of
unmistakable relief, she twinkled up at him.

"Your blade is blunt and mine is sharp. I'll not engage. But
if you will, I'll stand your second when you lunge again. I am
told there's a fair meeting-place in Bloomsbury that you"—she
watched him redden to his ears, and went on with gentle malice
—"are not loath to frequent in the company of one Belle Chuck,
who-lack-a-day——" she waved her hare's foot, sighing, "who
supplants me."

"Ods my life!" exploded St. John. "Who the devil are your
spies?"

She hunched a shoulder.

"Woman's instinct."

"Misdirected!"

"No," she flashed, "misled."

He advanced an eager step.

"If you would let me lead you——"

"I know my way, but"—she looked at him with meaning undisguised—"I think it is a way that you know better. A long way
and to its end, St. John, I am prepared to follow you."

He drew a breath.

"And if I follow *you* that way will lead to——"

He paused expectant, waiting for her whisper:

"To St. Germains. . . . And la route du Roi!"

Her maids were at the door, and St. John at her feet to kiss her
hand and huskily to tell her:

"We follow then united in one Cause. We must contrive——"

From an inner room adjoining Masham entered, halted; and unseen, stole away.

Her maids came in.

*   *   *

"I am sadly forgetful of late," said the Queen. "I have no memory for names. Doctor Arbuthnot says it is due to the gout in my stomach. Dear Duchess, are you not tired of tatting?"

And the Queen gazed with tenderest affection at the red-haired, sallow-visaged lady who sat on a stool at her feet.

"No, Madam, I enjoy my tatting."

"What are you making?"

"A purse, Madam."

"A purse!"

The Queen turned pink. A purse! Was there some sharp edge to that soft answer? The division of honours between the Duchess of Somerset, Mistress of the Robes, and Mrs. Masham, Keeper of the Purse, had occasioned some discussion, much dismay. The Whigs had hoped to have placed the Duchess in supreme command of the high offices vacated by her predecessor. Lord Oxford, however, had advised a careful dispensation, and the Queen, as always, had followed his advice. So:

"A purse! And such a pretty colour!"

"Orange, Madam, is my favourite."

The Queen eyed her doubtfully. Orange. A colour she abhorred; the colour flaunted by the Whigs in the Election which had turned them out in such a shattering minority. How tiresome of the dear Duchess to be so self-opinionated and . . . so tactless. But there was none now left to her in all the world to whom she could talk of her girlhood. The Duchess of Somerset had known her as a child, as a bride; had given her shelter at Syon House when to her everlasting sorrow, she had deserted her father, the King. It was sad that so few were left alive with whom she could share her early youth and her youth's memories.

The Queen glanced up and out of the window. Facing her in the rooms she now occupied pending the redecoration of her own, she could see the magnificent Palace built by Wren for the Duchess of Marlborough. How dreadful of Mrs. Free—— of the Duchess to have planted herself there in perpetual reminder of her presence. And what it must have cost! Every penny of the eighteen thousand on which she had insisted as repayment of her 'rights': that two thousand a year offered by the Queen as compensation for Parliament's refusal to grant a five thousand yearly income to the Duke and his heirs; a compensation which the

Duchess had high-handedly rejected. Yes, rejected and then, after so long a lapse of time, enforced. Still that was most thankfully over, and never more would she be troubled by those distressing scenes. The dear Duchess of Somerset was always so kind; her voice so quiet.

And in a voice so very quiet that she scarcely could be heard: "I am told," said the Duchess, "that Mr. St. John has submitted to Your Majesty the names of twelve new peers—among which is Mr. Masham."

The Queen's heart gave a bounce.

"Yes, I believe . . . Did Mr. St. John . . . but surely he did not tell you a State secret?"

"No, Madam," the Duchess palely smiled. "Mr. St. John did not tell me."

The Queen was greatly flustered. The Duchess of Somerset's calm could be at times more agitating than the Duchess of Marlborough's storms.

"Does Your Majesty consider it wise to make Mrs. Masham a peeress?"

"No," the Queen reluctantly admitted, "I do not. I have been over-ruled against my better judgment. I told Mr. St. John that it would be unseemly for a peeress to sleep on the floor at the foot of my bed, as she frequently does when I am ill. Nevertheless, I feel that the services of Mrs. Masham and her husband should be recognized."

"And the Tory Party in the Lords," said the quiet Duchess, "must be strengthened in order that Peace may be secured at any cost. Your Majesty looks to face a political crisis which will likely be unparalleled in the history, not only of your reign but of your Kingdom. Mr. St. John's twelve peers will gain a majority vote against the Whigs and determine the Tory efforts for a separate peace with France, which, Madam, I entreat you to believe, would be a Peace ill-won, with dishonour. Is Your Majesty prepared to desert your Allies in this nefarious scheme and retract your Treaty? I beg you, Madam, to consider . . ."

"I beg you, Madam, to consider." It was Abigail now who murmured in her ear. "The Whigs are at heart Republican. They are preparing a procession to burn effigies of the Pope, the devil, and Your Majesty's lawful successor, His Royal Highness, your brother, whom they so basely have labelled 'The Pretender'. But worse than all of this, the Whigs have hatched a conspiracy to depose Your Royal self and set up a Commonwealth, led by the Duke of Marlborough!"

"I beg you, Madam, to consider." It was Marlborough who spoke, "that my advanced age and the many fatigues I have undergone make me earnestly wish for retirement and repose. But I am bound to declare that I cannot, *will* not, join in any negotiation for a separate Peace with France, which would endanger the safeties and liberties of Europe."

"I beg you, Madam, to consider. Marlborough screens himself behind the Whigs in supporting their opposition to the Peace. The discoveries made by the Commissioners of Accounts show that the Duke has had illicit dealings with Sir Solomon Medina, and is caught in his own net of corruption. The term 'Extraordinary Contingent Expenses' is extremely wide—to the sum of two hundred thousand pounds of monies appertaining to the State. Again I beg you, Madam," said Lord Oxford, "to consider . . ."

Pacing her Green Closet, she considered. Marlborough! The greatest General the world had ever known, her friend, adviser, once so loved, to be brought so low, dishonoured; he, who had crowned her reign with glory, to stand accused, deprived of his employments and dismissed!

She shrank from immediate decision. She appealed to Oxford for redress. She could not even, on so serious a charge, dismiss one who for so long had served her faithfully.

"How, my lord, can I tell him to go?"

"Would Your Majesty prefer to write to the Duke?"

Yes. She would write to the Duke.

What the Queen wrote, to Oxford's dictation, has never been revealed, for Marlborough, in his first blaze of indignation at the Queen's injustice and ingratitude, flung the letter on the fire. But Swift gave his views on the Duke's dismissal to Stella, and posterity.

'The Queen and Lord Treasurer mortally hate the Duke of Marlborough, and to that he owes his fall more than to his other faults. . . . However it be, the world abroad will blame us. I confess my belief he has not one good quality besides that of a General, but we have had constant success in arms while he commanded. Opinion is a mighty matter in war, and I doubt but the French think it impossible to conquer an army while he leads. . . . I do not love to see personal resentment mix with public affairs.'

And on January 2:

'This being the day the Lords meet and the new peers to be intro-

duced. It was apprehended the Whigs would have raised difficulties, but nothing happened. I went to see Lady Masham at noon,
and wish her joy of her new honour. . . .'

Which may have, pardonably, somewhat turned her head. Her
hand held the key not only of the Privy Purse but of high politics.
Her position was unique, her influence behind the throne a
powerful weapon in the Tory armament against invidious attack
from the weakened Opposition; and the Whigs knew it. Duchess
'Carrots' knew it. St. John and Oxford knew it, and each played
their cards accordingly; yet neither knew they played a losing
game.

She invited them to dinner with Swift and Dr. Arbuthnot and
excused her husband's absence. "He is visiting his parents at
High Laver, but I cannot leave the Queen."

Arbuthnot nodded approval. "Ay! The Queen relies on your
ladyship's comfort to ease the gout in her belly and the pother
in her mind. This constant wrangling between hot Whigs and
lukewarm Tories on Peace to be or not to be"—the Doctor shot a
glance at Oxford, who looked along his nose—"is a sore tax upon
her failing health."

"Yes, Her Majesty sleeps ill of late," Abigail murmured. "She
will have none but me in her chamber at night."

"Which means," the Doctor eyed her shrewdly, "that ye don't
get much sleep yeself."

Alice, in a new gown of violet taffetas, flushed, opened her
mouth to speak and closed it upon a bite of broiled goose. She
had been brought in to support her sister and satisfy propriety.
"For I cannot," Abigail had told her, "entertain four gentlemen
alone."

"I do not understand why you entertain at all when your
husband is from home," had been Alice's curt answer. "And when
he is at home, which of late is far too seldom, you deny him your
bed and give others your company. Your lack of commonsense
and wifely sense, or any sense, looks like to wreck your marriage,
and if you ask me——"

"I don't ask you!" Which snappish rejoinder had immediately
preceded the arrival of Lady Masham's guests.

While she sat at her table, adding modest contribution to the
talk around it, Alice's outspokenness recurred again to prick
Pledged heart and soul in a Cause she believed to be just, had she
abandoned her primary duty to her husband and her children?
No! They were her life's first care, sole love; but he who had
begot them. What of him?

For the last few months he had spent his days at his Club and his nights in his own bed: not hers. She slept on a mattress at the foot of the Queen's, and only Dr. Arbuthnot knew that this particular care of Her Majesty's person was not, on medical grounds, a necessity; yet it served to stem the tide of gossip in Lady Masham's household and at Court.

And it seemed to her now that, since the birth of her son, the placid tenour of her marriage had been infected with a sudden blight; as if, on some fair September morning she had looked out at a green familiar orchard, to see its branches withered, its fruit fallen. From what evil seed had sprung this altered attitude of her forbearing husband? Had he become entangled in some tawdry light o' love? And if so, would she care? A leap, a dive, a frozen feeling in the region of her heart told her that undoubtedly she would.

She glanced aside at Oxford and her lips tightened till she looked to have none. Habitual drink was beginning to show in the droop of his facial muscles, in his exuberant speech, the over-emphasized gesture of his beautiful hands, the negligence of his once impeccable attire. His cravat was stained with the droppings of snuff, the front of his suit with grease. St. John had sneeringly dubbed him 'The Dragon': yes! a scaleless, crumbling dragon, who breathed not fire but the rank fumes of wine from his nostrils and mouth. And this was the man to whom she had rendered the fierce love of her youth, he who had taught her the dark witchery of passion and all of passion's loneliness; for him she had flamed and suffered, burned and died, and from those bitter ashes had sprung the phoenix of a far more poignant and more desperate desire: a thing implacable and rooted in the very fibres of her being—to destroy; to warp his life, at its supreme apex, as he had warped her girlhood's bud and blossom, and driven her for refuge to another man in what was now a mockery of marriage, as his had been a mockery of love.

At the sides of her chair she clenched her hands; and conscious of St. John's sardonic stare, she turned to give an order to a servant and her polite attention to Jonathan Swift. He was launching an imperious attack on the Mohocks—that dangerous gang of young ruffians who stampeded the town at night beating up helpless pedestrians. "And every one of them," Swift declared, "is a Whig with malicious intent against the Tory Ministers. I hear the Bishop of Salisbury's son is their leader. 'Tisn't safe to walk in the streets after dark."

"Nor to be carried through 'em neither," Oxford said. "They insult those in chairs more than those on foot. Who was it told me—Fountaine, I believe—that they ran his chair through with their swords and all but skewered him. What excellent wine this is! I congratulate you, lady, on your choice of vintage." To Abigail he bowed above his glass, emptied it in one draught, and bade a footman merrily: "Fill up again, sirrah, and pass it round."

Abigail held her smile fixed. St. John let his slide and said:

"Your ladyship should feel herself most complimented. Lord Oxford is the connoisseur par excellence—of wine."

"And a connoisseur," Abigail murmured, "of the arts."

A momentary silence fell, broken weightily by Alice.

"Is it true they have the plague at Hamburg? And if so, will it come here?"

St. John flourished a gold toothpick.

"Maybe—by way of Hanover."

Alice spooned a brandied cherry and laid the stone upon her plate among a dozen others. St. John, smiling, counted:

"Tinker, Tailor, Soldier, Sailor, Rich Man, Poor Man, Beggar Man——"

Said Oxford gently:

"Thief."

It was Arbuthnot now who broke the pause with studied heartiness.

"What of your lordship's South Sea Company? I'm of a mind to venture, cautiously, a hundred guineas."

"I advise you to venture all you have." Oxford's hooded eyes blinked hazily. "Every mickle makes a muckle, as they say in your Scots lingo. Our hostess here"—he peered into her face, "has put in—how much have you put in? A thousand of your good husband's hard won means?"

Abigail poised a perfumed almond at her lips before she answered:

"Five."

Arbuthnot screwed a look at her.

"Nay, lass, that's a bold risk ye run."

"No risk save a bold one," she said, "is worth a run."

"In," suggested Oxford, "double harness?" And he bestowed a sudden grin upon St. John, who cracked a walnut viciously between his fingers.

"Oh!" Abigail gave an affected little shriek and apologized: "I thought 'twas a pistol shot."

"Or a blunderbuss?" sneered Oxford.

"If so, 'twould be," said St. John rapidly, "a mighty loud explosion."

Abigail sent him a warning look. He shut his mouth, and

Oxford opened his to expound, in alcoholic volubility, his views on Marlborough's alliance with the Whigs, his subsequent political disgrace, and the recent illness of Godolphin, "which," he told the company at large, "will kill him. His blood is gravel-yellow. He'll die poor. Every guinea of his pension has been buried in horse-dung."

His words droned around the table while the company disguised their yawns, and Abigail nibbled comfits and released again her thoughts, besmeared with doubtful questioning. In her vowed allegiance and secret service to the Jacobites was she swayed by some more subtle urge than that of loyalty? In her pursuit of a lost, or losing Cause, did she seek to find surcease from the torment of a love turned sour?

She looked across at Oxford, who was talking in his slurred level voice, of the Peace negotiations, of the departure to Flanders of the Duke of Ormonde, Marlborough's successor—who," he said, "is motivated more by Mercury than Mars. He's too dev'lish impatient—has written me four times to know why—why our brilliant Secretary here"—and to his smile with a sting in it St. John, cold-eyed, bowed—"insists on a delay before he marches. Such orders of restraint, he writes, are sadly irksome. Ormonde is itching to make for Ghent." He twisted his long nose. "Mesnager has deliv—delivered me a paper full of propositions to the Allies' disadvantage. 'Fore Gad! 'Twill be a poxy Peace for 'em to swallow."

The elaborate movement of his hands, the frequent application of a furred tongue to moistened lips, denoted him to be far gone in drink, yet still sufficiently controlled to pass for sober. But Abigail who watched him, felt no pity for the pitiable devastation of that intellect which once had known no pareil in the Kingdom; that mind which hers had homaged, and before which her spirit had sunk.

She caught Alice's eye, and rising, told her guests gaily:

"Do not deprive us too long of your company, gentlemen. The card-table—and we—await you in the salon."

The remainder of the evening passed pleasantly at picquet. Swift, who always played low, won ten shillings from Alice, and declaring he would not play again to lose his little all, got up to go. The party dispersed, with Oxford complaining of lameness in his leg and a deafness in his ear. Arbuthnot took him by the arm and led him out.

Alice stayed and St. John, for a moment, to tell Abigail from a corner of his mouth:

"I have arranged with Her Majesty that you receive Mesnager,

the French envoy to-morrow. He will call upon you here at three
o'clock. I must not have a hand in this, but you, without prejudice, can. . . . Your servant, madam, and my thanks for a
most pleasurable evening."

"My duty, sir. Good-night."

While next day in her white parlour she waited the arrival of
the envoy, she carefully reviewed St. John's instruction. That his
choice had fallen upon her and not on one more qualified to deal
with so delicate a situation, both encouraged and alarmed her.
What if she blundered in her mission—or her French? St. John
had said that Mesnager spoke very little English, so she had
secreted a dictionary beneath a pillow of the couch. But above all
her fears and misgivings rose the thought triumphant—she and St.
John worked together to one end—to trick the Dragon! He, who
once had been so staunch a defender of James Stuart, had turned
traitor to denounce him in support of Hanover and that old
beldame, Sophia the Electress. She recalled how some months
ago St. John had told her that throughout the Peace negotiations
the name of the Queen's brother had been—he believed, deliberately—excluded by Oxford. His policy, St. John declared, was one
of double dealing to insure himself against, or for, a Restoration.
Oxford waited now to see which way the cat would jump—to
Guelph or Stuart. "But his lordship may find—" and St. John's
detestation of his once deeply revered Chief was undisguised—"he
may find the cat is turned on *him*—with nine tails!"

What could be the cause of this bitter enmity that had cut
across the friendship of those two? St. John's peerage, long
delayed and not yet forthcoming, may have contributed to his
antagonism, but surely there was more in it than that? Oxford's
inherent vacillation, his subtle trick of playing two instruments one
against the other as a flautist with two flutes, may have opened St.
John's hero-blinded eyes to these and other ingenious methods of
the 'man of mystery', which, to St. John, were equally abhorrent.
Strange, she reflected, that he and she who both had been Harley's
devoted disciples, should have undergone, and almost simultaneously so complete and utter a subversion; both imbued with
the same desire for . . . revenge.

And thinking that, a coldness came upon her. The room span,
dipped, heaved, and so did she, with sudden nausea. She covered
her eyes to block out the dancing specks that blurred her vision,
and sat down, weak-kneed and trembling; but her heart was racing
gladly, and she knew what for some weeks she had suspected:
that in December her third child would be born.

Then, in the midst of happy calculation, her joy fled. This had come to her before the chill of her husband's indifference had frosted their nuptial life and made of him a stranger to herself. But perhaps—with a delicate instinctive gesture she laid her hand against her body—perhaps this would clear the cloud between them when, in her own time, she would offer him her secret: and his.

Her eyes were glowing, her face flushed and beautified with a look of wistful expectation that, like a slow sunrise, may have lingered throughout her interview with Mesnager the envoy, who: 'wondered much that so mean a character, as some had made public, should be attributed to this lady who seemed to me more worthy of the favour of the Queen than any I have conversed with in my life. . . .'

Her footman announced him. He bowed himself in, pointing the toe, frilled with lace everywhere possible: a pot-bellied, highly rouged, grimacing little man whose English was atrocious, and whose overweening self-assurance deprived Lady Masham of hers.

In an excess of Gallic rapture he kissed her hands, waved his, and declared himself, in English, her minion, greatly honoured: shed rapid compliments in French upon her ladyship's appearance, feigned to be overcome by 'une ambassadrice si ravissante', and produced a sheaf of documents from: "Mon Maître, le Roi Soleil. Voici, madame, mes lettres de commission, mes témoignages juridiques. Enfin, miladi, mes credentials."

These she put aside and begged him to be seated.

"You must understand, monsieur, we are anxious on behalf of a certain Royal personage exiled in your country."

"Mais certainement, madame. His altesse le Prince, he suffer——"

Abigail started.

"Suffers?"

"Mais oui, madame." Displaying two rows of shining white porcelain teeth in a series of smiles, the envoy explained: "I have commission from the King, my Master, to know what is Her Majesty's pleasure to have done with son altesse le Chevalier, who suffer also the anxiety of suspense jusque son altesse can know where he will reside. Le Roi Louis Quatorze desire much que le Prince"—and to that name again Mesnager bowed—"be give une place d'honneur en Angleterre. That is the wish," Mesnager with dignity concluded, "of my King."

"And," said Lady Masham, "of my Queen. But we believe, monsieur, that the Whigs will endeavour to obstruct our intentions and destroy——"

"Mais—madame!" Mesnager raised ringed hands in horror. "C'est incroyable, formidable! Je suis stupéfié. Destroy!"

"J'ai dit," said Abigail desperately, "les Whig."

"Comment, madame? Wig?" The puzzled envoy touched his own, which was curled, blond, and reeked of eau d'espagne.

"Non! No! Not wig. Whig." Abigail dived beneath the cushion for her dictionary. What in heaven was the French for——?

"Ah! le Wig!" cried Mesnager profoundly. "It is the Wig who wish to destroy le Chevalier."

"Pray, monsieur, ne parlez pas de son altesse comme Chevalier. Nous l'appelons—we name him 'Prince of Wales'. The uncertain future of the Queen's brother is a great source of uneasiness to Her Majesty. If it could be possible with safety to the religion and liberties of Her Majesty's subjects"—she had this pat from St. John's notes and repeated it verbatim, but it was doubtful if the envoy understood a word—" to restore the Queen's brother to his rights after Her Majesty's decease, she would name him her successor. Do you follow me, monsieur?"

"Enchanté, madame!" He stood to bow and sat again; and since it was quite evident he had *not* followed her, she gave it up.

"I will submit to you a mode of correspondence, monsieur, which will be neither in English nor French. I have it here." She had placed a slip of paper, on which St. John had written a code, between the pages of the dictionary. Hastily she turned them over. The paper fluttered to the floor. The envoy leapt from his chair and stooped above his belly to retrieve it.

"Merci, monsieur. Voilà!" She was proud to air her few words of French, but she had none for 'code'. "This," she told him, "is a cipher."

"Pardon, madame?"

"A code. A . . . attendez s'il vous plait." Consulting the dictionary, she produced with triumph: "Zéro!"

"Mais, madame," Mesnager politely queried, "Zéro?"

Abigail held her patience.

"This, sir, is a cipher—a—wait a minute." She reverted to the dictionary. "Here is another word for it. Le chiffre."

"Ah, le chiffre!" Mesnager shrugged his padded shoulders to his ear lobes. "That now explains itself. Le chiffre!"

"Yes, monsieur, chiffre. A cipher. Code, we call it, and if you study this formula——"

"Ah oui! Ce formulaire!" Mesnager rose to take it from her with more bows. "Madame, je vous rends mille fois mes t'anks. Et maintenant if Madame will allow me to express la situation as from mon Maître, le Roi, to your Maîtresse, la Reine, in my own tongue which is more easy for me to speak——"

But not, she thought, for me to understand.

"Pray do, monsieur."

She understood little of it, yet enough to satisfy the Queen, to whom this interview was faithfully recorded, that if James Stuart were forbidden to set foot in his own country, he would at least be given domicile worthy of his Royal state, either in Lorraine or in the Rhineland. In token of her gratitude to Mesnager for this assurance, the Queen sent him by the hand of Lady Masham a miniature of herself set round with diamonds.

To Abigail and St. John, Oxford's flagging interest in the cause of the exiled Prince was not only a further indication of his marked degeneracy, but a challenge flung in stealthy opposition to the purpose St. John openly pursued. And while throughout that year of 1712 the preliminaries of Peace long sought, and by the Queen so long desired, were carefully preparing, war between St. John and Oxford was declared.

It broke in a thunder-clap from St. John, who, as reward for his services back and forth to Paris with Prior to treat with the French King and Torcy, now demanded from Oxford his 'plum'.

His letter was a masterpiece of mock humility. He had, he stated, no pretension. The post he filled already was more than he deserved, but he presumed to ask his lordship whether he might not hope that her Majesty would be so good as to revive in him the title of Earl of Bolingbroke, 'which is in the elder House of my family, and very lately extinct.'

St. John received his 'plum' to find crawling in its juicy flesh a maggot. The Queen, so Lord Oxford informed him, had announced her intention of creating Mr. St. John a Viscount, not an Earl.

To Abigail, his confederate and confidante, he rushed with his complaint. She sent for Alice. Not alone would she entertain this tiger-cub. Oh no!

Up and down her room he raged; and while she sat at her knitting and Alice at her tambour-frame, she heard:

"There's a low hog's trick to play me, hah? He won't have me at his level—thinks to plant his dragon's claw on my neck. But I'll bring him down, 'fore gad I will, for this insult he hands me."

Abigail hid her eyes and counted stitches. Alice innocently said:

"But surely, sir, a Viscount is little lower than an Earl? And to my mind 'Viscount St. John' is a most distinguished title."

"Distinguished my——"

St. John snapped his jaws upon obscenity, but only just in time. Abigail kept her lids demurely lowered.

"And truly, I can't see why you should be in such a pet, sir," persisted Alice with intent to sooth. "If I was your lady I'd be proud to be a Viscountess, I'm sure."

A fleck of spittle came to St. John's lip.

"And would ye so! Let me tell you, madam, had I known that I'd be offered what is nothing less than a courtesy prefix as thanks for my masterly Peace terms, I'd have left Oxford to twist France's tail and we'd have been at war another ten years. Why, ecod! I had that old buzzard Louis weeping tears upon my shoulder and vowing life-long love to Britain's Queen before I'd talked with him an hour. And this skim o' the Lords is all I'm handed as reward for keeping the balance of power in Europe, for raising the Netherlands Barrier, and extorting from Louis his promise that the crowns of France and Spain shall never be united on one head. 'Tis a tour de force that I've accomplished against the howling opposition of the Whigs, and with no support—only hindrance from that drunken sot, my Chief! 'Tis *I* who have set Britain where she sits—above the salt—served with the pick o' the dish, while France grovels on all fours beneath the table, and the Allies lick up the crumbs that I let fall from it! And does Harley think that after all I've done for England, I, who with my own hand"— he raised it high to clench it—"have paved the way for the Treaty at Utrecht, will stand lower in the House of Lords than Robert Harley, Earl of Oxford, Baron Wigmore——" St. John bared his teeth in a snarling grin. "Look you!" He ceased his rageful stride to plant himself firmly before the silent Abigail. "You can tell Anna Regina from me that I refuse her gracious offer of a Viscounty. You can go tell her—no, by God! I'll tell the Queen myself."

But he didn't.

When he finally had cooled enough to reconsider with coherence, he decided that half an earldom was better than none.

He took his plum and bit upon its stone and spat his grievance all around the town in every club and coffee-house, while the Whigs in the Kit-Cat split their sides to hear him. Nor did he know that the implacable vendetta he waged against his basic enemy who once had been his friend was watched, and when it flagged, rekindled, by the 'malice of a Queen's Bedchamber Woman', centred now upon 'the Dragon's' overthrow.

CHAPTER EIGHT

THE summer months were sultry with long drought; the Queen was fretful and impatient for the Peace. "So long delayed! Why do we wait? Dear Lady Masham, open a window. I must have air."

Lady Masham opened a window. The gardens of the Palace lay parched and shrivelled as did the too early ripened corn-fields through which that narrow stream, the West Bourne, wound its sluggish way from the blue heights of distant Hampstead down to the villages of Kensington and Knight's Bridge. The sweating gardeners with their watering-cans toiled vainly among the flower-beds to revive the dropped heads of lupins, wilting roses. Their voices grumbled upward. "This'll kill the harvest and the fruit. There's not enough water in the wells to feed the peaches."

In shadowy glades the panting deer sought shelter from the sun, and even the birds were silent as if too weary of the blazing heat to sing.

"Your brother," the Queen said languidly, "must find this weather very trying after the cold of Canada."

Abigail turned.

"He never reached Canada, Madam."

"Canadian *seas*, I should have said." The Queen unfurled a fan. "Such a brave soldier! We must compensate him, Masham, for that unhappy misadventure which was none of his fault."

"My brother, Madam, asks for no compensation other than Your Majesty's confidence."

The Queen gave her a harried look.

"He should know he has that, Hill."

"Yes, Madam. But," said Abigail clearly, "not since his return has he been received by Your Majesty, which oversight my brother believes to be an expression of Your Majesty's displeasure."

The Queen's underlip bulged.

"Brigadier Hill had but to ask for an audience, Masham. He cannot think that I hold him responsible for the Quebec disaster."

"No, Madam. But Lord Oxford does."

"Lord Oxford!" The Queen reddened. "How most ungracious and ungenerous—unkind——"

"Yes, Madam." Abigail lowered herself to a stool at her

Sovereign's feet and took up her knitting. Her needles clicked. The Queen puffed, fanned, and uncomfortably said:

"You must show me how to knit, Hill. A pleasant occupation. What a very tiny—is it one of a pair of shoes?"

"Yes, Madam."

"For your little boy?"

"Or"—Abigail raised her eyes—"my little girl."

"But are they not much too small for my god-daughter, Masham?"

"Yes, Madam. They are not for Anne."

"Not . . . Hill!" The Queen's bosom expanded. Her fan fluttered. A smile appeared. "Is it . . . are you?"

"Yes, Madam."

Thankful for this diversion from the unkindness of Lord Oxford, and other still more tiresome concerns, the Queen leaned confidentially nearer to ask: "When?"

"In December, Madam."

"I declare! I would never have suspected it from your appearance. These full petticoats. . . . How delighted Lord Masham must be!"

Abigail dropped a stitch.

"And how naughty of you to hide such glad news from me," pursued the Queen, playfully. "Dear creature! I must kiss you."

She was kissed.

"Madam, I was wondering," said Abigail, resuming her seat and her knitting, "since Your Majesty has been gracious enough to mention my brother, if you would consider granting him an appointment which Lord Bolingbroke advises and which Lord Oxford"—she said the name softly—"thinks fit to oppose."

"To oppose! Lord Oxford!" The Queen produced a handkerchief and wiped her face. "I cannot understand Lord Oxford's attitude of late. He seems to be determined to make difficulties where none exist. What appointment, Hill, does Lord Bolingbroke suggest for your brother?"

Abigail slid a look at the Queen's crimson countenance, and told her:

"The command of the British Garrison at Dunkirk, Madam. The occupation of Dunkirk by British troops is, as Your Majesty may remember, one of the salient points in the Armistice terms."

Her Majesty did not remember. She was heartily sick of *trying* to remember the tedious conferences held between herself and her two Ministers who seemed of late to stand at daggers drawn, the one against the other. Lord Bolingbroke, however, did at least attempt to clarify the almost incomprehensible documents he presented for perusal, and had indeed written the speech the Queen delivered to the Lords, which Lord Oxford had offered to write and then had forgotten to write. . . . And when she had somewhat sharply reminded him of his forgetfulness he had replied, with an indifference that verged upon the insolent: "I cannot see that my forgetfulness has rendered Your Majesty aught but a beneficial service. Bolingbroke has the gift—as they say—of the gab, far surpassing my own. His speech, in Your Majesty's mouth was received with tremendous acclamation."

And he had sat, without being asked to sit, in the Presence, and had dragged Minette to his knee by the scruff of her neck and said: "Madam, this elderly bitch of yours smells of her years. How old is she now? Ten? Twelve? Too old. We're *all* too old."

Lord Oxford's peculiar address had alarmed the Queen even more than it offended. Was it possible his lordship was sickening for a distemper? Were the cares of governance too great for his intellectual capacity? In short, was he out of his mind? He confessed to headache, dizziness, and once or twice the Queen had observed him to stumble as he entered or left the room; and recalling that most recent interview with him, the Queen said:

"Masham, I greatly fear Lord Oxford's health is giving way under the strain of the Peace negotiations."

"Yes, Madam." Abigail looked at her intently. "Which may account for Lord Oxford's attempt to sustain his failing health with—strong waters."

"Hill!" The Queen's high fontange quivered as she imbibed the significance of this gentle answer. "Do you mean to say——"

" 'Tis what others say, Madam, but I must confess that Lord Oxford has, to my certain knowledge, always been a heavy drinker."

The Queen's fan waved feverishly.

"Hill! This is most dreadful!"

"Dreadful, Madam, it is indeed"—the green eyes were cast up, the knitting laid down—"to see such woeful, sad deterioration in so great a statesman, and at such a time when the future of Your Majesty's throne is balanced on his word—the word, Madam, of a man whose loyalties and whose opinions vary with the weathercock, between the Whigs and Tories. A man, Your Majesty, who will sacrifice everything to private interest and personal gain. I have it, Madam, on the best authority, that while he woos Your Majesty's brother with the promise of His Royal Highness's succession, he is in constant communication with the Court of Hanover—and the Electress."

The Queen's head wobbled. The colour in her cheeks deepened to a duskier red.

"Not the Electress, Masham, surely? Lord Oxford knows where my heart is set. He has promised to secure my brother his succession if the Prince will agree to change his religion. I cannot believe Lord Oxford to be false."

"Nor, Madam," Abigail murmured, "can I." She returned, with complete absorption, to her knitting. The Queen let fall her fan to her lap.

"Hill?"

"Madam?"

"If Lord Oxford's . . . health should not permit him to retain his office, who other than Lord Bolingbroke would you suggest can replace him?"

"Madam, we trust," said Abigail evenly, "that his lordship's health *will* permit him to retain his office, but if not——"

"Yes, Hill?"

"If not, Madam, I can think of none other than Lord Bolingbroke to replace him." And she rose from her stool to help the Queen out of her chair, saying: "Your Majesty will find it cooler on this couch by the window. I will draw the curtains."

The Queen was couched and pillowed; her face bathed with scented lotion. Abigail resumed her seat and her knitting. The Queen closed her eyes. A bluebottle buzzed around the Royal head and was flapped away by a smite of the Royal hand. The Queen's voice said drowsily:

"If only the Duke of Shrewsbury were not so Hanoverian——"

Abigail's needles ceased to click.

"The Duke of Shrewsbury, Madam? The Lord Chamberlain?"

"He has always been my dear, good friend. . . . Hill, can you not rid me of this odious fly?"

Hill rid her of the odious fly, and while the Queen dozed Abigail sat, and in silence considered.

Shrewsbury! The 'King of Hearts', so named for his love of the ladies. She knew little more of him than that, since he had spent the first ten years of the Queen's reign in Italy where he had taken to himself an Italian wife who, it was said, had been his mistress. Rumour gave it that at the time of Godolphin's resignation he had been offered and declined the Lord Treasurership on the grounds that he refused to engage in an employment which he did not in the least understand. But he had accepted the office of Lord Chamberlain for which he was more eminently suited. The Queen showed him every indication of marked favour, for the same reason possibly that she favoured Duchess 'Carrots', having known them both in her early youth; and Shrewsbury, twelfth Earl and first Duke, was undoubtedly a charmer. Much of his charm, however, seemed to have waned before that of his vivacious, witty, wrinkled, but most attractive wife, with whom Shrewsbury was deep in love. The Duchess spoke but little English, and it was Shrewsbury's delight to teach her shocking words and hear her repetition of them at his table to his embarrassed guests. He was also inordinately jealous, and rumour gave it he had bought her a chastity belt from a Turkish pedlar in Milan. . . . And was this foolish, gay philanderer, the 'King of Hearts', to be the future holder, at the Queen's word, of the Lord Treasurer's White Staff? No! Abigail bit her lip. The Queen's word now is *my* word!

She glanced across at the dropsical hulk of flesh on the sofa, bedecked, bedizened with gold-threaded silk—she who was the Sovereign of England. Unexpected tears rushed to her eyes. While that unhappy, poor distorted body still existed, a Stuart reigned unquestioned, but . . . afterwards, who? Was all the secret work of Bolingbroke, of Ormonde, Arbuthnot, and herself, and that loyal band of staunch supporters North of the Tweed, to go for nothing—or for Shrewsbury?

She took her fears to Bolingbroke. He laughed at them.

"What! The King of Hearts? He'll never hold the Staff. When Harley goes I'll come in, and I'll pack Shrewsbury off to Ireland as Lord Lieutenant. They won't welcome a Whig over there, and one who truckles to George Lewis, but at least he'll be out of harm's way."

"I wonder," said Abigail quietly, "if Shrewsbury will ever be out of harm's way."

"Ph! Shrewsbury! He hasn't the bite of a bed-louse. Do you know that wrinkled wife of his? Ecod, she's a fascinator. These Italian women, though I speak from no experience"—he leered in Lady Masham's face—"have certain tricks, I'm told, that you English girls might envy."

She returned his braggart's stare with one of smiling chill, and quenched the scathing words upon her lips. She could not yet afford an open rupture with him to whom she was allied in the same ignoble purpose—to secure the downfall of the man they both had loved.

It must have been the strangest partnership, shared in mutual secrecy unvoiced, masked beneath the cloak of stronger issues which involved her sense of justice and her sentiment. No longer now was she an unacknowledged or unconscious factor in political manœuvres, but an active Jacobite whose attachment to the fallen line of Stuart was, unlike Bolingbroke's, entirely disinterested. He, completely reckless, did not care how far he went in the cause of James Edward, to reap, as he hoped, the undying gratitude in wealth and honours of Britain's future King. She, however, stood to gain nothing from her allegiance to the Prince whose succession half England supported and whose cause, unremittingly, she served.

She was so constituted that her flame-like energy which burnt white-hot to shorten her too short life, demanded always some dramatic focus point on which to seize and spend itself. As Harley once had fired her young imagination, so now was she possessed by the urge to 'right that wrong' to which end he too had been her first initiator. She remembered how he had consigned to her the safe delivery of that 'face from France' over which the Queen had wept and sorrowed, and, in secret, treasured. But Harley had apparently deserted his crusade. Although he still flaunted the Royal Stuart shield, he had lowered his lance. For whom did he wait to lift it? For the aged Electress Sophia? For her son? Or for himself? Did he, who had poisoned the Queen's mind with his careful hints of a Marlburian dictatorship, see himself in his turn a Dictator?

While in her white parlour she sewed her baby's garments, Abigail considered and rejected that improbability as too far-fetched. Harley, if she knew him—and who so well as she?—might aspire to the heights, but unaided he never could achieve them. It was she who had placed him on the pedestal he occupied; and she who in her own time would bring him down.

Her mind swerved then from further searching lest unimaginable memories be too vividly recalled. She had problems to contend with nearer and more sacred to her heart. The Queen's 'Enchantress,' that 'Ambassadrice si ravissante', who interviewed French envoys, who planned to fell a future dynasty and restore a past one, had naught to say to the concerns of Abigail Masham, wife and mother. As such it seemed that she had failed, not in her care of or devotion to her children, but in the attempt to serve two vocations.

From its lowliest beginnings she reviewed her life across the years and saw how, with patient scheming, she had laid the stepping-stones along the Queen's Highway to her present and unparalleled position. The orphaned waif, the bedroom slut who had emptied chamber-pots, defleaed an ape, received with the same humility her cousins' cast-off garments and their insults, had, by sheer unstinted perseverance, gained her goal. But at what penalty? Estrangement from her husband, between whom and herself the merest fissure on the surface of their marriage had widened to an abyss; and she stood upon its brink.

She was suddenly afraid. He, to whom in her disillusionment she had turned for sanctuary, and whom with certain intent if not in actual deed she had betrayed, now renounced her, shunned, deprived her of that intimate relationship she had come to cherish as her life's security. Was this then, his antagonism, the price she must pay for her ambition?

No word of reproach had been uttered. She could have borne it better if he had confronted her with accusations, reviled her for what she might have been, and which, through no attempted wiles of her own, she still was not. But although she guessed that he suspected her of infidelity, she could swear he had no thought of Harley. She had successfully removed that thorn. Had he picked up another? And if so, where? From whom?

Five months had passed since he had shared her bed or offered her the least encouragement to ask him why he didn't. Was ever wife in so uncomfortable a case! She who carried his child had not lain with him since it was first conceived. The situation had its comic side and she a sense of humour, but the laugh that escaped her was mirthless, and the colour that burned in her cheeks had sprung from the resolve to force from him an explanation of his conduct, or confession. If he had tired of her as a wife, or had taken to himself a mistress, or a dozen, or rebounded once again to his former fancy, Mrs. Forester, who for all her hard riding with the stag-hounds had not yet run a buck to the kill, she had a right to know the truth. And determined forthwith to probe it, she sought him in his sanctum.

He was writing at his bureau, and, as she entered, he turned to her a face expressive of the same surprised resentment with which he would have greeted the intrusion of a stranger.

Although distinctly dashed she brought a smile to her lips and the apology:

"Pray forgive me if I interrupt. Can you spare me a few moments?"

It was not the formal bow of his consent which caused her heart to shrink, but the icy unmistakable contempt in his eyes that for an instant met hers. Shame, alarm, compunction, were followed by a swift sense of injustice.

"What? Why do you——" anger struggled with her incoherence. "I demand to know why you treat me as if I were a leper. Do I no longer hold any place in your life? What have I done to deserve——" She stopped herself.

"Done?"

A slight stiffening of his figure, his face unmoved save for a contraction of those lines around his mouth that never surely had been there before, accompanied that single repetition of her words.

She flung it back at him.

"Yes, done! Your avoidance of me is so marked that in order to account for it and to discourage gossip in my household, I resort to lies and subterfuge."

Again he echoed: "Subterfuge—at which you have always excelled."

His frosted gaze removed itself while with incredulous attention she regarded him. His flaxen blond peruke, immaculately curled, his cinnamon cloth coat ornate with silver lace on cuffs and pockets, the fall of batiste at throat and wrist, the whole point-device extravagant appearance of a man of fashion presented a startling anomaly, as if a waxwork had been suddenly endowed with animation to tear apart its finery and expose the nakedness of human flesh, scarred, bleeding. But even as that bizarre notion flashed upon her she heard him speak to quell it.

"If that is all you have to say, may I be permitted to resume my work?" He indicated his desk, strewn with documents bearing the Royal Seal; and going to the door he opened it, stood waiting there for her to pass.

She did not move. Her face had whitened and her voice was a whisper to tell him:

"This is all I have to say. I think you do not know I am going to have a child."

She could feel his eyes upon her in so chill a look that her own fell before it; protectively she raised her arms from her sides and folded them with her elbows in her hands, as if to shield her body and herself. Then from some far-off vacancy she heard him answer:

"Whose?"

The door creaked as he closed it behind her. He stood gazing at it for a moment as if asking it a question before he returned to his desk; but not to his work.

Till daylight faded there he sat and, with a brooding cynical detachment wholly foreign to his nature, surveyed this blighting of his faith, his life, his honour. He did not query his suspicion. Her unchallenged acceptance of his accusation hurled at her in that one word confirmed her guilt. He sought the obvious solution. What to do? Scandal must at all costs be avoided, but there were other ways of severance from marriage than by public juris-diction. His situation was not singular. Half the Court was married in name only. St. John had been separated from his wife for the past year. St. John! . . . Something seemed to grip him by the throat. He felt a craving for strong drink to lull him to in- difference or rouse him to kill. St. John's charming face with its supercilious air of mockery rose up before him: St. John on his knees to her in her bedroom; she, in little more than her shift, and he with his hand to her lips and those words, a lover's words, upon them. 'We must contrive——'

Masham covered his ears to shut out the whisper of that recur- rent memory. Must all his life be haunted by these doubts? Could he endure again the horror of that night when she had borne his son, whose unmistakable resemblance to himself was the sole proof he possessed of her fidelity? And now this—to heat again his smouldering half-laid mistrust and bring about the devastation of his life and hers; their children's.

And the more he brooded the more deeply did he suffer, past all sanity and wisdom, the victim, in his self-afflicted torment, of tradition.

That possessive instinct inherited from a line of forbears whose wives were as much their sole monopoly as the lands they over- lorded, could not reject those compulsions implicit to the squire- archy of ownership. Nor did he see himself as inconsistent, in that while he had applauded and encouraged his wife's endeavours which had raised her to the heights, she was still his chattel whose infringement of her individual liberties must be leashed within the bounds of legalized concubinage. Beyond this last imagined out- rage to his sense of property and wounded pride he did not look. Yet he may have had some dim awareness of a conflict deeper than the jealousy of a suspicious husband.

He did not know that the first call to arms had sounded here in his home, in his heart; or that the battle of the beaux and belles, which began in the reign of Anne, would be waged to its climax two hundred years later across that arid no-man's land of sex antagonism: a war whose way to victory was led by those two outstanding pioneers of feminine enfranchisement, each born two centuries before her time: Mary Wortley Montague and Abigail Hill.

But Abigail's husband was no seer. He only knew his immediate reaction in hostility unsheathed, of man to woman's right as a careerist. He could accept no more than the ruffled surface of his questioning which revealed his wife as the woman taken in adultery, and that short of whipping her to Bridewell at the end of the cart's tail he could appeal to the Church for divorce.

A divorce!

The thought paralysed him. How could he bring himself to

jettison his name and that of his heir? Must his children—and these first two—by their likeness to him and to his family, were indubitably his—must they be branded by their mother's degradation? What was the alternative? To take for his own another man's bastard? Blind himself to the truth, as a 'complaisant' husband should?

From behind his closed lips issued a queer moaning sound, and stretching his arms along his desk he laid his head upon them, and so sat huddled, very still, seeing her face float before him in the darkness of his thoughts. . . . Her face! The pain-twisted horror of that little pointed face grown old, he fancied, at his spoken word. He could see it now, her face, lifeless suddenly, as if indeed that word had killed her dead, and her arms holding her body as though they held within them, what? His child or . . . whose?

"My lord!"

Her maid was in the doorway wringing hands and sobbing out a tale with lugubrious enjoyment.

"My lady—she has fallen in the courtyard, and oh, my lord, she looks—may God a' mercy—to be dying! Will your lordship —ow!" The girl let out a yelp as his lordship's hand descended on her shoulder to swing her round.

"What's this you say?"

"My lord—'tis her lady—they've carried in—had a fall——" gabbled the maid, too scared by his look and his voice to talk sense. "Mrs. Hill is with her and she says——"

Masham did not wait to hear what Mrs. Hill had said. Thrusting the frightened maid aside, he rushed from the room and into his wife's.

She lay on the bed. Her face was no paler than when he had last seen it, but the eyes were closed and there was blood on her forehead, on the pillow. Alice, with a basin of pinkish water and a cloth in her hand, was bending over her while a maid burnt feathers under her nose. He could smell vinegar. As he approached the bed Alice gave him a look half-menacing, half-frightened, and said in a hushed voice: "The doctor is on his way. You had better go."

He drew nearer, and, with a dry mouth, asked: "What has happened?"

"She fell."

"How?"

To that question Alice made no answer other than what seemed to him to be a movement of repulsion; and as she turned again to bathe that streak of blood, he heard from the maid a gasping sound and the words: "Madam! My lady has stopped breathing!"

"No. She still breathes, but only just."

Masham marvelled at the calm of Alice. He stood very still, smothering the upward surge of his thoughts. She had fallen. How? Why did her sister look at him with such bitter condemnation as if he were the cause of—— How long had she lain there in this living death, so ghastly white and breathing, 'only just'?

The window was closed. He went to open it, saying stonily: "She could have air." And he stayed with his back to that bed looking down upon the courtyard where some few grey pigeons picked among the cobbles. It was growing dark outside. A fog-misted twilight blurred the bared tree-branches of Kensington's gardens. The pigeons fluttered, to soar on startled wings at the thud of galloping hoofs. The rider clattered into the court and dismounted.

"The doctor is come," Masham heard himself say; and Alice's quiet, "Thank God."

For two days and nights she lay there, tranced, unliving, yet alive. For two days and nights Arbuthnot fought to save her and her unborn child. Alice, Mrs. Abrahal, and her two maids, shared the vigil at her bedside with Masham, who refused to leave that room. He would not eat; he could not sleep. He sat watching for the first sign of her return to consciousness from that dark world where her flown spirit wandered.

The doctor had given his brief verdict, "Concussion," and his orders: "Ice to her head, hot bricks to her feet. No stimulants. Nothing to be done till she revives, then——" More orders, broth, complete repose. "On no account must she speak."

And to Masham's strangled question: "Will she ever speak again?" Arbuthnot with unwonted sternness answered:

"I am no prophet, sir. Your wife lies at death's door. All that can be done for her is done."

It was on the morning of the second day that Alice, who had snatched some hours' sleep, beckoned Masham from that bedside and out of the room. They stood in the corridor together. Alice looked worn and wasted; she seemed to have shed her plumpness overnight. She drew him to a window-seat and holding his eyes with hers, said steadily: "I think you ought to know that I saw Abigail immediately after she left you the day before yesterday. She appeared to be half-dazed. What occurred between you? Did you quarrel?"

"No."

"From what I understand, you did. She told me little, but

enough for me to know that if she dies you will have destroyed her and your child as surely as if you had murdered them."

At the passionless deliberation of those words, repeating as in some awful dream his own self-accusatory conviction, Masham covered his eyes.

"She had ordered her chair," Alice's voice went on. "She said she had to make a call. She didn't say where. I watched her from my window. Her chair was waiting but she passed it by. One of the chairmen spoke to her. I saw her shake her head. She wore no cloak nor hood and she walked quickly. Then, of a sudden, she put out both her hands as if she were"—Alice paused to swallow something—"as if she were blind. And then she stumbled and fell sideways. She knocked her head against that mounting-block—you can see it from here if you look."

Masham did not look.

"She must," continued Alice, "have turned dizzy. The chairmen carried her in. She was bleeding. Her right side is bruised from shoulder to hip. If you"—and Alice's studied quietude gave way to a sort of savage gloom—"if you believe, as I think you do, that she and Bolingbroke——"

Masham dropped his hands; his face was grey, his lips a closed hard line. He opened them to say on a deep intake of breath:

"I believe nothing . . . now."

Alice blinked, and lifting a finger brushed a tear from under her eyelid; and when she spoke again her tone was softer.

"I am sorry I said what I did. I had no right——"

"Every right."

A shudder passed over him. Alice laid her hand on his and held it there. "But this I beg you to believe. You are mistaken if you think her interest in Bolingbroke is personal. It isn't. I have often warned her she would lay herself open to evil misconstruction from this gossiping cesspool of a Court if she entered into partnership with him." And seeing Masham's haggard look turned upon her with a tense appeal, she hastened to explain. "Maybe you don't know that for the last half year she has been in constant communication with the Pretender." Avoiding the astonishment, and, it seemed to her the almost frenzied light of relief that leapt to Masham's eyes, Alice added with the ghost of a smile, "she's a raging Jack, and so is Bolingbroke. But I am not, for from what I've heard I don't think he'd be at all a proper King, being as he is a Papist, and 'twould be Bloody Mary all over again if *he* came to the Throne. Abbie and I never have agreed about him, but she and Bolingbroke do, and are of one mind together in what they call 'the Cause'. And that's as far as it goes." She gave him a sidelong glance and said bluntly: "I can tell you this, if it'll make you any easier. She don't like him. Bolingbroke I mean. She says he's a conceited puppy. So he is." She got up. "I must go back to her now, and you'd best get some sleep. I'll call you if"—she faltered—"if you're wanted."

She slipped away and left him sitting with his head in his hands, a sob in his throat, and in his heart a prayer.

* * *

Extract from Swift's Journal to Stella:

'Lady Masham, poor creature, she fell down in the court here t'other day. She would needs walk across it, upon some displeasure with her chairman, and was like to be spoil'd so near her time, but we hope all is over, for a black eye and a sore side . . .'

And on December 12, *this:*

'Lady Masham's month of lying-in is within two days of being out. I was at the church on Monday. I could not get the child named Robin after Lord Treasurer. It is named Samuel after the father.'

CHAPTER NINE

THE flags and banners in the cities of London and Westminster hung limp and faded at windows where a year before they had waved in joyous celebration of the Peace. But in Parliament at secret sessions, and in the Queen's Green Closet, the last decisive struggle for the future of a dynasty continued unassuaged.

The greater part of the population had now rallied to the side of the Elector since it had become known that the Queen's brother, James III, had refused the Crown offered on condition that he 'dissimulated his religion or changed it entirely'. Yet he, to his honour, stayed firm to his Faith, while every kind of rumour was floated into legend by the Whigs.

The 'Pretender' and a squadron of French warships carrying thousands of armed troops, were preparing to invade the English coast. Queen Anne was ill, was dying; dead. Bolingbroke and Lady Masham had declared themselves joint Regents, to plunge the country into Civil War.

Over their ale-mugs old men spun out tales of their boyhood

when brothers, fathers, nearest kin were at each others' throats, in
Cromwell's day. But if this war came, so went the doleful pro-
phecy, it would be a fight between two Kings—the lawful heir to
Britain and the German.

Opinion stood divided, with a balance in the favour of George
Lewis, whose mother, the octagenarian Electress Sophia, niece of
the martyred Charles I, would wear the Crown before the Hanoverian should she outlive Queen Anne. That looked more than
likely. The old lady's grip on life was strengthened by her own
determination to inscribe upon her tombstone 'Queen of England'.

Dismal forecasts of the health of the reigning Queen had been
lately issued by her doctors. At Christmas-tide a chill attacked her,
laid her low. Her end was near, and the Restoration of the Stuart
hung upon her word. Would that word be spoken?

The quiet Duchess 'Carrots', mouthpiece of the Whigs, sat
beside the Queen's sick-bed to conjure bogies of bloodshed,
Popery, and treasonable dealings with St. Germains. On the
Queen's other side sat Lady Masham full of gentle warnings, and
reminder of a plot to bring over the Elector or his son to take his
place at Court.

"Madam, you should not be so pestered. Will you not write
to the Princess Sophia expressing Your Majesty's displeasure at
these ill-timed anticipations that cause you such anxiety?"

Yes. The Queen, unwillingly, would write.

She was propped upon her pillows, her swollen hand unbound
from its wrappings, the faltering quill guided, the words dictated:

'Madam, Cousin, Aunt,

'Since the right of succession to my Kingdom has been declared
to belong to you and your family, there have always been disaffected persons who by particular views of their own interest have
entered into measures to fix a Prince of your blood in my Domi-
nions, even while I am yet living. I never thought till now that
this project would have gone so far as to make the least impression
on your mind——"

The Queen stayed her pen.

"Masham, I dare not write so strongly. I must consult Lord
Oxford in this matter before I——"

"Madam, Lord Oxford has declared himself for Hanover by
his marked exclusion of your Royal brother's interests in the Peace
terms. It was Lord Bolingbroke who succeeded in effecting a
compromise with France to His Royal Highness's advantage. If
Your Majesty seeks the advice of Lord Oxford you will forsake

your brother's cause. Dear Madam, will you jeopardize the
Prince's royal heritage and your dead father's memory?"

"O, God!" The red-rimmed eyes gazed up in fretted inde-
cision. The loose lips trembled. "Yes, his beloved memory. I
must. . . . What more, Hill, shall I say?"

"Say this, Madam. Let me hold the pen. Is that easier for you?
Now . . . 'There are here, such is our misfortune, a great many
people that are seditiously disposed. I leave you to judge what
tumults they will raise if they should have a pretext to begin
a——.' "

"Revolution?" queried Anne fearfully as the pen paused.

"No, Madam. 'Commotion.' Two M's, Your Majesty. . . .
'I persuade myself therefore you will never consent that the least
thing should be done to disturb the repose of me or my subjects.' "

"How shall I sign myself, Masham?"

" 'With a great deal of affection,' Your Majesty?"

" 'Twill be a written lie."

But the Queen wrote it, and sent it post-haste by courier. And
its contents were duly recorded to that secret circle over which
Lord Bolingbroke presided; and Tom D'Urfey, the Queen's lyrist,
put it into song to be bawled in every Tory Club in town.

> 'The Crown's far too weighty
> For shoulders of eighty;
> She could not sustain such a trophy.
> Her hand, too, already,
> Has grown so unsteady,
> She can't hold a sceptre,
> So Providence kept her
> Away—poor old Dowager Sophie.'

Providence, or Abigail's letter, did indeed keep her away, for
no sooner had she read that message of renunciation from her
widowed relative in England than 'poor old Dowager Sophie'
fell down in a fit and died, in ten minutes, of shock.

The race was beginning: the starters were ready with jockeys
up and odds even on Stuart and Guelph. While to the old tune of
'Lilliburlero' was shouted the song of the Whigs.

> 'Over, over, Hanover, over,
> Haste and assist our Queen and our State,
> Haste over Hanover,
> Fast as you can over,
> Put in your claim before 'tis too late.'

Was it too late? The Commons stood divided on that issue, about to be forced by Bolingbroke's vigorous endeavours in opposition to Oxford's wavering resistance. But he still held his Lord Treasurer's Staff, 'with a dead gripe', as Arbuthnot described it to Swift, and 'was kicking and cuffing about him like the devil' in defence of his office, though not in defence of King James or King George; nor in defence of Queen Anne. She must fend for herself. And she did.

Unaided, ill, deserted by her Ministers, whose concerns were centred no longer in her cause but in their own, she rose from her sick-bed to attend the opening of Parliament. There, for the last time, she spoke to them in a voice that, by the sheer effort of her Stuart will, rose strong and clear to: 'Tell you plainly that the prosperity and liberties of my subjects can never be attained unless all groundless jealousies between you be laid aside. . . .'

In her heart she may have known such jealousies could never more be laid aside. The savage feud that had split the friendship of her two leading statesmen was taken up in arms to split the Tory Party. The followers of Oxford joined with Shrewsbury in support of Hanover, while Bolingbroke, Arbuthnot, and the Duke of Ormonde led for Stuart: and behind them stood one other, waiting, working silently, to strike.

*   *   *

"You sent for me? An unexpected honour."

"Yes. I sent for you. Be seated."

With slow deliberation Oxford took the chair to which Abigail waved him, and crossing his knees leaned back in it. From under her eyelids she watched him. His mouth was twitching, his restless fingers alternately fiddled with his snuff-stained cravat and a buckle of his breeches that had come unfastened. His stockings were mud-splashed about the ankles; the lace of his cuffs was frayed, his face lined, haggard, old, much older than when she last had seen it, with a mildewy tinge about his cheeks that were a little sunken, and his eyes a little filmed.

She offered him wine. He refused it, saying jauntily:

"I must keep my wits about me to match yours—and drown 'em later. To what freak of fortune am I indebted for your invitation? Are you softened? Do you repent?"

"Of what," she asked with sudden energy, "should I repent?"

His shoulders wriggled slightly, as if at that question he restrained a laugh.

"Of your studied churlishness," said Oxford carelessly. "Or have you come to your senses at last, to know that while you seek to make of me your fool—and Bolingbroke's—mine is the whip hand to whip you out of office were I so minded: which I'm not. You and I, my dear, are too close entwined to break asunder."

Folding her lips she smiled. He went on: "My stomach is proud, little cousin. It does not sink before the foul insinuations you and your disciple hatch in your joint nest against me. You don't honestly believe—if you can believe with honesty"—and on that word he laid a satirical stress—"that I have been in correspondence with Marlborough and intend to bring him back?"

"I do not know what may be your intent," she told him calmly. "I only know mine."

"Which means"—and he uncrossed his legs—"that I may hope?"

Her eyes were fastened upon his in a look of fear, hate, contempt, that mingled with a haunting triumph as she echoed softly: "Hope?" Then her face, so pale, crimsoned as if lit by some inward flame. "I have this to say"—and on a breath she said it, while that colour faded from her cheeks leaving them deathly white—"that, beyond my hope, beyond all expectation, you have fulfilled the office which you hold and owe to me. Beyond my prayers you have succeeded."

With supercilious gravity he bowed.

"Did you bring me here to tell me so?"

"And more." She sat rigid with hands so tightly fisted that the nails cut into her flesh. "You have succeeded in proving my judgment infallible. I placed you where you stand, up there"—her chin lifted, and her eyes, with an eager predatory light in them—"knowing well that you would bring yourself, in your own weakness, down."

His head turned. Glancing up and sideways at her, he luxuriously stretched himself and chuckled. "Sublime, sublime! 'Cod, to see and hear her! Why, 'tis excellent. 'Tis high dramatics. She should take to play-acting upon the board—and not behind the scenes—to make her fame and fortune. So the nymph would fight the dragon, hey? A female St. George—or St. John. Which? Madam," and again from his chair he tauntingly bowed, "any service you have rendered me, I promise you, will be returned with interest."

"Careful, Harley, how you threaten." She nodded, as if in smiling playfulness, but there was blood in the palms of her hands.

"Careful, my Enchantress," he mocked her, "how you tempt. I love your spirit. Mine goes out to meet it."

"Your spirit," she countered, "is cuffed. Your tail's whisking but your fangs are drawn!"

"Drawn though they be," he exposed them, "and decayed—as I am—they can bite."

"Maybe. On stones." She looked at him with an air of invincible innocence, and rising from her seat she glided to the bellrope, laid a hand upon it, and said in a small, almost a child's voice: "I was your friend. You were my life. I loved you—loved you, Harley, and you crossed me. Yes, I rendered you my service, but you have rendered no one any service. Not yourself, nor the Queen . . . nor me."

And to the footman at the door she said: "His lordship's coach."

He had left a glove behind him on the chair he had vacated; a worn, embroidered glove with a tarnished crest, its gold fringe tattered. She took it, pulled apart its crushed fingers, held it, gazing down, while something strangled crept from her throat to her lips in a deep cry: and one tear fell. She brushed it away and going to the window which was open, she dropped from it the crumpled thing she held.

*   *   *

"I cannot possibly attend the Council meeting, Masham. I am not well."

"Sweet Mistress, I think it is advisable—imperative—that you attend."

The bandaged hands moved helplessly.

"I cannot walk—so shaming—for all the world to see."

"Only your Ministers, Madam, and they understand. Let me call the dressers."

The dressers were called, the swathed hands hidden in filmy scarves. The face, red and bloated from erysipelas, was bathed in cooling lotion, the piteous, distorted hulk disguised beneath a cloak.

"Now, Madam, your drops."

"So nasty tasting, Hill."

"Not on a lump of sugar, dear. And afterwards a piece of this delicious preserved ginger which Dr. Arbuthnot has prescribed for the pains. There! Not so nasty, is it?"

The sugar, soaked in 'drops', was dutifully scrunched; the ginger swallowed.

"Masham?"

"Your Majesty?"

"Such a shock, Masham. Lord Oxford—I hardly like to mention it, but was he not in drink when we received him yesterday?"

"Yes, Madam. He——" Abigail paused to add, "the floor *is* slippery."

Over the Queen's distended features swept a look of shuddering reminiscence.

"It was so dreadful, Hill. He fell, didn't he? Fell! He reeled as he backed. I did not believe his excuse of sudden vertigo. The floor may be slippery, but nobody else has fallen down. Even I, when"—the Queen's underlip trembled—"when I had the use of my legs I never fell down, however tottery. And my darling angel boy, he *was*, God bless him, tottery. But he never fell down. No, Masham, Lord Oxford was drunk. Offensively drunk. He smelt. His speech was unintelligible." The Queen's head moved helplessly from side to side. "How can I meet him? What can I say to him? My Lord Treasurer! Disgraced."

A bandaged hand, uncovered from its swathings, lifted to wipe away the pouring moisture from those sore, caked eyes. "I am tired, Hill. So weary. . . . To think I have the gift of healing, yet I cannot heal myself. What *am* I to say?"

"There, sweet one, don't cry." The relationship between Majesty and servant had changed of late to that of nurse and nursling. "Let Masham wipe your face. Your Majesty won't have to say. Let *him* say. Your Majesty is always just. His lordship has the right to plead his cause against the accusation that he has invited the Duke of Marlborough—and the Duchess—to return to England."

"Do you believe that accusation, Hill?"

Abigail's eyelids dropped.

"Madam, I am so bewildered by these brawls in and out of Parliament that I do not know what to believe."

From her harassed depths the Queen fetched a great sigh.

"Tell the men to come."

Four attendants entered. The Queen was too heavy now to be carried; her chair had to be lowered through a trap door to the Council Chamber and hauled up again by ropes and pulleys. The lid of the trap was raised. The chair with that nightmarish shape in it, slowly descended; and to Abigail's curtsy the swollen lips smiled, and one of those mummified hands was raised in a gesture that seemed to linger.

At that debate in the Cabinet, within a few feet of drooping Majesty, Oxford and Bolingbroke met and fought their last fight to its end.

Those who watched that final contest between these two on whose divided leadership the fate of nations swung, saw how the sottish wreck of Harley rallied to the challenge to denounce with vituperative passion the man who sought to break him.

The galvanized Queen, the stunned Council, heard the Premier tell of financial corruption, of the pilfering of Secret Service funds to swell Lord Bolingbroke's estate: of practices, public and private, to bring over the Pretender—"on whose head," thundered Oxford, "a price has been placed for the safety of Britain and by Her Majesty's grace."

The bowed figure in the Queen's chair bent its head. Yes, she had been swayed against her will, her heart, and her desire, under threat of Revolution to declare herself against the Prince, her brother, unless he could be persuaded to change his religion. But he would never change. He was of the Faithful.

"Your Majesty, my lords. I charge this man of treason to the State!"

A buzz of indignation rose in protest, but Bolingbroke gripped the table's edge and sat in silence.

"I charge Lord Bolingbroke," cried Oxford, "of intrigue with the Jacobites and France, with whom, by the unscrupulous devices of a certain lady whose name——"

"Must not be spoken!"

Bolingbroke was on his feet, his hand upon his sword-hilt, and red fury in his eyes.

"Your Majesty! My lords! There sits the man who accuses me of his own crimes and peculations. I refute these charges and demand immediate redress and—satisfaction!"

But his lips had scarcely clenched upon those words when from the stupefied spectators rose a cry: "The Queen!"

Her attempt to rise and quell, by an assertion of her Sovereignty, this unprecedented outrage to herself and the Council, was too much for her. She staggered back, slumped fainting in her seat.

The Queen's women, hastily summoned, revived her. Four footmen hoisted her chair on its pulleys to the Bedchamber. The interrupted belligerents, both now rather sheepish, conserved their mutual hatred for later revenge. And Oxford went home to write letters: one to Swift.

'I send you an imitation of Dryden composed on my way from Kensington.

> To serve with love
> And shed your blood,
> Approved is above.
> But here below,
> Th' examples show
> 'Tis fatal to be good.'

The next day Abigail also wrote to Swift:

'Dear Friend,
    'I own it looks unkind in me not to thank you all this time
for your sincere, kind letter; but I was resolved to stay till I
could tell you the Queen had got so far better of the Dragon to
take his power out of his hands. The poor lady has been
barbarously used. . . . I cannot have so much time now to
write all my mind, because my dear Mistress is not well and I
must go to her. . . .'

The long struggle was over; the short reign of cloud and
tempest drawing to its close, brought to its speedier end by that
violent scene in the Council Chamber and Oxford's subsequent
dismissal.

It had been a cruel wrench to part with him—her last decisive
action before her crippled mind and body sank beneath their
burden, not of years, but of the cares and strife of Sovereignty too
great for her endurance.

The news of the Queen's impending death flew like fire over
London, with the whisper that the displaced Lord Oxford had
sent a private circular to every Whig Lord within call to stand
prepared to fight for Hanover against the Jacobites, and Bolingbroke.

The race was on, the starters off; which now would be the
first to reach the winning-post?

The supporters of the Stuart were assembled in an ante-room
awaiting the signal to proclaim James Edward King at Charing
Cross. Their last hope hung upon the Queen's last word. As
when, a century before, another greater Queen lay dying, so now,
while breath was in her body, the name of her successor must be
spoken—could she speak.

The Favourite was sent for, hotly questioned.

"Speak? She cannot speak. She is dead, from her feet upward."

"You must make her speak—or write. Can you not guide
her hand to write his name?"

"My lords, I tell you, she is going—all but gone. I die for her
if she lives until to-morrow."

"Who is with her?"

"None but I and her women."

But in Abigail's absence from that room two others had come
there. The Duke of Shrewsbury and the Duchess of Somerset
were at the bedside when she returned, and at the doorway halted.

A sound, dreadful, such as she had never heard, broke from that inert mass beneath the gold-encrusted velvet; and as Abigail sank to her knees, her shrinking eyes saw Shrewsbury lean over that ponderous bulk, raise aloft its lifeless bandaged hand, and take from it the Lord Treasurer's White Staff.

The last coach rattled out of the Palace yard. The gates were shut, the curtains drawn: and darkness fell.

*   *   *

Bells were pealing, banners flying, cannon booming, beacons flaring, and a stout little rosy-faced German King riding through the thronged streets of his capital. Cheers and rejoicing, trumpeters, heralds, body-guards, outriders, the Duke of Shrewsbury, the new Lord Treasurer, on his knees; the Duke of Marlborough —with his happy Duchess—on their knees; the Archbishop of Canterbury, giving thanks to the Head of his Church, on his knees, and every Whig throat roaring welcome. The silence of the Tories passed unnoticed in that din.

Queen Anne is dead, and in two weeks forgotten. God save King George the First!

Here he comes in his golden coach, swaying and bumping over the cobbles, rolling about on his red velvet cushions like a pea in a very large pod.

The King drives alone. He has a wife, but she has misbehaved herself with a Swedish adventurer and is shut up for her sins in a castle. Behind him, for his sins, come his two hideous middle-aged mistresses, the ladies Kielsmansegge and Schulenberg: the one tall and thin, the other round and fat, both soon to be English peeresses: Countess of Darlington, Duchess of Kendal.

Send up a cheer for them. We all have our mistresses—why not the King? Hip-pip huzza! The King, God bless him, come from Hanover to save the Church of England—and us—from Popery. Huzza, huzza for Hanover!

He wears a scarlet uniform emblazoned with stars, ribbons, German Orders, gold everywhere and a white wig. Oho! An innovation. And every blade in St. James's is off to Old Drury to order himself a white wig.

"Off with the old Whig and on with the new," giggles Sir Andrew Fountaine from the window of White's Chocolate House, and tells his groaning fellows, "I must find another housekeeper. My Mrs. South has gone, in a rare huff, to Ireland. She won't stay, she said, in this island to see a German on the—— Hush! Tee-hee! And Dr. Swift is going to—where he belongs. And Boling-broke is gone to Paris, and the Mashams go to Hertfordshire."

"Who cares," hiccuped Lord Oxford, "if the Mashams go to hell?"

The windows of Lady Masham's suite in St. James's Palace were closed, the rooms dismantled and uncarpeted. Her personal belongings and her husband's had been sent in advance to Langley Manor, the house Lord Masham had bought for a song and furnished for a fortune.

She was dressed in deepest black with a cloak about her shoulders, and a white rose, the badge of the Stuart, in her hair. Her coach waited at the door and her husband at her side in some impatience.

"Dearest, must you stay? We won't be there till midnight."

"I must stay until he comes; and then we'll go." Her eyes travelled round the almost empty room and alighted on a table where stood a bottle and two glasses. "I'll drink a glass of wine, love. So will you. Pour it."

Masham poured it.

She unlatched the casement, and as she swung it open a multitudinous yell rose up to hit the sky, "The King!"

Her body stiffened. Masham slipped a glance at his watch and one at his wife, and drank his wine at a draught. She held her glass untasted; raised it, whispered: "Look!"

Along St. James's Street swept the enormous gilded coach with the little man inside doffing his cocked hat and grinning, sweating, bowing. Trumpets blared, horses pranced, pennons fluttered in the breeze; sun-shafts struck gleams from silver harness, trappings, and gold lace. The coloured crowds that lined the way were one thick jostling mass.

"God save the King!"

And as that lusty shout went up, Abigail cried its echo to:

"The King . . . over the water!"

Then she drained her glass and flung it down and set her heel upon it, and turning to her husband said:

"Now take me home."

AFTERWORD

WHILE Sarah, Duchess of Marlborough, has always been a popular subject for biographers, none to my knowledge has written the life of her less glamorous, but not less successful cousin, Abigail Hill, named by Queen Anne 'That Enchantress'.

It is true that no biography of Anne Stuart or of the Duchess of Marlborough is complete without some allusion, almost always opprobrious, to Lady Masham, her intrigue with Harley, her crass ingratitude to the Duchess, and to the evil works of Abigail generally. But against these accusations, founded chiefly on Sarah Marlborough's embittered memoirs, we have the opinion of Swift who knew her well and who describes her as 'a person of great truth and sincerity: of an honest boldness and courage superior to her sex . . . full of love, duty and veneration for the Queen, her mistress.'

We have also the eulogy—for what it is worth—of Mesnager, the French envoy, in his *Minutes of Negotiation*, quoted on page 313.

And finally, Winston Churchill in *Marlborough, his Life and Times*, tells us that: 'Abigail was probably the smallest person who ever consciously attempted to decide, and did in fact decide the history of Europe.'

In writing this life of Abigail Hill which is based entirely on fact, I do not seek to vindicate her character but to present her as she emerges from my deductions. She has been much maligned, but whether rightly or wrongly let the reader judge for himself.

After the accession of George I, Lady Masham lived in retirement with her husband and their family at Langley Manor.

Of their five children, two girls and three boys, only two outlived them; Francis, their youngest, and Samuel, their second son, who succeeded to his father's peerage and died without issue in 1761. At his death the barony became extinct.

Abigail died in 1734 at the comparatively young age of forty-nine, and her brother Jack in the following year. Alice died, unmarried, at the ripe old age of seventy-seven.

Lord Masham survived his wife for five and twenty years, and did not remarry.

All characters, all letters and verses quoted are entirely authentic, and wherever possible the actual dialogue has been reproduced.

To my husband, for his patience, interest, and careful criticism throughout the writing of this book, and to those authorities, living and dead, whose works have aided my research I am most gratefully indebted.

DORIS LESLIE.

COOMBE HILL. *September* 1948—*September* 1949.

BIBLIOGRAPHY

England under Queen Anne	G. M. Trevelyan
Lives of the Queens of England	Agnes Strickland
Anne of England	M. R. Hopkinson
Social Life in the Reign of Queen Anne	John Ashton
Memoirs of Marlborough	Archdeacon Coxe
Marlborough, his Life and Times	The Right Hon. Winston Churchill
John and Sarah Marlborough	Stuart J. Reid
Sarah, Duchess of Marlborough	Kathleen Campbell
Conduct of the Dowager Duchess of Marlborough	Edited by Hooke
History of My Own Times	G. Burnet
Robert Harley, Earl of Oxford	E. S. Roscoe
Bolingbroke	Sir Charles Petrie
The Jacobite Movement	Sir Charles Petrie
The London Spy	Ned Ward: with introduction by Ralph Straus
Journal to Stella	Jonathan Swift, edited by Harold Williams
Arbuthnot, Life and Works	George Aitken